MW01644255

THE REALM OF NIGHTMARES

Book One of The Shadow King

SHAYHA OBERT-HICKEY

This book is a work of fiction. Names, characters, places, and incidents are the product of the author's imagination and are used fictionally. Any resemblance to people, events, or places is coincidental.

Dedicated to my children:
Jack and Alice, always follow your dreams
no matter how long it takes.

Also dedicated to my mother, Haley.
I couldn't have done this without your help.

THE REALM OF NIGHTMARES

Shayha Obert-Hickey

PROLOGUE

I remember standing in the tower looking across the land that once burst with life, of hope and richness for our people, the realm that Mavi Ivar, our King had created for us in a time of need and destruction. It was to be a prison, but it changed. It grew hopeful, sprouting a realm of beauty that not even the darkness could touch, or so I thought...

I watch the flickering torches of Dentro's army moving closer to our kingdom. My kingdom. The place I hoped would allow me to have peace one day was ending. Soon the place I wished to grow old with my love would be crumbled to dust and ash.

We had evacuated most of the town, but some refused to leave their homes. The fools, they didn't stand a chance against him. He was why we were here in this realm.

Dentro was the first Nightmare to be born into the human realm. He was a simple nightmare turned into a powerful evil;

the person who dreamed of him couldn't help but release Dentro into the world and bow down to the god he had created.

Dentro would haunt the minds of other humans, creating new Nightmares to bring into the world to serve him. As long as Dentro could bend the minds of the weak and fearful, he could produce nightmares that bled into the world, covering it in darkness. But as the world grew dark, a spark of hope was born. Mavi Ivar, my king, and our hope.

Dreams of those who would not go silently to the grave or let fear take over their minds created him. He became a noble warrior against Dentro, creating an army of those who would not flee from the shadows, gifting them a power of strength and light, and we began calling ourselves Ivars after our protector and king.

Mavi, using his power, created a new realm that could trap Dentro within and protect humans from the darkness. He blinded the humans from seeing what was beyond their world and naming the new realm, Hatheya, where we still fight Dentro and the years of fighting have brought many deaths and pain to all of us who wish for peace, Nightmares, and Ivars alike.

The war has raged on for centuries, and the human world soon forgot about the darkness and Dentro, but Mavi still searched for a way to destroy Dentro and his power, traveling to the darkest corners of their lands calling on all the creatures of the realm until a powerful Enchantress, Kanna, came before him begging him to sacrifice himself so that his blood would flow through the land and fill their realm with the hope that had been born within him. With her came her sister Navara, the most beautiful woman a man could see, but a dark heart was within her and she betrayed the King and her sister, siding with Dentro and his power.

Today Mavi will lay upon the stone and sacrifice his blood for our land.

"Gannon! What are you doing?" A guard from the tower called.

Gannon held up the journal and noticed the man trying to hide his laugh, "You write while Dentro marches to us?"

He glanced out across the land at the torches coming closer.

"We should meet them before the border of the town, smite the Nightmares down before they kill our people. Why does Mavi have us hiding in this tower?"

Shrugging, Gannon replied, "He knows what he is doing." Then he bid farewell to the guards in the tower and started his long descent down the spiral staircase, his thoughts wrapped around what was about to happen. Though Mavi was his king, he was also his brother through battle. They had been by each other's side for centuries and he had named Gannon the Realm Keeper of Hatheya. He was the only one besides Mavi who was able to unlock the Realm and enter the Human Realm. Though he saw no purpose for this title, as he never wanted to return, and the humans had long forgotten them, Mavi insisted upon it. Mavi always seemed to be one step ahead of all of them and would share only what he had to and only with whom he wanted. Gannon felt as if he was just a chess piece in Mavi's realm, but he trusted him, nevertheless.

Stopping outside Mavi's chamber door, he hesitated. The King had asked not to be disturbed and for utter quietness. Perhaps he was preparing himself for the spell Kanna was to perform, but he wished to speak to his brother, his friend, and King to maybe find another way to stop Dentro that did not involve Mavi's death. His hands shook, along with his heart at the thought of never seeing Mavi again. How was he supposed to pretend Mavi was not about to die to give his life for them? Gannon gave a quick knock, praying he would open the door and they could speak one last time to share stories and laugh, as they had done many times.

"He will not answer." Kandem stepped from the shadows with deathly quietness. "I've knocked and called out, but…"

Gannon sighed and rubbed his tired eyes, "Do you know when he will begin? The army is moving closer." He didn't want to sound cold, but he needed to find out what Mavi's intentions were in waiting until the last moment.

"I'm unsure. I don't think Mavi is alone in there either. I heard a strange noise as if someone moaned in pain."

"Why did you not break down the door?" Gannon moved to the door again, ready to charge into the wood and splinter it. Mavi was the strongest man that Gannon knew, but even the strong had weaknesses.

"He yelled to leave him be, that he was fine." Kandem leaned against the cold stone wall and placed a casual hand on the hilt of his sword, clearly not as upset as Gannon was about the noises. Perhaps he knew something Gannon didn't.

"And what if he's not?" Gannon questioned, eyeing the man and his body language.

Kandem's jaw feathered, "He is our king, and we will do as he says, even if that means being annoyed by it."

Scoffing, Gannon grabbed Kandem's shoulder, "You say that because Mavi has appointed you the next king and you wish for me to follow you," he smiled, letting the tension flow out of him. He had known Kandem just as long as he had known Mavi, another brother of battle, stronger than blood.

"A troublemaker like you follow orders?" He laughed.

"You will be a great king, Kandem."

"Make sure you write that in your journal."

"I will and I will share it with everyone I see on the streets! We will all drink to your name!"

Kandem's smile faded slightly, "And to Mavi for his bravery and sacrifice."

Gannon nodded solemnly, "For all the Ivars and their sacrifices."

He bowed his head, "For our realm, we must survive and fight with our every breath."

"Never waver in the strength." Gannon thumped his breastplate with a fist.

Kandan did the same, "Never waver in the strength."

The tower high above us trumpeted with a warning. It erupted through the halls, causing us to draw our swords. Gannon banged on the door with force, "Mavi! They've reached the border!" He banged again.

Mavi swung open the door breathing heavily, "Kandem, lead the men, give me as much time as you can." He slammed the door shut again, leaving Gannon fuming.

"You heard him!" Kandem's voice was commanding, "Get to your post!"

Gannon ran to the door yelling to the others to bar the door. He didn't know how much time Mavi needed, but he was determined to give him all of it. Gannon could hear Kandem's voice echoing through the castle as he prepared the other Ivars and a few Nightmares that had sided with Mavi for a battle.

Arrows began to fly down to the enemies below, trying to stop as many as they could before they reached the castle.

The earth quivered underfoot. Gannon knocked against the wall at the sudden force, "Dentro," He breathed, tightening the grip on his sword. It would be useless against the creature that could kill with just a movement of his hand, but it would slaughter those who followed him.

The door pounded with the fists of the Nightmares. They roared and screamed threats of blood. The ground shook again. Dentro's shadows were upon them. "Brace yourselves!" Gannon shouted. The door shattered open, sending wood and metal shards around the entrance. Gannon ducked behind a chair, receiving only a few splinters to his back.

In a blur, the fighting began. Gannon's sword was through the head of a Nightmare then through the chest of another. He dodged axes and maces and sharp teeth.

Sweat burned Gannon's eyes, and the smell of smoke filled his lungs. Just outside the castle, the town burned wildly. Gannon felt his heart tighten at the sickening sight. His home was turning to ash.

"Gannon!" a soldier called above the roar of battle. "Gannon go to Mavi!"

Bewildered, Gannon started to fight his way to the stairs. Coldness filled the room. Gannon stood straighter, his heart pounding hard against his ribs as smoky shadows flowed across the ground. Ivars backed away, screaming in pain as the darkness leaped upon them. The darkness tore at their minds until they ran themselves through with their own weapons, trying to rid the madness from their minds.

Gannon slipped on the bloody stairs, catching himself before he could draw the attention of the Nightmare that walked in.

The Nightmare stood tall among the quivering Ivars, his shadows flirting around him and blocking most of his body, but Gannon swore he could see Dentro's fiery eyes burning into him, a sickening smile showing sharp teeth. Gannon turned away not waiting to be taken by shadows, and darted to Mavi's rooms.

Mavi was standing in the doorway, blood covered his shirt and something small tucked close to his chest. "Dentro is here!" Gannon gasped, "He's here!"

"Don't worry about that right now. I have something more pressing for you to handle." He looked down at the tangle of blankets.

"More pressing than Dentro?" Gannon blanched, "What is that?"

"I need you to do something for me, Gannon. You cannot tell anyone, not even Kandem." Mavi's brown eyes bore into him. "I need you to take-" His voice caught, "Take her and leave Hatheya." He handed Gannon the bundle that was now wiggling around. Gannon dropped his sword as he awkwardly held the newborn baby.

Gannon gawked down at the child, "Mavi?" He breathed, "What is this?"

Mavi somehow managed a chuckle and brushed his knuckles across the baby's cheek as she settled comfortably in Gannon's arms.

"Who's!" He glanced into Mavi's room, but couldn't see anyone, but bloody towels and blankets laid on the floor.

"Do as I have commanded, Gannon." His voice could have shaken stone, "Do it without questioning me, do it without looking back."

Gannon nodded, "I promise." Panic was filling every part of his body. What was he going to do with this tiny thing that he could barely hold? How would he even feed this thing?

"She is yours now." Mavi gripped Gannon's shoulder, "I have to go to Kanna and complete the spell. Goodbye, brother."

Gannon nodded again, unable to speak. His tongue was too dry and his head spun; his heart ached.

Mavi gave the baby one last glance before darting off.

Gannon used one of the secret passageways to escape from the castle. It was sickening for him to abandon his friends, but what else could he do? He had promised his king.

The baby wiggled and screamed under his cape as he mounted a horse and kicked it into a gallop.

Tears streamed down Gannon's face as he rode past cries of help from the Ivars, as he rode past his family being slaughtered, and at the sight of Kandem who stood on the battlefield drenched in blood screaming at him to stop to help him and the others.

"Gannon!" Kandem cried, "Gannon! You traitor!"

Gannon kicked again, squeezing his heels into the already exhausted animal till it bolted faster away from Kandem and his pleas and till he could no longer hear the sounds of battle and he could safely enter the human
realm without being followed.

I have spoken to a few across the realm in Hatheya about what happened that night, paying a large sum for their silence about me and their watchful eyes on Hatheya. They told me that Mavi has won, and the tower crumbled upon the spell. Dentro and

many are dead. Kandem is living on, a powerful and hopeful king.

I will try to live my life here; I will try to obtain what I so desperately wanted when I was in Hatheya, as I will never be able to go back. My name was slandered as a traitor, and I feel as if I am one.

I awake every night dreaming of the battle that forced me away from Hatheya. It has only been a year here in the human realm, but many years in Hatheya, or what I would assume would be many years. Time flows differently here. It's slower, painfully slow. Hatheya has no time,. Night comes when it wants, you sleep when you need, and awake when you want, and seasons would pass quickly or not at all. Unlike the human realm, we did not concentrate on what we could not control.

I have grown tired of writing about my homesickness, about the past. I need to look forward to the future, to the strength within me, not just for myself, but for my child. I will teach her to be an Ivar to be brave even when afraid, to fight even when weak, and to never waver in the strength.

I wish dearly that she could see Hatheya, to see that land thriving, a land that Mavi gave his life for, but I don't think that will ever be possible.

Gannon stood, closing the journal before throwing it into the fire. The flames gripped the pages till they were ash. Gannon walked away to tend to the crying baby that lay in the make-shift crib.

ONE

*M*ost children read stories about princesses and princes, about how good trumps evil, how a shoe can make your dreams come true, not of monsters, and how they became men. Stories not of knights, princesses, and romance, but instead of the creatures that lurked in the dark, under beds, and in closets.

Written in dark ink diligently sprawled across the leather-bound journals were stories that consumed me. These stories, which spun tight webs across my mind, were not for the faint of heart. Not for those who dreamed of happy endings, even when the brave fought and won. There was still so much death. How could one rejoice in victory? They could only take a breath before more violence was there again. It was always there, waiting until you let down your guard, until you started healing again, and like a wolf waiting silently for its prey, it was suddenly there destroying everything you had built. Life, it was life, and no one likes reading about the truth and pain. That's why they read fairy tales and happily ever after. These were not those stories, and maybe that was why I was like this. Painfully pessimistic and burning to find quiet in my mind that never stopped turning noise.

Tonight, like most nights, I sat down in front of the round window, gazing out at the moonlit forest. The wind crashed against the house like ocean waves, shuddering the branches of trees that brushed across the roof and shook the windows, making it sound like the old house could collapse to the ground at any moment. The moon cast shadows across the yard, creating shapes around the forest that could be mistaken for monsters themselves. A chill ran down my spine, forcing me to look away from the darkness, but for only a moment. This little window was where I would curl up and watch the shadows run free. Something my body ached for, and my soul craved to be as free as the darkness that could go anywhere and was quiet and content with itself. Maybe even proud to be able to cast such a foreboding feeling on people.

This is where I belonged, in the ghostly realm, huddled in the dark with just a small flashlight and one of the leather journals in my lap.

My father claimed these were his journals, where he wrote everything he knew about Hatheya and drew maps and sketches of what he remembered it to be like. As a child, I had begged to go there until my mother said it was all fake, a world he had created for fun to entertain me. I was heartbroken then, but I still read the journals as if it was air in my lungs. They called to me. Perhaps it was because I didn't fit in here and longed for a place, any place besides here.

We moved from place to place, so I never could make friends. My father kept me busy, "training" me to defend myself with swords, archery, hand to hand. He would make me run for miles until my lungs screamed, my heart pounded wildly, and the world spun.

He took me camping almost every weekend no matter the weather and taught me how to rock climb, how to start a fire, and how to hunt. Though I was no good at the hunting. I had a challenging time killing an innocent animal. They always seemed to know I was there, turning to look at me with their wide eyes. Their breathing changed, slowing as if they were ready to die, but I was never ready for the kill. More often than not, I would let them go and deal with the tongue-lashing from my father the extra few miles of running he made me do and the extra wood he made me chop.

"You can't be weak, Farren. One moment of regret, one pause could kill you."

I didn't know who was out to kill me or him, but he always told me to watch my back and not to linger in one place for too long. He was paranoid about everything, and it was becoming worse.

I told him I didn't believe in the stories he had written, but he scoffed and called me a fool. Perhaps I was.

I curled my fingers around the edge of the book and shuddered at the thought of Dentro. The beautiful Nightmare that had a taste for blood and power would forever haunt my thoughts. The first time my father had read to me about him as a child had me sleeping in their bed for weeks.

I snapped the book closed and leaned my head against the cool glass window, trying to rid my mind of all thoughts of Dentro, but I couldn't free my mind from them. I wanted to dream of their world, to be lost within it for just a bit longer. My raven black hair fell around me like a tent blocking me from the real world.

I traced a bony finger down the spine of the journal I had selected and sighed deeply. My body ached from the grueling hike we had taken that morning and then my mother whisked me away for shopping, claiming I needed to do normal teenage things, which entailed six stores and a visit to her friend's home for gossip. When we were in town, we had to get everything done that day before returning to our hidden home in the mountains.

The door creaked open, and my father stood in the hallway light. "Ferren," he said gruffly.

I hadn't heard the stairs creak as my mind had been fuzzy with thoughts of Nightmares. I blinked at the light and gave him a tight smile.

He stepped into the room and gave a huff, "hiding?"

I shrugged, "Maybe."

He nodded, understanding.

"How can you truly believe in these stories and why must I?"

He reached for the journal and skimmed the pages, frowning at the sketches of Kandem and Mavi.

"Why do you insist on me learning all of this? What good is learning about politics from a place that isn't real?"

Sighing, he handed the journal back, "We need to get more wood before the storm sets in."

I leaned back against the window, glancing at my watch. It was almost ten and I still had homework to do, but if I mentioned that he would ask why I didn't do it earlier, "I'll be down in a minute."

He stopped at the door, "something wrong?"

I shook my head and placed the journal back on the shelf. I didn't want to leave the dark office and the quietness of a book that helped me keep my thoughts at bay. I was always thinking, always in my head, my thoughts overtaking me and distracting me from the world.

"Ferren?"

I turned to him, "No, I'm fine." For the moment.

"Let's go camping tomorrow."

"I have school."

He shrugged and smiled, "Skip it, you need the break and I know you haven't done your homework yet either."

I laughed, "Of course you do." As I turned toward him, I took a double take back to the window as something caught my eye, but he pulled me away before I could make out what I had just seen.

He shut the door behind us with a tight click and led me down the stairs to where my mother was watching the news, a ball of yarn in her lap. Her knitting made a relaxing tink sound as she worked on another project.

"We'll be back shortly," my dad started coughing and went to the kitchen to get some water.

"Now? It's so dark out," my mom called from the couch, not looking away from the TV.

He didn't answer as his coughing increased. I could hear him shifting through the medicine cabinet.

"Gannon?" she called again, "Maybe you should go to the doctor?"

He came back to the living room and waved off her worried look, clearing his throat, "I'm fine."

She gave a skeptical look but went back to her show. I understood her worry. We had never seen my dad sick.

"Come on," he pulled on a jacket and grabbed the axes off the porch.

We lived in the mountains in a clearing of trees. A pond was just two miles from our house. We had found plenty of cliffs to climb and caves to explore on our land. My favorite part was the wildflowers that grew in our fields, which always calmed me with their scent. It was a beautiful home, but too far away from the town

for my liking. It took me an hour to get to school, and we rarely left our land due to having to drive an hour to reach one store. I had to beg my parents to be able to go to a public school and since we were so isolated up in the mountains, they reluctantly let me go.

My mom had a garden where she tended to chickens that were meant for food, but she fell in love with them, and now they were pets that happened to lay eggs. Horses that I spent most of my time with, and a cow that was grumpier than my dad.

"Go grab some wood and I'll start chopping this pile." He grunted, grabbing a log.

I laid the axe down and headed to the little path which we had thrown some logs earlier today. It was dark, but my dad had installed lamps around the pathways and the house, saying it would frighten away some of the weaker nightmares if they ever broke free of Hatheya. I had just nodded and accepted the crazy like I had always done, but secretly I wanted to see one, to see if it was true.

I picked up a few logs, balancing them in one arm, and tried to reach for another. A shadow darted across my eyes, making me drop the wood. I stood straight back, staring into the dark at nothing.

The chickens began squawking angrily. My heart calmed as I took a breath. "Those damn foxes," I mumbled under my breath, walking to the chicken coop. The squeak of their cage door stopped me in my tracks for a moment.

My dad must have seen the fox and gone to check on the chickens. I chewed on my lip, wishing I hadn't left my axe by the porch. I took slow steps to the chicken coop. The little lanterns around their coop had been broken, making it hard to see with just the moonlight. Listening to the forest noise around me, the chickens had gone eerily quiet as I approached the coop and peered in. The stench hit me first before my eyes settled on what I was seeing. It reeked of decaying flesh, reminding me of fish left out in the sun too long or when we found a half-eaten deer in the woods.

Don't scream. The words rushed to me in my panicked mind as I stared at a disfigured animal standing on its hind legs, tearing into one chicken with a sickening squelch. I backed away from the coop quietly, with steady feet and a pounding heart. I raced back to my dad.

"The chickens." I grabbed his arm, stopping him before he sunk his axe into another piece of wood, "There's…there's something over there." I tried to keep my voice down to keep the fear from shaking my words, but my mind was still trying to figure out what I had seen.

He grabbed my shoulder, trying to calm me, "Take a breath, Ferren."

I pointed to the path of the chicken coop, "There's something there. It ate the chickens."

"What type of animal was it?" He grabbed his axe again, eyeing the darkness.

"It was- "a dog? A bear? It was too large to have been a fox, but the way it stood, the way it tore into the chickens. It was holding the chicken in a claw, "I'm not sure, it was too dark to see."

"Get your axe," He commanded, grabbing a flashlight and charging to the coop.

I gripped the handle and reluctantly followed, keeping a few feet behind him. I didn't want to see that beast again.

"It's gone," he called over his shoulder. "You must have scared it off."

I moved closer to him, looking over his shoulder at what remained of the chickens. One chick stood stunned in the coop with the other five that had been torn apart and plucked. I grimaced, turning away.

"Your mother isn't going to be happy about this." He sighed, "How did it get in here?" He checked the latch on the door.

"It opened the door. I heard it." The latch wasn't broken. Nothing but the chickens had been touched. "But it had claws like an animal…I think."

He rubbed his chin and eyed me doubtfully, "Did you remember to latch the door before dinner?"

I dropped the axe to my side, "Yes, and I told you, I heard the door to the coop open. The animal or whatever it was opened the door."

He scooped up the stunned chicken and handed her to me, "Tell your mom it was a wild dog."

"It wasn't-"

He raised a hand, "I know, I believe you. I need to check the rest of the lights and get my gun. Quickly now." He shoved me back to the house.

"What was it?" I whispered suddenly afraid that my voice might draw it back, but a thrill of excitement raced through me. Fear always brought that about in me.

He coughed hard and shook his head, "It can't be. It's not possible."

"What's not possible?" I reached the door, welcoming the light that flowed over us.

"A Nightmare."

"What are you doing to my chicken?" My mom took the hen from me. "Why is there blood on her?" her eyes widened at us.

"Wild dog," He grabbed his shotgun and darted back out, "I'll be back." He called over his shoulder.

I counted down the minutes by pacing in the living room while my mom cried over her animals. We would need to clean the coop tomorrow, so she wouldn't have to see the horrendous scene. "Find anything?" I asked the moment my dad walked through the door.

He shook his head. Dark circles lined his eyes and his shoulders sagged from the weight of the gun. He suddenly looked very old.

After a while of watching my dad constantly check out every window, I went to my room, thinking I could at least try to get some rest.

I couldn't rest or even try to rest while thinking about what my dad had said. A nightmare? A creature from his journal, from Hatheya, was here? I scoffed. Even if that was true, how had it gotten here? Hatheya was locked away by Mavi's power, or at least that is what my dad had claimed in his stories.

I sat in front of my window wrapped tightly in a blanket, watching the rain. The storm had come just like my dad had said it would.

I watched the shadows move across the yard, waiting for them to spring to life, to become Nightmares hungry for more than just the chickens.

One lantern fell to the ground as the wind picked up. It bounced across the grass and rolled to the boot of a man. I jumped up, throwing my blanket to the floor before moving closer to the window. It was hard to see through the rain. Maybe it had been a trick of the eye.

With a flash of lightning, I could see the figure walking closer to the house, a man with pale marbled skin that seemed to glow, gray-white hair that fell just around his broad shoulders, and a build that could easily tower over any man. His tattered clothes were soaked through from the rain, but he didn't seem to notice the coldness or the howling wind that tore at his body.

I couldn't look away as he walked closer to the house, the forest becoming a blur behind him. The moon fell across his face, highlighting his ghostly features and empty silver eyes. He rolled his head back to look up at me, his mouth slightly open, his hair falling back behind his shoulders. My pulse began to race, and before I could think properly about it. I was out of my room and down the steps, avoiding the last one that always squeaked, and into the rain. I was instantly soaked, my clothes clung to me tight, my hair was plastered down and heavy.

There, there he was, standing a few feet away from me. A ghostly blur in the blinding rain. "Who are you!" I yelled.

He didn't move or answer.

"Are you one of them!"

A cry came from inside. I looked at the office window, unsure if I heard a scream or if this was a trick of my mind.

The creature raised a hand and stroked me across my face, bringing me back to his hollow eyes. I took a step back, my scream drowned out by thunder. He was so close now, but he still looked far away. My eyes couldn't focus properly on him.

"Stay." His voice was carried to me on the wind.

My eyes snapped up to the window as I heard a shout from inside again.

He grabbed my arm, his marbled skin burning cold. "Let go of me!" I screamed, trying to peel his fingers from my arm. He let go suddenly. I fell backward onto the wet ground. My head collided with something hard, another shout from inside the house, my name being yelled. The man stood over me as blurs spun around me before I fell into darkness.

TWO

I squinted up at the clouds moving across the early morning sky. Moaning at my stiff and freezing body, I sat up rubbing my pounded head. I was sitting in the yard covered in mud and a bit of dry blood that must have come from my head. I stared into the forest, trying to focus on what had happened. A shiver ran down my spine as flashes of what had to have been a dream knotted in my stomach. I could still feel the icy touch of the man's hand against my cheek, the horrible beauty of him still shown in my eyes.

Slowly, I stood, hearing my mother screaming my name and running towards me. Her eyes were wide with fear and confusion. "Ferren!" She pulled me into a hug. Her heart hammered against mine before pulling away. "Where is he?" She clutched my arm with a powerful grip. I winced and pulled my arm away. Black and blue blisters from frostbite circled my arm. I felt the rising panic in my body.

"Why are you out here!" Her eyes were wide with panic as they searched mine for answers.

"Where's who?" I swayed on my bare feet, shaking, teeth clacking together. All I wanted was to go inside and stand in a hot shower, wash away the mud and the dream that made me sick, then lock myself away in my room avoiding the world and my father's talk of Nightmares and Hatheya.

I gave a quick look up at the office window and gasped. The window had a thick spiderweb crack across the glass as if someone or something had slammed across it. My dream flashed across my mind, screaming from the office and a flash of movement. It was just a dream; it had been just a dream. I yelled to myself. I began to shake harder as my mother dug her fingers into my arm, bringing me out of a tranced state of panic.

"Your Father! He's not here! I woke and he-he was gone. The office is a mess. Then you were gone as well!" As if she just noticed that we were outside, she glanced around wildly and then down at my bare feet and my mess of pajamas. "What happened?" She croaked hoarsely, dragging me into the house. "Why were you outside?" she brushed my bloody hair to the side and checked my wound.

It took me a beat to answer as my head continued to spin. "I think it was a dream," I whispered. "Perhaps he just left for a bit. Went fishing?"

She shook her head, "No-no, he was up and down all night complaining about hearing noises, but with my medication, I fell asleep without a care." She collapsed into the chair, grabbing her phone. "The office," she pointed up the stairs. "It's destroyed; there's blood."

I rushed up the stairs, slipping on my wet feet, and crawled the rest of the way.

I gaped at the surrounding mess. The desk chair was broken across the floor. Items that once had a home on the desk were now scattered over the room. Shelves were knocked over, and their items were broken. I stared at the fireplace filled with burned pages of the journals, their leather covers torn with viciousness and scorched with ash. Blood was on the window and the floor. My father's knife was beside it. The air smelled foul and sick, just like it had when I saw the animal in the chicken coop.

I turned away, tears filling my eyes as I ran down the stairs, my feet slapping against the wood floor, then I was on the grass running into the woods that surrounded the cabin.

I only stopped when my breath turned ragged, and my heart pounded against my ribs screaming at me to take a break to breathe. Reluctantly listening, I fell to the ground, letting the earth cool my sweating body. I sobbed out a few cries before the exhaustion forced me to stop.

He was gone. He was truly gone. Closing my eyes, I blocked out the sun that was trying to dry the earth. I knew he was gone; I could feel it…the emptiness that surrounded me. I should have listened to him last night when he claimed it was a Nightmare I had seen. That it wasn't an animal at all, but a killer coming for him. The thing he was always looking over his shoulder afraid to see. I had seen it in his eyes last night. I should have stayed up, should have been the one protecting him. He had called my name; he had screamed it last night when I was in the yard. Was the man a nightmare as well? Had he lured me down away from my parents? Why hadn't he taken me like the other thing took my dad?

When I finally appeared from the woods, the police were there. My mother clutched me in a tight embrace, shaking with cries of anger that I had run away and with tears of fear of what might have happened to my father.

A missing person's case was opened for him after questioning us. I didn't tell them about the man I had seen or what was in the chicken coop. They wouldn't have believed me, anyway. They searched the woods for a body and when one wasn't found and no news surfaced of his disappearance. It became a cold case, and they left us with the conclusion that he was forever gone, and it was time to move on.

I tried talking to my mother about that night about the man, and what my dad had said, but she shut me out, ignoring my questions, getting angry at the mention of Hatheya or Nightmares. She cried herself to sleep every night. I couldn't cry; I couldn't grieve. I felt angry at myself and the creatures that had taken him. If I had just been there, I could have saved him. I could have at least tried.

I sat in the office next to the window, tracing the spiderweb crack that ran around it. I had cleaned up the room a few weeks earlier with protests from my mother that I should just stay out of there, but I ignored her as I swept up the ashes from the journals and reorganized the desk with what little hadn't been broken beyond repair. The shelf that once held those beautiful journals remained empty, a reminder that I had lost more than just my father, but the whole world that I grew up with.

"Your Father was a great man; he loved you so much."

I turned around to look at my mother who seemed so fragile, broken, and alone. Her brown hair hung limp at her shoulders and her eyes had turned gray with grief.

I didn't respond. I could barely talk anymore. I didn't leave the cabin to hike or camp and suffered through taking care of the animals. The silence of doing my chores alone was a reminder that my dad was gone.

She placed a hand on the empty shelf. "He told me all those stories about Hatheya." She gave a small smile, "though, I didn't quite like them as much as you do or did." She looked around the office, tears showing in her eyes, but she didn't let them fall as she took in a shaky breath.

I angled myself so that I was facing her. "They were actually quite disturbing."

She laughed haughtily, "He tried to convince me that it was real. That he had lived there, that he fought Dentro and was in the wars."

"He told me the same…do you think- "

"No," she said flatly, "He just made them up. He had a talent for that. We've had this conversation before, Ferren." She sat beside me, draping a comforting arm around my shoulder. I leaned my head against hers and breathed in her comforting scent.

After a moment, I asked, "Do you know what Mavi gave him? What was in that bundle that drove him to come here? And why didn't he write that story down in one of his journals?"

"He never said, only that it would remain a secret forever. I'm surprised he never told you. You loved those stories." She brushed a piece of hair from my eyes.

"But, then again, there was a lot he never told you," she mumbled.

"What if this is real?" I asked, "What if that place does exist? What if he's there now because of this secret mission?"

She rolled her eyes. "Goodness, child, I don't want you flying off the handle like he did with these stories." She pulled her arm from around me.

"What if they're not just stories? What if he's still alive and we need to help him?" I needed her to agree with me, to tell me he was still alive and that one day it would be okay. I needed her to say all the right things to make my mind stop screaming terror at me all day.

She shot to her feet. "There is no grand quest planned for you because of this. Stop thinking that you need to figure this out. He is gone, and that's the end of it." She stormed from the room with a huff, slamming the door as she went.

I clicked my tongue against my teeth. Anger seethed out of me. Perhaps she was directing her haughtiness at me because of her grief. I would bite my tongue because of that. We had been drifting apart, and I didn't want to damage our relationship even more.

I knew what I saw that night. I knew it was real. Those creatures I had seen proved to me that it was true. Every story, every map, every sketch I had seen had been real.

I pushed the chair away from the desk, slamming it into the shelf, causing something to fall between the wall and the shelf. Reaching my hand between the two, I grabbed a cold chain and pulled it out, gingerly a small golden locket swung at the end of it. I laid the round locket in my hand, looking it over. Carved on the front in curling letters was the initials A&A, inside was a faded black-and-white picture of a young woman with long hair and wild eyes smiling brightly at me. Her face was slender but had strong cheekbones. I couldn't tell if she had freckles or if the picture was aging. It looked like she was caught mid-laugh. I studied the locket, looking for more clues as to whom this woman could be. It clearly wasn't my mother, and the initials weren't hers or my father's. I tucked it into my pocket. Perhaps *this* was the last thing that connected me to my father. Another part of these stories that he had yet to tell me. It was a beautiful secret that I longed to figure out.

THREE

Seven years later, I stood in front of the cabin. It looked like I had just stepped into a horror movie. The siding was falling off, the gray paint was chipped and peeling, and the windows gaped open with broken glass framing the edges like sharp teeth.

I shuttered as I walked up the cracking front porch feeling the steps buckle under my weight. I was afraid of what I would find within the ageing walls of this once lovely place.

We had moved to a small town to be with my great aunt a year after my father disappeared, only visiting the cabin once more to lock it up. She had refused to sell it. I guess it was her last connection to her husband, but she could no longer take care of it or the animals.

I had made a promise to my mother that I wouldn't come back here, her health was slowly declining and I didn't want to cause her any more stress than she was under, but when she died just last year, family secrets had come out thanks to my great aunt's loose lips.

I had found out that my mother wasn't my biological mother, but rather when she married my father, he already had me. That whoever was my actual mother had passed away when I was born, and they didn't want to burden me with it. I asked my aunt about the locket I still clung to, wondering if perhaps the woman was my mother, but she hadn't a clue.

When that bit of news came out, I rushed here, putting my studies on hold, not caring to say goodbye to anyone. I needed to see my home. I missed it, but I understood why my mother had to move, had to leave the cabin and my father's memories here.

The front door was broken, swinging open easily with a slight push. I stepped into the house and my heart plummeted. This once beautiful home that I felt safe in, the only place I felt safe in, was now ruined. The little blue couch that had sat under the living room window was torn apart; stuffing was thrown everywhere. Surely an animal had claimed it as their new home. The grandfather clock that had once stood tall in the corner lay on its side, broken into pieces. The house that once smelled of freshly baked bread and lilac now smelled of mold and dust. Squatters have been in and out of the house, taking what they could, enjoying the fireplace and warm blankets. I knew that this place wasn't going to be the same. That it would be a rotting, forgotten mess that would bring me pain. I was getting used to that feeling. That never-ending sickness that clenched my heart.

I clicked on the flashlight and trudged up the old stairs to the office door, not expecting to find much, but didn't know where else to start. I wasn't even sure what I was looking for. Maybe something about my biological mom, Hatheya, other secrets that had been kept from me?

A bang erupted through the house. I jumped back, dropping the flashlight. It tumbled down the stairs, casting flashes of shadows across the walls. I stared down at the flashlight, afraid to turn around as the office door squeaked open. I had probably just walked in on someone camping out in the house or a group of teens who had been enjoying a long weekend. Slowly I turned around when no one struck me, passing it off as the wind or the house settling, and entered the open office.

Something was calming about stepping into it, but that was pulled away as I looked around at my empty surroundings. There was no oak desk covered in papers and a lamp, there was no oversized couch or old paintings that hung across the walls. My mother must have had someone come and clean out the office, destroying any clues that would have helped me find out about the locket, about my mother, about my life. I had so many questions filling my head I couldn't breathe anymore. They consumed me, eating away at my mind and filling me with anxiety.

I searched the cabin for anything that would help me, but was brought to dead end after dead end. There was nothing left of my dad. It was as if he had been wiped clean from here. Maybe that is what he had wanted. After a while, I stopped searching and sat in the living room staring at a candle that I lit, wishing there was something, anything, that would have helped me.

The door squeaked upstairs. I sat up straight. Adrenalin coursed through my veins as the noise echoed throughout the house, shaking dirt down from the ceiling. I jumped to my feet unsure of what to do. I had just been up there; it had been empty and there was no place to hide. Another board squealed under the weight of someone. Picking up the flashlight, and shined it up the stairs at the open door, tracing a shadowy figure. I tried moving, but shock overtook my mind as I stood there watching as a man dressed in black and silver appeared from the doorway, staring down at me. Across his chest, he bore a gold-threaded symbol of a tree growing through a crown. His dark hood hid his face.

"Ivar," I breathed, instantly recognizing the uniform from the sketches my dad had drawn of them many times. The man swung his legs over the railing and smoothly jumped down, landing just in front of me with a soft thud on his feet. I slid backward until I slammed into the door. "You're Ivar," I said again, a grin spread across my face. "I can't believe it! You're real."

He grabbed my arm and slammed me to the ground. Pinning my arm behind me. My jaw hit the ground, making me bite my tongue. "Wait." I spit out blood that swelled from my tongue. "I know what you are!"

He ignored me, wrapping my wrist in a rope. Before he could grab my other wrist, I rolled, kicking his shin, causing him to stumble just enough to get to my feet. He grabbed the back of my hair, screaming in pain. I shoved backwards against him, making both of us collide with the coffee table. The lit candle fell against the couch and quickly started to flame. I was up before him. Turning on my heels, I kicked him in the head, just like my dad had taught me, and then darted out the door. I did a quick check of my pockets and realized I left my keys inside. I cursed, forcing myself to run, to not look back at the burning cabin, my burning home. He was after me within a second. I pushed harder, faster, forcing my tired legs to leap over broken branches and climb over rocks. I ignored the bile that rose in my throat, the scream of my lungs. I hadn't run like this since I was a kid. I darted to the road leading down the mountain and was struck with a burst of coldness. It was as if I had just jumped into a pool of water, but my skin remained dry and began to tingle all over. My hair stood on end. At some point, I must have slowed down. The man tackled me and together we tumbled down a steep mountain slope.

FOUR

I stared up at the trees as they gave way to little patches of the sky through their thick canopy of branches. It was a dark blue, darker than normal, with gray clouds that hung low in the sky. Thunder rumbled, making the trees shake. Roll after roll of thunder thudded throughout the forest. Mud seeped into my clothes, making my bones ache. What had happened to the beautiful hot summer day?

The man lying next to me was thankfully unconscious.

Lightning struck across the sky, sending electric waves through the forest. I jolted up. This was not the woods that surrounded my cabin. The trees stretched up into the sky as if they were touching the clouds. Thick vines of moss hung between them, dangling down like spider webs. I felt so insignificant standing in the large forest. Dead leaves clung to my hair, mud, and blood covered my body, and then the genuine pain and panic filled me as I realized I wasn't anywhere near the cabin. I had no clue where I was or how I had gotten here.

The sky turned from dark blue to black in a matter of moments, a crack of lightning and thunder, fog covered the ground, and then came the rain. It poured out of the sky with giant drops that pelted me like razors. I couldn't see more than a few inches in front of me as the rain and mud splashed into my eyes.

"Don't move!" The man clutched me tightly around the chest, pinning my arms down at my sides. He pressed a knife against my throat.

"What do you want with me! Who are you!" I trembled in his grip, suddenly more afraid of being lost in this forest than to be with the stranger who was hurriedly binding my hands.

He pushed and pulled me through the rain. We fell into mud pits and ran into trees that seemed to come out of nowhere. I clung to the stranger, afraid that if I fell into the fog I would be lost in the rain forever. I was unsure what would be worse, to find out where this man was taking me or to be stuck here in the icy rain, unable to see.

"This way!" He dragged me into a small cavern. Even though the cavern was freezing, I was thankful for its protection from the pelting rain. It was just barely big enough for both of us to fit, having to crawl in and huddle close together. He finally let go of the rope around my wrists. They were bruised and bleeding from him pulling me around the forest. I shivered violently at the wind that snuck its way in, and with nerves that crawled through me.

He kneeled in front of the exit, watching the sky before turning his attention to me, flipping his hood off his face, revealing a young man with deep brown hair that was cut short and choppy, like he had done it himself. He had brown eyes, and his nose was too big for his face, but maybe that was because the rest of his face seemed to be pinched together in disgust

"Once the rain stops we move." He snarled, "No more games." He unclipped his cape, reaming out the water. It splashed across the ground, soaking our only dry ground. I scooted as far back as I could until the rocks bit into me.

"Where are you taking me?" I fought against my soggy bindings, causing my wrists to bleed, but the ropes were loosening slowly.

"You'll find out, eventually."

"Where are we?" A violent shiver coursed through my body, my teeth clacking together. I tried to stop it, so he wouldn't see how cold and exhausted I was. "Who are you?"

"Evir." He said flatly.

"Are you an Ivar?"

He grinned, "Sure."

"You aren't a Nightmare, are you?" My teeth clicked together again. I needed warmth to help calm my nervousness and adrenalin.

"No," he snarled. Lighting a small candle, he had dug out from his pocket.

I studied his uniform again. It was caked in mud, but the silver and gold threads seemed to glow in the candlelight. Mavi's symbol of a silver weeping willow growing through a golden crown was in the center of the black uniform, but something differed from the sketches I had seen. The crown had a picture of a dove standing on a skull stitched in the center. "What does that mean?" I asked, pointing to the symbol. He didn't answer. "What do you plan on doing with me when we get to wherever we are going? You can at least answer that."

His voice was scratchy and bitter. "I was told to fetch you, other than that…" He shrugged again. "I don't get paid to ask questions. It's a waste of breath."

"If you're an Ivar, then why are you doing this to me?" I had been taught that Ivars were the protectors of all. They wouldn't hurt a human, wouldn't drag them through the rain, wrist bound and bleeding. Lightning flashed outside; the sky lit up for a moment and something large jumped from one tree to another. The trees groaned under the weight. "What was that?" I whispered just above a breath.

"A Mammoth Araneae?" He tried to pull his sword, but the cavern was too small to angle it out without cutting me. He instead pulled out a long silver knife and blew out the candle, plunging us into darkness.

My shiver stopped instantly. "What?" A Mammoth Araneae, in other words, a large ass spider. I had read about it in one of the journals. A creature that was supposed to be fake, like the Ivar sitting in front of me, "I'm in Hatheya?" Maybe I fell and hit my head, maybe I was delusional and still sitting on the blue couch at the cabin, but the cold that raked through my body felt real. The terror and excitement that coursed through my veins felt even more real.

"If there's one, there's more." Evir said, peering out into the dark, "The bastards like to hunt together."

They were skilled predators who could smell out their prey from miles away and enjoyed the hunt as much as the kill. Many Ivars and Nightmares had lost their lives to the creatures.

"They must have a nest around here somewhere." He twirled the knife in his hand, "Looks like we're stuck till morning."

"They still hunt during the day."

"They can't see as well during the day." He cut back.

"Are we really in Hatheya?" I asked after a moment. Thunder shook the ground and trees creaked around us. Panic was settling in from being stuck in a small space, and hunger was gnawing at my stomach.

"Yes." He was cleaning his nails with his knife now.

"How did you open a doorway to the human realm?" Only Mavi and Gannon could open a doorway, and since Mavi was dead, maybe that meant my dad was here somewhere, but that wouldn't explain how Evir got through one or why I was being taken unless my dad had been taken captive and forced to open the doorways. I was suddenly giddy thinking about my dad possessing such an ability, to be the Gannon I had read about and learned about.

"I didn't." He rubbed his brow.

"Then who opened it?" I pressed, trying to keep the eagerness from my voice. He didn't answer. "Was it Gannon? Is he here? Did you take him too?"

"Enough," he drove his knife into the ground, "I told you I don't ask questions, and those types of questions," he pulled the knife from the ground and pointed it at me, "could get you killed."

"Killed by who?" I leaned forward, glaring.

He flicked his wrist, sending the tip of his knife across my cheek. My hands flew to my face on instinct. Warm blood dotted my fingers and face.

"No more questions, or I'll gag you." Lightning lit up the sky, tracing his dark features.

I leaned back against the cold rocks, closing my eyes and I concentrated on the ropes around my wrist. What knots he had used to tie me and how I would get out of it, out of this situation altogether. My dad was here somewhere. I felt it. I would find him, find answers.

FIVE

A hand clamped over my mouth, jolting me awake; Evir placed a finger to his lips. I choked a scream down as the world slid back into place. The freezing cave was filled with silence and moonlight. The storm finally ended.

Evir was clutching a knife in his gloved hand, his cloak still lay on the ground in front of the exit. "Stay quiet, don't scream," he whispered in my ear.

Panic sprung within. I grabbed his hand, trying to push him away. His body tensed against my grip. "Quiet," He hissed, glancing out the cavern.

I followed his gaze. I couldn't see anything, but I could feel eyes on us, many eyes. Evir removed his hand from my mouth and grabbed the hilt of his sword. He would have to leave the small cavern to pull it. I desperately wanted a weapon, anything that I could cling to, something that would give me a fighting chance against what prowled outside. I worked the knots of the ropes while Evir watched a large spider scurry across the forest. I pulled the rope looser until it fell to the ground; Evir scowled at the rope as he turned back to the opening.

A long black spider leg slipped inside, followed by another. I pulled my legs up to my chest and gave slow, shallow breaths to help myself not to pass out. I wasn't afraid of spiders when they were normal-sized, but this one was something out of a nightmare. I didn't want to see what its body looked like, how large its fangs were, or stare into the eight hungry eyes.

The spider moved its legs around until it landed on Evir and started pulling at his clothes with a sharp claw. Evir swiped his knife across the leg. Warm blood splashed my face and a roar of pain shook the ground. The spider swept its leg around knocking into me, then quickly pulled it from the cavern. I slammed into the wall. My vision blurred for just a moment as my head ricocheted off the wall. Evir pulled me closer to him, trying to angle himself just in front of me in the small space before the spider lunged a leg back in receiving another slash from Evir's knife.

I heard movement above us, trees creaking, a chattering noise, then silence that cut deeper than Evir's knife had.

It had been silent for some time now as we sat huddled against the wall, Evir never lowering his guard, watching our only way out. The sun began to rise, warming our cavern. Finally, the shivers subsided, but the hunger and dehydration came in full force, slamming into my exhausted body. "Do you have any water?" I whispered.

Evir glanced over his shoulder snarling a bit, "We would have been at the camp already if you hadn't caused us such a delay."

I scoffed, "Are you blaming me for the spiders or the weather?"

"For the running." He snapped harshly.

I glared at the back of his head. "We're in this situation because of you," I seethed with anger.

"Stay close to me unless you prefer to die." He started to edge forward. The sunshine beamed across his face as he finally exited the cavern.

"If I stay with you, will I die when we get to this camp place?" My voice was icy. I watched the sun flicker off the silver blade. I had to get my hands on that.

Evir signaled for me to follow him. I slowly made my way out into the bright sun, quickly glancing around. No sign of the spider or anything else that could potentially kill us.

I expected to see a lush land, filled with towering trees and flowers with rich colors like my dad had always described it, but as I crawled out and looked at the tall trees, I noticed they were covered with rot. Their branches hung low and heavy; the grass and moss were a sickening brown. Even the sky looked sick and tired. Perhaps it was just this part of the forest that looked like this? I was lost in my thoughts until Evir grabbed my hoody, slamming me to the ground, his sword swinging above me.

A million yellow eyes peered down at me. I rolled to my feet and stared up at the large, hairy spider. It chattered at us, smacking its fangs in hunger. It has been waiting for us. We were easy prey in its many eyes.

I quickly rolled to my feet, as the spider lunged forward; its fangs nearly missed Evir as he dodged left, pushing me away. I backed away until my back was pressed into a tree. My skin prickled, feeling as if my body was being overrun by insects. I spun around, brushing my arms wildly trying to get the feeling off me. What I was standing next to was not a tree, but another spider. It was a little smaller than the one Evir was facing, but still large enough to swallow me whole. It studied me for a moment before lunging at my face. I jumped out of the way, slamming to the ground and quickly regaining my feet. Adrenalin pumped through me as I faced the spider again. Its limbs hit the ground, shaking the earth as it started after me. "Give me a knife!" I shouted at Evir who was slashing wildly at the spider.

He snarled at me and turned back to his spider. I franticly looked around for a weapon as the spiders moved closer. Grabbing a stick with a sharp end, I jabbed at the mouth of the spider, sending it back a few steps. It lunged again, shooting a leg at my side. I blocked it with the stick but was knocked down by the force. It snapped its fangs at my face. I rolled under it and raised the stick high above my head. With a quick jab, I stuck it into the underbelly of the spider. It sliced through the skin, deep into the belly. Blood poured out as I retracted the stick, stabbing it once more. Blood slid down my arms and body, a metallic smell burned my nose. I pressed my lips tightly together, trying not to swallow the sticky crimson.

It backed off of me, screeching. I turned and ran as it screeched again, vibrating my bones and making my ears ring. It snagged my hoody, jerking me to a forceful stop. I stabbed its leg, twisting the wood down to the spider's bone. It threw me against a tree, knocking the breath from my already tired lungs. The stick was still embedded in its leg as it thrashed around until the stick flew through the air and landed next to Evir, who had managed to blind two of his spiders' eyes.

"Hang on to your weapon!" He yelled, throwing the stick back at me as he jabbed another eye blind.

I wheezed a thanks ducking as the spider jumped back, clawing at me, but it caught me in its other leg, dragging me towards its fangs. I slashed the stick across its eyes. It screeched again, but didn't let go, instead it reared back angrily grabbing me with another leg I stabbed at it desperately until it loosened its grip enough for me to dart under it as it came back down and raised my stick again using its weight to help me stab it deep in the head. This time I knew to step back as the blood came pooling out.

Its legs buckled as it tried to get away from the pain before it collapsed to the ground, sending a thundering sound through the forest. I turned back to Evir who was momentarily distracted by the noise. Shock covered his face as he saw the dead spider.

"Evir!" The other spider had launched itself across the ground at incredible speed, slamming Evir to the ground and piercing him with its long fangs. He screamed, slicing his blade into the spider repeatedly, but it didn't release its grip on his arm until it ripped from Evir. Bile sprung to my stomach; the world hissed around me. Maybe I was screaming with Evir. His arm dangled out of the spider's mouth. Blood gushed from Evir as he pulled himself across the grass closer to me. He looked up at me, choked sobs racking through his body. He tossed the bagger at my feet.

I couldn't move. This couldn't be happening; this couldn't be real, but silent tears streamed down my face, the smell of blood was everywhere and my eyes wouldn't move from Evir's body.

The spider stepped closer and plunged a clawed leg into Evir's back, stilling him instantly, and pulled him closer. I slowly bent down and grabbed the knife trying not to make a noise as it began to wrap Evir in its webs. I was too close to move fast, too close to make a sound. Another step back and another, followed by the sickening sound of a stick breaking beneath my shoe. I stopped, instantly my heart plunging into my stomach as the spider's remaining eyes shot at me.

I threw the stick, knocking it against its eyes. It screeched as I turned and ran. I pumped my sore legs to go faster, but there was no outrunning the monster that was quickly gaining on me. Trees became tighter together as I ran deeper into the forest, their branches tangled together, and they were taller than anything I had ever seen blocking out the sky above, making it seem like night had fallen around me. Vines grew across the ground in thick bunches and the earth sunk beneath my feet as thick mud grabbed at my shoes.

I took a quick look behind me. The spider didn't have a problem with the mud; it ran through it like it was nothing, but it began to slow as the trees tightened around us. I zigzagged around the trees, feeling a brush from the spider's long limbs reaching out to me, ripping the back of my shirt, sending a chilly breeze down my spine. I turned to the right, diving into a thick of trees that spiked out in all directions and fell to the ground and slid across the muddy ground. The spider followed me, lunging its heavy body against the trees, impaling itself on the branches. It released a horrifying sound that echoed throughout the forest before stilling.

Coughing out the spider's blood that had splashed into my mouth, I rolled to my side and stared up at a man standing a few feet away watching me with an amused smile.

SIX

He casually leaned against a tree, his hand on the hilt of his sword that was strapped to his side. He wore a black jacket that hung loosely over a dark blue shirt and jeans, and strapped across his chest were two knives and another knife tucked into his black boots. Sitting at his feet was a small pure white fox with red eyes. It cocked its head to the side and sniffed the air.

I tried to push up, to get to my feet, but my muscles screamed for rest. My stomach cried with hunger, my mouth was too dry to call for help. The adrenaline had spent all my remaining energy and the image of Evir's body imprinted on my mind was just as draining. He may have abducted me, but that death would forever haunt me. I ground my teeth together, pushing that out of my mind as I focused on the new threat that stood a few steps away.

Glaring was the only energy I could muster up as he started toward me, the fox trailing at his side. He had a mess of brown hair that caught the reflection of the sun. It was just long enough to hit the tips of his ears. His tan skin highlighted his sharp features and scruffy face. His eyes were black, darker than night itself. Not a calm, beautiful night that I used to watch from the cabin, but a night filled with terror, death, and hunger. I shivered and looked away; this man was a Nightmare. And I was lying on the ground, too exhausted to run. I took a steady breath, calming my anxiety. I didn't know what they were like now that Dentro was gone, but Evir hadn't been what I had imagined Ivars to be.

He nodded toward the spider, "Quite a kill, though it wasn't gracefully performed."

I glanced over my shoulder at the impaled spider and then back at him. He was studying me with those dark eyes. I could suddenly feel how disgusting I was, covered head to toe with blood and mud, my arms mutilated with cuts, leaves were stuck to me, sticks tangled in my hair. "Water?" I choked out.

He gestured toward the trees he had come from. "I have some in my pack."

I laid my head down against the muddy ground. I wasn't going to move another inch. Thankfully, he returned with a canteen of water and what looked like a bit of jerky. He slid his pack off his shoulder, crouched down next to me, tilting his head to the side, studying his prey. I looked away, focusing on the cool water that ran down my throat. Nothing had ever tasted better. Even the overly dried jerky was wonderful. The shakes subsided, as did the pounding headache. I sat up slowly, "Thank you." I handed him back his canteen.

He tossed the now empty canteen in his bag. "You're lost."

It wasn't a question; he clearly knew I was lost. I didn't know where to go from here. How to get back to the cabin or find my father. I couldn't leave this horrid place without trying to find him, or even to find out if he was here. I was tired of my life leading to one dead end after another, filled with questions that would never be answered. I was so very lost. Perhaps I could use this Nightmare? He hadn't just left me here to die, "I'm Ferren."

There was a long, awkward pause before he answered, "I'm Asher. This is Eira," he brushed the white fox. Standing, he threw his pack over his shoulder. "Where are you from, Ren?"

I stood with him, my legs shaking a bit at the weight. "It's Ferren. Around, and yes, lost. I'm looking for someone."

"In the woods?" He started walking away.

"I'm not sure where they are. Perhaps you could help?" I stumbled after him, feeling every pain and ache that coursed through my body. The smell of blood still burned my nose, making it hard to breathe. "I could pay you. I don't have much, but I'm sure I could get something."

He stopped twisting me. "Where are you from?"

"I'm not from around here," I said slowly. "I'm from somewhere far away." It was against their laws for a human to be in Hatheya, for them to be in the human realm for everyone's protection. My dad told me the realm was sealed so that neither could go from one realm to another; clearly, he was wrong or lied.

Asher looked me up and down. "Why are you out here alone?" His black eyes grew even darker, swimming with curiosity and frustration.

I swallowed the guilt down again. "I was with someone, but they were killed."

He nodded slowly again. "So, you are alone and lost, looking for someone and you don't have any idea where they are?" He chuckled, "Good luck." He turned away again.

"Listen!" I grabbed the sleeve of his jacket, pulling him back around to me. "I have to find him, and soon." Eira made a small growling noise, pulling back her lips to show her pointed teeth.

He ripped his arm from my grip, his face growing dark. Shadowed hands reached out around him, contorting his features in a gruesome way. They swarmed around his feet and hands. I could see faces screaming, biting at each other, begging for help yet hungry to devour me.

I tripped over my feet as I backed away from him and fell to the ground, scooting even farther away, and raised a hand and screamed. "Dentro!" Those shadows would consume me, trapping me in their hell of faces, forcing me to feed upon victims to grow his power.

The shadows disappeared back into nothingness. The sun was back and shining down on us.

I stared up at him, my breath caught in my chest as I tried to figure out what to do. I had known that there were other Shadow Nightmares, but I also thought Dentro had devoured them all to gain their power. Carefully, I rose to my feet. "Do you have a map I could have?" I asked quietly, as if standing in front of a wild animal.

"No."

"Okay," I didn't like the way he watched me, "Do you know where the closest town is?" Perhaps if I started there, I could find a map or some supplies, and figure out where my father is. If he was here at all.

His face started to soften, "Yes, Sonder is the closest Nightmare town to here. Are you from the farms?"

I nodded. "Yes, a farm extremely far away from here. I came here looking for someone and…" I gestured at the spider. "Haven't had the best of luck, so if you would just point me toward that town, I would really appreciate it."

There was a long stretch of awkward silence again before he nodded and turned around, heading back the way I had just come. "I'll show you."

"No, no." I shook my head quickly. "I can go alone."

He continued walking. I stood there a moment scanning the trees, my chest beating with anxiety as unknown sounds filled my ears. After a terrifying moment, I followed a few steps back from him, just in case he decided to turn on me again.

He glanced back at me. "Who are you looking for?"

"My dad." What else was I supposed to say about him? Definitely not that he was Gannon, an Ivar soldier.

"And you don't know where he is?"

"Ummm…" I chewed on my bottom lip. "All I know is he was taken."

"Taken by the Ivars? For what crimes?"

Did he think I was a Nightmare? I blinked at my stupidity. If he thought I was Ivar, he wouldn't have hesitated to kill me. "He didn't do anything, but they took him anyway. I'm hoping to bring him home."

He laughed, "I'm sorry to say, but I'm sure he's dead unless they took him to do a public execution, which they only do to the worst of us."

A public execution? Ivars and Nightmares still live separately?

What my dad had dreamed Hatheya would grow into hadn't happened. The land still looked dead as we walked on. No birds sang, no lovely smells of wildflowers or trees, just rot and sickness touched everything that lay before us. "Is there an Ivar town around here?" Maybe Ivar towns would be filled with the beauty I had learned about.

He stopped walking and checked his compass. "They're mostly by the farms."

I gave him a tight smile. "Not anywhere near my farm."

Asher pointed through a thickening of threes. "Did you kill that one as well?"

I walked to the opening of trees and saw the other spider's body lying in a pool of blood. I stood still, staring at the spider thinking of Evir. Should I go back and bury his body or just leave it? I didn't think I could handle looking at the body again, and why should I? He abducted me and brought me into a land of danger. I wasn't the one that killed him, but before I could move on, Asher cut through the trees.

"Two kills are impressive. Oh, looks like I found your friend." He walked away from my line of sight, then came back, his eyes as black as coal again. Before I could react, he grabbed me. "Who are you!"

"I told you already." I tried pulling away, but he tightened his grip.

"Your friend is an Ivar Soldier. You claimed to be from the farms but didn't know that was where Ivar towns were." His fingers dug into me. "You're an Ivar aren't you?"

I didn't waver, even though panic rose inside me. Was I? If my father was, wouldn't that make me one as well? What did it make me if my mother wasn't? Was I just a half-breed then? These thoughts captured my mind until he shook me harshly. "No." I finally sputtered out, "He took me captive!"

Asher let go of my arm, pushing me away, "He took you and your father?"

"No, I don't know who took my dad." I ran a hand through my messy hair, trying to calm my mind. "I don't know what happened to him."

I readied myself for Asher to have the shadows trace around us again. For him to lunge at me with a weapon even. I knew how to defend myself against a weapon, but the darkness that spawned from him was something that would surely devour me.

"Which town was he taking you to?"

"He didn't say a town, he said a camp?"

"You said town earlier." He crossed his arms. "Which is it?

I took a breath, clearing my thoughts and forcing my exhaustion down and out of my mind before answering, "I wanted to go to an Ivar town and see if I could find out anything about my dad, maybe find out if he is at this camp and where it is."

He narrowed his eyes, "How do you expect to do that? Just walk up to an Ivar and ask?"

"I'll be fine." Unless all the Ivars are now like Evir and no longer protected humans, or whatever I was.

"If you want to get yourself killed, then Finara is that way." He pointed behind me, "Three days' walk if you walk all night, which wouldn't be wise."

I crossed my arms and matched his stance, "I'm not going to run off in a random direction. I need a map and supplies. Take me to Sonder; it's close, right?"

"Why should I help you? I'm still not convinced you're not Ivar." He studied me again, his cold eyes taking in every part of me, "There's something off about you." His shadows swept around him.

I screamed, feeling death curl around me. "Stop please!" I almost sobbed with relief when they stopped creeping toward me and stayed behind him.

He turned away quickly and cleared his throat, "I'll take you to Sonder."

"Oh," His sudden change of heart shocked me, "Thank you." I sputtered, breathing hard and regretting the fact that I was going to have to follow him.

He just nodded.

I trudged over fallen trees and rough terrain. My feet were sore; blisters were forming from rubbing against my wet shoes; my back was freezing from where the spider had ripped my shirt and jacket, and my arms burned from all the scratches.

Asher had given me more water and food as we walked; we didn't take breaks as the sun started to set. He said we didn't want to be out here past dark unless I wanted to meet something worse than the spiders.

I kept a close eye on him. Clutching Evir's knife to me, just in case. Eira walked ahead of us, sniffing the air, sometimes disappearing, and returning with a mouse. Her blood-red eyes were always watching, her large ears picking up on sounds I couldn't hear, making me clutch the knife with white knuckles.

He paused, and he handed me his jacket. "Put this on. I don't want you drawing attention to us."

"Won't all the blood draw attention?" I gestured down my body, which was painted with crimson. My clothes were tattered and grimy and sticking to my overly bruised body.

"No, that will help you fit in." He forced the jacket into my hands and didn't wait for me as he headed down the hill.

I scoffed and pulled the jacket on and hugged it close to my body, sighing with relief as I instantly felt warmer. The jacket was much too large for me. I rolled the sleeves up and pulled the hood over my head, blocking out the wind.

"Cover your face more and don't talk." He called over his shoulder.

I swallowed my fear. He obviously knew something was way off about me, yet he continued helping me unless he was leading me somewhere to kill me, or worse. *Just get supplies and get out.* Sleep and food would be nice as well.

We continued our walk in silence. I watched the forest begin to thin out and bend over at the weight of their leaves, and heavy mud covered our path. Chimney smoke filled the sky. I looked back into the thick of the forest that we had just come from, "Asher." I hissed as I saw bright eyes watching me from behind. "Something is watching us."

"Probably." He didn't look back or seem concerned.

These weren't just eyes, there was a figure standing deep in the forest. My nerves stood on edge; my heart pounded in my ears. I started walking faster, glancing over my shoulder until we finally walked into a small town. If you could call it that. Broken-down houses lined a muddy, worn street on either side. They all seemed to be caving in or tilting precariously to one side. Many lacked doors and shutters allowing the wind to whip around inside. "Was there a fire?" I asked, noticing that farther up the road were burned houses that swayed dangerously with the wind.

"Yes, many still live in the burned homes, but others," He pointed to an alleyway lined with makeshift tents, "They survive any way they can and some are just passing through to another place, no one stays long unless you work in the mines for the Ivars or you have nowhere else to go. Just stick close to me." Asher pulled me toward a larger building that seemed like a house stacked onto another one. The heavy weather-beaten sign hanging out front that read *Jovie's.* This was by far the nicest place they had in this town.

"Why don't you rebuild?" I asked, my heart sinking for the people shivering in the cold.

"That would cost money, a thing a lot of us don't have." He kept his face neutral, not a hit of sadness for this town shown on his dark face.

"What about Eira?" I hadn't seen her return after her last hunt.

"She'll be fine." He pulled open the door and shoved me into the dusky bar. I blinked a few times, waiting for my eyes to adjust to darkness, then gaped at the creatures. Everyone inside was talking loudly, passing drinks around, and shoving food into their mouths. There was a man with three arms and a face on the back of his head who was talking to an ogre, a woman who was bleeding from a gaping hole in the middle of her stomach and eyes leaning against the back wall staring into the dark and a creature sitting in the very back that had faces covering his body that were all talking or eating, sharp teeth hacked away at a piece of meat. Every type of Nightmare that I had seen crawling around in my dreams and my father's journals were here in this small, suffocating bar.

A metallic pungent smell lofted through the bar. I had to bite my tongue to keep from gagging. These were nightmares, actual nightmares come to life. I folded my shoulders down and hugged the jacket closer. I wanted to disappear, to never look back at the creatures that sat around me, but my feet felt glued to the floor, not out of fear, but out of curiosity. Pure disgusting curiosity to watch these creatures.

"Hello there," a woman sauntered towards me. She was dressed in black leather that barely covered any part of her as it crisscrossed across her chest, leaving her stomach bare and a pair of shredded pants (if you could call them that with how thread-bearing and thin they were).

The woman's ribs were pressed tight against her pale skin as if at any moment they would slice through her thin skin. Her eyes were black and red orbs that hung in narrow slits in her sunken face and her overly large lips were bright red, with four piercings along the bottom. "Well, I see Asher here has a new friend," she smiled at me, showing off her yellowed, pointed teeth.

"Hello Jovie," Asher sighed and looked around the bar, "Tell TJ that I'm taking a room."

I gave a sharp look at Asher, "A room?" I glanced out one of the dirty windows. Night had fallen quickly, and it had brought out many more Nightmares that crowded the streets.

"Really?" Jovie smiled at me again, "Did you find a new toy?" She brushed a piece of hair out of my eyes, her long nails brushed against my skin. I took a step back, slapping her hand away. She leaned forward sniffing the air around me, "You reek of spider blood." Jovie glanced at Asher and then back at me, "Been playing in the forest, have you?" She gave a light laugh.

"Back off Jovie." Asher grabbed my arm, pulling me away from her, but she caught my other arm.

"Where ya from sweetie?" Her nails were digging into my skin, "The way you're looking around at everyone, it's like you've haven't seen anything like us."

I pulled away from both, "Are you always this nosy?" I sneered at Jovie, wishing for a moment I had deadly teeth like her.

"Yes, she is," Asher grabbed me again, pulling me up the stairs like a child. She watched us until we disappeared. We walked along a tight hallway until we got to a room at the end. The room was small, with a twin-size bed under a crooked window. A bathroom with a bucket of water hanging on a hook with a sponge, and another bucket in the corner, I assumed, was to be the toilet. I wrinkled my nose; I would rather go behind a tree. At least the room had a fireplace, or at least what I assumed was a fireplace. I had never seen one so small before. "Lovely." I hovered in the hallway, "Thank you for getting me here. Is there a back way out?"

"No," He shoved me into the room.

My knee slammed into the bed, and I swore under my breath, "Would you stop man-handling me!" I rubbed my knee.

He moved over to the fire and soon a flame of warmth filled the small room.

"Get some rest. You have a long trip coming up." He extended his hand. "You can have the bed. Give me back my jacket."

I slipped it off, feeling the chill returning to my bones, "You're staying in here, with me?"

He tossed his jacket on the small spot on the floor. "Yes, sorry *princess,* but I could only afford one room and just like you, I'm exhausted." He kicked off his boots. "Just don't stab me in my sleep or I won't help you find supplies." He gestured to the knife I had tucked into my waistband. "Might want to hide that better, since it's an Ivar blade."

I hissed, making my way to the so-called bathroom. I stood in front of the dirty, cracked mirror, dunking the sponge in and out of the bucket and wiping off everything that I was covered in. There was no way to save my clothes, but at least my face wasn't such a mess anymore. I ditched my hoody at the end of the bed, grabbed the blankets, wrapped them around me, and laid down on the dust-filled mattress, praying bedbugs wouldn't eat me.

I held the blade in my hand, tracing the etching of Mavi's symbol that was around the handle. The Willow tree meant growth from pain, and the crown meant a kingdom for all…or at least that's what my dad told me, but seeing Hatheya like this, there was no growth, maybe that's why the skull and dove were added.

Asher sat quietly, watching the fire. It reflected in his dark eyes like a mirror. It was breathtaking. I watched until my eyes grew heavy and my body relaxed in the bed, trying to ignore the pain that was running through my body. I laid there, feeling every muscle in my body ache as I was drifting in and out of sleep. Nightmares about Evir filled the darkness of the room. The crackling sound of the fire sounded like bones breaking. His screams echoed through me. I awoke to a sweet scent of flavor floating across the room. I opened my eyes and sat up, pushing Evir from my mind as quickly as possible.

The sky was a hazy blue, rain was falling in giant drops, splattering across the dirty ground outside. Nightmares ran from shack to shack trying to avoid getting wet, and others walked in the middle not caring about it as mud caked their boots. There was a leak in the middle of the room. It was pounding down on the floor like a quick tick of a clock. Asher was gone, as were his jacket and boot.

SEVEN

*K*eeping the blanket wrapped around my shoulders, I stood. My body screamed in protest. I hadn't felt this way since camping with my father or after he would make me spend the day running through the woods. Maybe this is why he made me go through all that pain, so I would be ready for this.

I stared out the window for a while, stretching out my sore joints before finally opening the door to the hallway. The sweet scent hit me again, reminding me of Sunday mornings when my mom would make baked goods for church.

I ditched the blanket and snuck quietly down the stairs into the once-crowded bar. The sight was quite different from last night. There were Nightmares passed out all across the bar. Others were huddled together in small groups, picking at their breakfasts and murmuring. Some were still drinking. I avoided staring this time as I sat down at the bar. The bartender walked up to me. He was a troll, a literal troll, with a horn on top of his long, thin head. His hands were huge, with sharp little claws on the tips, his skin a pale orange. "What do you want?" he mumbled.

I looked around, trying to figure out what everyone else was eating.

"Food or drink?" He leaned forward, eyeing me closely. "Where you from?"

"Food." I avoided his second question. Did I have the words *might be human* stamped on my forehead? "What kind of food do you have?"

He snorted and walked back to the kitchen, returning a moment later with a platter of meat and dropping it in front of me. The blackened meat was unfamiliar, but its smell still made my mouth water.

I grabbed a piece of meat ready to take a big bite, but he slapped it out of my hand, "Hey, you got to pay first." He glared down at me, his nostrils flaring in and out reminding me of a bull.

Panic filled my chest; I had nothing to give this man. He was going to kick me out or kill me. He would wonder why I had nothing, why I was covered in spider blood, why I didn't know anything.

"She doesn't want that anyway, TJ." Jovie came out from the back, handing me a plate of bacon and some muffins, winking at TJ. That wonderful, sweet smell of muffins filled my nose. "On the house."

TJ walked off with the tray of meat huffing angrily as I stuffed my face as quickly as I could with a muffin and prayed this bacon wasn't made from something other than a pig. I wasn't even sure if they had pigs in Hatheya.

"You still smell of spider blood." Jovie made a disgusted look. "Did you roll around in it or something?"

I simply nodded and shoved another piece in my mouth. The sweet blueberries burst into my mouth.

She tapped her nails against the wooden bar, "You never told me where ya from."

I didn't answer and tried to keep from cringing at how loud she spoke. Nightmares across the room could hear her interrogating me.

"Oh, I see. The new girl doesn't want to make friends. You must be from the western town. Everyone over there is a little weirder," she giggled loudly. "How did you meet Asher?" She stopped smiling. "He was down here at the bar all night, so clearly he didn't buy you."

I choked on the bacon, "Excuse me! Why would you think that?" I gave her a once over and realized that perhaps she wasn't just a girl who owned the place. She glared at me, her cat-like eyes piercing in the morning sun. "Oh, don't worry, I'm not taking your place."

She flicked her long black hair behind her shoulder, making her bracelets clink against each other. "Huh, thanks for the reassurance, honey." She moved closer to me, "I don't know why you're here, but I can tell something is off about you."

I finished eating and slid the plate away from me as TJ walked by grabbing it, "Don't worry I'm leaving." I watched her eyes fill with even more curiosity.

Her long earrings swung with the tilt of her head. "Where are you going?"

"Why are you so interested in me," I snarled.

"I'm interested in everyone that comes into my bar," She looked me up and down, batting her eyelashes.

"Thanks for the food." I smiled haughtily. Jovie rolled her eyes as she moved away to another table, striking up a conversation with a woman who was reading a paper, not caring that she was interrupting her.

Even with food in my stomach, I felt hollow inside from the anxiety that pulled at me endlessly. I guess Asher was right about me needing to keep my head down, but I could only go so long without food. I looked around the pub as Jovie continued to talk about something else, glancing over her shoulder at me and spotted a man asleep at a table, a white fox curled at his feet.

I slid into the seat across from him. Eira slinked out from under the table and jumped into the chair next to me. Asher raised his head, "I see you found me." His voice was gravelly.

"Wasn't hard. We need to leave; your friend Jovie is becoming very nosy."

He leaned back in his chair, cracking his neck to the side, "She's always nosy. Don't worry, no one will believe a word she says. She's a gossip, likes creating drama." He stroked Eira.

"There isn't anything to be said about me." I forced my leg to stop bouncing.

"Then why worry about her being nosy?"

I clicked my tongue against my teeth. "Why did you sleep down here?"

"You were uncomfortable with me sleeping in the room." He smirked at me with his dark eyes. "Plus, I wasn't sleeping down here. I was drinking. It's a bar, after all." He lifted a glass with a few sips of beer left in it. "We'll be on our way shortly."

I leaned back in the chair, "I need supplies."

He sipped at the beer. "I will get you some."

I sighed impatiently as he took another small sip of his drink.

"Hey TJ!" A Nightmare with a rat face walked into the pub shaking the rain off his jacket. "Did you hear another one got killed by the Ivars at the Eastern border? They said he crossed into their land, killed him right there."

I sat up straighter, watching the two men and Jovie at the bar.

"That doesn't surprise me. It's getting worse." Tj poured the rat man a drink of something thick and dark, "The Ivar think it's a sport killing us. Yet, if we kill back, we get hunted and executed."

The rat man shook his head and leaned into them, "There were rumors that Gannon, the old keeper, was spotted back in the realm with the Ivars."

Jovie gasped dramatically, "Don't spread rumors like that, especially around here."

TJ snorted, "Gannon the famous gatekeeper, or now known as the traitor. Might be getting an execution a grand one at that!"

The rat man snickered in excitement; his whiskers twitched on his face.

I swallowed slowly, keeping my face blank. Gannon was here! My dad was spotted within this realm and most likely in danger. Would he tell the other Ivar why he left, and that it was under the orders of Mavi? I prayed he would, or at least he would live until I found him and helped him. Then we could get out of this rotting realm and go home, back to our cabin that we would rebuild and get chickens to remember Mom by.

"I also heard that they've been looking for someone. A woman," said the rat man excitably.

Jovie shot a quick glance over at me. "Why are they looking for her?"

Even Asher was watching me now.

I raised a brow at him, "What?" I leaned back in my chair, trying to relax as my heart pounded in my chest, making it hard to sit still.

A hint of a smirk or grimace flicked across his lips.

Rat man shrugged, "Don't know, just know they're in a hissy about finding her. Some Ivars came to the mine to question some of the well-known slavers there. The Ivars dragged them out by their necks after they denied everything, naturally. Won't be seeing them again." He laughed and dug into the food TJ had just brought out for him.

TJ said, leaning on the counter with his meaty arms, "Good riddance. They weren't just taking Ivars anymore. They crossed a line taking their own."

Jovie flipped her hair over her bony shoulder, "They shouldn't have been taking anyone. Is this woman Ivar or Nightmare, then?" she asked, ignoring TJ's glare.

"Not sure," He said with a full mouth, "Maybe she's another shadow Nightmare." He looked over at Asher. His beady little eyes watched Asher as he stood stretching, then walked to the stairs with Eira on his heels. Shadows played at his fingers, dripping off like dark paint. The rat man flinched back quickly, looking away.

I made my way after Asher, keeping a healthy distance from him. "Where should I go to get supplies?" It didn't look as if there were stores in this crumbling town.

"I'm assuming you're the woman the Ivars are looking for?" He laid down on the bed with a groan, "Why might I ask, are they so intent on having you?"

I leaned against the wall rubbing my tired eyes, "I'm not sure."

"What about your father? Why would they take him?" Eira jumped onto his chest and gave a soft purr as Asher ran a hand over her white fur.

I slid to the ground and rubbed my blistered feet, thinking about how to answer. Nightmares had to have taken him. I saw two that night and now he was here in Hatheya, but Evir an Ivar had taken me. None of it made any sense, especially in taking me. I was a nobody, where my father was the realm keeper and considered a traitor of the Ivar, "I think if we find Gannon we'll find my dad."

He rolled over and propped himself up on an elbow, making Eira jump to the floor. She wandered around the room, looking for a place to nap. "And why would that be?" He raised an eyebrow.

I sighed deeply, "I'm not sure. I just know that they are somehow connected. If I find one, I find the other; I don't know why and I don't know what I have to do with all of this either." I was sick of the questions.

"Really?" he rolled onto his back again. Shadows buzzed around his head, "Lots of Nightmares will be searching for Gannon."

"Why?" I asked puzzled. "It's not like they need him to move around realms they clearly can do that." I snapped my mouth shut. Dread coursed through my veins like ice. "I heard they could, at least some could." Like the ones who took my dad and me.

He narrowed his eyes at me, "Haven't heard that rumor before."

I shrugged and looked down at my callused feet, avoiding his dark eyes.

"Find your father? Find Gannon?" He mumbled under his breath; the shadows swirled darker around him. "Alright," He finally sat up, his shadows settling a bit, "We find Gannon and hopefully your father." He said the last part flippantly.

"Eager to find Gannon, are you?" I slipped my shoes back on, wincing.

"Eager to get out of this hell of a realm and Gannon is just the Ivar to help," He stood, "Unless you know how these said Nightmares got out of the realm."

I walked to the door, "Nope, just a rumor."

He huffed.

"And what makes you think Gannon will let you out of the realm? He won't let you out to terrorize people." My voice came out more bitterly than I intended. I scolded myself for letting my emotions slip again. I was going to have to live with the lies I was telling. Asher thought of me as a Nightmare and apparently, they still hated Ivars. I glimpsed myself in the bathroom mirror now thankful for my gaunt, pale body, dark hair, and too-large eyes. They helped me fit in. Though I still had too many features of a natural human, or Ivar, I guess.

"We'll just let him decide that when we get to him. Perhaps a gift for helping him escape from the treacherous Ivars that want to see him dead." He reached out a hand, "Do we have a deal?"

"Going to the human realm is this important to you? So important to you that you're willing to drag me around Hatheya until we find him?"

He nodded slowly, his hand still reaching out. I placed my hand in his and gave him a quick shake.

"Fantastic! You just made a deal with the devil." He gave a snarky smirk.

"Ugh," I pulled open the door and marched out. My skin crawled from shaking his hand.

"Here, you're going to want this." He handed me back his jacket.

I reluctantly took it, tucking the jacket around myself, thankful for the warmth from the icy rain. The streets were slick with mud and crowded with Nightmares that shoved and pushed. No one gave me a second glance, but always seemed to be watching Asher and his shadows that encircled him. I couldn't blame them. He carried Dentro's dark gift.

A little girl stared out from a tent that lined the alleyway. She shook from the wind, her cheeks turning rosy and her many eyes watering as her mother struggled with tying down the tent flaps. Children. They had children here. That thought never occurred to me that Nightmares had families. They shopped together on the muddy streets, going from vendor to vendor trying to get food. A couple held hands, an older lady haggled with a vendor about a price, and kids splashed in puddles and received tongue lashings from parents. The normalcy of their actions struck me. I never thought of Nightmares this way.

Asher directed me into a small shop. The front window was shattered, the glass still scattered across the floor. Water leaked from the ceiling into large metal buckets. The clothes were piled onto dusty shelves or on the floor. It was too dark to see much unless you stood next to the shattered window. The woman behind the counter was an older lady with large brown eyes and deep sagging wrinkles lined her skin. She was missing all her teeth and constantly coughed into a rag. I wrinkled my nose, taking a few steps away from her.

"You can get clothes here." Asher pointed to the back of the shop.

I stared into the darkness for a minute, wondering where the least moldy and musty clothes would be. Wandering over to a shelf of clothes, I pulled out a pair of cotton pants and a long-sleeved red shirt that hung well below my hips with a black corset in the middle.

Digging through a pile of random pieces, I found gloves that could pass as matching and a heavy black jacket that would still require me to roll the sleeves a bit. I entered the dressing room. There was a moth-eaten curtain in the back corner, lit by a dying candle. I pulled my wet clothes off; glad I was finally rid of them. The gold locket fell out of my pants pocket. I picked it up. Rubbing my thumb across the initials, I could see a faint reflection of myself in the scuffed gold. I shoved the locket in the pocket of my new pants. If I found my father, I would ask him who the woman in the locket was, and so many more questions I had.

I handed Asher back his jacket, and he handed me a pair of riding boots. "A friend owed me. They might be a little big, but you can double up on socks. Keep your other pair handy when the weather gets warmer."

"Is it going to get warmer?" I asked, now doubting my choice of outfit.

He shrugged, "Who knows? The weather does what it wants."

I felt much better now that I was clean and in warm clothes. It wasn't something I would normally wear, but you had to take what you could get.

"Where to next?" I asked as we walked down the street. The rain was now creating a little river down the middle of the road. "Does it always rain here?" I was sick of the mud that pulled down my feet, making them feel heavy.

Asher nodded, "Always cold and rainy. Sometimes it snows. Whatever makes this place more unbearable." He pulled his jacket tighter around him. "We're heading out now. There was spotting of some Ivar soldiers down at the stream just east of here. They might be the ones looking for you."

"And they might have information about where Gannon is." I huffed as we walked up a steep hill.

"Are you positive Gannon and your dad would be together? Wouldn't they keep them separate?"

I shook my head, "No, they need them together."

He glanced over his shoulder, "Are you going to tell me why?"

"Tell me your secrets and I'll tell you mine," I smirked as he turned away. "Any ideas on how to get my dad free once we find him?"

Asher lifted his hand. Shadows moved in closer to us. Leaping about, excited to have been called. "I have a few, and we need Gannon free as well. Don't forget about my debt."

A debt I had no problem not filling and neither would my dad. It was just a question of how to get rid of Asher once I found my dad.

I pulled myself up the rest of the hill and gazed upon a field with glowing purple trees. A few were leaning heavily down. Their beautiful leaves were shaken loose by the wind and their branches snapped and broken. "Why is everything dying here?" Even the ones that stood up tall and proud seemed to waver in the breeze. Dark rot eating away at the surrounding ground.

"I'm not sure. It started a while ago and only infected the grass and smaller plants. Our crops started having a hard time growing…and now the trees."

Eira ran to the trees smelling the air, then darted away back into the covering of the bushes.

"Is it like this in Ivar towns as well?" I circled a tree, looking up into the glowing branches. A dark animal jumped from a high branch, landing in front of me. I stumbled back, yelping in surprise.

The creature looked like a hairless cat with large, owl-like eyes. It made a soft clicking noise and pawed at the branch with its talons. More appeared high above in the branches, all staring down at me with their large, hungry eyes.

"Careful," Asher pulled my hand away as I reached out to touch one of the curious creatures, "They like to bite."

I quickly stuck my hand in my coat pocket, ridding myself of the curiosity to touch one. They jumped higher into the tree and tucked themselves into the leaves only their owl eyes could be seen.

I looked back at the dying purple trees, wondering what they would have looked like when my dad used to live in this realm. Did he know everything was dying or was it a shock to him as well?

We walked until the sun began to set. My back and legs screaming in exhaustion. I hadn't hiked like this since I was a kid, and I was paying for giving it up now.

"We'll camp here." Asher's voice cut through the silence, making me jump a bit.

I threw my pack on the ground and pulled a blanket out, laying across the dry grass before throwing myself on it and moaning in pain. I had camped many times at home. Occasionally, my father would hand me just a sleeping bag and some food and send me out into the forest to sleep under the stars and wake with the sun, but I doubt I would sleep tonight knowing about the dangers in the woods that Asher kept mentioning. He had given me a bow for protection, but I was a bit rusty and doubted we would have time for practice. Another thing I guess I shouldn't have given up, but if I did have Ivar blood in me like my dad, using a weapon of any kind would be easy to do. I had read many times that a weapon to an Ivar was considered an extension of themselves. They could pick it up and know how to use it, no matter what it was. I stood and weighed the bow in my hand, tracing the curve of the wood and the pull of the string. It felt right to have it in my hand, and I was suddenly excited to pull the string back to send the arrow flying across the land and strike a target.

"Save the arrows." Asher said, crouching down to start a fire, "We only have a few."

I dropped the arrow back into the quiver with a huff and sat down on my thin blanket, the dry grass poking through nipping at my skin. I suddenly wished for my thick sleeping bag and comfortable pillow.

"Sorry, no tent princess." He pulled out another blanket and handed it to me.

I scowled at him, "I'll be okay without one. I used to camp all the time. Another thing Ivars have in the blood. They rarely get cold or hot. Their bodies adapt to their circumstances. I pulled the blanket over my shoulders. I still got cold, just not as much. Perhaps I wasn't full Ivar. I still got sick, cold, and hot, and I couldn't heal nearly as fast as my dad could. I felt the weight of the locket in my pocket. Her smile and her laughing eyes were etched into my mind. I didn't look anything like her, but the possibility of her being my biological mother still lingered comically in my mind.

A deep ache sliced through me for my mother, the woman who raised me even though I wasn't hers. I missed her hugs and her baking. I just missed her with everything I had. If I could get my dad back, I would at least heal a little of my aching heart.

Eira slinked out from behind bushes, sniffing at the food that Asher just pulled from his pack. "Thinking of home?" He asked, casually flipping a piece of dried meat to Eira. She gracefully leaped up and snapped the food, then scurried away with it.

"Yes, and no." I swallowed the lump that rose in my throat and took a breath, clearing my mind of my parents' faces, the smell of home, and the feeling of comfort that I haven't had in so long. "Just to have family back would be nice."

Asher looked deep into the fire. Night had just settled on us as well as heavy clouds that blocked the moon and stars. "What are you thinking of?" I asked, looking for something to distract me from my bleak thoughts.

He sighed and laid down on his gray blanket, looking up at the starless sky, "The human realm."

I rubbed my head, regretting asking him anything. That was the one thing I wanted to forget at this moment. "What do you want with that realm? To terrorize the humans?"

He gave a short laugh, "No. Well, maybe just a little for fun, but I'm looking for someone."

I looked him over, shocked by this, "You're looking for who?"

"I'll tell you my secrets if you tell me yours," he said mockingly.

I rolled my eyes, "You've been to the human realm?" I was curious about the Nightmare I was traveling with and what his intentions were.

"Yes, a few times before Mavi sealed the realm for good."

I laid down, pulling the extra blanket over me, "How? Once Mavi created the realm, Nightmares were forbidden to leave. They kept the walls guarded." My dad was one of those guards.

"There were ways to sneak through, and everyone was more concerned about Dentro than me sneaking into the human realm once in a while." He yawned, "I would have stayed there too if I wasn't dragged back by the mighty Ivar."

"You know the human realm's time works differently than it does here. Whoever you are looking for is probably long gone." I wanted to be nice about it. I didn't know who he was looking for or what their connection could have been.

"I know," he breathed. "You're on first watch." He pulled the blanket over his head.

I nodded and curled down as best as I could and watched the fire flicker into the sky. Asher's breathing became heavy. I tucked the blanket around me as rain started to fall. I watched Asher shift under his blanket, but he stayed asleep. Eira tucked up close next to Asher,

her red eyes glowing in the flames of the fire. I pulled the gold locket out and stared at the flame-lit picture, wishing it were instead a picture of my parents. Soon the rain put out our fire, leaving the dark to swallow me and my running imagination. I saw shadows everywhere I looked, monsters with sharp claws and long fangs. I shook my head and sat up. It was all in my head; I was creating monsters through my fear.

I watched the wind take leaves into the air with great gusts. They rose and swirled in the wind, dancing in the darkness. Then I saw him, the man, with the marble skin and white snow hair. The man who had been there the night my father was taken. He stood still, staring at me as I stared back. Eira growled and looked around wildly. I rose to my feet, my hands shaking with anger. Every night since then, I would see a flash of him in my dream, haunting me, mocking me. I grabbed my bow as he turned away, walking deeper into the darkness. He was glowing like a ghost walking deeper into the woods away from me. I lurched forward ready to run after him, to send an arrow through him if he didn't tell me about my dad.

"Where are you going?" Asher sat up, grabbing my leg.

"I need to figure out who that is." The man was getting farther away, "I need to go. Now, I pulled away from him, never taking my eyes off of the darkness and the swaying light that was drifting out of view as I started to run. I dodged around fallen branches and large puddles, ignoring the bite of the branches against my face and arms as they lashed out at me, trying to stay quiet, to not draw anything else to me. Asher was behind me and Eira quickly caught up to me. Before long, I lost my direction as the man disappeared into nothing. I stopped short; Asher grabbed my shoulder, swinging me around to face him. "What are you doing!" He whispered, "This could be a trap for all we know." Even in the darkness, I could see his shadows, their icy touch against me. I wondered then if they were all just shadows or if Asher had taken the souls of other Nightmares trapping them within his darkness. I pushed him away, but his shadows continued to swarm around my legs, "Stop it." They didn't move. I knocked an arrow and steadied it on him. This was not like hunting for food as I had been forced to many times. This was protection. I could do this. I took a breath, calmed my heartbeat, and focused only on the weight of the bow and the direction of the wind.

He calmly took a step back, muttering something under his breath. His shadows finally followed and settled on the forest floor like a river of tar. "They won't hurt you."

"Unless you command them to." I snarled.

His voice was calm. "And I won't." I couldn't see his face. He could be smiling at my fear. "What did you go chasing after?"

"I saw someone. I think they had something to do with my dad being taken."

"Would you mind lowering the bow? I prefer not to have a conversation with a weapon pointed in my face." He stepped forward, pushing the bow down.

I moved the bow down, but didn't relax the string.

Asher ran a hand through his already messy hair, "You can't just go running off after something in these woods. You can't trust your eyes here."

Eira gave a soft growl, treading forward a bit, her ears pinched back. "Eira saw it too." Or more likely sensed it. I followed after as she walked along the wet forest. Asher sighed deeply in distaste, but followed along in silence as I trailed Eira through the thick forest. "Stick close to Eira. She'll let us know if there's something wrong. She'll also know how to get back to the camp and the town. If we ever get split up, stick with her." Asher whispered; his hot breath tickled my neck, making goosebumps rise. We stopped when we saw flames from a fire. Ducking down into the bushes, we crawled our way up closer. One fire turned into three and all were surrounded by people warming themselves or eating whatever was in a large cooking pot over a fire. Tents littered the area, people shuffled in and out of them. Horses and a barred wagon lay just beyond the circle of fires.

"Ivars" I breathed. They walked with such grace and power. Everything they did seemed to be filled with it. Just standing there, you could sense the strength that flowed through their veins. I shrank back a bit in remembering Evir and the coldness in his eyes.

I watched the group closest to me. I could hear bits and pieces of their conversation as their voices rose and fell.

"Another one was killed this morning, and who do they blame? Us!" A man was standing next to the group watering the horses. "They don't think maybe someone murdered their own! What fools!"

The group raised their cups in agreement and then went silent for just a moment before the man sat down on a log. "There's something strange going on. You can see it in Bexley's eyes. He's hiding something," he eyed his group. "Everyone is."

Some people nodded; others just stared down at the fire. "Rumors of a war are on the lips of many people," another soldier said, "That a great evil is emerging once again, and that is why our land is dying and the realm keeper has returned."

I sucked in a quick breath and strained to hear better, wishing my heart wasn't pounding so loud. This was what I needed to find my father, and it sounded like he was still alive. Asher shifted next to me.

A tall lanky woman gave a harsh laugh, "That traitor probably has something to do with our land dying!"

"And what of this woman we have to hunt for?" Another asked, "Why is she so important that she needs to go to camp WinWord? The same place I remind you that Gannon is being held at." He took a swig from his canteen.

I felt Asher's eyes on me. I looked at him and shrugged. We were both pretty sure I was the woman they were looking for. I eyed the barred wagon again, swallowing my fear. I would not end up there.

"None of us have even seen Gannon since his supposed reappearance." A woman added, "Could just be rumors."

"Guess the lucky few that are going there tomorrow will find out." He laughed, "Say hello to the King for us while you trek through the Deadlands!" They all laughed and started in on other conversations.

I sat there staring at them, hoping they would say more about my father and this camp. The hoot of an owl brought me out of my trance. I noticed a man pulling his cloak on. The silver symbol of a crown and tree flashed in the light. "Do you know where WinWord is?" I asked once we were cleared away from the Ivars.

Asher shook his head, "Never heard of it, but they mentioned the Deadlands," He scratched his chin, "Seems a bit weird that they're holding Gannon there and with the King?"

I shrugged, "I don't know. Don't give me that look. I don't." I marched ahead, aggravated and tired. My shoes were caked in mud, my hands were freezing even with my new gloves, and I desperately wanted to find WinWord no matter what.

We reached our little camp; I collapsed down on the blankets, my mind reeling with everything we heard and still wondering where that ghost of a man went. "I guess we need to figure out where WinWord is."

"Sound like suicide." Asher responded, "If the King is there, it's going to be heavily guarded and if it's truly in the Deadlands, we'll have to get more gear. A tent, extra water canteens, food, and arrows. There's no water or animals out there, just emptiness."

I leaned back against my pack. It could be a good thing for me and my dad that the King was there. Kandem was best friends with Gannon. Their bond was greater than blood, and perhaps he had forgiven Gannon, especially if my dad told him why he left. Kandem would have to honor Mavi's wishes for what Gannon did. "If you don't want to come with me, that's fine." I said, hoping he wouldn't, "They said some from the camp were going. I can follow them."

"If they see us following them, we're dead. They're also going to have horses. How are we going to keep up with them?"

"We? So, you're still coming?" I frowned.

He ignored me, "I haven't been out to the Deadlands for a while, but if the Ivars are sloppy with covering their tracks, I should be able to find WinWord easily enough." He sighed, lying down. "There's nowhere out there to hide a large camp, anyway. We should be able to spot them easily enough."

I tried to lay down, to calm my mind as Asher said he would be on watch, but my body leaped with excitement for being a step closer to finding my dad, to finding answers. I just hoped Kandem and my dad had worked things out, that he was safe and well taken care of. Then again, wasn't it King Kandem who oversaw Ivars? Ivars like Evir and those with a barred wagon?

In a few hours, we would head out to the Deadlands and try to pick up a trail to the camp. There we would spend time watching the camp until we figured out where they were holding my dad and how to get him out, and then Asher would find out my dad was Ivar. There was no way around that. My dad looked at it, walked like one, spoke like one, and was the overwhelming presence of one. I just didn't realize that until I saw the camp of Ivars. He would fit right in. Me, on the other hand…that was still a question that burned into my brain. I didn't fit in with any of them.

EIGHT

I jerked awake with a kick from Asher to my leg. I had just fallen asleep and awoke dizzy. My mind screamed for more sleep, but I packed my stuff, ignoring my sore muscles, and trudged after Asher who seemed just fine with his lack of sleep.

The sky was still dark, but the clouds had moved on, letting the stars and moon shine down on us. It should have been morning already. I scanned the sky, but not even a note of a sunrise was trying to pierce the night. It didn't help with the chill in the air that seemed to take hold of the weather. I focused my mind on other things, trying to understand how I was still cold or sore when Ivars could endure so much. "Where is the sun?" I finally asked, breaking the silence as Asher studied for signs of the Ivars. They had moved out long before us, but we hung back, not wanting to be caught by them.

"I guess it hasn't decided to rise yet." He pulled on a pair of black wool gloves, "It's going to be a cold day."

I buried myself deep into my coat and tucked my hands under my arms, concentrating on helping Asher track the Ivars. The cold soon drifted away as the excitement of wandering through the forest closer to my dad set in. It was, in a way, refreshing to be out in the wilderness again, pushing myself to the limit until my muscles screamed.

"How are you fairing?" Asher asked, taking my pack from me and setting it against a tree. I stretched for a moment, groaning at my stiff back. "Fine, I'm used to it. Or I was used to it and am now getting reused to it." I gulped down the water. The lack of sleep was beginning to catch up to me. My legs shook with exhaustion and my head swam. I leaned against a tree, feeling my eyes grow heavy, but I forbade myself to sleep. I should have slept last night, forced myself, and I was now paying the price for that.

I had to get up and carry on, no matter how sore or tired I was. Asher was squatting next to Eira, running a hand through her fur, his calloused hands looking harsh against her soft fur. He didn't seem tired; he was on guard. Ready to move in an instant. He stood, reaching out a hand to help me up.

I gratefully took it, ignoring my shaky legs. "How much farther is the Deadlands?"

He shrugged, staring out into the bundles of trees that surrounded us. "Four-day walk straight east, but we're stopping in Linord for more supplies. We're almost there, maybe a couple of more miles before we hit it."

I sighed, "Alright, let's get as far as we can today." I swayed on my feet, "Maybe we should eat first."

He smirked, setting down his pack again and digging out our food. I started the fire while he checked our surroundings and came back with a rabbit that had fangs and bulging round eyes. My stomach tossed with the disturbing sight, but my hunger prayed it would taste the same as a normal rabbit.

"It's quiet," I said, chewing on the gamey rabbit. I couldn't hear birds or crickets as I could at the cabin. It was almost disturbing how quiet it was. I suddenly wished for one of my father's stories, something to keep my mind from wandering down the dark paths it always took. "Know any good stories, perhaps some about your travels to the human realm?"

"None that end in a happy ever after." His dark eyes found mine. "Plus, words destroy the quietness of nature."

"Are you saying I'm destroying your peace?" I tried to sound upset, even hurt, but I couldn't help but smile. "I don't think I talk a lot."

He shook his head, "You don't, but I think that's because you're either exhausted or confused. I'm sure in your head you're having a constant dialog of thoughts."

I bit my cheek and nodded to myself. He wasn't wrong. I felt like I had a stream, no, a waterfall of thoughts pouring through me ever since I got here. I couldn't just ignore the looming death that surrounded me, the fact that my father was most likely in danger as well, and the confusion about what was going on with the Ivars. Not to forget, I had no idea who to trust here, but I needed help to survive. I was stuck in a horrible situation that was beginning to weigh heavily on me. I chewed my lip, trying to clear my mind away from it all.

"You're in deep troubling thoughts again, aren't you? "Asher smirked, "You need to start being more aware of your environment. Don't get so lost in your head. Notice the surrounding sounds. The smells, your surroundings."

I scoffed, "You're beginning to sound like my dad."

He shoved dirt across the fire, the flame sputtered, and winked out, taking our light with it. "I'll be first watch. Get some rest."

The moment I laid my head against my pack, I was thrown into a dreamless sleep that didn't last long enough before Asher woke me for my watch. I felt a little better as I stood and walked around, trying to keep the cold from settling back into my bones.

I wasn't sure if Asher was awake or talking in his sleep. His shadows would slide around him like a blanket. A whisper of a word would disturb my silence and the shadows would flow back down to the soggy ground. I couldn't take my eyes off the smoky darkness, feeling the cold across my skin and the dread that loomed around me when they appeared. When I couldn't take it anymore, I finally woke Asher by loudly coughing and throwing things back into my pack.

He opened an eye, "Ready to go, I see."

"Yup, and the sun has decided to rise as well." It has risen fast. Pushing its way high into the sky, driving away the stars and night sky.

"Good," He sat up, "It will make it easier to find Linord."

We shoved our blankets into our packs and started back onto the winding trail.

I cleared my throat, "Did you know you talk in your sleep?" I said, without looking at him.

"No, I don't." We were now walking down a steep trail, sliding occasionally on the loose rocks.

"Well, you were last night." I skidded to a stop at the bottom of the mountain. "A lot."

He looked taken aback, "That wasn't me."

I gave a sharp laugh, "Then who was it?"

I saw him swallow before turning away from me, "There should be a small stream just beyond those trees. We can stop and refill our canteens."

"Good, I need to wash off some of this mud." It was beginning to itch where it had caked along my pants and my shoes had enough mud on them to weigh down my feet. The trek was already grueling. I didn't need added weight.

At the stream, I stripped off my coat and boots, sat in the sun, and began scraping mud from my clothes. The sun warmed my back, and the water was warm enough to dip my feet into. I sighed, enjoying the water moving around my feet and helping soothe my blisters.

Asher walked down the stream, disappearing behind a few trees. I laid down, feet dangling in the water, and the sun shining on my face, enjoying the solitude. Now all I needed was a book and a coffee to enjoy this moment.

I swallowed my heartache over suddenly wanting to read one of my dad's journals. Did he ache for them too, or was he writing more? Writing about the new Hatheya that didn't bloom into beauty and peace, which didn't bring about a new society of Nightmares and Ivars that coexist…

I stood quickly, wanting to be done with this trip. I wanted to see my dad. Wanted to go home and be blissfully ignorant again.

I threw my coat and boots on and started to look for Asher. I turned, pushing dead branches out of the way, and stopped short. Asher kneeled by the stream, washing his shirt. His tan back was lashed with long scars. They stood out fiercely against his tan skin, slicing down his back from his shoulders to the center, reminding me of wings. He turned as I stepped closer. "Sorry," I said, chewing my lip, "I was just seeing if you were ready to go."

"The scars are from being whipped." He said, throwing on his now damp shirt.

I opened my mouth to protest that he didn't need to tell me, but he shook his head and smirked, "Don't worry, everyone is curious about them and how a shadow nightmare would allow himself to be whipped by the Ivar."

"What?" I breathed.

"It's okay. I wanted the scars; I wanted a reminder." He gathered his pack.

"Reminder of what?"

His shadows flowed around him like wind, "Nothing you should know about." His voice was soft, almost painful as whatever memory overtook the moment. He shook his shadows off, "I allowed Bexley to do this to me for leaving the realm and visiting the human realm before the realm was fully closed off."

"And now you want to go back?" I asked.

"The scars aren't a reminder to not leave the realm." He looked at me deeply, making my skin flush before turning away, "They're for something else."

I just nodded. We all had our secrets and now, or maybe, never would be the time to talk about them. We were traveling together, both trying to get what we wanted, not to grow a friendship, and I was fine with that.

NINE

We fell back into our comfortable silence with Asher Occasionally pointing out the signs the Ivars had been here. I did eventually tell him I could track too but wasn't the greatest as I always seemed to become distracted by my wandering thoughts.

Asher's shadows jumped from the ground, running down his shoulders and darted out to the trees and hidden covers. Asher grabbed me, pulling me to the ground behind a clump of bushes. I collapsed on top of him. Our bodies slammed into the ground, knees knocking into each other.

"Why did you do that?" I ripped my arm away from him, cursing as my bow dug into my hip.

He placed a finger to his lips and then pointed at his ear. I fell silent, straining my ears to hear what he was listening to, but all I could hear was my breathing. I watched Asher as he stared down the path his shadows had run to. He moved closer to me with his lips right next to my ear. I held my breath as he whispered, "Stay low and follow me" I was about to pry his hands from me when I heard voices just up ahead.

We untangled from each other and scooted around a tree. Just a small group of Ivars stood around, letting their horses rest and graze on some of the grass. A short woman stood at the front of the group, holding a piece of paper and talking to a man who stood close by her. They seemed to be in an intense argument. Their voices rising and settling, trying to keep to a hush. Their group threw them curious glances.

"Looks like we're camping here tonight." Asher's voice was tense, "I don't want to risk being seen."

"Won't they let us pass? We're just going to Linord."

He eyed me, "Better not risk it. When they move forward, we'll go to the town and they should be far enough away that it will be back to easy tracking."

I was anxious to get moving. We had rested enough and had sat behind these trees for far too long. I stripped leaves into pieces, trying not to let the annoyance of having to sit still drive me mad.

My legs burned with exhaustion as I shifted behind the bush to find a comfortable position. Sleep was a long way off for us. Asher never let down his guard as he watched the smoke rise from the Ivars' fire. I offered to take the first watch, but he scoffed at me. Eira was curled up on the pack fast asleep without a care, "Do you think we're going to be okay here?" I whispered, thinking of Asher's scarred back.

Asher shrugged. "The sun is going down and that should help cover us. Just stay quiet."

We chewed on dry meat and bread, watched the sunset, and watched Eira hunt a mouse. The Ivar's voices rose louder with their laughter and boastful stories.

"Quiet!" An Ivar yelled "This is not a party! Do your rounds, now! Keane, take the lead, do your job." She stomped away, leaving the soldiers quiet for a moment before footsteps and shuffling pots sounded.

"Asher," my voice was barely more than a breath. Two soldiers were walking our way. Their torches lit their path as they glanced around, clearing the perimeter. Asher scrunched down closer to the ground; I mimicked him, my heart pounded. I held my breath, trying to be as quiet as I could. The torches grew brighter. I wanted to run and get as far away from them as I could, as fast as I could before they could capture us. Asher grabbed my hand, a silent way to tell me to calm down. The soldiers turned before they reached us. The flame of the torches flicked away from us. I let my breath out and relaxed the grip on my knife that I hadn't noticed I had taken it out. I wasn't sure what I would have done if the Ivar found us huddled in the dark. I would hope they wouldn't kill us on the spot, wouldn't drag us away, and throw us into the barred wagon just for camping here, but then again, I wasn't sure what to believe or who to trust. My father always told me to question everything until I was completely satisfied with the answer and knowledge I had. I pulled my hood tightly over my head and turned my back to the camp.

I couldn't see Asher's face in darkness, but I felt his eyes on me. Studying me. "I'm sorry they took your father. It's hard to be around them."

"Oh," I was shocked at his kind words and that he had noticed my pain even in the dark, "It's been a while since he's been gone. I just recently learned he might still be alive." I swallowed the hard lump that had risen in my throat.

"How long?"

"Seven years," I whispered, trying not to let those long years come tumbling back into my memories.

"And what will you do if he isn't at camp WinWord?" he asked after a moment.

"I don't know, I guess find out if he's even alive."

Asher jumped to his feet, pulling two daggers from his side. My heart jumped into my throat as a firm hand wrapped around my neck, pulling me into an awkward leaning back position.

"Move and she dies." A woman spat. Her blade was pressed against the side of my neck. Even with the freezing weather, I felt sweat tickle down my back. I stared at Asher's shadowy outline as they faced off with each other.

"Lower your weapons," she commanded.

He did as he was told, but his shadows crept around him, bringing an overwhelming sense of fear and ice-coldness that nipped at my fingers. I pushed back against the woman, watching the shadows swallow the light of the moon and stars.

"Enough with the shadows!" yelled the woman as she pressed the blade against my skin, drawing a drop of blood. I made a choking noise that was embarrassing. Asher's shadows fell back but still lingered just behind him.

"Get up," she nudged my back, "Slowly." I rose to my feet, "Rider! Get over here!" A younger man ran to us carrying a torch. He drew his sword and helped escort us back to the camp.

We approached the crackling fire, and I felt grateful for that quick moment that we had been taken just to warm my freezing fingers and to be rid of those shadows. My stomach turned acidic at the thought of them. Asher tried to catch my eye, but I looked away as stories of Dentro circled my mind.

After stripping us of our weapons, another Ivar approached us, clutching the rope. He was the perfect height with wide shoulders and a perfectly shaped face with a strong jaw, stunning sky-blue eyes, and dusty blond hair. He was like the men you see on the cover of a magazine. The only thing off about this perfect man was he had two very crooked teeth that were obvious on his handsome face. He glanced at me quickly and gave a small timid smile that disappeared the moment the woman looked over at us.

"You have no right taking us. We're not in the Ivar's territory." Asher bit as an Ivar pressed a blade to our backs at the woman's command to end us quickly if Asher's shadows showed even a bit.

"You creatures were spying on us." The woman snapped back, "Why else were you huddled in the dark on a freezing night without a fire?"

"You see, a Nightmare and you assume we're all out to kill you," Asher snarled.

Two soldiers grabbed Asher, pushing him back. He struggled against them. I shook my head; it would not make our situation any better if he stabbed someone or caused any type of injury.

"We weren't spying." I stepped in, "We were just passing through this part of the forest and noticed your camp and didn't want you to think we were up to something, so we stayed quiet. We're sorry we disturb you."

The woman clicked her teeth and walked around us like we were her prey. She was a muscular woman with a pixie cut. Her dark skin glittered with sweat as she closed in on me. She came up to just my nose, but she radiated with confidence and power. Her brown eyes burned into me as she looked me up and down, "Interesting. Spider blood? Nasty stuff to get off. The scent will linger for days." She stepped back, wrinkling her nose at me. "Especially if one hasn't bathed in days."

I instantly felt the mud and sweat that covered my body and worried about my stench and crossed my arms over my chest, shrinking down into my coat.

"I'm Zyra Brinn. I'm sadly the one in charge of these bunch of morons. This is Keane Zavian, my second." She nodded to the man with the ropes and a soft smile, "And you are?"

"Ferren Vair and this is Asher," I said calmly, trying not to think of the blade against my back or the terror of uncertainty coursing through me. Asher shot daggers into me, his eyes burning black.

"Asher Dagon?" She gave a clipped laugh, "Calm yourself, Nightmare." She walked to Asher and looked up at his towering frame and gave her cat smile. "Yes, I've heard of you."

"We're headed to Linord for the winter." Asher gritted out. He looked like he was struggling to keep his shadows at bay as they tumbled around his feet like excited dogs ready for a hunt.

Zyra scoffed, turning her attention back to him, "Quite a way to travel and you seem to have started your trip off late in the season if you're hoping to beat the snow."

"Anything is better than dealing with the winter in Sonder. "

"Ferren?" She turned to me again, "Where are you from?"

"Sonder."

"Keane, take them to the tent and tie their wrists."

He nodded briskly. Grabbing my arm. He led me into a tent, followed by Asher being dragged by two men. They threw him to the ground, he glanced at me, and the blade now held to my throat by Keane and stopped fighting back as a few soldiers tied our wrists and then exited the tent leaving us each guarded by one Ivar and Zyra in front of us.

"You were not what I was expecting." She said.

"Oh?" I watched her circle me again, then headed to Asher. She had to know that I was a human. That's why she was circling us, questioning us away from her soldiers.

"I do have to say I was surprised that you are traveling with the shadow nightmare. Bexley will be surprised as well."

Asher tensed at the name; a shadow dipped into the tent, earning us both a jab of a sword. He closed his eyes for a moment and the shadow retreated.

Zyra watched with a smile on her face, "I see you remember him."

He grounded his teeth together, "What would Bexley want with her?"

She shrugged sarcastically, "Oh, who knows?"

"Did Bexley send Evir after me as well?" I stepped forward, knocking Keane from the loose grip he had on me. He took a rocking step back and didn't seem too shocked that I broke from his grip or was too threatened by my now raised voice at Zyra. "What do you want with me and my dad?"

She cocked her head to the side, "Evir? Interesting choice." She said, more to herself than to us.

"Zyra?" A woman threw open the tent flaps and rushed in, "Oh." She stopped short. "I did not realize we had guests." Her hood was pulled tightly over her head, blocking her face. A heavy white dress hung loosely across her body.

"I am busy, Nilsa." Zyra hissed, "Take your concerns to someone else."

Nilsa pulled her hood down. Turning toward us, Asher took a sharp intake of breath. Nilsa was a young woman with soft, sun-kissed skin and rosy cheeks. Her curly red hair was swept halfway up, framing her heart-shaped face. She had a large tattoo of wildflowers and vines swirling across her neck up to the back of her pointed ears. "Hello," She tilted her head gingerly to the side, blinking her green eyes at Asher. "You are a Nightmare?" she gasped.

I nudged Asher in the ribs as he stood staring, "Yes." He cleared his throat, "So are you. A Nightmare captive, to be exact."

Zyra ran her tongue over her teeth smiling at Asher, "They are not our captives, but I would understand how a simple-minded Nightmare like yourself would think that."

Asher tensed again, his hands knotting in tight fists, "and I would understand how a high and mighty Ivar would think she wasn't."

She smiled again, but it didn't reach her eyes.

"I am an Ivar Enchantress. A protector of Ivars." Nilsa said in a sickly sweet voice, "I have never met a Nightmare before." She smiled, showing off a set of pointed teeth.

I could hear Asher scoffing.

"But you." She blinked her large eyes at me, "Are quite different from what I have ever imagined a Nightmare to be like." She threw a glance at Zyra who was ignoring her.

I swallowed hard. It felt like I had rocks in my throat suffocating me, "We're all very different, us Nightmares." I managed to choke out. She was an Enchantress! Just like in the journals about Navara and Kanna! I had to quip my excitement before they saw it across my face.

"Is she different, Zyra?" Nilsa asked, twisting her hands together, stepping farther into the tent, her eyes wide as she looked at me.

Zyra turned to her, "Why? Does she seem different to you?" she asked darkly.

Nilsa shrugged, "I was just wondering since so many Ivars are looking for her."

"You agree she is the woman we are looking for, then?"

Nilsa nodded eagerly, "Yes, is it because she is *different*? An Ivmare perhaps?" She gasped and closely watched Zyra's expression, but the woman's face stayed blank.

"She is not an Ivmare!" Asher stepped forward, "Why would one of our kind mate with yours?"

"Seduction, a love spell, and many things worse than that." Seethed Zyra.

I caught Keane staring at me, he didn't seem disgusted by me, more curious than anything. He flicked his eyes away quickly when he caught me staring back. I felt like a freakshow, everyone staring at me, talking about me, and I was silent, checking my surroundings for any way out, anyway away from these people. I knew being whatever I was would soon be shown, but I knew I wasn't an Ivmare. Born of Nightmares and Ivar. There was no way my father would have been with a Nightmare. I looked between Nilsa and Asher and thought back to the families I saw in Sonder. I guess it wouldn't be too bad to be both…maybe. But the way they looked at me perhaps was best if I was one or the other.

"How fascinating," Nilsa gawked at me, "I thought they were all killed after Mavi's death."

I wanted to tear her eyes out as she continued to stare at me.

"Nilsa, get out and keep your sickening stories to yourself." Zyra shoved the Enchantress out and snapped at a guard to keep her out. "Keane, we're taking them to see Bexley in Finara. His hunch was right." She snapped, coming back into the tent. "Let the others know we're changing course."

"Both of them?"

"That's what I said, isn't it?"

Asher's shadows grew, "You are not taking me to Bexley!"

Keane stepped back, but Zyra advanced, grabbing me by the elbow. I tried to pull away, but the rope dug into my skin and she had an iron grip. For being even smaller than I was, she was strong.

"Fine, we'll just take the girl, and you can stay here with the other Ivars." She pulled me out, keeping the blade close to my body.

Asher hissed and allowed Keane to lead him out as well. We were brought to the barred wagon.

Nilsa stood just beside it, watching us. "Are we taking them to WinWord, then?"

Zyra huffed a sound of annoyance at her, "Take care of the Shadow Nightmare. Now."

Nilsa rushed up to Asher and touched his temple, muttering something quickly. Asher flinched back, allowing his shadows to rise this time. The guards quickly stepped back; their faces drawn with fear.

"Shhh," Nilsa said softly, "Sleep."

Asher fell to the ground, and the soldier grabbed him, throwing him into the wagon. His shadows leaped after him, surrounding him like a thick blanket.

"Asher!" I yelled, "What did you do to him?" I turned to Nilsa, who gave me a pout look.

"I just made him sleep. I didn't hurt him. Promise," she said, gathering her dress in her hands, looking like a child that was just scolded. I choked out a disgusted snarl. I always thought

Enchantresses to be cunning and brave, but this girl who stood before me was no better than a young child.

Zyra shoved me forward, "In, and I would stay away from his shadows. They're trying to protect him while he sleeps."

I climbed up into the wagon and huddled in one corner, watching the darkness swirl around Asher. I wondered how long he would sleep and what would happen when we meet Bexley, the man who gave Asher his scars.

TEN

I tried pacing in the wagon as it bumped along the road, but eventually gave up and sat near the window, watching the trees go by. We had stayed a couple of hours back at the camp until Zyra announced they all had enough rest and needed to get on with it. They let me out once to relieve myself and to eat, but I was soon shoved back into the darkness of the cold wagon with the unconscious Asher and his jumpy shadows.

He moaned slightly and rolled over onto his side clutching his head, "What the hell did that Enchantress do to me?" He closed his eyes tightly and winced at the rocking wagon as it hit divots and rocks. "They're taking us to Finara?"

I nodded, then realized his eyes were still closed. "Yes," I whispered.

"The opposite way we were traveling. Straight into the heart of the beast itself," He snarled.

"Don't be so dramatic,"

He scoffed, "You clearly don't know what they do to Nightmares, let alone someone they think is an Ivmare. Our deaths will not be quick, Ren, but I won't die locked in some cell. I'll make sure of that."

"Is that what you think I am?" I asked, my voice catching in my throat. He had noticed something was off with me the first time he saw me; he threatened me when he thought I was an Ivar traveling with Evir. What did he think of me now?

He pushed himself up and leaned against the wall still cradling his head, "No, I know you're not, I know…" His dark eyes found me for a fleeting moment, "You can't be something as despicable and cruel as them. Your… not Ivmare." It sounded like he wanted to say more, but instead closed his eyes again.

The constant rocking of the wagon wasn't helping the sickness that spread through my nerves and ate at what little confidence I had been clinging to. I prayed that not all Ivars were like this. There had to be someone out there who would listen to my story to see that I was, in fact, the victim. Ivars were made to protect humans, to protect anyone who called for their aid. I thought of Keane and his kind smile and the calmness that encircled him. Surely he couldn't be the only Ivar out there like that.

Asher had moved closer and laid a hand on my shoulder, shocking me from my thoughts, "Deep troubling thoughts again? Don't worry, I'll get you out of here, Ren."

Guilt slammed into me, taking my breath with it. I gave him a tight lip smile. I was using him. At first I felt fine with it, but he was suddenly determined to protect me, to keep his word about getting me to my father, and I had no way to repay him. I let him cling to the fake thought that Gannon would help him, that I wasn't Ivar, that I was just another Nightmare wronged by them. "Can't you get us out of here?" I whispered.

"I could kill them, sure, but we would still be locked in here with no way out." He stretched, "Sadly, shadows can't pick locks."

It wasn't until hours later that Asher threatened to kill everyone his shadows could reach if they didn't feed us soon and, sure enough, food slid through the window. I gratefully gnawed on the hard bread while Asher explained a bit of his shadows. He could only kill. They won't do anything else, as he put it. They refused to do anything else, which gave me pause, "What do you mean by that?" I asked steadily.

He cleared his throat before answering, "Think of them like their own Nightmare that is attached to me."

My eyes widened, thinking about how Dentro would pull the souls of other Shadow Nightmares, collecting them to grow stronger.

"I know what you're thinking and no, I have never done what Dentro has done." He said harshly.

I wondered how many others constantly compared him to Dentro just because they happened to have the same power. It wounded him; I could tell even when he let it roll off his shoulders and continued with the conversation.

"When I was born, the shadows that lived in Hatheya found me and attached themselves to me and they were unable to do anything on their own except watch the surrounding land." He cleared his throat, "They are the anger of the dead. If someone dies in a horrific way that leaves their soul scared. Their anger becomes a shadow, searching for vengeance. That's why they can only kill. Why they only want to kill." He scrubbed a hand across his face, "It's hard to control their blood lust, to not let it overcome me and give into what they want."

I leaned forward in awe of this news, none of this stuff was in the journals, and perhaps even my dad didn't know any of this stuff, "Do you feel it?" I asked, watching his face contort in discomfort at my question.

"Sometimes, only if I kill with them…sometimes their shadows become bound to me. They're angrier and harder to train to listen to me. Their murderer."

I reared back, "I thought you said-"

He raised his hands to stop me, "No, I said I would never take shadows from another shadow Nightmare, and I don't want their anger attached to me. I try not to take it, but sometimes." He rubbed the back of his neck, "sometimes they just stick. I could take every shadow from everyone I have ever killed, but I don't want that."

I couldn't help myself from wide eyes and a panicked expression as I opened my mouth to speak.

"Don't." He breathed. "Don't ask how many." He turned away from me.

I waited for my heart to calm, for my breathing to return to normal, but it never did. I was trapped in a cage with a Nightmare that could trap me with him forever, hungry for death forever. It truly was a nightmare.

We finally reached the border of Finara. I pressed my face against the bars of the window, trying to get a glimpse of the Ivar town. The horses slowed down to a steady trot, allowing me to get a better look. The city was quiet and a few candles lit up windows, but that was it. No one was bustling around the clean roads or in any of the pearl-white buildings that crowded the streets. Half-empty garden beds were in almost every yard, empty flower boxes lined every window, and tree stumps littered the dying areas around us. My heart ached. I desperately wanted to smell the flowers and see the blooming trees that my dad had written about. I mourned the things I would never see.

I gaped at the castle that came into view. The large white and blue castle reached to the starry sky reflecting the moon, reminding me of ocean waves. It had dead vines climbing up and around that had surely been filled with bright blooming flowers once. The stained-glass windows were graced with beautiful stories of how Hatheya was created. All were brightly lit so that even at the border, you could see them.

I grew giddy as we drew closer, excited I was actually going to see the inside of a castle, but that quickly passed as I remembered I was a prisoner and that the only part of the castle I would be seeing was the dungeon. "Where is everyone? It seems like a ghost town."

"There is a town curfew." Responded, Keane riding up to me.

Zyre hissed at him, "Do not talk to *them.*"

He pulled his horse away with a huff, leaving me to continue to gawk at the looming castle, the enormous wall that surrounded it, and the metal gate guarded by Ivars. Asher ignored me as his shadows wound around his hands like a pet cat.

We approached the castle; a man came out asking for papers. Zyra handed him a well-worn paper before he called to others to pull open the gate. I could hear gears turning within the wall, grinding and moaning at the large gate until it finally swung open to a sad courtyard with dying trees and wilting flowers. The grass had patches of green and brown littering across the yard that stretched far into the darkness. The earth smelled old and moldy. It reminded me of the smell at Jovie's. I had thought that it was the smell of the Nightmares, but now I realized it was the realm. It smelled this way everywhere, but it was stronger in some places than others.

We bounced on the cobblestone before coming to a quick stop. They threw open the doors and instantly had arrows on us. Well, mostly on Asher, who sighed before slowly exiting the wagon, with me right behind.

A middle-aged woman stepped up to Asher, her hands in front of her as if she was holding an invisible shield. She was strikingly beautiful, with her red hair pulled back harshly and her eyes on fire. "Another Enchantress?" I asked no one in particular. She instantly reminded me of an older version of Nilsa, but she held power in her eyes. This was the type of Enchantress I had wanted to meet. This was the type of woman I imagined all Enchantresses would be like.

"Take him down to the cells," Zyra said. "Keane, stay here with her." She walked away.

Asher snared, but the Ivars didn't step away. The Enchantress pushed him forward. "Come on, make this easy for the both of us."

"We can step inside," Keane said after binding my hands. We stepped through a thin door that I assumed was for the workers of the castles and into a large hallway lined with doors and paintings. The soft whispers of the workers bounced lightly across the halls.

I took a breath, calming my nerves, and listened to sounds around me. I searched for another exit with my eyes, having to squint into darkness. The hallway was lit only by candles.

I counted how many servants were around. Five plus one that just walked up the spiraling stairs. Keane's heavy hand on my shoulder also kept me in place. I knew Ivar servants were also trained to protect themselves and how to use weapons. Which made an escape harder, would threaten no one in this town.

"Who are you?" Keane whispered. "Why are you so important?"

I craned my neck around to look at him. "I don't know." It could be because my dad was Gannon, but I wasn't sure. And like hell was I going to mention that to anyone. It would put a target on my back to be the child of a so-called 'traitor.'

"Tell me what you know. Tell me the truth," His hand tightened for a second on my shoulder.

"If I told you the truth, you wouldn't believe that either."

He spun me around to face him, his face now hard, "Listen very carefully to me, this is the last place you want to be right now."

"Here in Finara or in Hatheya?"

"Keane!" Zyra yelled, breaking us apart from the whispers, "Bring the girl!" She watched us closely for a second until turning back to the doorway and marching in.

Keane shoved me to get me walking, clearly peeved about me not telling him who I was.

I followed Zyra into a cold room with floor-to-ceiling windows that looked over a bare courtyard with the sun struggling to rise.

A large oak table that barely covered any floor space sat in the middle of the room. The fireplace was burned down to soot. The smell of smoke still lingered in the air. There were boards with maps, shelves overflowing with books, and pictures of what I assumed to be important people framed across the walls.

There were just two heavy chairs at either end of the table and a tray with hot tea sitting at the far end, with a man looking curiously at me.

He was an older man with a deep brown beard and long brown hair that was tied up in a bun, wide shoulders, and dark eyes that looked deeply tired. Zyra must have just woken him, as he didn't look completely put together, but he wore his Ivar uniform adorned with black and silver buttons on his right sleeve.

"I'm General Bexley," the man stood up as his deep voice echoed around the room. He had to have stood a good two inches above Keane and looked like a giant standing next to Zyra.

I took a step back thinking of Asher's scars, and bumped into Keane; he placed a light hand on my back and pushed me back to my spot. "You may untie her."

Keane followed the order and quickly untied my wrists. I rubbed at the chapped skin the rope had rubbed raw.

"You said you were from Sonder?" Bexley walked around the table, towering over me as he studied me closely. Panic filtered through me, pounding my heart against my ribs. The world tilted around me, and my mind spun in a chaotic web of trying to figure out what to do, what to say. I felt like I had been standing in the dizzy silence for years, his fierce eyes boring into my skin.

I relaxed my shoulders and turned my eyes up to him, forcing the panic down and out of my mind. Schooling my features into neutral and forcing my body from fidgeting even the slightest. I became a stone statue. "I did say that, yes." I cleared my throat, "I'm Ferren. Though, I suppose, you already knew that."

Zyra shook her head, "Who are you really? Why does-"

The man raised a hand, and she instantly silenced, but her eyes screamed murder at me.

"I'm no one. Just happened to be in the wrong place at the wrong time."

He gave a slow nod and walked back to his chair. "Zyra told me who you were traveling with. Interesting choice." He poured himself a cup of tea, "Now, I know the King is looking for you. He has sent us on a wild chase to find you. Can you tell me why?" He took a sip and the steam danced around his face, reminding me of a dragon from a story my mom told me once.

"I don't know," I said, matching Bexley's calmness. He acted as if this wasn't an interrogation, and I wasn't a prisoner and even had the gall to offer me some tea, which I took with a small smile. He was trying to make me feel comfortable with him so I would open up more. I knew this game my dad had taught it to me. Let him think I was gullible and naïve. I sipped the tea and thanked him again.

He nodded and sat down with a grunt, "Zyra said, Nilsa, you remember the Enchantress?"

I sipped at the tea and leaned back in the chair, "Of course."

"She said Nilsa thinks you're an Ivmare." He gave a light laugh, his deep voice rumbled in his throat, "If you are, I don't believe that is why the King would be so desperate to find you. No, there is another reason."

"Shouldn't you know? You are his general, after all." I wrapped a loose string from my shirt around my finger repeatedly as he stared down the table at me. I quickly stopped and laid my hands flat on my legs.

He stirred his tea and sighed, "The King has terrible secrets, and I think you're one of them."

"I know nothing." I shrugged, "I was taken from my home and have been hunted ever since Evir died."

He took another sip of tea and finally set the cup back on the tray after staring at me for much too long. "Yes, I did hear about Evir. He won't be missed." He gave a gruff noise deep in his throat.

"I have many questions for you, but it seems like you don't know many answers." He raised a heavy eyebrow at me.

"I also have a lot of questions myself," that was beyond the truth, I wanted every question that was buzzing through my head answered, and I didn't want to play any more games of tricking or deal-making, but I knew that wasn't going to happen. I also found it odd that the King's General thought the King had terrible secrets and willingly admitted it.

"Oh?" He leaned back in his chair. "May I ask a question first?"

"Do I have a choice?" I smiled, leaning forward and grasping my hands together.

"Is there anything you could think of as to why the King would want you?"

"Why would I answer that truthfully?" I scoffed.

"Because you rather trust us than him," Zyra said.

I looked between the two of them, "I choose to trust no one. No one has given me a reason to trust them over anyone else. Frankly, everyone in this realm seems to be corrupted and insane."

"Are other realms different?" He leaned just slightly forward, his eyes alight.

I leaned back in my chair, narrowing my eyes at him, "I wouldn't know." I cursed silently at myself. My dad would be dissatisfied with how I was playing this game.

He folded his hands together, "Do you have anything to do with Gannon being found?"

My pulse quickened, but I made sure my face stayed flat, "No."

"Yet, you were following my Ivars to WinWord. My hunch was right that you would want to go there."

"We were heading to Linord." I kept my voice neutral, even a little bored at his questions, but I silently begged for him to keep talking. To say if Gannan was alive or not, to say if he was okay. I just wanted to know if he was okay.

He poured himself another cup of tea, "The King is also there, the man who is looking so desperately for you. Do you wish to be found by him?"

"No."

"Do you wish to find Gannon there?"

"No."

Bexley cocked his head ever so slightly. My pulse quickened. Had my voice changed? Did he read something on my face? I didn't move, didn't breathe until my lungs screamed for air.

"Are you an Ivmare?"

"No," I said again.

"Are you perhaps human?" Bexley stirred honey into his tea and took a long sip before looking at me. "Ivar and human? We've never had one of those before."

My heart stopped beating for just a moment, "No." I said with more force than I intended.

"Some say that when Gannon abandoned the battle at the tower he fled to the human realm and now has returned with young women in toe." A slow smile built across his face as he watched me. "Would you want to go home because we can send you home right now? You can forget about us and about the dangers that you have faced."

I wanted desperately to go home, but he couldn't send me home, and I wouldn't go without my dad.

"Oh, I see, you don't want to go home." Bexley laughed, "You are trying to get to Gannon." He tapped his fingers on the table like he was in deep thought, "Let us be honest with each other." He sat up straight and smoothed down his uniform, "I know that you have some connection to Gannon, I wasn't able to find out what exactly, but I know you're looking for him and that the King is looking for you because of it. We both know the King has Gannon at the camp and that he is up to something, and Gannon is helping him."

I didn't move I glanced around the room, shuffling my thoughts around as I tried to figure out what to say. If what Bexley was telling me was true, then my dad and Kandem had made up in some ways and were working together and if that was true, Kandem wouldn't have sent Evir to abduct me. No, he would have sent someone to explain things to me and invite me to Hatheya, "Did you send Evir?"

Bexley smiled, wrinkles forming around his eyes. "It was not me who told Evir to get you, no that was King Kanden Elide himself." He paused as there was a knock on the door. "Zyra." He didn't look away from me as she stepped out, and a hushed voice filled the room as she opened the door. "Wait." She snapped, then closed the door behind her.

"Sir." She opened the door, leaning in slightly, "We need to speak with you for a moment."

Bexley politely excused himself and shut the door behind him, leaving me once again alone with Keane.

"Human?" Keane breathed lightly, "An actual human." He looked at me in awe.

I sighed haughtily, "I never said I was. Bexley is just grasping at anything. Trying to connect me with Gannon."

"Don't trust them," he whispered.

"I wasn't going to." I rubbed at my pounding head, wishing for some water. I took another sip of the bitter tea that didn't quench my thirst and pushed away the cup as Keane came around to stand next to my chair.

"Do you really know Gannon?" He asked, eyeing the door. His hand was still resting on his sword, but he seemed more relaxed than earlier.

I sighed in disgust; I was sick of the same questions. "You don't trust them either?"

"No, not anymore." Something broke in him as he said that. His relaxed body turned ridged and tense again. "I don't trust Bexley, and I don't know if I trust the King anymore, but it's still my job to protect Hatheya, to protect the people, and to do that I need to figure out what is happening within it, to figure out why our lands are dying, and I believe that you have something to do with it."

"I've done nothing to Hatheya." I stood clenching my fists at my side. "I don't know what is happening to your land or why, and I have nothing to do with it. You could ask me a million questions and I wouldn't have an answer to any of them."

"Fine," He scrubbed a hand across his face, "Let's just *pretend* you are human or even half-human for a moment. How would you have gotten here? Why would Gannon bring you here or even come back himself? It's dangerous here for both of you."

I braced my hands against the table, "I can't change your mind about thinking I'm human, can I?" I said harshly.

He gave me a small shrug and smile.

"Fine, I didn't come here with Gannon, don't know how I got here if Gannon helped with that or not, but I trust him and if he wanted me here, then he brought me here for a reason or against his will. I need to find him and then we can go home, and you can go on with your noble quest to figuring out what is wrong with Hatheya, but we have nothing to do with it."

He wrinkled his nose as if my words were foul, "He betrayed the Ivars."

"No, he didn't, that is a lie that has been fed to all of you!." I sagged my shoulders, "I know I sound crazy, but I have to get to him and then we can go home. I just want to go home."

"Who is he to you?"

I looked down at the table.

Bexley and Zyra burst into the room, making Keane snap back to his soldier self, sliding off the table to a hard stance.

"Seems our time has been cut short" Bexley wrapped his large hand around my forearm, and bruises appeared instantly between his fingers. My poor pale skin was already so bruised, and now I had a handprint across my arm. "What are the King and Gannon looking for?"

"I don't know what the King is looking for," I tried prying his hand from my arm, making him squeeze me tighter.

"I no longer have time to play these games. It's not a coincidence that you show up here, wanted by the King and knowing Gannon. You were caught following some of my soldiers. You are all up to something."

"I know nothing!" I tried pulling away again as he dragged me out of the room and down hallways and stairs.

"You aren't telling me something, so until we leave, you can stay down here." I tripped, making Bexley pull up on my shoulder. I heard it pop. Shearing pain exploded through my shoulder and down my back. I whimpered as he pulled me back up. An icy breeze hit us as he flung a heavy door open. Inside there was a row of six cells on either side of the room, no windows, only cement floor, and walls.

Asher was leaning against the bars of one of them. A flash of worry crossed his face. Bexley tossed me into the one across from Asher's. "Don't fret, someone will be down to talk to you," He snarled, "Either that or we'll just forget about you." He walked away, slamming the heavy door behind him. I turned to look at my jail. There was a simple gray cot in the corner with a tattered blanket across it, a bucket in the corner, and some hay. I wandered over to the cot and laid down, clutching my shoulder tight to my body.

I didn't know how to get myself out of this one…I was truly trapped at this point.

"What happened?" Asher's voice echoed across the cells.

I wrapped the blanket around me and then tossed it off just as the itchy fabric touched my skin. "They think I know more than what I am saying."

Asher didn't respond. We were tired from our nerves being on edge for days. I stared at the soft flame dancing in the lantern by the door. I rolled over to the other side, staring at the grimy wall. That matched how I felt much better. I don't know if I slipped in and out of sleep or if I just stared at the wall until my mind went numb from trying to think of a way out of this. Asher called my name, but I ignored it, my thoughts tumbling down a dark hole. I started to wonder if my dad had been the one to bring me here and had known the king had sent Evir. I closed my eyes tight, trying to banish the thoughts, but I couldn't. They clung tight to me.

"Ferren, we've got company," mumbled Asher.

ELEVEN

I rolled over onto my bad shoulder and winced at the movement. Keane was standing outside of my cell, holding a tray of food. Asher was already holding his and picking at the bread and soup. I'm sure he was wondering if it was poisoned. I got to my feet, eager to have something to stop my hunger pains. I could smell the spices that made up the soup and the butter that coated the bread. My mouth watered; this wasn't the meal I had expected to get in a prison cell.

"I will help you find Gannon, but you must be completely honest with me." Keane gave me a tight-lipped smile. "I know where WinWord is and can lead you directly there."

I gripped the bars and leaned forward, "I already said the truth."

"What about you being a- "

I snapped my eyes to Asher and then back to Keane trying to will him not to finish that sentence. Keane caught my eye and stopped.

"Being a what? An Ivmare?" Asher scoffed.

Keane nodded, "Right an Ivmare, but I'm beginning to think you're not." He slid the tray of food through a slot in the bars. "Strange things are happening. Bexley looks like he's getting ready to leave and I don't know why or where to. The King has taken many soldiers from Finara and has been wandering with camp WinWord for longer than he should. I want to know what he's looking for and if it can help Hatheya."

"Strange things are always happening." Asher abandoned his food on his cot and reluctantly sipped at the water.

"Not like this."

"I honestly don't know, but I do need to find Gannon."

"What is your connection to him?"

"I find him, I find my dad," I grinded out, laying my head on the cold bars.

"Is that why you trust Gannon?"

Asher stepped forward, "That's new information." He smirked at me, but I ignored it. "Why don't you trust your commanders?" Asher questioned before Keane could say another word. "Aren't you Ivars trained not to question anything your high and mighty leaders do or say?"

Keane huffed out a low breath, glaring at Asher, "Something is going on at camp WinWord and I plan to find out what."

"Why?" Asher asked.

"As I told Ferren, I have to protect Hatheya to stop whatever is happening."

"To protect all of Hatheya, or just the Ivars in Hatheya?" Asher leaned against the bars.

"All of it," Keane said, his jaw tight, "If you haven't noticed, things are dying everywhere. Aren't you wondering why or if it's ever going to stop?"

"You think the King is looking for the answer?" I asked, nibbling on the bread.

"Maybe." He scrunched his brow together.

"Get us out of here and help me find Gannon and I will help you figure out what going on in Hatheya." One more promise I probably couldn't keep, but it came out easy. I was beginning to breathe lies.

He narrowed his eyes at me. "I can't get you out just yet. They're going to notice."

Asher gave a haughty laugh, "He's not on our side Ren. Don't be a fool."

"No one is on my side." I seethed.

I paced the small cell, trying not to go crazy as time ticked by. I watched a mouse across the room nibble on some crumbles until it ran away, noticing that I was watching it.

"Please stop sighing," Asher groaned, "It's making this day feel even longer than it already is."

I responded with an eye roll. The door to the dungeon squeaked open. I was expecting Keane to come through the darkness, but a heavy-set man with large round eyes and hairy arms stood in his place. He gave me a wicked smile, looking from me to Asher and then back again. Asher was now on guard, His arms crossed across his chest, he stood straight and glared back at the man. The man chuckled and walked over to my cell. I took a step back as he opened the cell and harshly pulled me out, "There are ways to make you talk if you don't want to talk to General Bexley nicely," his voice was gravelly and hard to understand.

"Ren!" Asher called out. His shadow grew around us like it had when Zyra had me. The man chuckled, hugging me tight against his sweaty chest, his arms coiling around my throat, and backed away, leading me to a hidden hallway that stretched on and on. Finally, we came to a small room that Asher's shadows couldn't reach.

My stomach tightened at the sight. There in the middle sat a chair. It looked like a wooden dentist chair, with bloody spots staining the chipped wood. A large, wooded cabinet in one corner and a fireplace in the other. The rest of the room was empty and cold.

I tried to backtrack, but the man was easily triple my size. He threw his weight into me, pinning me to the chair, strapping me down. My shoulder popped again. I screamed at the sudden force of pain that echoed down my arm and back, but then the pain vanished, leaving a dull throb in its place.

There was a strap covering my legs, arms, chest, and forehead. I already wanted to scream, cry, and beg for help, but I took a breath and stared up at the man, what would begging do? I needed to be strong and get through this. If I could.

He lit a fire; sweltering heat quickly filled the small room, making it hard to breathe. I ran my tongue across my dry lips. Water would have been a beautiful gift at this moment.

"Tell us why the King wants you." The man bellowed.

"I don't know." My voice came out shakier than I would have liked, "I already told Bexley everything I know."

The man took a dagger and heated the blade over the fire, "Do you really want to do this? Or do you want to tell us the truth?" He turned back to me, welding the glowing hot knife over me.

Sweat dripped down my forehead. I squirmed in the straps trying to break them, "Evir brought me here. Bexley knows that I don't know anything else. I told him that."

"Brought you from where?"

I met his eyes and glared, "From my home."

He dug the tip of the blade into my arm. It sizzled my blood, I screamed, I couldn't help myself. I've never felt this kind of pain before. My flesh burned, ached, and itched all at the same time. I couldn't pull away or fight back; I was trapped. The room tilted and swayed, reminding me of being on a boat.

"Why does King Kandem want you?"

I couldn't answer the questions. He was talking too fast. My head was spinning, trying to put all the information together about what he was asking. I screamed again as he slashed the knife up my arm. I couldn't tell how deep he cut it; I was in too much pain to concentrate on anything besides not passing out in the suffocating hot room.

"Do you know what is in the King's possession?" He growled, "Does it have something to do with what he's searching for?"

Footsteps, and then the heavy-set man was on his back. Keane and Asher were standing over me, undoing the straps across my arms. The man was on his feet slashing the knife in the air as Keane dodged around, and Asher was reaching for a weapon from the cabinet.

I could sit up. I winced as I reached forward, undoing the foot straps. Crimson covered my arms; sharp red slashes of burned flesh were crisscrossed on my wrists; I gagged a little at the smell of my burned flesh.

Asher jumped on the man's back, slamming the hilt of his newly found sword against the man's head as they tumbled to the ground. He flipped Asher off him, grabbing his throat. Keane was back on his feet, slamming his full weight into the man. He let go. Asher seemed to glide over to him, ready to slice the sword across his throat. "Wait!" Keane's pleading voice echoed off the walls. The large man stood still, watching the blade that was just inches from his neck. The shadows melted into the room. I breathed in the cold that they brought with them. The fire flicked out, the room grew dark and blinding. I heard the large man's panicked breathing.

"Asher!" Keane said, "Please, no one deserves to die like this. We'll put him in a cell."

The shadows retreated to Asher's side. The man, still on his knees, didn't move; his chest heaved up and down, his eyes wide. Keane took a step back as the shadows crawled forward. The man pleaded he scooted away on his knees. Sweat beaded on his body, even though the room was ice cold again. "Asher. I know you don't want to do this." I could already see the pain forming on his face. If he did this, the man's shadow could stick with him for life. I slid off the table. Shaking, I raised my arms, looking at the wounds that would turn into scars.

Asher shuttered and pulled his shadows back.

The man jumped forward nearly slicing me across the back. Asher's eyes flamed with anger.

Keane yelled to stop.

I tried to look away, but I couldn't. I watched as the shadows jumped forward, covering the man. He screamed, his gravelly voice cut short as the shadows swarmed over him. The man tossed and turned, trying to fight off the monsters he couldn't grab. The man went still, and the shadows melted away completely. They didn't even swirl around Asher like they always did. The man lay curled in a ball, his eyes were clawed out, and he had ripped his ear off and was clutching it in a bloody hand.

"What did you do?" Shaking, I noticed that I was clinging to Keane, dripping blood onto his clean Ivar uniform.

I let go of him quickly and grabbed a rag to help stop the bleeding. Asher stepped forward to help, but I flinched away, still shaking at what I had just seen.

Asher quickly turned away from me and stepped out of the small room, and Keane stepped forward to help me wrap the cloth around my wrists. "What did he do?" I asked again quietly.

"He made the man kill himself by showing him fear itself. He could have killed him quickly; could have been merciful." Keane seethed and then took a breath. "Here, I got your knife back. It's an Ivar blade, you know."

I gingerly took the knife, "I know. Thank you. We need to go now before Bexley comes looking for his information and finds one of his men…" I took a final look at the lifeless man before stepping out. It was much cooler here and I let the cold wash over me, driving out the horrendous scene I had just witnessed. I was in the realm filled with nightmares. Death here was going to be worse than in my realm.

Keane's shoulders were still tense, and he stood like a soldier ready for the war. "We need to go through the tunnels and around to the stables. I have a wagon of supplies going north. We can get out of the city that way, but we must be cautious, especially you, Asher. Your face is well known among the guards."

"I'm going to take that as a compliment," he mumbled, turning his back once more to us.

"This way, quickly." Keane flew down the hall with hushed feet.

We crept through a doorway on the other half of the dungeon. The hallway was cold and damp. I could hear footsteps above us, bustling around. He led us through a winding staircase that led to the back of the house where it seemed to be the staff's rooms and kitchen. It was deserted except for a few voices down the hall.

"The staff is in a meeting; that's why I wanted to wait till now to get you out." Keane pushed open a back door, letting the wind whip around us. "This way to the barn."

We kept our feet light and our steps quick as we rushed to the barn. An elderly man stood in the barn readying a horse that was pulling a wagon full of produce. I stopped quickly seeing him, but he waved me forward.

"In here, hurry." He helped me up into the wagon and covered us in a thick blanket that smelled horribly like a horse. They laid a few items of produce across us. Asher grunted as a box was not so gently thrown onto his stomach. Surely that had been Keane's doing.

"Do not thank me for sending you to your death." He took in a shaky breath, "But I am thankful for your faith in the ways the Ivars should be. May your faith protect you."

"You as well, Father, and the family."

My gut twisted. I felt immensely guilty for having Keane help us and pull his family into it as well. I hadn't taken a second look at the man who was helping us; I was focused on getting out of here. I was pulling more and more people into my problems.

"Quickly, boy, I must not be late for the next delivery. I've already been here too long."

After a silent moment that seemed to drag on forever, the wagon lurched forward. I held my breath and listened to the clopping of the horse's hooves change from walking against the soft barn floor to the loud cobblestone that made me grind my teeth together with every clomping step. The blanket was suffocating with all the boxes piled around us. My skin was clammy where Asher's arm touched mine. It was like being buried alive or what I assumed it would be like.

The wagon came to a stop, and the boxes of food shifted above us as the older man moved about, taking some and moving the others so that we were always covered.

Asher tensed a bit as a mumble of voices talked. I couldn't make out what he was saying, but the wagon was rolling forward once again.

I heard music and wagons around us, surrounded by a mumble of many voices. Laughter bubbled throughout the air. I wanted to peek up from the cover of the blankets and see where the music was coming from and why the streets were filled with laughter. It was much different from Sonder. Warmer with both life and weather. It was even beginning to grow hot underneath the thick blanket and piles of boxes. I so desperately wanted to shift and move, to throw the blanket off and breathe in the fresh air that I heard people running around in.

We made a couple more stops, always waiting for the man to pull up the blanket and tell us to get out, but after three more stops, I began to feel like he forgot about us. There was no way of communicating with him either unless we wanted to give ourselves away and by now the guards had realized we were gone and had found the body we left behind.

I had just begun to view Asher differently than the Nightmares I read about in the journals, but I was fearful again. Afraid of what he might do to me if he found out that I was part Ivar and knew my dad had no intention of helping him get to the human realm.

We finally pulled into a stable. The smell of animals filled my nose as the blanket was lifted off of us, "It's safe now but stay quiet." Keane's dad whispered. His salt and pepper hair was slicked with sweat, and he was breathing heavier now than he was when we first met him.

I took a deep breath, regretting it instantly as the stench of the animals filled my lungs. I gagged before standing and stretching my legs.

Asher jumped out, then Keane. Asher bristled at the sight of him.

Keane ignored him, "Thank you, Father."

"Yes, truly, thank you." I could now see their resemblance. Their eyes were the same, and they held themselves the same, the way they tilted their head or talked.

"My father has packed us things for our trip to WinWord. We should hurry."

"Still planning on abandoning your post and helping fugitives?" Asher asked flatly.

I twisted, popping my joints in any way I could till I felt satisfied and readied myself to have to pull the two off of each other. Even Keane's dad stopped his hurried chores of taking care of the horses, turning back to us, eyeing Asher.

"I am not abandoning anything." Keane was now in Asher's face. He stood a good two inches above Asher, his stance screamed he was combat trained. "I am trying to save my people, protecting them." He sized him up, then stepped back with a smirk on his face. "At least I have people to protect. You Nightmares kill each other, tear down what each other built, destroying everything. You're fractured people." He laughed, "No, you're not people at all."

I jumped from the cart having to catch myself as my legs wobbled from being cramped all day, but before I could step in, Keane's father did.

"Enough," The horse he was brushing shook its mane and stomped the ground, agitated at the sudden boom of the old man's voice. "Keane, your arrogance will not get you far if you challenge your companions like this." He pointed at Asher, "The same goes for you as well."

Asher huffed, "We are not companions."

"Fate believes you are, or it would not have shoved you all together. Now you either can work together and figure out what the hell is going on here, or work against each other and create more blood and war."

"I vote we work together and get out of here now before someone finds us." I stepped up to the old man and laid a gentle hand on his, "Thank you for helping, but if they know Keane helped us escape, they will guess you helped as well."

He nodded, "We must all do our parts to end this," He sighed, "End whatever is happening to our land and my people," He looked at Keane who was now staring down at the floor like a scolded child, "Keane told me who you are looking for, I knew him. I was in training camp with him when we were much younger." His eyes crinkled as he smiled. "You need to get on your way."

TWELVE

The house was backed up next to the edge of the forest, making it easy to sneak out from the barn and down the small path that led to the woods.

"There shouldn't be a patrol out this far, but once we hit the border, I'm not sure what or who we'll run into, especially since by now they will know you two are missing." Keane led us, clearly knowing this part of the woods. Asher fell behind me, glancing over his shoulder now and again, his eyes cold and black, his shadows following after him, darting around bushes and trees. Excitedly jumping over fallen branches. They were ecstatic about their last kill still. I shivered violently.

"You're being too loud." Asher grimaced at Keane.

Keane shot him a look but didn't say anything. He trudged on. I suddenly notice that his steps were louder than Asher's, but not enough to cause us to worry. My steps were louder than both, and Asher hadn't said anything to me. I sighed to myself, angry that the two people I was stuck with hated each other and would surely cause drama on the way to the camp.

"We're coming up to the border now," Keane slowed into an army crawl across the ground, checking his surroundings quickly before scurrying across the ground again. I struggled to keep up and keep quiet, I cursed myself for not keeping up with the practices my father had taught me, for one, I would be in much better shape than I was in, and on another I wouldn't feel so silly crawling across the wet mud in an awkward snake-like maneuver. I could practically feel Asher's laughing eyes on me as I swung my hips side to side, trying not to stick my butt up too much.

Keane raised a hand, signaling us to stop. He lay there waiting, listening for anything. A bush rustled near us. I sucked in a breath, reaching for my knife, not sure what I would do with it even if someone or something attacked us.

Red eyes peeked out from behind the bush.

"Eira," Whispered Asher. I could tell there was a small smile on his face. "I was wondering when you were going to show up."

"Is this your pet?" Keane asked, eyeing the white fox suspiciously.

"She's not a pet," He grumbled back, "Get moving."

"Shhh!" I glanced over my shoulder as shouts erupted behind us. "It's back at the house."

"Move now, stay low." Keane pushed up to a low crouch and burst forward. I tried to focus on my feet, where to put them to avoid branches and not to bring them down too heavily. We didn't stop running, even when we could no longer hear the shouts from Keane's house. I wondered if we were running because they thought we were being followed or if Keane was running away from the shouts of his father and the rest of the family. My breath was turning ragged, but I didn't stop. I could handle being pushed beyond and above anything. Mentally and physically. If it meant getting closer to finding my father, I could do it.

"Keane," Asher loudly whispered. His voice came out dry. "We're far enough away and if we keep running, we'll draw attention to ourselves." He slowed his pace.

I slowed to a stop and leaned against the tree; my lungs felt like they were on fire. I took slow, even breaths, trying not to show that all I wanted to do was collapse to the ground and chug a gallon of water. I checked the stitching in my arm that Keane's father had done up quickly; it burned, but at least it wasn't bleeding, and they were healing rather quickly. "Will your family be okay?" I asked slowly, trying not to sound too winded.

Keane turned away from us, looking up at the sky. Its dark gray clouds covered it, preparing us for more rain and a chilled wind. I pulled the jacket closer around me, buttoning one of the middle buttons so it wouldn't hang off my body. It was a much nicer jacket than the one I had picked up in Sonder. Keane had packed a bag for us, each full of clothes. I'm assuming he got my clothes from his mother or sister then, food and water, and had reluctantly given Asher a bow and a quiver full of arrows. He had handed me mine without a second thought.

"We need to hurry," Keane grabbed his water from his pack. "The sooner we figure out what the hell is going on, the sooner I can help my family."

"They could have come with us," I shrugged, trying to keep it light.

He shook his head, taking a swig of water.

"We need to travel light, not with a group of people," Asher interjected.

I waited for Keane to bite back, to start another verbal battle, but he stayed silent as he pulled on his pack. As did I. I shouldn't have said anything. I regretted bringing up his family.

"Don't worry. He's a soldier. He's used to pain." Asher came up beside me, "But it's wise not to bring it up again. Listen, don't talk. Remember."

I nodded, taking a step back. My skin was crawling with fear. "Perhaps you should take your own advice sometimes," my voice rasped.

"You're afraid of me now, aren't you?"

"That was-I'm-I" I stumbled over my words. I didn't know what to tell him. Would telling him yes, I was frightened of him from the moment I met him help any of this?

"Don't worry. I promised I would help you find Gannon and your father, and I will do that. We have a deal, and I don't go back on my deals."

I studied him a moment, his shadows at his feet, his shoulders were hunched as they had been since what his shadows had done to that man. "I cannot promise he will send you to the human realm, but I promise I will ask and I'll tell him about what you've done for me." I stuck out my hand. "That's all I can do."

He nodded and shook my hand, "I'm sorry, you had to see that. Sometimes their anger wins." He turned and walked away.

We didn't stop until night was surrounding us, and the frigid air drew us to make a small fire within the cave just enough to warm our frost-bit fingers, then we put it out, wrapping ourselves in the thick wool blankets.

"Are you cold?" Keane crouched down and wrapped his blanket around me.

"Aren't you? Even for an Ivar, this is rough." Or at least for a half Ivar like me.

He shrugged, "I'm used to it. Being in the Ivar army requires us to be out in the cold. If we're in the Nightmare territory, we don't have fires."

"Perhaps if you didn't come into our territory, you could have your fires." Asher tossed Eira a bit of his leftover food. She snapped it up quickly and ran to the other end of the cave, tearing it to pieces with her razor-sharp teeth.

Keane ignored Asher, sinking to the ground, "We were scouts looking for some of our troops that have gone missing. They had been sent out into the dead lands farther than most of us go. It's inhabited by the worst of the Nightmares, and we do not need to go out that far."

"Who sent them?" Asher asked.

"Bexley?" I guessed.

"No, the King did, then Bexley sent us after them. We couldn't find them or a sign of them."

Asher ran a hand across his tired face, "They were a part of camp WinWord?"

Keane nodded, "Yes, and all part of Bexley's favorites too. Seems odd that they suddenly disappear."

"Clearly those two aren't on good terms," I said. A stream of silence filled the cave as we all stared out the mouth of it. After a while, I fell in and out of a sleepy daze until Asher broke the silence, making me jump.

"A lot of Nightmares believe that the Tower could be out in the deadlands, or what remains of the Tower."

"Why would the King look for that?" Keane asked, "What could he possibly want with a crumbled tower?"

"Just a thought." Asher laid down and draped an arm over his eyes, "I've met the King, and that man is eviler than some Nightmares. He reeks of it."

"My Dad thought Kandem would be a righteous king. A just king for both the Nightmares and Ivars." I tightened the blanket around me. "Maybe he is, and Bexley is making it look like the King is the one in the wrong?" Maybe they're all wrong and this entire realm was a twisted, sick place where no one was morally caring.

Asher sat up casually and took a drink of water, "Does your dad know Kandem just as well as he knows Gannon?"

I raised my eyes to Asher.

"Are they all old buddies? Two powerful Ivars and a Nightmare?" He said it calmly, but poison lay just beneath his words. "Tell me, Ren, how do they know each other?"

Keane had asked the same question, and I gave them both the same answer. "You'll find out soon enough." I had already filled Keane in about how if we found Gannon we would find my dad and what I had supposedly promised Asher in return for helping me. Keane gaped at me and told me I couldn't promise such a thing. I already knew that I didn't need to be told.

Then I rolled over and flipped the blanket over my head. They mumbled in the dark at each other, but I ignored it and let sleep come for me and my tired body.

We left the cave before the sun was even up, even though I was still tired. The faster we moved, the faster I could see my father.

In the night, the men decided we needed horses to travel faster. Keane tried to convince Asher that we could buy horses, but Asher didn't want to see or waste time haggling with someone about the horses. Keane reluctantly agreed with that, but he was set on returning it to the person after we were done with them. I scoffed at that. It was a nice thought, but didn't seem realistic at a time like this. I felt guilty for stealing, but Keane was sick with it, trying to think of anything we could do besides that, but Asher ignored him and soon I had to as well to stop the guilt from building within me.

"Keane, you're driving me insane. Please shut up!" I whispered loudly as we approached a small field. A few horses were tied up along a fence. The workers must have been off within the field somewhere.

Asher crept across the edge of the field, staying hidden within the trees as much as he could.

"Doesn't he know that you are a human?" Keane asked, never letting his eyes leave Asher.

I sighed, "No he doesn't."

He tilted his head toward me, "Why tell me and not your friend?"

"Because," I said a little too loud, I took a breath, "It's all very complicated and confusing. Asher seems to hate everyone, and I lied to protect myself and others."

"To protect your dad?" Keane asked, following me along the tree line, watching Asher.

"Yes," I tossed him a look over my shoulder, "Don't breathe a word about it to Asher."

"Maybe you should. He's going to figure it out, and it's better to tell him now, and you obviously don't trust him. You could have asked me to leave him behind, but you didn't."

"How do you feel about working with a Nightmare?" I asked, trying to steer the conversation away from me and the guilt.

He thought for a moment, "There was a time I thought the King would have brought us together like Mavi wanted, and there has been some push for it, but it gets torn down. My parents taught me that the only way for Hatheya to grow and become healthy again was for us to live in peace with each other. Though, as you've seen, both Nightmares and Ivars have been taught to continue to hate each other, and I have let the pettiness take over." He looked down ashamed, "I truly want peace for both of us, and healing our realm, and revealing the true evilness could bring us together."

"What is the true evilness?" I turned to him.

"I'm not sure. But I want to find out. I just want peace. For once in my life, I want peace." He sounded exhausted, not physically, but emotionally. His shoulders fell, his face tightened at his words. "I hope that happens, for all of you." My heart ached at his words, "I thought that is what Hatheya would have been like. I was shocked when I saw it. Nothing had truly changed from the stories my dad told me. I'm sure his heart broke over it as well." I crept over to where Asher was bringing the horses. "Excellent thievery, Asher."

I gave him a smirk, trying not to think about his shadows, about what happened back in Finara. He gave me a small one back

"I don't think we should be praising such a thing," Keane patted the horse. It was a young horse, with white and brown spots across its body. It bumped his hands excitedly.

"Would it have made you feel any better if it was the property of a Nightmare?" Asher stroked the horse and checked his saddle.

"Would it have made you feel guilty if it was?" Keane shot back.

"Perhaps, but that's only because Ivars have the money to replace a horse. A Nightmare doesn't."

Keane's face wrinkled in disgust, "Your knowledge of the Ivars is highly lacking."

I took the opportunity to choose my horse, a dark black one with white around its eyes and a long black mane that he constantly shook. I swung my leg over the saddle and pulled myself up, smiling. The horse seemed well-behaved, and since I hadn't ridden since I was a child, it would be nice to have a calm animal. Keane and Asher looked up at me. "Will you both be riding the other horse, or will one of you be walking?" I laughed.

"Do you know how to ride?" Asher handed the reins he had been holding over to me.

"Yes, we owned a horse when I was younger." It was one of the best parts of living away from everyone. I could ride for what seemed like hours and always find something new to gaze upon. I patted the horse again as it huffed at Asher.

"I can ride with Ferren, and you can have the other horse," Keane said.

Asher opened his mouth and then closed it quickly before mounting his horse behind us.

It was uncomfortable riding with Keane. The saddle dug into me and every time the horse lurched a little we were slammed together.

"Just lean your weight back into me and you won't be jostled around so much," Keane said, sighing as I slammed back into him again. I was leaning slightly forward, trying not to have too much connection with him, but I reluctantly gave in and leaned back, trying to relax my aching back and shoulders. It helped a bit, but I was still tense from having to sit so intimately with a man I had just met.

I hadn't ridden in years, but it came back naturally as we started forward. The sway of the horse, the connection to nature as I rode up high. I could reach out and touch the low-hanging branches. Every type of tree I had ever seen filled this part of the forest and more that I didn't recognize. I tried to keep my awe and wonder to myself, not wanting Asher to know that I was shocked at this area as well.

Now that the trail had widened just a bit Asher could ride next to us. I could feel his eyes glancing over me and I had caught him once, but quickly looked away, unsure if it was a friendly look or he was still peeved about me not telling him about the connection between my father and Gannon. He had brought it up once more, but it was quickly shut down by Keane who wanted lunch and Asher offered to hunt for us, saying he needed peace and quiet for a while.

We ate a strange animal Asher had caught, and I tried to ignore the weird aftertaste of it. But it lingered in my mouth even as we started off again.

My thighs began to chafe as I rode along the not-too-gentle path that Keane had claimed led to WinWord. I shifted around in the saddle, trying different positions that would soothe my aching body, and tried to relax. It wasn't until the chilly wind started and the moon was high in the sky that I suggested that we give the horses a break for the night. There was no need to run them ragged like we were doing to ourselves.

The next morning was the same. We kept quiet and hurried through the forest. The wind was growing colder, and we were met with icy rain that bit into any skin that was exposed. It grew stronger, shaking the trees around us and starting rivers in the middle of the forest. The horses slowly tripping over branches and rocks that they couldn't see.

"We need to find cover!" Keane yelled, his voice being carried off by the wind.

I squinted my eyes against the harsh rain as it blurred everything around me. I heard a snap of a branch to the left and peered up to the small ledge. A shadow jumped from the ledge, grabbing me and knocking Keane and me to the ground. The horse bucked and screamed as it regained its balance, then took off into the roaring storm.

I struggled under the weight of the thing that pinned me to the ground. Its hood had flipped up, revealing its hideous face. It had tentacles like an octopus and sharp razor teeth that were off to one side of its face. I wasn't sure where its mouth was. I pressed my body against the wet ground, trying to wrestle the thing off. Its sharp claws dug into my wrists.

I managed to get a knee under it and push it off enough that it let go of one of my wrists. I grabbed my knife and sliced it across the eyes. It yelped, tumbling to the ground, grabbing at its face.

Asher's horse was bucking around, screaming as thunder rolled across the sky. Asher and Keane were entangled in their own fights as I leaped to my feet, readying myself for another attack from the creature as it stood screaming with rage, one eye bleeding and pinched closed.

Shadows launched themselves across the creature. This time I knew to look away. I listened to the sound of rain instead of the cries of pain.

We were surrounded by hooded figures that pushed us back. The horses were gone. The rain pounded down harder now, and it was turning into large balls of hail. They struck my head, leaving the icy feeling of pain.

A tall figure stepped forward; Keane swung his sword toward him as a warning.

The figure raised a hand, signaling to the others. They raised all their weapons at once. There had to have been at least twenty of them surrounding us, more in the shadows of the rain. All ugly creatures that sneered and laughed as we backed into each other.

The figure laughed deep in his throat, "Asher Dagon, the Shadow." He gave a mocking bow to him and laughed deeply again. "Oh, what a treat this is!"

"Bhaltair," Asher tightened his grip on his bow.

"I've missed you, boy!" He shouted, "Take them! Let's get the hell out of this rain!"

The circle closed in tighter, their weapons dangerously close. I dropped my knife and was pushed to my knees. My hands were brought to my back and wrapped in thick rope.

"Asher, let's not cause a scene. We'll get out of this rain and talk about it like men!" The man laughed again.

Asher glanced around then threw his bow into the mud; his shadows settling at his feet.

"Excellent choice, Shadow." The man turned away from us, disappearing into a blur of rain.

We were shoved to our feet, forced to follow the man. I wanted to get closer to Asher to ask him who the man was, how much danger we were in, and why he hadn't simply let his shadows tear the rest of Nightmares apart. They had been swarming at his side, killing quickly, then suddenly fell away.

My arms were tied behind my back. My hair mopped over my eyes, blocking my view even more. I had just gotten free from one situation and was back with my hands tied and my future uncertain again. I wanted to lie down on the cold ground and scream. I just wanted a break, a simple walk to WinWord. Between the weather and the fact that everyone seemed to be after me, my hope of even seeing a glimpse of my dad was becoming a fleeting thought.

We ducked into a large cave packed with tents and roaring fires. A few other creatures were there roasting meat over the flames or sleeping. The cave echoed as the Nightmares greeted each other and shook the rain from their jackets, causing muddy spots around us.

"Prisoners or food?" One sitting by the flames asked, eyeing us with hunger. He licked his green lips with a forked tongue.

The tall man laughed, "Profit!" He pulled off his hood, revealing a sunken face with sickly green and black flesh hanging from it. His eyes were bloodshot and almost looked calloused over. His lips bled and cracked open whenever he smiled wide and let out a deep choking laugh that resulted in him spewing blood and mucus from his unhinged jaw. When he moved his body, it cracked and crunched like broken bones. He sauntered over to me and brushed the wet hair from my eyes. I choked down a gag at the man's stench. His smell reminded me of the time I stumbled upon the rotting deer's corpse. It was full of maggots eating away its black flesh and I suddenly feared that was what this Nightmare looked like under his cloak. "I haven't seen a pretty Nightmare like you in a while." He studied me a bit more, "Or are you Ivar?"

Asher pulled forward but was stopped by a large creature that reminded me somewhat of TJ. He wagged a finger at Asher and laughed when his shadows jumped up to Asher's shoulders.

"And I have never seen anything as rancid as you." I tried to breathe through just my mouth.

He threw his head back, laughing and making a great show about it. "My, how I do like them feisty." His nose started bleeding, coming out in a thick stream of crimson. He wiped it away with the back of his bony hand before approaching Keane. "Asher Dagon traveling with an Ivar? I never thought I would see that in a million years." The surrounding creatures hissed and snarled at Keane.

"Pardon our behavior, but we don't get many guests around here. My name is Bhaltair, this." He gestured around him, "is my clan. I would introduce you, but I can't remember their names." He chuckled at his joke and was joined by some others.

"I wouldn't say we're guests, but more of captives," Keane said after the laughter had died down.

Bhaltair popped his knuckles and nodded, "Let's not dwell on the darkness of the situation, but rather on the glorious profit that will come from it." He raised his arms in a dramatic show as his clan cheered.

"Who are you working for now, Bhaltair?" Asher's voice echoed off the cave walls, bringing all the attention to him. Some Nightmares dipped their heads with whispers, and others glared and spat in his direction.

"A high payer that was very determined to have her." He pointed at me, "Very determined. But now I'm not too sure what to do with you two." He trailed his eyes over Keane and Asher, "Unless dear Asher you would like to come back to the family?" He chuckled, coughing up a bit of blood, letting it run down his chin.

"That payer wouldn't happen to be Bexley, now would it?" I asked dryly.

He smiled, cracking his lips, "I know not to work with the Ivar. They can't be trusted." He sauntered away to the fire where food was being dished up. Everyone moved out of his way as he grabbed at the largest piece of meat that was still bloody. His rotting teeth gnawed on the raw meat like a rabid animal.

The men who had us by the arms pushed us to the ground just behind the food they were roasting. "Stay," the creature ordered, then sat down to a plate of food.

"You know this group?" I leaned over to Asher and then pulled back as his shadows still circled his shoulders.

Asher nodded, "it's a renegade group that lives outside both the Ivar and the Nightmare laws."

"And you were part of this group?" Keane gave a concerned look.

"At one time, yes." He seemed to be studying every Nightmare that sat around the fire.

"Why didn't you use your shadows before they took us?" I snapped. I was furious at him. He had immense power but just failed to use it to save us.

"I can't just kill everyone. Even I have limits." He snapped back, causing Bhaltair to glance our way. "If I feed them too much, they become harder to control." He dropped his eyes from mine and stared down at the fire, "Perhaps I can talk to Bhaltair."

Keane scooted closer to us, "What do you hope to accomplish by doing that? He wants money, so unless either of you are secretly rich, we're not getting out of this."

"Enough whispering!" Bhaltair grabbed a handful of food from another Nightmare's plate and stuffed it in his mouth and continued to stare at us as he slowly chewed. I had to look away as he spit out a tooth, his or someone else's I didn't know, and I didn't want to know.

Bhaltair grabbed the back of my hair, pulling me up. I bit in a scream, meeting his sunken, dead eyes.

"Did I say you could talk?" He traced a finger down my chin as I snarled at him.

I would not be afraid.

Asher's voice boomed through the cave, "Bhaltair!"

Bhaltair's eyes drifted slowly over to Asher and Keane, who were held down and surrounded by weapons.

Bhaltair threw me to the side. I grunted in pain as my knees collided with the hard ground, blood blooming across them.

Asher pushed to his feet, his eyes deadly dark. His shadows leaped forward. A rock slammed into the side of his head with a sickening crack Asher crumbled to the ground.

"No!" I screamed, trying to rise, but Bhaltair shoved me back down.

Keane couldn't make a move before the Nightmares jumped him, beating him with their fists till his screams mixed with mine.

"Enough!" Bhaltair yelled, breaking up the brutal beating. Keane lay there blood covered and unmoving.

They're dead. They're both dead, I thought.

Keane groaned.

"Keane!" I barely made it through his name before Bhaltair backhanded me. I fell backward. A taste of crimson brushed across my tongue.

Bhaltair kneeled grabbing my face forcing me to look at his, "Did I say you could talk?" he asked again. "If you speak again, I will let my men kill your Ivar soldier." He pulled my face closer, "Do you understand?"

My heart raced with anger and fear. I wanted to spit on him but feared that Keane or Asher would take the punishment, so instead I gave an awkward nod in his hand.

He pushed me away, "Take the men to the back of the cave. I'll be watching this one."

The Nightmare snickered as they dragged the two men away. Keane struggled a bit, but a kick to the gut silenced him.

I scooted back against the cave wall, watching Bhaltair as he finished his food and laughed with the others as Keane's cries of pain echoed in the cave. He was being tortured. I rose slowly to my feet, watching Bhaltair, then darted towards Keane's screams. I didn't know what I was going to do or how to help, but I couldn't just sit there and listen to his pain.

I made it to a back tent before a Nightmare grabbed me around the throat and slammed me to the ground. I gasped, but no air filled my lungs.

Asher was leaning against the back wall of the cave unmoving. His head dripped blood. "Asher." I tried calling, but my lungs burned. I tried clawing at the Nightmare's hand and yelling for Asher again, but black spots started filling my vision.

Asher stirred, his hand twitched, and a small groan escaped his lips before a Nightmare stuck him in the head. Asher slumped to the floor.

Bhaltair leaned over me and the Nightmare that was pinning me. He placed a finger to his lips and shook his head. The hand around my throat was gone. Air rushed into my lungs. I coughed, sucking in as much air as I could get, then they were dragging me away by my legs back to my spot next to the fires.

Keane had stopped screaming in the night and I only hoped it wasn't because he was dead.

"Up and at them boys!" Bhaltair yelled.

I hadn't slept. I watched the rebel Nightmares throughout the storm and now that it was over, Bhaltair was kicking his group awake and throwing things at them.

He grabbed me and stomped out of the cave and stood now in the shining sun. In the bright warmth of the light, he looked even more disturbingly sick. A warming, decaying carcass.

Keane and Asher stumbled out, looking worse than before. Keane's right eye was swollen, his lip cut open and swollen, and every part of his skin I saw contained a bruise. He fell to the ground, groaning and breathing hard before he was pulled to his feet again. Asher grabbed his arm, standing him the best he could with bound hands.

Asher's head and face were sticky with dried blood. His eyes bore into Bhaltair's. A darkness so deep it enveloped his face.

"Asher, Keane." I breathed out.

Asher turned to me, relief flooded his face, "Are you okay?"

Bhaltair shoved me away from me, shaking a finger at Asher and tisking at him.

I gave both men a reassuring nod before we were shoved forward, hands still bound.

I was able to help Asher hold up Keane as he stumbled over the trail. His breathing sounded better than it was in the beginning, and I was hoping his Ivar strength was healing him as fast it could.

"We're still heading towards the Deadlands," Asher whispered. "Kandem or Gannon could be the payer?"

"Not Gannon," I breathed in a huff, "He would never do this to me."

Asher's eyes narrowed, but he kept his questions to himself.

"Do you think the King would hire any Nightmares? Especially this one?" Keane wrinkled his nose and pulled his lips back showing off his crooked teeth.

Bhaltair came up behind us smiling smugly, "And as I said before, I do not trust Ivars." Bhaltair put his arm over Asher's shoulders, "Glad to see you again, boy, even in this circumstance. I've missed my Shadow," he said dramatically, gushing like a proud father, "The Shadow is back! And I'll convince you to stay this time!" He hugged Asher's shoulder tighter and leaned his head against his for a brief moment.

Asher stayed quiet but grimaced angrily as Bhaltair continued talking loudly, waving his arms around as if he was giving a poetic speech in a play. It was comical how this feared and dangerous renegade talked and moved about.

"Now, I know why you left us the first time," he sighed heavily, "But the girl is gone now, she can no longer warp your mind and as for this one," He looked over at me, "Doesn't seem like your type." He stage whispered.

Asher stopped walking his breathing became quick, "How did you know of Amber?" He asked deadly quietly.

Bhaltair crossed his lanky arms, "I know everything, Shadow. Why did you even try to hide it from me? I cared about you and have raised you before you had your shadows and yet you keep secrets from me." He jutted his chin.

"Did you do it?" Asher stumbled over his words as rage built, "Did- did you do it to her?" He let go of Keane.

Coldness bit at our arms, then an explosion of yells erupted behind us. A wave of shadows threw the Nightmares aside and surged over others. I pulled Keane back, telling him to go as they were distracted by Asher and his sudden unmanageable rage.

Asher's hands struggled in the bindings; his body shook as the wave of darkness overtook more. The Nightmares darted around in all directions, trying to avoid the shadows.

Bhaltair didn't move. He looked down his nose at Asher, "Simply giving up control to the shadows because of a dead girl?" He stepped close to Asher, "Rein it in or let them finally overtake you."

"We need to unbind our hands," Keane stumbled over a rocky layer of ground, his eyesight surely slowing him.

I looked back at Asher, who fell to his knees, panting, his body shaking. His shadows slowly crawled to his side.

Keane shoved me again, "Go, you have to go Ferren." Keane was tackled from the right, knocking him hard to the ground. I stumbled to a stop and turned to help him.

"No!" he shouted, trying to fight the creature off without his hands. "Run!"

I kicked the thing off of him, but it jumped to its feet. Keane was just as quick to get to his feet and they knocked each other back to the ground. I knew others were close as their thunderous cries filled the air.

"Run!" Keane ordered again.

I grunted in frustration, but turned and ran. If I could just unbind my hands, I could do something. I zig-zagged through the thick foliage of trees and bushes until an arm suddenly appeared from behind a tree and closed-lined me at full force, knocking me to my back. My head collided with the ground, blurring my vision for a second. I was pulled to my feet, causing my eyes to go black and fuzzy.

I shook my head, clearing my vision and stared up at the Nightmare. He held the hood of my jacket as we waited for Bhaltair to make his way to us.

Bhaltair gave me a lip-splitting smile as he gingerly walked up to me and placed his hands on my shoulders. "Come girl, we must make haste." He dropped his arms to his side.

"Where is Asher?" I seethed. "And Keane?"

"Asher ran off, probably to rest after exerting too much energy, and the other one?" He tapped his chin, "Dead, I believe, unsure and I don't care."

I sputtered. My mind was frozen at the fact that Keane died trying to save me and Asher would leave me. Leave me in the hands of this creature. He smiled down at me. His cheeks ripped from his grin.

THIRTEEN

Bhaltair decided to place a rope around my neck and pull me along like a dog. He hummed to himself and pulled on the rope now and again, causing it to rub my skin raw. He allowed me to take small sips of water and a few bites of food just to keep my strength up, but not enough to get energy to try to escape again. I trudged alongside him, feeling weak but waiting for any type of opportunity to run or to fight. I checked my surroundings hoping that Asher would appear, but I wasn't sure how long he needed to rest after using the shadows so much. He had killed or wounded half of Bhaltair's men, and quickly. The journals had never said that after Dentro used the shadows, he would have to rest, but then again, he was the strongest nightmare to live. He was said to have been part of the shadows themselves.

"Here!" Bhaltair pointed to a lake that shimmered in the sunlight. "Avoid the waters, men!" He shoved me to the ground then sat on a rock, stretching out his legs and exhaling. "Beautiful lake, isn't it?"

The water stretched out to meet a mountain at one end and us at a small rocky cove. Dense trees surrounded the other sides. The sun seemed to shine directly in the middle of the lake, where boulders jutted out sharply.

A fin flipped through the lake, spraying water into the air.

"Mermaids," I breathed in awe, standing to get a better view as it flipped its fin again.

Bhaltair laughed loudly, "If that is what you would like to call the flesh-eating creatures that occupy this lake, then sure."

"Of course, they are flesh-eating…" I sat down again. Nothing in this realm could just be normal.

One man approached the lake carefully, canteen in hand. He bent down to the water and slowly filled it.

"Watch." Bhaltair smiled like an excited child and leaned forward rubbing his hands together.

A fin peaked out from the water and was gone in a second. The man stood, taking a sip from his canteen. A splash of water rose from the lake and with it, a creature jumped out. It had the tail of a mermaid. Beautiful and reflective of many colors, but the rest of it was that of a drowning person. Puffy and blue skin. Its eyes rolled around in its collapsed skull. It made an awful gasping noise as it tilted its head back, revealing a mouth with rows and rows of needle-like teeth.

The man tried to run, but he slipped on the mud, falling face-first to the ground. He clawed at the ground and screamed as the creature fell on him, its teeth digging in his back, and began to drag the man back into the water. He screamed, punched, and pulled at the creature, but the creature's waterlogged arms wrapped around him, pulling him deeper until they were both underwater. Bubbles and ripples covered the surface of the water. More fins peeked out swimming towards the blood.

Bhaltair's laugh broke the silence. "Told you all to stay away from the water!" The others laughed with him.

I was suddenly thankful my stomach was empty, "Why didn't anyone help him?"

"Because I did not tell them to. I am the leader, and they don't act without me giving them the go." He said it like it was common knowledge, "You always follow the leader."

"What if the leader is wrong?"

He shook his head, "I'm never wrong."

"A little full of yourself, aren't you?" I turned from the lake, looking at the sky instead, praying I wouldn't see anything man-eating leap from the clouds down to us. I had many new fears since coming to this hell of a place. Perhaps it would have been better if my dad had left it forgotten.

"I am confident." He jumped to his feet. "Hello, gentlemen!"

Two men wearing the Ivar uniforms and clutching bows appeared from the forest. Bhaltair's men pulled their weapons, stepping closer to us and guarding Bhaltair.

His fingers cracked and popped as he folded his hands together, "Out for a stroll, Ivars?" He said pleasantly, "Glad the sun has risen today to chase away the rain clouds."

The Ivars exchanged a glance, "We noticed you have a slave. That is against the King's laws," the older one said. He wore a thick beard flaked in gray.

"She is a Nightmare, not Ivar, so I do not understand what the King and his laws have to do with this?" Bhaltair stepped forward, still clutching the rope around my neck, pulling me to my feet.

"The King's laws apply to everyone and everything within this realm. You will let her go."

Bhaltair pulled the rope around my neck, causing me to stumble forward into his outstretched hand, "She is too precious to let go." He gripped me tighter.

"You know our soldiers surround you." The younger Ivar stepped forward, "Spare the lives of your men and let the girl go."

Bhaltair smiled, "My my my, why do you all care about her so deeply?" He clicked his tongue, "Not even death could stop me from taking her to where she belongs."

I pulled against his grip, "Where would that be?" I pulled forward again, but his grip was gone and I stumbled to the ground with a grunt as the air was knocked from my lungs. I spit dirt out and glared up at Bhaltair before wiggling myself up on my knees, trying to get air back into my lungs.

The older Ivar raised his hand as a signal to the other Ivars who were hidden somewhere within the trees and rocks. Bhaltair didn't move, didn't blink, but his men shuffled nervously around us.

Looking around, tightening their grips on their weapons. Bhaltair would die before giving me up, but I wasn't too sure about his men.

"Give her up, Bhaltair!" The older Ivar shouted. "Last chance."

Bhaltair placed a hand on his temple and sighed deeply before letting go of the rope around my neck. "Don't worry, I'll find you again." He whispered before stepping back, his eyes alight with hunger.

The Ivars slowly inched their way forward as Bhaltair inched his way back.

The older one helped me to my feet. They stayed quiet as they gently pulled me away into the forest where there was a small group of the others hidden within the thick trees, arrows pointed at Bhaltair's group.

A woman with shoulder-length black hair and warm olive skin approached me, shaking her head, "What did they do to you?" She untied the rope from around my neck and wrists. "Get her some water!" she inspected the rope burns around my neck and the cut across my lip.

Someone handed me a canteen of water and I gulped it down selfishly. The woman gave me a sad smile and turned away, collecting her bow. "Come along, we have some horses just up head, and the camp is not that far from here. Just a brief ride and then you can rest."

I stared at them not moving, "Where are we going?"

She turned back to me, this time with an apple in hand for me, "WinWord."

"WinWord!" I jumped to my feet and then settled my excitement. "Why there?"

"We've been looking for you since the King and Gannon caught word that you might be in Hatheya. We got lucky when someone spotted you traveling with Asher and that led us to Bhaltair."

"Gannon sent you?" I couldn't believe it; this was all too good to be true. I had found the Ivars, good Ivars, who wanted to bring me to my father. Who was alive! "I thought the camp was in the dead lands?"

"It was, but we moved it." She said.

"Why?"

She shrugged and walked on, leading me to the others, "Guess the king was done looking out there."

"Looking?"

I was still on guard and skeptical as I followed close behind them. They talked among themselves and glanced back at me occasionally, handing me water and asking how I was doing.

"How did you become tangled in traveling with Asher Dagon?" The woman asked, walking slowly beside me.

A man with dark skin and fiery eyes stepped to my other side. "Only fools would travel with such a creature. He probably led you straight to Bhaltair and his group. I'm sure he got a big payout for it."

"You think I'm ignorant then?" I asked.

"You are human, you know nothing." He said with confidence.

"Excuse me?" I wasn't sure which part I was saying it to. The part where I was apparently stupid because I was human or the part where they *knew* I was human.

"We are the king's most trusted. Don't fear that we know you are human." The woman said kindly. "I am Margret, by the way, this is Brice."

"Ferren," I bit into another apple Margret had given me.

"We know," Brice said, exasperated.

Once the forest began to settle, we could ride the horses the rest of the way. The wind was whipping around us as icy snow began to fall. I was tucked down into my heavy jacket, watching my surroundings like Asher had taught me. It helped me keep my mind off my numb hands and aching back. I was on my way to see the King, the man I wasn't sure I could trust, but if my dad was with him, and had sent these Ivars out after me, that had to be a good sign.

Out of the corner of my eye, I saw a little white tuff of fur scurry into a bush. Could that have been Eira? Which could mean that Asher was around. Was he following me hoping I was safe or hoping that they would lead him to Gannon?

He would become angry at me soon. Seeing me there not as a prisoner but as a rescue and as an Ivar…His shadows could tear me apart. His anger would be because of me lying to him, but a part of me wanted desperately to continue to trust him. As Keane's father said, fate had thrust us together.

A short while later, we came upon a camp that was congested with tents and soldiers. It was in a small clearing of trees. Mud coated the ground where foot traffic seemed to be heavy. Horses grazed further off, tended to by young Ivars that laughed as a horse nickered and shook its mane in their faces.

Others glanced up at us as we rode to the largest tent in the field. It was three times as large as the tents the soldiers had to sleep in.

As soon as we came to a stop, I slid off my horse and approached Margret, "Where is he? Where is Gannon?"

"I need to inform the King that you are here first." She said with a smile. "Then I can find Gannon for you."

I hopped from one foot to the other, anxious to find him to throw my arms around my dad and tell him of the things I had seen and had been through.

"Ferren! Ferren!"

I turned at the shouts, "Dad!" I yelled, running to him, weaving through soldiers, and ran into his open arms. I couldn't help the tears that fell when I heard him give out a sob and clutch me tighter.

"Oh Ferren, I never thought I would see you again!" He pulled away and cupped my face in his hands, "How I have missed you!"

"I can't believe you are alive! For years, I thought you were gone forever!" I sobbed, not caring about the on-looking Ivars. He was older-looking now. His beard was graying, his face freckled with age, his hands much rougher than before.

"I thought I was too until Kamden found me." He pulled me into another hug.

"The King?"

He nodded eagerly, "Yes, I had been taken by a group and was tortured for many days, then hope came." He looked over my shoulder, his face tensing.

"How did the Nightmares get through to our realm?"

He pulled me in for another hug, "We must talk privately." He whispered softly.

"Gannon! Is this her? Is this your daughter?"

I turned around and saw a man leaning on a walking stick. He had a short, thick white beard and graying hair that was cut short. The man who stood before me did not remind me of a king. He was pale and thin and had a faint smell of bitterness around him. His brown eyes seemed faded and underwhelming. Much like the land, he seemed to be fading away.

My Father nodded, "Yes, she finally arrived."

"I am so thankful you were found alive! I feared the worst for you and then came to find out you were captured by Bhaltair and Asher and I knew we must act fast." He beamed at me.

"I was *not* captured by Asher. He was helping me get here. I didn't know who to trust and Evir and Bexley did not help me trust the Ivar at all," I crossed my arms.

Kamden looked shocked, "Why? What did they do, dear?"

I pursed my lips, "For starters, Bexley had me tortured to try to get information about you."

"What!" He bellowed and stormed off into the overly large tent.

"Are you alright?" My Father put an arm around my shoulder, leading me to his tent. It had a small cot and two saddlebags of clothes and food inside. I gratefully sat on the cot, relaxing into my father's embrace, feeling like a child again.

"I have been through a lot, and I have learned a lot, but the truth of everything is still muddled about." My eyes and throat burned with tears.

He nodded somberly, "Yes, this place will do that to people, especially now with all that has changed." He grabbed a rag to wipe my face with and kissed the top of my head.

Warmth radiated from my chest. "What is it that you wanted to talk about privately?" I wiped my sniffy face. I wanted to stop crying, but I couldn't help it every time I looked at him, tears pricked my eyes again.

"Shhhh," He pressed a finger to his lips "Not here." He moved to the entrance of the tent and looked around.

I instantly sobered up, "Is there anything you can tell me, like why you were taken?"

"Many reasons." He rubbed his hands together nervously, "The sword and why I fled the tower that day."

"They wanted to know about a sword?" I raised a brow.

"Later we will talk, later," He patted my hands, "Your mom must be so worried about you."

I looked away at the mention of her.

"What? What is wrong?" I could hear the panic in his voice even as his face stayed calm.

"She's gone." I closed my eyes, not wanting to see his heartbreak at my words. "I found out she wasn't my birth mother."

"I'm sorry we lied about that to you, but at the time it seemed like the easiest thing." I let him stay silent for a while. He didn't cry or ask more questions, he just stared at the ground. "The night I was taken I had made peace with the fact I would never see her or you again and then when I was rescued I knew I had to stay and help heal this place."

"You chose to let us believe you were dead?" I tried to keep my voice hushed in the thin tent. "You chose this place over us?"

"I couldn't let Kandem know I could open a portal. I had told him that I had lost the power after being in the human realm for so long."

"Then who is opening the portals?"

"No one. The realm is breaking down and so is the wall around it keeping the human realm safe. It's becoming easier to find a breach in the realm and slip through it."

"Why?"

His brow crinkled, "I'm not sure…"

My frustration mounted, "Who is my birth mother? Was she an Ivar too?"

He shook his head, "That's not important."

"Are you my real father or is that a lie, too?" I jumped to my feet, knowing it was important. Every question I had burning my brain was important.

He narrowed his eyes at me for a second, then looked away as I didn't back down from my anger.

"Why did the Ivars bring me here?" I seethed.

"The Ivars?" He knitted his brows together.

"Yes, Evir was an Ivar. He abducted me.

He grabbed my hands, "Tell me everything."

FOURTEEN

"No wonder you look like you have been chewed up and spit out." He shook his head and closed his eyes for a moment.

I gave a light laugh and stood, stretching. I needed to clear my head of everything.

"You have become brave." He smiled proudly at me. "Though traveling with that Nightmare." He ran a hand through his beard, "I do remember him."

"What do you remember?" I asked, watching his face.

"He supposedly did something terrible." He cleared his throat, "I once had something of his when he was captured that I was to return, but I can't remember now what it was."

"Gannon! Ferren!" Kamden rushed into the tent. "I'm sorry to disturb you, but I must question you more about Commander Bexley. I sent Brice back to Finara to investigate what is happening there. I shouldn't have left and for so long!" his voice was grave. "I thought I was leaving them well cared for, but if what Ferren says is true, it makes me worry. We are peaceful people. We do not torture. We are not Nightmares." He twisted the cane in his hand making a small hole in the dirt.

"It is true." I snapped.

"Yes, yes, I'm sorry. I do not mean to doubt you. I just can't believe that he would do such a thing. Perhaps he didn't know who you were and thought you were an enemy?" He said in a rush.

"Bexley thought I was working for you, wanted to know what you were doing out here." I shot a glance at my dad. He seemed calm, but something was hidden just under the surface.

"Come to my tent and we will brief you on what is happening." Kandem hobbled off, leaning stiffly on his walking stick.

We entered his lavish tent with a large table in the middle with many maps folded on top of it. The other half held a bed, a small trunk, a bedside table, and a soft rug. I knew kings traveled in luxury, but it seemed weird to carry around such stuff. A small fire was in the corner with fish being grilled on top by a young servant. She smiled at me and gave a stiff smile to my dad before disappearing out of the tent. People must still be warming up to him.

"Please tell me everything Bexley said and did." Kandem sat down and rubbed his knee.

"Why don't you tell me what you're looking for first, then I'll decide who to trust." It came out harsh and satisfying.

"Ferren!" my dad shook his head at me.

Kandem laughed and raised his palms to me, "I understand the hostility. What you have been through would cause anyone not to trust." He poured himself some water, "Did your father tell you we fought alongside Mavi? That I was handpicked by Mavi Ivar to serve as king. Though I love being king, I would rather have Mavi here with us instead. We fought against Dentro together." He gestured to the stools that sat around the map table. "I'm sure you have heard that story a million times?"

He sounded boastful, as though knowing Mavi should make me trust him more easily, "I have." I sat on one of the wooden stools and looked at the maps. They were outlining the places around Camp WinWord. Some had large Xs on spots, others were scribbled through with anger.

"But you have not heard the ending." He said frankly, "How would you know when your dad wasn't there to see it?" He laughed.

My dad gave a tightlipped grimace and settled into a chair next to me.

Kandem patted him on the back, "When I found Gannon back in Hatheya, I was overcome with many emotions and unsure what to do with him, but I always knew there was a reason he left the battle."

"And what was that reason?" I asked coarsely. My head spun slightly from the smell that was wafting off the King. It burned my mouth and eyes. My dad didn't seem to be affected by it or he was hiding the fact that it was bugging him.

Kandem waited for my dad to say, but as the silence dragged on, Kandem finally spoke, "He won't say more than Mavi sent him away. True to the King even in his death."

"It is what Mavi wanted," Gannon crossed his arms, "No matter how many times you ask, I cannot tell you."

Kandem humphed and turned back to me, "I am out here because Dentro did not die like in the story…he was not killed in the crashing of the tower. We told people that so that they would not be afraid any longer."

"Then, where is he?" I asked slowly, unsure if I wanted to know.

"He is still trapped in the tower. Kanna Asena placed a spell on the tower and locked him inside after the battle, then confused the minds of anyone who had seen the tower to forget where it was. Mavi was unable to complete the spell before he died and simply crumbling a tower on Dentro wouldn't have killed something so powerful."

"We are afraid that some nightmares have finally found the tower and are searching for a way to break him out." Kamden sighed, running a hand over his brow, "I also fear it is not just the Nightmares that are looking for the tower."

"You believe some Ivar are as well? Why would they?" I narrowed my eyes at him.

"Ferren," My Father leaned forward, "Before the final battle, Mavi had made a weapon that would allow control over the Nightmares."

"Then why didn't he use it to stop Dentro? To stop the army from attacking the Tower?"

Kandem sighed, "Something was not right with it. When Mavi tried to use it, it hurt him, but I did see Dentro bend to its will till Mavi tossed it aside, unable to continue to wield it." He took a shaky breath, "We are unsure, but believe it is in the tower trapped with Dentro, and whoever is foolish enough to go in and retrieve it can control the worst Nightmare there is and will cause havoc upon us all. That is why Gannon and I think that some Ivar are looking for it."

"And that is what you're looking for?" I stood, "You want to control all the Nightmares?" I thought of Asher being controlled, unable to think for himself, and following the orders of this man that reeked of distrust and vileness. "If it didn't work for the most powerful Ivar, then why would it work for you or anyone else who is much weaker?"

Kandem's face flashed anger, "I am looking for it because I want to guard it from others. The land is failing and soon everyone will remember where the tower is." He rose to his feet, matching my glare, "I fear even Kanna's spell keeping Dentro locked away might be failing and then we'll have another war on our hands. We must be prepared and if we can then we must fix the sword."

"To control Dentro or to control all Nightmares? Even the ones who don't want to follow Dentro?"

Kandem rubbed his eyes, "I think that is enough for today. I must deal with Finara. Goodnight to you both."

I was ushered briskly out of the tent and took a breath of the clean fresh air. My head instantly cleared.

My dad clapped me on the shoulder, "I feel like I should scold you, but I realized you aren't a child anymore, but a woman rightfully demanding answers," He lowered his voice, "But be careful, Kandem is not who I thought he was. Something has changed within him."

We walked in silence for a moment, mulling over what the King had said, "This land, even when Dentro was at constant war with us, still held beauty and hope for a better future, but now there is no hope, no light within the Ivars or Nightmares. They're going back to the way things were and not the way Mavi wanted them to be. There's just no hope anymore."

No hope, no peace. Keane just wanted peace and now he's dead. I clung to my dad's arm. "We'll find some."

I thought I would have slept soundly even while sleeping on the ground in my dad's tent, but I tossed and turned, awakening at all noises. I peeked out the tent flap, watching the Ivars tend to their duties, hoping to tire my mind but perked up at the sight of Kandem mounting his horse, riding away with two other Ivars.

I moved the tent flap aside when a hand grabbed my shoulder. I jumped and turned to my dad who was shaking his head at me, "Stay here," He whispered, "I'll follow them."

"I'll go with you," I whispered back, eager to see what the King was up to in the middle of the night.

"No, stay here. I don't want you to be caught by him." He pulled on his boots, "I will find you when I get back."

I bit the inside of my cheek to keep from arguing. It was no use when he got like this.

When the sun rose, I wandered around the camp looking for food and keeping an eye out for my dad. Margret found me and led me to a food wagon. I ate a bit of crackers and cheese before heading over to the stream with Margret to bathe. She led me to the stream and then to a small pool that flowed into. It was surrounded by rocks and thick red vines that trailed their way around the pool.

"This is for your neck." She handed me a small container of clear gel. "It will help with the pain while it heals."

"Thank you," I warily looked down into the water. "There's no man-eating creatures in the stream, are there?"

She laughed lightly, "No, they prefer large lakes not shallow streams, but you should always be cautious of your surroundings." She stripped out of her clothes and jumped into the pool. "Though some large snakes creep into the water sometimes."

"How large of snakes?" I hesitate at the edge of the water.

"You don't want to know." She laughed again.

I stared down into the water and decided I would risk it just to get clean. I sank into the water, dunked my head under the water and let the coolness of it relax me and started to scrub off the dirt and blood and whatever else covered me. Dirt ran from my tangled hair as I combed it out with a brush I borrowed from Margret.

I floated through the water, staring at the white tulip-like flowers that bloomed around the vines and the clouds that ran across the sky. It was beautiful and peaceful. Even after Margret got dressed, I stayed in the pool. She sat on a rock, watching the forest and soaking in the sun.

"Look at that little white fox." She pointed across the pond to a fox watching from the cover of a dead shrub.

I snapped my head over to where she was pointing.

"It's beautiful, isn't it? Even with its red eyes. It looks like it's staring right at you." She smiled and waved to it. "Hey there little fox!"

My cheeks grow hot. "Will you hand me my towel?" I swam up to Margret and grabbed it from her.

"Are you all right? It won't hurt you." She helped me out of the pond.

I gripped my towel tightly around my chest and found a tree to dress behind. "Just cold." I dressed awkwardly behind a towel, glancing around looking for Asher while Margret stared at me like I had lost my mind.

"Are you sure you're okay?"

I nodded, my ears still hot.

Back at the camp I found my father asleep in his tent and settled in on the floor, wrapping a blanket around me and sighing with relief that he was back safely. Now I could just worry about Asher. I desperately wanted to believe he wouldn't try to hurt me as he found out who my dad was, and I felt compelled to at least try to talk to my dad about the bargain I had made with Asher. Even though I knew he would say no to letting Asher out of the Hatheya.

"Where has he gone!" Kandem's booming voice sounded through the camp.

I darted out of the tent with my dad half asleep following after. He rubbed his eyes and squinted at Kandem and Brice.

Brice had returned from Finara. He stood panting and shaking his head, "I don't know my king. When I got to Finara, soldiers said that Commander Bexley had fled, and some soldiers left with him, even commoners. Women and children had left in the dead of the night. I'm unsure if they too left with Commander Bexley or on their own."

"Why would Bexley flee?" I asked as we approached them.

"Probably because he knew I was on to him." Kandem ran a hand through his beard repeatedly. "I trusted him. I treated him like a son and now I fear he has started a revolt against me. I can only pray he is not looking for the tower." He patted Brice on the shoulder, "Thank you, Brice, for the urgency. You are excused." He turned to us, "Gannon, please join me in my tent." He gave me a slight bow of his head before turning away with my father right on his heels.

There were too many people around to sneak up to the tent to listen, and Brice had his eyes on me, trying to glare me down. I turned away and started to the little pond Margret had taken me to. Perhaps I would see Eira again and find Asher lurking around, waiting for the truth of who I was.

I circled back around and cut through the trees to get to the path of the pond, then waited to get a sight of Eira. Suddenly something gleamed in the sunlight where I had last seen the fox. I stood and walked over to the shrubs. There my knife stood planted in the dirt, an Ivar's knife.

"Asher?" I shouted softly looking around waiting for him to make an appearance, "I'm still going to talk to Gannon about getting you out of here, especially with everything that's going on and what is to come, but I'm not sure if he'll agree." I took a breath, "I'll be back tomorrow with an answer." I tucked the knife into my belt and headed back, hoping my dad was done with Kandem and we could finally talk.

"There you are." My Father said embracing me, "I was beginning to worry."

"We need to talk soon. I'm tired of the games and secrets."

"I understand." He led me to the horses that were feeding on the grass, then glanced around. Not too many people were around, and they were far enough away that they couldn't hear if we whispered.

"I know you have many questions. I wish I could answer all of them."

"Start with the biggest ones," I whispered haughtily. "My mother? Am I half Ivar? When are we leaving this place?"

He shook his head, "Oh Ferren," He cupped my face in his hands and leaned his forehead against mine. "My sweet daughter, I wish I could keep you hid away from the things that are about to take hold."

"What is going on?" I swallowed the lump that had risen in my throat, "I need answers."

He let go of me, "Kandem has changed. It feels as if he isn't even the same man I grew up with. He is not the man Mavi chose to rule. Something dark runs through his veins now."

"Where did he go last night?" I asked softly as I watched him struggle with that realization.

"He found it. He found the tower." Gannon walked to one horse and patted it gently.

I gaped at his words, unsure what question to ask next.

"He went around the cliff side, and I didn't see him come back for many hours. I'm not sure what he was doing there, but I believe he is looking for the sword."

"What about Dentro?"

"I didn't get close to the tower, but if he had gotten out, we would know."

"We need to leave this place, Dad, please." My heart ached at the words. I wasn't sure if it was because a part of me wanted to stay and keep the King away from the sword and try to figure out how to heal the land, or if I wanted desperately to fall back into the normal life of my realm.

"I told you," He pitched the bridge of his nose. "I'm not going back. This land called you back as well."

I opened my mouth to ask a question, but I didn't know what to say.

He swallowed loudly, "You must not utter this to a soul, Ferren. Promise me."

I nodded.

"No, promise." He gripped my shoulders tightly.

"I promise. Now what is it that you have to tell me?" I pushed his hands off my shoulders.

"The night of the battle, Mavi handed me a baby and told me to flee to the human realm and never come back."

"A baby?" I managed to squeak it out.

He rubbed the back of his neck, "You, he gave me you."

I began to shake and teeter on my feet.

He grabbed my arm and started to walk me, "Be calm, Ferren, don't draw attention to us. I know this is a lot to take in at the moment."

My stomach dropped, my skin lined with sweat and my heart pounded at his words, just like they had when I found out my mother wasn't my biological mother. "So, you're not my real dad?"

"I'm not," He choked out, "But I'm still the one who raised you and treated you like a daughter. I still love you like you're mine."

I took a shaky breath that didn't help calm my pounding heart. "Who are they? Who are my parents?"

"You must calm yourself before I tell you."

I just nodded, dreading his words.

"After Navara betrayed us, her sister Kanna tried many times to find her and bring her back safely. Kanna soon found out that Navara was pregnant."

"With me?" My voice came out so soft I was unsure if he had heard me.

"Yes." He kissed the top of my head, "Navara gave birth to you the night of the battle. That's why Kanna and Mavi waited so long to start the spell. They were tending to Navara and you."

"Who is my dad, then? Why was Navara there and not with Dentro?"

"I don't know."

"Tell me?" I snapped, "No more secrets."

"I am telling the truth. I don't know, but Mavi told me to protect you and keep you away from here."

"Why? Who am I?" collapsed down as my legs began to shake, "I'm not Ivar then? Not even partly?"

He shrugged, "I do not know." He rubbed his neck again, "I asked Mavi that night who your father was, and he would not answer."

"Who do you believe it is?" I looked up at him, tears lining my eyes, "She was with Dentro when she got pregnant."

He shook his head quickly, "Don't think that Ferren, don't ever think that."

"I have to. It's possible I could be his…" I coughed out a disgusted choke. The thought of that monster being able to be a father turned my stomach. "That's why Mavi wanted me away from Hatheya and he didn't have the heart to kill a baby. Even Dentro's child."

He kneeled in front of me, "You couldn't be his child; you are nothing like him."

"Gannon!" Kandem shouted and rode out to us on a large black horse.

I swore under my breath and turned away. Surely my face revealed an emotional upset.

"I have looked for you everywhere!" He huffed. Dark circles lay under his eyes. He looked down at me and gave me a small nod, smiling, his eyes suddenly alight with something mischievous. "We are set to move camp,"

"Where?" Gannon rose stiffly.

"Come along. We must discuss many things." He rode away.

My dad patted my back, "We can talk more in a little. I won't be gone long."

I watched him walk slowly back to the crowd of tents and shuffling of Ivars. I tried to stand to follow, but I couldn't force my legs to move until night was falling again and rapidly. The wind picked up and the frigid air threatened snow or icy rain.

The camp was in full action with people packing and shouting out orders. I scurried off to the tent and prayed they would stop soon so I could rest.

My dad wasn't in the tent, so I laid on the hard cot and stared at the flapping fabric of what made the tent up, repeating the story he told me over and over until my mind went numb.

I couldn't sleep with all the noise in my mind and the camp, so I walked around looking for my father to bombard him with more questions.

A group of riders shouted off into the distance and then raced into the trees. I ignored their shouts and continued my search. They were not in Kamden's tent, and I began to worry as more soldiers mounted horses and grabbed weapons. "What is going on!" I shouted to a soldier who was passing by.

"A large group of Nightmares at the edge of camp!" He hurried off.

I started running through the camp shouting for my dad. An arrow of fire flew through the air and planted into a tent, causing it to set ablaze. It crumbled into a close by tent, making the wicked flame swallow that one as well.

More arrows followed after that until the camp was burning all around me. I pulled my shirt over my mouth and coughed out my dad's name. Shouting it as loud as I could over the yells and cries of the soldiers.

Some were tossing buckets of water onto the tents and then quickly giving up. I grabbed a sword from a woman who was handing them out to the soldiers.

I looked into the tree line where the riders had gone, but it was too dark to see anything.

It was only seconds when a flood of Nightmares broke into the camp. I was suddenly face to face with cries and shouts of battle. Blood spatter and the harsh clinking of swords filled the air.

I tried to avoid most of it, skirting through it, looking for my dad.

I was knocked to my back by a Nightmare with two heads, each of them growling and panting with anger. I rolled to my side as his mace struck the ground and jumped to my feet, and ran; I didn't have the time or the energy to deal with it.

"Gannon!" I screamed. "Kandem!" Surely Kandem wouldn't leave my father alone in this mess.

I raised my blade, blocking a sword from connecting with my head, and shoved them back. Another blade sliced through him.

"You attract violence!" Asher pulled his blade out of the Nightmare.

"Asher!" I blocked another blow, "Are you with these Nightmares?" I stepped back.

"No, but they were the perfect cover to get into the camp." He pushed me out of the way of a sword.

"I need to find my dad." I panted, panic filling me as more Nightmares and Ivars began to fall.

"You lost him again?" He swung his blade at his attacker, knocking him to the ground.

"Follow me." I pushed and shoved my way through the fighting. Blocking what I could and letting Asher handle the rest.

"You need to fight, Ren!" He growled. Blood coated his swords, his shadows danced happily around his body, excited for the next kill, but Asher kept them from diving too deep into the bloodshed.

"I'm trying!" I knew what he meant he wanted me to kill them, to help stop them from coming back again and again. Asher was sweating now, his arms shook as his shadows leaped onto three more Nightmares devouring them with grace.

I caught his eye, backing away from the fight. I couldn't even kill an animal while hunting. How was I expected to kill anything else?

I received a slice of a blade across my arm, making me drop my sword. I gripped my arm, trying to stop the oozing blood, and jumped back as another blade almost got my middle. Asher's dark shadows were there instantly engulfing the other Nightmares in a darkness so black I couldn't tell if it was truly there or if they had simply disappeared. Then the shadows were pulled away like a rabid dog. They would fall to the ground, a look of fear frozen on their face, their eyes wide, mouths open with a scream that would never come.

Some other nightmares seemed to have abilities as well, one looked like it was sucking the life out of the Ivars by placing a hand on their face until they turned gray falling to the ground, and another one seemed to be in every spot I looked. Every time I ran, he would be in front of me, but he never seemed to move. I would swing my blade and without moving he would be just out of reach. My arm ached from the wound I had received, and the blood loss had my head spinning, but I stayed on my feet, trying to outrun the chaos.

I continued to scan the crowds in search of my father and avoided many fights to save my energy in case he needed me. He was a better fighter and a strong Ivar, but the feeling of worry and dread wouldn't leave my mind.

Asher stuck by me. A few times, I had to push back Ivars from attacking Asher and direct them to another threat.

"Do you see Keane!" Asher shouted.

I didn't respond. He must not have known that Keane had been killed.

"We need to push back into the forest! Wait till this dies out if there is any chance of finding your dad! Especially if you won't fight!" Yelled Asher

"I am fighting!"

He seethed at me but didn't say another word.

I didn't find my dad as the sun rose and the battle was beginning to thin. Many Nightmares fled. Their forces weren't as large as ours. Finally, it seemed like the storm had passed. Blood and bodies covered the ground, a mix of Nightmares, and Ivars. I scanned the bodies and sighed in relief that none of them were him.

Asher was shoved quickly to the ground. Brice stood above, blade raised. Shadows flinch around me as if waiting for their master to give word to let them protect him. Ivars that were nearby clung to their swords and others grabbed at torches to rid the area of shadows.

"Wait!" I shouted, "He helped us!" The shadows stilled a bit. Asher looked up at me. His eyes were a pit of blackness and bloodshed. A chill ran through me, and I had to look away at Brice, who puffed out a breath of disgust.

"He is the one who helped me! He even fought alongside all of you!" I shouted. Others had now started to gather.

Brice shoved him over and laughed, "Listen here, human!" That caused looks of astonishment and confusion among the crowd. I refused to look at Asher.

"I know you're simple-minded and don't understand the sheer evilness of a Nightmare, but I surely thought that after you saw that attack from them you wouldn't stand by and protect a monster like him."

"I did see the attack, and I saw him fighting with us. Not against us." I stepped closer to Brice, clutching my sword. A cold smile spread across his chapped lips at the sight of my nearly clean sword.

"Why would a creature like you do such a thing?" He shoved Asher away, snarling.

Asher stood and casually dusted some dirt off his jacket.

"Kill it!" someone in the crowd shouted and was met with a few cheers.

"Let the King speak with him!" another shout.

"Kill it! Kill the monster!"

"No!" I pulled forward and was instantly grabbed by a group, pulling me back and ripping the sword from my grasp.

"Raise your sword!" Brice commanded at Asher, "Fight me like a man, without your shadows."

Asher tossed his sword to the ground at Brice's feet. His eyes were now calm.

The crowd jeered at him.

Brice laughed, "Afraid to fight without them?"

Asher stayed silent, earning another jeer from the crowd.

"What is going on here!" Kandem yelled as he galloped up to us on a horse that was still on edge from the battle. The King was holding a shield in one hand and cradling his left side a bit. He flinched when he saw Asher.

The crowd let go of me, and I lunged at Kandem, blocking his path to Asher. "He fought with us! He has saved me many times! Do not kill him!"

"Brice, explain!" Kandem gave me a sideways glance.

"This human expects us to believe that he fought alongside Ivars! That he saved her and protected her! She understands nothing of these creatures!"

"Brice!" The King slid off his horse, handed the shield to a soldier, then grabbed his walking stick, leaning heavily on it. He limped over to Brice, pulling him close by his shirt, and whispered loudly into his ear, "What did I say about keeping her true identity a secret!" He shoved him away and turned to me with an apologetic look. "If what you say is true, then I don't know what to believe anymore!"

"Just let him go!" I pleaded. "Just let him go and he won't bother any of you."

He derided, shaking his head and mumbling to himself, "He is one of Bhaltair's men. They are the ones who attacked." He stepped close to me, looking me dead in the eyes, "And you know why," He whispered.

The tower…Bhaltair wanted to go to the tower, and I suddenly dreaded the fact that he wanted to take me there. "Yes, but Asher is no longer with that group. Just let him go. Please."

Kandem looked over at him, then back at me, then at his soldiers. He scratched his beard and shook his head. "Brice, bring him to my tent. And the rest of you get back to work. We have bodies to identify and burn the Nightmare's corpses!"

"What do you intend on doing to him?" I grabbed Kandem's arm, stopping him mid-stride.

"I don't know yet," he drawled, looking down at my hand that was still clinging to him.

I tightened my grip, "Is my dad not with you?"

"No, is he not with you?"

I shook my head and let go, "Where is he?"

"I don't know, but I fear the worst. He hasn't fought in many years…" He beckoned to some of his troops. "Find Gannon! Tell the others to find him at once!" They raced over, checking the dead and telling others as they passed. "We will find him soon." He said with reassurance.

I watched Asher let Brice drag him into the King's half-burned tent. He could handle himself. I needed to find my father.

Anxiety was filling me with every step I took around the camp. Checking the brushes, the burned tents, and the bodies of everyone I came across. It was beginning to smell as the heat baked the dead. Their lifeless eyes stared up at me, a cry caught in their lips. I would close their eyes and feel guilty for the happiness that tingled through me when it wasn't my dad.

"Help!" A raspy faint voice caught my attention.

I turned to the covering of trees that were a distance from the camp. The voice came again, lower and weaker this time.

I pushed through the brush and tangles of branches and nearly stumbled onto my dad. He was leaning against a tree, his face bloody and bruised. He gripped his stomach tightly, blood oozed between his fingers.

"Dad!" I fell to his side and grabbed his shaking hand. He rolled his head over to look at me. His eyes were dark, and his skin pale. There was so much blood, it covered him like a blanket. I moved his hand to check his wound and gasped at the slice that cut deep, threatening to let his stomach spill out. I think I screamed and gagged, but I couldn't hear over my ears rushing with panic. How was he still alive? How was I going to move him?

He coughed, "The key." His voice was barely a horsed whisper. "Blood."

"Help! Someone! Over here!" Tears burned my vision.

He shook my hands, bringing my attention back to him. "He knows," he coughed out again.

"Help!" I screamed with desperation, the word ripping at my tight throat.

"Stay away from." He coughed.

"Save your strength, I'll get Kandem."

He grabbed me with his other hand. His bloody stumps of missing fingers dug into me.

"No!" He shook me again, "Stay away from him." He coughed harshly, black blood dribbling down his chin. "He knows."

"Kandem knows what?"

His grip began to weaken on my hands, but he nodded, desperation in his fading eyes.

"You're getting cold." I pulled my jacket off and laid it over his broken body. "Who did this to you?"

Tears flooded down his face, "I failed Mavi."

"No," I said gently, "No, you protected me and cared for me just like he wanted. I'm going to be okay. Everything is going to be okay, Daddy." I choked out.

He reached for my hand again and I grabbed it quickly.

"Kandem."

"Kandem did this?"

He nodded. Bringing my hand to his lips, he gave it a quick peck and tried to smile. "I see your mother and all my friends," he said, looking into the sky and taking a shaky breath, shutting his eyes.

"No!" I screamed. A flock of birds shot from the trees. "You do not get to leave me again! You have so many questions to answer! So many more things to teach me!" I sobbed, clutching his limp hand. "Please don't leave me again!" The world stilled, the wind stopped brushing against the trees, the birds quit their songs and the air became cold. It felt like my heart had stopped for just a moment, as if it were willing to take his place.

"Ferren?" Margret pulled me into a hug as I still clutched my father's hand. "Tell the King!" she shouted over her shoulder to the closest person. "It looks like he was tortured…"

"He's truly gone this time…" I whispered, more to myself than Margret, "I can't find him this time."

FIFTEEN

Margret let me throw myself upon my father's still chest and scream. I didn't know how long I had laid there screaming and begging for him to come back, but as she pulled me away, I was soaked in his cold blood. The taste of metal filled my mouth. My ears were ringing, my body ached, and my fingers were ice.

They moved his body. Margret said something to me, and then we were walking somewhere. Kandem was there shaking my shoulders trying to ask me something, but I stared up at the sky watching the clouds floating by with no care, just like I had done the first time I had lost my father.

I clutched the locket, letting it bite into my skin, imprinting the shape on my palm. I never got to ask him about it, or anything, really.

"Ferren!" Kandem's voice shook the surrounding air. I snapped my eyes to him. He was breathing heavily and the fierce look on his ageing face could have frightened even the worse Nightmare. He wasn't used to being ignored. I wanted to wrap my hands around his throat to drain the life from him, but I would be killed in an instant. There was a guard just outside the tent. My attempt would be pointless. No one else knew about him killing and torturing my father, and I had to know why he did it in the first place.

I glanced around his tent. I didn't remember walking here, "Where is Asher?" My voice burned my throat. It seemed too loud. How long had I been crying? I looked out one of the scorched holes of the tent. The sunset was just beginning, but that didn't help to keep time here.

"He is with Brice and a few of my trusted soldiers. Do not worry about the Nightmare right now." His face changed to tenderness as he looked at me. I was sitting in a hard-wooden chair that smelled of burned smoke, which was more pleasant than the smell that drifted into the air. Large smoke clouds rose high into the dimming sky. My heart jumped with me as I jumped from the chair.

"It's okay." He placed a light hand on my shoulder, "We're burning the Nightmare's bodies."

"The bodies…"

"Gannon will be buried with the other soldiers within the Ivar Forest."

I blinked back tears; he had no right to talk about him like he cared.

"We bury our soldiers there so they may become one with Hatheya and protect our land."

I choked on tears. Tears of anger, of sadness, of revenge.

Kandem handed me a rag and patted my shoulder again, "Death is never easy, but he will be with you as you walk our land."

The tears wouldn't stop as they poured out of my burning eyes again. I turned away from the king, pressing the rag hard against my eyes, creating blurred spots of bursting blackness, and let one more sob escape before turning back to him.

"He was alive when I found him." I watched his expression. It was cool and calculating. He didn't flinch.

"Oh? Did he have the strength to say anything?" he asked gently.

"No," I said flatly.

I still felt Kandem's eyes watching me, waiting for me to say anything, to let something slip up, "Take me to Asher." I walked out of the tent.

Kandem wouldn't look away from me, eyeing me, waiting for me to confide in him again, but I stayed silent watching the sky cloud with smoke. "I do not trust Brice with Asher."

He cleared his throat, "Brice wouldn't do anything without my command."

"Like announce that I was human?"

"That was an unfortunate mistake."

"Take me to him, now." Kandem's forehead knotted again, but he led me to a tent where Asher sat. He was bleeding from his eye and lip, but did not look like he was in pain.

I looked at Kandem, "Yes, very trustworthy men you have here."

"It happened in the battle," Brice spat.

Asher stood making everyone but me flinch to the ready position, "Would it matter if it hadn't?" He directed the question to the king.

"Why would you help Ferren? What did you have to gain from it?" The King's harsh voice was back. The voice that commanded soldiers and ruled over the land. He stepped up to Asher and pointed at the chair. A silent command for his prisoner to sit.

Asher didn't move, "Maybe, I'm just a nice guy."

Brice sneered at him and pushed him back down into the chair.

"I haven't killed your foolish men here, now have I?" Asher crossed his arms.

"That proves nothing if you haven't received what you want for taking care of Farren." The king studied Asher.

"He wanted nothing. I had nothing to give him, anyway. He just wanted to help me find my father." I said.

"Did you know who her father was? That you were helping an Ivar?"

"I thought she was human?" Asher didn't look away from the king.

"I am. Gannon adopted me." My chest tightened at the words.

His eyes flicked over to mine, then back to the king, "Is that why you are so interested in her? The daughter of a traitor."

Before I could speak, the King jumped in, "He was no traitor. He was an honorable man and was helping me try to heal this land."

"Was?" Asher asked.

"He's dead now," I said, surprising myself by keeping the tears in. Now that I couldn't honor our deal about Gannon opening the human realm for him, I waited to see if his eyes would darken and if his shadows would strike us all dead. A part of me knew they wouldn't. I wished they would at least strike the King.

Asher didn't blink. He gave a quick nod of condolences to me and waited for the King's next question.

Kandem stroked his beard, "Do you trust him, Ferren?"

I cleared my throat, "Yes." Not completely, but I trusted him more than the King, and having a shadow nightmare on my side still worked for my benefit.

"Alright then, let him go," He white-knuckled his cane. "He can't stay here; it would cause more harm than good right now."

Asher's black eyes found mine before Brice shoved him away from his chair and toward the forest. "Get lost creature," One Ivar spat.

"Thank you for the help," I said. A part of me wanted to plead with him to stay to tell him I was in danger and that the King had killed my father, but I couldn't. I wouldn't. I would be putting his life in danger as well, and I couldn't stomach that.

"Get going!" Brice shoved Asher hard with the butt of his sword. "Now!"

Asher's eyes turned swirling black; his features contorted; an Ivar stepped back.

"Asher just go." I swallowed the same fear that filled me the first time I saw him do that. Nightmares were unpredictable, and I was trying to get him out of here before he killed someone.

He turned away, storming into the trees, a black shadow following him.

I found my way back to my father's tent, which was now just a charred piece of fabric and sticks. It looked like how I felt. A crumpled mess of burned confusion and brokenness. Where did I go from here?

"I guess you don't have much to pack." Margret handed me the jacket that I had laid across my father. "I cleaned it for you. You look like you could use a bath yourself before we move out."

"What are you talking about? Where are we going?"

"More news from our scouts about the tower."

"And you expect me to come with?"

"Oh, I'm sorry. Did you have other plans?" She gave a soft smile.

I snorted, "I guess not, but…I don't know…"

"Kandem told me to find you. He wants you to come. He is sending some people to find breaks in the wall to send you home."

"Really?" I doubted that he was sending me home. He wanted me here for some reason, but I could stay close to Kandem if he was after the sword to control the Nightmares, to kill them, or to enslave everyone. If he could control Dentro and all the Nightmares, he could also control the Ivars. He would have all the power.

"Yes, but it could take a while. I guess it took a while to find one to get to you the first time. But now that Gannon is gone, he doesn't believe Nightmares will be looking for you now…"

I nodded, "Thank you, Margret." I swung my coat over my shoulders. It still smelled of blood and death, but it was one of the few things I still had besides the clothes on my back.

I began to help pack what little was left of the camp, numbly moving around with the Ivars, and was placed on a wagon with others who seemed just as exhausted as I was. I looked for Margret but didn't see anyone I recognized. "Where is the King?"

A soldier pointed to another wagon going in the opposite direction of us. "I thought I was to go with him?" I gripped the side of the wagon, anger sizzling in me.

The soldier shrugged, "Not what we were told."

I watched the other wagon until it was out of sight, letting my anger blissfully fill my thoughts with revenge.

SIXTEEN

"Are we headed to the town of Gantrick?" A soldier asked while watching the road.

An Ivar with plump round cheeks and curly brown hair nodded, "We got lucky with this assignment!"

The others cheered in agreement.

"What is Gantrick?" I was becoming nauseous of the bumpy ride and clung to the side trying to steady myself before I lost everything in my stomach. It didn't seem to be bothering anyone else.

"Oh human," the Ivar chuckled, "The richest of the rich live there! Parties constantly!"

"The food and drinks never stop flowing!" another chimed in, "And all the pretty ladies want to dance." The men snickered at each other.

"It's the aristocrats, the nobles, and the gamblers!" the curly-haired Ivar said making his cheeks blush.

"Why are we going there?" I asked. Besides the fact that Kandem wants me away from him but in sight of his spies.

"I'm not sure," He shrugged, "It's known for its eccentric nightlife, nothing else. And it's not the best-guarded place around. Nightmares are constantly sneaking in. Perhaps he's upping the soldiers there for safety."

"You can't blame them!" A lanky dark-haired woman said, "As a kid, I tried sneaking into some of the underground poker clubs."

They snickered together again and passed along more stories to each other.

I listened to as much as I could. It sounded like these parties and poker games were hard to get into, and that it was very much invite-only and affluent people were only allowed. Others told stories of underground games and dancing and fraternizing with Nightmares as well.

"That's not true!" An Ivar barked. A few nodded in agreement.

"No, Ivar would be caught dead with a Nightmare!" Another shouted

"For the right price, they would be! That place runs on money and power." A woman added matter of fact and earned some glares.

An argument broke out within the group as we set for camp. We had no tents, so we settled under the stars with a small fire, cooking whatever animal they had hunted down.

"Don't worry about Gantrick. It's truly not as scandalous as they play it up to be." The curly-haired Ivar sat beside me near the fire. It reminded me of camping with Asher, the stars, the smoke, and the eerie feeling of being watched. I looked around for the white fox. "I have more to worry about than a silly, flashy town." Perhaps I should try to find Asher again. If anyone would help me murder the king, it would be him. Then again, did I want him to know about the weapon and that Dentro was alive? Who knew how he truly felt about the greatest Nightmare that lived?

He smiled, "Don't go worrying too much, it's not good for you."

I laughed lightly, "I'll try to remember that."

It was two more days of travel until we reached Gantrick. Every minute grew colder as winter pushed itself closer to us. I hoped this town would have a proper clothing store. One where they sold winter clothing and boots. I could barely feel my toes anymore and the blood smell of my jacket haunted me with every intake of breath.

We reached a border marked with a large sign reading *Gantrick, Ivar Territory* In thick black letters. I was expecting the same stone pathway and little brick cottages like in Farina, but the streets were glittering bricks of silver and green. Large flowers bloomed across purple trees that looked like they shimmered with magic. The houses were more like townhouses built on top of each other, each with large yards filled with plants and flowers of every kind, all glimmering with silver from the setting sun.

"We will be staying there." I breathed in awe, suddenly understanding the excitement that had come from the Ivar soldiers.

A tall castle sat on a rocky cliff. A section of the castle jutted out over the cliff, clinging to the part of the castle that was on solid ground giving the illusion that it was floating over the edge. On the other side was a large waterfall that reached to the sky. It flooded down onto a windmill, pushing the cranking gears around.

"That's how they power their electricity for the town." The curly-haired Ivar said. "No candles for them here."

"They're lucky then." The wagon pulled to a stop in the front and a few servants in green dresses and purple aprons flooded out of the open double doors to greet us.

"Welcome! Welcome!" A bubbly servant wrapped her arm around mine, "you must be Ferren! The King said you were our special guest, and that we were to treat you as such."

I gave her a tired smile, "That's kind of him." Keep me locked in a castle with your workers around spying on me. That was smart.

"I will show you to your room."

"I can just go with the other soldiers."

She shook her head, making her dirty blonde hair bounce, "They will stay in the service quarters."

"But I don't have to?"

She shook her head again, and gave a soft laugh, "Of course not! You are not a servant!"

I got rude looks from the others as I followed the bubbly servant away from the Ivars. I kept my eyes forward and refused to look guilty. It wasn't my idea. They should be glaring at their king, not the prisoner.

The servant pulled me away into the cool castle with walls that were a bright glittering silver. A staircase lined the wall on one side and full-grown trees lined the other. Birds were singing within the castle while servants bustled around feeding them and watering the flowers.

My room was on the third floor, facing the waterfall, and I could see a bit of the courtyard from another window. My room was decorated with white linens and rugs that felt like clouds to walk on and a giant bed that could fit six people with room to spare. A plush couch and armchair faced a roaring fire that smelled of cinnamon and pine wood. I instantly took a deep breath and wanted to fall into the bed.

"A hot bath has been drawn for you, miss," she opened a door, revealing a small bathroom.

I could have screamed and danced with joy at the site of it. "Thank you. I think I can handle everything from here."

She nodded, bouncing her curls again, and left, closing the door behind her.

I soaked in the tub for a while until the water turned muddy. I didn't know what to do after getting out. The servant had brought me a lacy pink dress with puffy tool sleeves and a tight corset top that made it hard to breath. A note was left with it that said dinner was at eight in the social room.

I eyed the lacy dress and dreaded the word 'social' on the note. I wasn't ready to see people or make small talk with anyone, but I was also starving and didn't have any other clothes to wear. Reluctantly, I slipped on the dress and stood before the window, craning my neck to check the crowd gathering at the castle for dinner. "Keane?" I blinked a couple of times trying to make sure that I was really seeing him, then shut the curtains. It wasn't him. It couldn't be.

I wandered out of my room and found a servant cleaning a room down the hall.

"Hello," she smiled.

"I was wondering where the soldiers were staying. Or if any others showed up before or after us?"

She blinked at me and looked uncomfortable.

"I'm looking for a friend, that's all."

"Oh," Her shoulders relaxed a bit, "well, you shouldn't go down there, dear. I will find him for you."

"I think I could manage if you just point me in the right direction."

Her smile tightened.

"Will they be at the dinner this evening?" I tried keeping the annoyance out of my voice.

She laughed, "A few of them will be there since you will be going."

"What do you mean?"

"They are here to guard you. That is what I was told."

"Who told you that?"

Her smile fully faded away, "The King, of course. He sent word of you coming."

"When?" My corset was becoming tighter.

"A half a month ago, I believe." She shifted uncomfortably.

"Was someone else supposed to be here with me?" Like my father.

She shook her head, "No miss, I was supposed to get just a room for you." She wrung her hands together, "The King didn't mention someone else. Should I prepare them a room?"

I shook my head. I wasn't at his camp until a week ago, they didn't even know where I was. Half a month ago, I was still in the human world.

"Can I help you with anything else? Anything with your room?" Her face was a blotchy red now.

"No," I swallowed, wanting to pull the fluffy heavy dress off, "The room is perfect." I turned away quickly. My legs felt like lead after pacing the floor repeatedly, and I finally gave in to lying down on the bed and collapsing into a fitted sleep. I hadn't slept the whole time we were traveling here. I couldn't. Every time I closed my heavy eyes, I saw my father's face, or the anger in Asher's eyes when I told him to leave. Only after he had left did I realize the guilt I harbored. I wanted to help him like he had helped me, but what could I do? I was a nobody…at least that's what everyone thought. I was still unsure of who I was or what I was. Perhaps the guilt that was tearing at me was because I had more in common with Asher than I thought. I was most likely half Nightmare, if not full.

A knock on the door awoke me. I didn't realize that I had fallen asleep. I rolled off the bed as the knock came louder. The sheets were tangled around my legs, pulling me to the ground. I sat on the ground untangling myself. The knock now sounded annoyed as it came quick and loud.

I threw open the door holding the sheet in one hand, my hair surely a mess of tangles and my dress a crinkled disaster.

"Oh, someone woke up on the wrong side of the bed." Nilsa the Enchantress stood at my door and smiled at me like we were best friends. She wore a floor-length lavender dress that had a row of bows that went from her neck to the bottom of the dress. It had a high neck and capped sleeves. Her hair was in a loose braid that came to her hips. "Don't worry, I'll help you get ready for dinner!" She pushed me aside and grabbed a brush from the bathroom.

"What are you doing here? Weren't you one of Bexley's?"

She stiffened a little, "No, I was not *his*. I came here before he fled and I'm glad I did."

"How did you know I was here?"

She giggled, "Everyone knows you are here?"

"Did Kandem want you here because of me?"

She sat on the bed and patted the spot next to her, "No, but I'm incredibly happy that I am here. Now we can get to know each other."

I sat and let her brush the knots from my hair. "How long have you known the King?" I was trying to keep my voice light, as if we were best friends doing each other's hair.

"I was born into the Ivar court. My family has always served the King."

"So, you know a lot about the history of this place and Kandem?"

She pulled a knot harshly from my hair. "Sorry, that one was tangled," she smiled. "There, now you look much better. Come with me. I will take you to the dining room." She tried flattening the wrinkles from my dress.

"I will be down in a minute," I opened the door for her.

"Okay." She bounced off the bed and to the door, but before she left, she leaned over to me, her lips near my ear.

"The walls have ears. Be careful of what you say and what you ask." She pulled away, a smile on her pink lips. "See you soon, Farren!" and then bounced down the hall quickly, her red hair a blur.

Before I ventured down the stairs to find the dining room, I walked around my room, suddenly feeling as if eyes were watching me. If I thought about it, I felt that way since I had gotten here. Something lurking just behind me, just in the shadows, just out of reach.

I eyed every servant I passed while following the smell of food. It led me to a large banquet room with hundreds of people. They were standing around laughing, drinking, and stuffing their faces with fancy food from a long table filled with every type of food I could have dreamed about.

I filled a plate and watched the guests. I saw Nilsa's red hair in a group of men who were laughing loudly with her. It wasn't an appropriate time to approach her about what she said and maybe it never would be wherever she went a group of people followed her.

"You look lovely," Keane said, sneaking in beside me.

"Keane?" I said with a mouth full of food. I swallowed down the now dry food, begging it not to get stuck in my throat, "You really are here, but how? I wanted to throw my arms around him and make sure he was real and wasn't a ghost or my exhausted mind playing a trick on me, but I couldn't draw attention to ourselves. "How…how did you escape and know where to find me?"

"Asher helped me fight off Bhaltair's men, and we found the group that attacked the camp. Where is he hiding out now?"

"I made him leave…my father…" My lip quivered stopping the words.

"I heard what happened. I'm so sorry," sympathy shook across his eyes.

I glanced away, driving my thoughts away from the pain. "Did you hear of Bexley fleeing from Finara as well?"

He nodded, "Yes, camps like to gossip, predict where they will be assigned to next. I'm sure many fear for their families there. Why would you make Asher leave?"

"Because he was only helping me to get to my father, and now that Gannon is gone well, I had nothing else to offer to him. Plus, Ivars would have killed him if he stayed."

"I've come to believe that wasn't the only reason he was helping."

I looked up at his blue eyes. "Why do you say that?"

"Asher is different. I do think he wanted to find Gannon, but he wasn't stupid. He could see that something was going on, just like I can. Our world is dying, Ferren and even the Nightmares care about that."

"Do you honestly believe that?" I shoved food into my mouth.

He shrugged slightly, "Very little, but he saved me when he could have left me for dead and so I would like to give him the benefit of the doubt. My father said we were brought together for a reason and my father is always right." He beamed another smile at me.

"He couldn't stay here anyway, and you know that."

His smile turned down at the edges a bit, "I do."

"And what of you? Aren't you considered a deserter?" I whispered.

"At this point, with what is going on with Bexley, it's unsure where I stand in the eyes of the other Ivars. Perhaps I need to speak with the King."

"Do you think that would be wise? Most already think Bhaltair killed you."

"It wouldn't be wise to hide from him."

"I think it might be, actually." I glanced nervously around the room, "We need to talk, somewhere private."

"You might want to leave the food behind if you want to make a haste escape."

I placed my mountain of food on a table and weaved my way through people until we were out of the room and heading to the doors. It felt good to breathe in the crisp air and feel the coolness bite into the skin. "The King killed my dad." I blurted out.

Keane's breath hitched as I told him who Gannon was to me and what happened at camp, leaving out the parts that I still didn't understand or want to think about.

"Gannon and Kandem were friends. Their names are in history books together." He ran a hand across his tired eyes.

"Power can make people do horrendous things. Like, kill their friends." I suddenly found myself desperate to make Keane believe me. I just wanted someone to believe me to have them hate the King as much as I did. "If my dad was trying to stop Kandem from getting the sword or if Kandem knew he was hiding something, that would give him the motive to kill him."

Keane was silent for some time, leaning against the brick railing and staring up at the stars, then across at the matching little houses that you could see through the gates. "I slightly understand why the King wants the sword, but," he held up a hand to stop me from cutting in, "Controlling them wouldn't help us learn how to coexist together it would only drive the wedge further and risk setting Dentro free for the sword is not worth anything." He took a breath, "If you go after the King, you will die, and if you tell anyone else this they won't believe you or…"

"If Nightmares find out, they'll start a war."

"Our land can't take a war it's already dying."

"There you are." Nilsa came floating from the door, "I was wondering where you were, and I found you sneaking around with a boy. And not the same boy from before, either." She looked Keane up and down, fluttering her lashes, "Why you're the boy from Bexley's camp! I remember seeing you around!"

He nodded and gave me a worried look, "Keane Zavian." He gave a bow of his head to her.

"Where is that other boy you were with? The one with the dark eyes?" She blinked her eyelashes at me like a girl asking about her schoolgirl crush.

"He was a Nightmare. Why would he be here?" I asked carefully.

She pouted a bit, "That's too bad, he was very handsome. Well," she clapped her hands together, "Let's get back to the party!"

Keane and I couldn't talk. We were being pulled around with Nilsa, and people talked too loudly, they laughed too much, and I was being watched by the servants and the soldiers and the guests.

The party began to end, and Nilsa pulled me into a hug to say good night. "Sneaking away was stupid." She pulled away and nodded a goodnight to Keane before heading up the stairs.

I was escorted back to my room by a servant. I ripped my dress off and placed the thin nightgown on that had been left for me.

Nilsa was right. I had been stupid, but how else was I able to talk to Keane about anything? I was a prisoner in this place! I threw a vase full of purple flowers across the room. It exploded into sharp pieces across the carpet.

I collapsed onto the bed, wanting to scream and throw more things, but I didn't want more attention on myself.

Others had to know about Kandem being corrupted. They had to have information about where he was, when he would be back, anything that would help me get to him. People talked, and this place seemed like a place full of gossip and loose lips.

I pulled myself off the bed and to the window. I opened it and invited the cooled mountain air in the world was drowned out by the noise of the waterfall. Little red eyes blinked at me on the ledge of the window. I jumped back, grabbing my dagger from the bed. A white fluffy face peered up at me, looking completely bored. "How did I know you would be around here somewhere, Eira?" She blinked at me again. "What is Asher up to now?" I stepped aside and let her into the warmth of the room before scanning the ground for Asher. I closed the window and the curtains and crawled into bed, still clutching my dagger. It felt comforting to have it close. I shouldn't leave it lying around. I'm sure it would disappear the instant one if the king's spies saw it.

Eira jumped up with me, her red eyes scanning the room. "Make sure no one comes in to kill me." I patted her head, earning myself a swipe of her claws and a hiss before she curled up on the very edge of the bed.

SEVENTEEN

I sat in an empty field, stars shining down at me on one side and on the other, the sun was shining high in the sky. I looked around at the dying field and began to walk, but the field never ended. "Hello!" My voice echoing like a cannon. I covered my ears, the sound pounding through my head. My blood turned to ice, my skin prickled, and my head swayed. I turned in a tight circle until my eyes landed on him. The pale ghost of a man off in the distance. The same man that I had chased in the forest and when my dad disappeared.

"What do you want!" I screamed, my throat ripping.

He didn't move. I tried walking towards him, but he never grew closer. He was always in the distance, staring at me. I stopped and fell to the ground, exhausted. My body begged for sleep, but I refused to look away from the ghost.

He raised his arm high above him, a sword suddenly in his pale hand. I watched the glowing sword pulse with light, following my heartbeat. The man blurred, the field swayed, and I opened my eyes to the blinding light.

I was standing in the castle bedroom, looking out the window. Eira was on the windowsill, staring up at me. Her tail wrapped around her body, her piercing glare traced me over as if she knew what I had dreamed.

I quickly dressed back in the awful dress I had worn last night and threw my red coat over it. I need to escape my prison, even just for a few minutes. Before I left, I opened the window for Eira and then raced out of the room, down the stairs, and out the door before someone could stop me. The air had grown chillier overnight, which appropriately matched my emotions. I didn't know what time it was, but it must have been early. The streets were dead as I walked along them looking for a clothing store. I needed to get out of the hideous dress and death-covered coat.

I stumbled across one down a white-rocked path that shimmered in the sun. It was covered with flowers and lovely little windows that showed the many clothes within. The door chimed with a bell as I entered the empty shop. "Hello!" I shouted. I wasn't met with an answer. "Hello!"

"Just a moment!" A chipper voice called from the back then a round woman with rosy cheeks bustled in with a bit of fabric over her shoulder and holding a box of sewing items. "Well, hello there! I'm not used to having customers this early!"

"Oh, I'm sorry. I just need to grab a few things."

She looked me up and down, "Take your time."

"Thanks." I wandered away, browsing the bursting racks as the lady followed me with her eyes. The racks were filled with dresses and skirts of every type and shirts that glittered and had feathers and beads covering every part.

"Looking for something in particular?"

"Pants and something warm." I sighed.

She nodded, "You don't seem like a party dress type of girl."

"Perhaps at another time of my life." Like when I wasn't worried about getting killed or having to run for my life, I could have twirled around in a fluffy dress and giggled with the men like the women had down at the dinner last night.

"Come with me." She led me to a back room full of boxes and scraps of fabric thrown around. "Here, they're on the house, dear. No one around here was interested in such clothes and they're just gathering dust being back here." She handed me a large dress box.

I balanced the box carefully on a stool before I opened it and pulled out a dark pair of pants lined with pockets and a shirt that was forest green. It was low cut and had a ribbon sewn into the long sleeves. "Thank you." I shuffled through the other clothes for a moment before closing the box. They weren't the type of clothes I particularly wore, but at least they weren't all dresses and skirts.

"Not a problem, dear." She tied the box with a black ribbon, beaming a smile at me.

"I just need a coat now."

"Oh?" She eyed mine, "well I don't have anything like that, but the shop next door carries some."

I thanked her again, before heading next door and picking out a plain black coat with a thick wool lining. The woman behind the counter charged it to the castle for me with a sickly sweet smile on her lips and told me to come back soon. Probably hoping I would spend more of the king's money.

I carried the box back to the castle and was greeted by the bubbly servant with the curls, "There you are! I went to your room earlier, and you weren't there, and your window was open! I feared the worst!"

"And what was that?"

She opened and closed her mouth quickly.

"I'm fine. I just need clothes." I raised the box at her.

"Well, I could have sent for some! No need to do that on your own!" She held the door open for me and then straightened out the bottom of my dress, her forehead wrinkled with worry.

"I think I'm capable of getting clothes." I didn't want to get her in trouble with the King if she was supposed to keep tabs on me, but I wasn't going to let the King control me either.

Her smile dipped a little, "Yes, you are very different from the others that stay here."

"You don't even know." I muttered under my breath, "Have you heard from the King? Or perhaps know how to contact him?"

She shook her head, "No Miss."

I clicked my tongue against my teeth. She probably wouldn't tell me if she had, anyway.

Once back in my room, I reopened the window making sure Eira could get in when she wanted and pulled out the clothes and decided to go with a dark plum pair of pants that had sharp slashing black lining them reminding me of the night in my dream and a long black sleeve shirt that hung down to my ankle at one side and barely hit my hip on the other side. It had a purple corset middle that latched together with ribbons matching the pants. I stood in front of the mirror for a moment, checking my movement in the outfit. It was a flattering outfit, but what I cared about was being able to run or defend myself in it.

Next, I needed to find Nilsa. If anyone would have answers it was her. I asked a servant where she was, and they led me up another flight of stairs and into a long hallway that was filled with paintings of what was supposed to be the last battle with Dentro. I studied them quietly while we passed. Their elegant watercolor images clouded my vision as I saw the depiction of Gannon *fleeing* the battle. If it was historically accurate, I should be tucked in his arms as he took me to safety.

The servant cleared her throat. I blinked, realizing that I had stopped in front of the painting.

I waited till she left to knock loudly on the door of Nilsa's room until she answered. She was in a heavy robe that was baby pink and had little flowers circling her hips. "Oh, it's you." She looked down the hall at the servants who were dusting the paintings. "I just awoke. I'll send for you later!" She smiled sweetly and gave a fake yawn before closing the door in my face. I grinded my teeth together before turning haughtily away. If I couldn't talk to her, I needed to find Keane next, see if he'd overheard anything from the servants. I made my way down the flights of stairs and started searching for the servant's courters when an Ivar soldier found me. "Hello, Farren, I'll be your guard today." He was short but broad and had deep olive skin.

"I don't need a guard."

"The King thinks you do and since you keep wandering away, the servants agreed."

I pinched my lips together, trying to smile, but I couldn't make it happen. "Then I would like Keane to be my guard."

"We are on rotation. I'm assigned first."

"Fantastic" I tried not to come off too pissy. I sat in my room with a guard named Dex just outside. He would be with me all night and escort me to the dinner that night as well. The window was too high to jump from and the vines that trailed down it weren't strong enough to hold my weight. The other window was dangerously surrounded by jutting rocks slick with water from the falls. It would be suicide to try to climb down either window. I threw myself on the bed with a sigh of frustration.

Eira jumped through the window. "Show off," I growled. She was wearing a collar made of purple baby's breaths woven together. "What's this?" I pulled it off her, examining the collar closely. It didn't strike me as a thing Asher would do, but I doubted Eira would have let anyone else put it on her. One flower was facing inward. I pulled it out and a small piece of paper fell onto my lap. It was wounded tightly together. I unrolled it.

Talked to Keane. Others know.

Was written across it. I sat up, heart pounding. He talked to Keane? Talked to him about what and who are these others? I ripped the note up and threw the remains in the fire. I was sure the servants were searching my room whenever I left.

I went to the window and took a breath of the cool air, scanning the yards filled with people. I needed to get out of here and figure out what the note meant, figure out what was happening beyond this little town.

Nilsa crossed the grounds of the castle, floating along with some servants and other nobles. They seemed to all be talking at once, giggling about everything they said. They leaned close to each other's ears and whispered.

I smiled; I could still snoop in plain view. "I'm going to join the other women in the yard," I told Dex as he trailed after me.

I waved to them, "Hello ladies."

They studied my outfit for a bit then smiled as Nilsa greeted me warmly as if she didn't just slam the door in my face a minute ago.

Dex stayed a bit away as he looked annoyed by the gossip and giggling, but Nilsa latched arms with me and gave me a wide smile, saying how wonderful it was to have a new friend.

I spent the day with them but didn't learn anything of importance besides who liked who and who threw the best parties with the most drinks. I pretended to lap it up, hoping their tongues would loosen and maybe say something about the King or Bexley. Some started to talk about Bexley and him deserting, but then shut it down quickly as those around them became antsy.

As the sun began to set, the women retired to their homes to change for dinner and the parties that would happen afterward.

"Come, I'll walk with you back to your room." Nilsa winked at me, "How lucky are we that we get to stay in the King's castle, all the girls are jealous of us."

"I would think they would feel lucky just living in such a beautiful town. Especially after what has happened in Finara. With Bexley and the King being so far away from his castle and them leaving it unprotected."

Sighing, she laid her head on my shoulder as we walked, "Such a shame someone so devoted to the Ivar and to protecting Hatheya would do such a horrendous thing. It seems like it isn't even real, that he perhaps fled for a different reason, but that is only a wish." She pulled away and skipped up the rest of the stairs.

I chewed on my bottom lip as I walked to my room. Did she not believe Bexley was against the Ivars like everyone whispered about? Perhaps he thought like how I did about the King. Perhaps he didn't trust him, and he fled with those who believed him? Or he fled because he wanted the power of the weapon as well? If Nilsa and I could just talk freely, then I could figure out what the hell was happening.

Again, a hideous party dress was waiting for me on the bed when I got back to my room. It was light blue with pink lace covering the long, heavy bottom. There were even matching gloves that I refused to wear as they made my hands itch. I stood with the women from earlier today pretending my feet weren't killing me and watched the partygoers.

"Poor Linda, she still won't come out of her house. She says that Bexley never would have done anything like what has been said."

I snapped my attention to the woman who was talking. She was a tall, thin woman who stood above the rest of us. Her face reminded me of a bird with a large nose and pouty lips.

"Who is Linda?"

"Oh, she is Bexley's sister. She lives here just a few blocks from the candy shop owned by Mr. Bradly."

I had no idea what she was speaking of but nodded anyway, "That poor girl, perhaps we should visit her and bring her a treat? I don't think she should be alone."

The ladies gave each other nervous looks, "I don't know how it is in the Farm Country you reside from, but we don't want to be seen with someone like that at the moment." A woman with short legs and a heavy face said.

"What Milly means," Nilsa said, stepping in, "Is that Bexley and Linda were awfully close, and some believe she knew about his plans and whatnot. So, it's best not to be seen with her at the moment."

The women nodded, and I nodded back making a mental note about it. Somehow, some way, I needed to see Linda and figure out if she knew anything. I glanced over at the guard, watching closely. I hadn't seen Keane for a while, and I didn't know how to get to him without causing suspicion among the other Ivars. I nibbled on food and listened in on other conversations and learned that others were also worried about the King not being in Finara and wondered why he was traveling with the army. Some thought it was because the Nightmares were building their own army and that's why so many Ivars had gone missing. Some even whispered that a resistance against the King had started with both Ivars and Nightmares. The woman listening to the rumors blanched at such a thing and stormed out of the party. A few glanced over their shoulders at her but didn't seem to care much as another round of champion was served and music filled the room sending people twirling and laughing around.

"Come dance!" Nilsa pulled me to the center of the room surrounded by flowing dresses and flaring hands. "Word that the King might stop here is spreading."

"He is?" Nilsa turned to me and moved away from the guards' prying eyes.

"Yes, I told some *friends* that he was coming to the Fallen Moon Festival. That is when our moon rises and then sets within an hour of its time. It is the darkest night of the year, as there are no stars in the sky either. It was once ruled by the Nightmares, but after Dentro fell, it became a night of celebration for us. The King comes here every year to celebrate, and I plan on making sure he comes this year as well."

"How will you do that?" I tried to keep in step with the dancing, but I seemed to be the only one who didn't know the dance.

"His people are already fearful of what is happening around them. He must come if he doesn't want them asking more questions. Feed the fear." She smiled wickedly, "In a month, he will be here." She spun away, taking the hand of a man, and giggled with excitement.

I reluctantly danced with others until my feet felt like they were blistering, then retired to my room. The quietness of my room surrounded me with a bit of peace. I could still hear a bit of the music from downstairs, but as I opened the windows, the sound of crickets and water flowing covered it. I sat on the window ledge watching bats catching bugs.

Eira jumped onto my lap startling me, "I wish I could move as silent as you." I ran a hand through her fur, expecting a swat of her paw, but she slid her head against my hand instead. I placed her on the bed and searched the room for a pad and pen, then wrote a quick note to Asher about the Fallen Moon Festival and hoped that he could also get a message to Keane.

I tied the note around the flowered collar and waved her out the window. She got to the bottom and stared up at me. Her red eyes never blinked, then she turned away and disappeared into the darkness.

I fell onto the bed exhausted, but I couldn't calm my mind. The thought of the King's arrival was all that I could think about. What would I say to him when I saw him? I had no proof of anything, but I had to look him in the eye when I accused him of my father's murder. I had to see his expression. I spun my blade in my hand, imagining running it through him.

I untied my hair from the bun and ran a brush through it lazily. The weight of the world suddenly felt heavy on my shoulders. Escaping with Asher and Keane would have been easy, but I stayed to confront the King not only about my father, but to prevent further bloodshed and stop him from finding the sword. I clutched the hairbrush tightly, my knuckles turning white.

I would find proof of his wrongdoings, of his betrayals, his murdering, and then I would kill him. I slammed the brush down, cracking the handle.

EIGHTEEN

I stood in a grand room decorated with floating lights that hung far above my head. They barely lit down to the cold stone floor that I stood barefoot on. I held a bloodied knife in my shaking hands. It dripped down onto a stone floor, flowing away as if it were running from me. It ran to the foot of a man who sat in front of me on a throne. The throne seemed to be scurrying around, hissing. I blink into the darkness unable to scream as I realized the throne was made of beetles and snakes that feasted upon each other but seemed to ignore the man. He uncrossed his tall legs, reaching a hand for me.

I stumbled back, anxiety gnawing at every nerve in my body. This was not the pale man that usually haunted my dreams. This creature was darker. His body towered over me, constantly growing, suffocating the space, until he was everywhere at once. I fell to the ground clutching my throat as air seemed impossible to breathe in the shrinking space. Echoes of laughter sounded, sending the insects and snakes from the throne tumbling down on me. They bit my skin, scratched my eyes, and slithered down my throat.

I jerked awake, my stomach retching. I barely made it to the bathroom before expelling everything from my stomach.

I laid on the floor, my skin sticky with sweat, my head pounding as nausea rolled around my body. I must have fallen asleep again because as I opened my eyes. A servant stood over me, her face white and filled with panic.

"Should I call the physician?"

I sat up slowly, shaking my head and instantly regretting it, "No, I'm fine, I just need some water and not to be disturbed today."

She helped me up and back to bed before getting me a glass and a pitcher of water.

I heard a commotion at my door, but no knock came as I peeked out from the blankets and saw a note had been slipped under my door. I rolled ungracefully out of bed, dragging the blankets with me as I picked up the rose-scented envelope. My name was scrawled across the front of it in swirls and curls of a very graceful hand.

I popped open the letter.

"Dear Farren, I did miss you today at our lunch and other assorted gatherings. Perhaps if you are feeling better, we could meet tonight at 7 pm sharp, in my room for tea.

Best wishes, your friend, Nilsa."

I took a glance at the clock and sighed. One hour until she wanted to meet. Even though my head was pounding, and my body ached as it had when I was camping with Asher, I got dressed and brushed my hair with the cracked brush, then went to see Nilsa with my guard trailing behind me.

I still hadn't seen Keane since that first day and I had to keep my anxiety that something was wrong to a minimum. I had too much to worry about and asking around about him might put him in a worse situation than he was already in. He could handle himself, and he had to.

In front of Nilsa's door stood another Ivar guard. I smiled at him as I approached, and he stepped aside so I could give a quick knock.

Nilsa rarely had a guard at her door. They kept an eye on her, but not so close. Was this her doing or Kamden's?

I knocked again, expecting her singsong voice to tell me to come in or her to throw open the door and show off her horrific pink outfit, but neither came.

The guard raised a brow at me. I gave him another smile and tried the door. It was unlocked. I slipped in and closed the door without giving another look at either guard.

Irritation was building in me; she just gave me the note. Did she already forget I was coming?

I looked around; her room was three times the size of mine and truly what I pictured a princess room to be. I gasped a little at the drapes of white glittering fabric that hung around the walls, a white luxury couch and armchairs sat in front of a fireplace made of marble, and small angels were etched into it. A bed with silk sheets and a chiffon canopy sat exactly across from an equally enormous bathtub in the center of a wall of windows facing the white peak mountains. I wanted to drape across the bed and feel the softness of such an amazing bed. I gave a pillow a small pat; the exhaustion returning to my body instantly. I couldn't imagine you would ever have nightmares in a bed that grand.

I drifted deeper into the room. The overly soft white carpet quieted my steps as I rounded a corner and heard something thud to the floor, then pages of a book being quickly flipped through.

"Nilsa?" No response, "Hello?" I said gruffly, pushing open a door.

"Must you be so loud?" Nilsa sat on the floor of a large closet with a book in her lap and another lying beside her. Her hair was scrunched up into a bun dripping with water and a robe slung across her. Tattoos of black trees trailed down her legs.

"Every tree signifies the death of an Enchantress from my family line. Doesn't matter if they're Fairies, Sprites, or Enchantress. We believe that our bodies return to the forest and grow into a tree so tall and thick that no one dares to cut it down."

"Like the Ivar?"

"No." She said haughtily, "They become the soil of our souls so we may grow. They are not the trees." She narrowed her eyes at me. "I have nearly twenty trees across me. The Enchantresses keep them hidden. Especially from the Ivar.

Would you like to sit, or do you want to continue to stare at me like I am some kind of Nightmare?"

"You are a Nightmare, apparently."

She tisked at me and smiled, "Not in the palace, not while the King needs his Enchantress." She gave a laugh, showing her full set of sharp teeth. "Fairies are harder for him to control, so he sets his eye on us Enchantresses. The sprites don't contain much power in their tiny bodies and are easily crushed," she slammed a hand down on the book, making me jump, "Often."

"What ruses are you playing with me?" I should have left Asher a message about where I was going. This woman seemed off her hinges. Was this her true personality or was it the wide-eyed doe that was just a little smart?

"The kind of ruses that keep me alive. That gives me a place like this," She threw her hands around and stood quickly.

I clutched the dagger that I had hidden in my waistband.

"Ferren, if I was planning on killing you, I certainly wouldn't do so in my room. I don't want my quarters haunted by your disgruntled soul."

I let go of my dagger, "That's not fully comforting."

"It shouldn't be, I wasn't trying to comfort you."

I narrowed my eyes at her, "I knew there was something off about you."

She rolled her eyes and flipped a loose piece of hair out of her face, "That's because I wanted you to. Now out."

"Excuse me?" Did she just invite me over to show off her second personality and then throw me out?

"I need to dress. Get out of my closet." She shoved me out and slammed the door in my face.

I knotted my hands into fists and then threw them into the air. I didn't like either of her personalities. One made me want to vomit, and the other made me want to punch her. I walked to the window and looked down at the dizzying view below us until Nilsa emerged wearing a silk red nightgown that flowed to the floor and a fur shawl that was wrapped around her shoulders. "I'm sure you're wondering why I asked you here."

"I'm assuming it wasn't for tea."

She waved a hand at me, "Of course, we will have tea; I enjoy tea."

"Okay then- "

She placed a finger to her lips silencing me, then tossed the large book she was reading on the bed and flipped to a page.

It was in a language I had never seen before. I crept forward, looking at the ruin-like symbols and strange pictures that were squashed onto a dog-eared page.

Nilsa started to whisper strange words, then placed two fingers up and brushed her lips. A gray light followed her fingers then spread silently around the room until it vanished.

I stood there with my mouth gaping, staring at Nilsa. Magic. I just saw real magic!

"Now we can talk freely without *those* guards hearing us." She slammed the book shut, "Now as you know, I have spread the word the King is coming in a month's time."

"Why do you want him here?"

"Because I hate him as much as you do, and I, unlike most of his people, am not blind to how much he has changed over time." Her eyes darkened with pain, "He was once a very noble king, but now when I look into his eyes all I see is his hunger for power. His secrets grow every day, unexplained deaths, and now you."

"Me?"

"Yes, a human in our world and your adopted father, Gannon, the gatekeeper. Strange." She lounged across the couch, glaring at me.

"How many of you know I am human?" I crossed my arms, sizing her up as she was doing to me.

"Very few. I have spies of my own that gave me word about you. I had my guesses the first time I saw you, but still…strange." She looked at me and shuttered, "Tell me what you know about the King and what is happening. You were at the camp; you must have seen or heard something."

"Heard of what?"

"Anything. War, Nightmares, the land, about Gannon's death?" She intoned.

"Why should I trust you? Perhaps you'll run to the King and tell him everything. I am not quick to trust. Especially someone so good at lying," I walked to the fireplace watching the dancing flames light up the small angels.

"You trusted the Shadow Nightmare, did you not? An immensely powerful and dangerous creature." She sounded excited by it.

"And you aren't dangerous?" I turned back to her. She was now standing close to me. I jumped, grabbing my blade. I never heard her move, never felt her breath on my neck even as she stood just a beat away.

She laughed and fell gracefully into an armchair, "Oh I am, and as you notice powerful too." She nodded to the chair across from me, "We will work together because sadly we're all that we have at the moment. And I noticed they are keeping the handsome Ivar soldier away from you, so they know something is up with you two. He's out of the question of helping you at the moment, is he not?."

I slid into the chair and crossed my legs, blade still in hand. "At the moment." I cursed under my breath. I had hoped they hadn't noticed Keane so early. Any chance of communicating with him was gone, and now I had to worry if they had seen Eira and Asher as well. I needed to be more careful.

"And what of the Shadow Nightmare? Do you know where he is?" The giddiness was back in her voice.

"I'm assuming drinking his nights away at a bar," I said flippantly.

She gave me a suspicious look, "Shame, he would have been useful."

Yes, and that is why I plan on keeping him a secret. I wasn't a fool and showing my complete hand to such a flawless deceiver. We smiled at each other tightly as we each made our cups of tea and politely nibbled on crackers.

"Now," she took a sip, "Tell me everything. I'm growing bored with crackers and suspicion in your eyes." She took another sip of the burning tea, "I know the King is looking for something."

I told her most. I kept my father's last words to myself and the sword, pretending I didn't know what exactly he was after in the tower. My Father trusted me with that knowledge, and I wasn't planning on telling everyone. Especially someone I didn't particularly like.

She set her cup down, leaning back in the chair and staring at the ceiling, "Interesting. I wonder what he is after in that tower."

I shrugged, "I'm more concerned about Dentro."

"Why? He's stuck in that tower and done so by a very powerful Enchantress." She waved a perfectly manicured hand at me.

"Can't spells be broken?" I rebuffed.

She nodded thinking, "Yes, but it's extremely hard and that was blood magic and not just any blood, Mavi's blood. It would be extremely hard. It would take many types of Enchantresses to break."

"But it can be done." I pressed.

"He would have to have a dozen Enchantress willing to do it, and not only that, Dentro wouldn't be thankful and let him live. He would slaughter all the Ivars and anyone else that was in his way. The King would be idiotic to do that, and Kamden is a practical man. Cruel yes, but he thinks through every decision he makes."

"No, he's not, but all I can tell you is he has a plan to avoid slaughter."

She looked away from the ceiling, settling her eyes on me, "Does he know?"

I took a sip of my tea, ignoring her piercing gaze.

"Well, if that is the case, then we have much more to worry about."

"Yes, so tell me how getting the King here will help us?"

"We'll kill him, of course," she said calmly and set her cup down.

I choked on my tea. I had been thinking the same thing, but having it said out loud suddenly made it real.

"And hopefully he doesn't find the tower before the festival." She sighed dramatically.

"How do you plan on killing the most powerful and protected man in Hatheya?" I tried to calmly set my tea down as Nilsa did, but a bit slopped over the edges.

"*We* are in for a challenge, but I do love challenges." She smiled like a cat who just caught a mouse and was now playing with it.

I cleared my throat, giving my mind a minute to catch up with what was happening. "I can tell you that when he gets here, he'll want to speak with me."

She arched her brows and sat forward, "Why is that?"

"Because he killed my father, and he knows I know and I also know something else."

She waited.

"Just tell one of your spies to tell him that I know what is in the tower."

"And what is that?" She was on the edge of her seat now.

"Does it matter? Just as long as it gets him here and he'll want to speak with me alone."

"You know for sure he'll want to speak with you alone?"

"Yes."

"You do know we probably won't make it out of this alive."

I looked down at my spilled tea. Of course, I knew, but it would stop him from finding the tower and doing whatever he had planned with the sword. Thousands or maybe millions could die by his hand. "Yes."

We finished talking over a basic outline of a plan and then parted ways. It was getting late, and we didn't want to rouse suspicion. Nilsa said the guard that was now watching her was sent by the King since she started spreading the news that he was coming. He apparently didn't like that she was saying that and found it in his best interests to keep an eye on her. She was, of course, a Nightmare even though she grew up in Ivar territory that still made her a threat.

"Do you think he'll ask you to help him break the spell on the tower," I asked before leaving.

She rolled her head back and forth, "No, he thinks I'm dumb-witted. He doesn't know that I have books about Hatheya magic. A gift from a family member."

"You trust me enough to tell me?"

"A secret for a secret. Goodnight." She blew out the candles and crawled into bed before I was even out the door.

I laid in my bed braiding and unbraiding a few pieces of my hair as I thought about what Nilsa and I had planned.

Could I really take a life? He was evil, and most likely he was going to kill thousands in the near future if he got his hands on that sword, but what if I was wrong? What if I was jumping to conclusions and letting Nilsa lead me down a very dark path?

My stomach knotted as I fell in and out of sleep.

NINETEEN

The next day I dressed in warm clothes as the snow was now knee-deep out and the coldness seemed to seep through every crack and window in the castle.

I pulled on a heavy violet sweater and pants, thankful for the warmth that rushed to my skin. I was most thankful for the boots that Nilsa brought me. They were fur-lined and warm enough to thaw my icy feet.

My stomach grumbled, reminding me that it was indeed time for breakfast and that I hadn't eaten anything yesterday. I still felt anxious and on edge, but I had to pull myself together. Sitting scared in my room over a dream wouldn't help Hatheya.

I threw open my door and without looking at my guard I headed down the hall. The guard was walking particularly closer than usual and had his head down. They mostly kept their distance and acted annoyed they had to trail me around all day. He stepped closer to me; I came to a quick stop, turning on my heels to face him. "Ever heard of personal space?"

He raised his head a bit, "We need to talk soon."

"Keane?" I nervously looked around, "You shouldn't be here. They know we're friends, and if anyone sees you talking to me, you'll be in danger."

"Listen," he took a quick breath, "Take a walk-through town today. Don't worry about me. I still have friends in the guard that are helping us as much as possible. I don't know how often we'll be able to communicate, but you need to get out of the castle. The King is coming."

"I know." I swallowed, "And don't worry about that. We have a plan."

"We who? I know it's not Asher. I just spoke with him."

"You spoke with him? How?" I turned away quickly and walked down the hall as a servant came up the stairs. I stopped at the top stair, gaping down at the entryway. The once tall and beautiful trees were dying. Their leaves were gone, their branches hung low their trunks seemed to be leaking something black. The birds were all dead. Servants in masks and gloves were picking up the dead animals and quickly shoving them and the leaves into bags. Other guests stood back covering their mouths and whispering quickly to each other.

"It's spreading to the animals," Keane said quietly.

I swallowed and ambled down the stairs.

I wasn't hungry anymore and only ate for show. Trying not to glance at Keane who stood at the edge of the room with some other guards keeping to himself as much as he could. I swallowed a lump in my throat.

Nilsa tapped my hand, "I said, have you gotten your dress for the ball yet?"

"What?" My head snapped around to where she was sitting, "Oh, no no." I took a sip of water, trying to help my dry throat.

"Well, you better get on it! It's going to be here sooner than you think!" She giggled her fake little laugh.

I smiled tightly at her. "I'll go today."

"Do you want me to go with you?"

"No," I said too quickly, "I think I can manage it and a quiet walk would be nice."

She side-eyed me for a moment then turned back to her food and the gossiping gentleman beside her.

After breakfast, I quickly fetched my jacket and gloves and with Keane right behind me, we headed out.

"So, you're getting all dressed up for the festival?" He asked when we were far enough away from the castle. "I don't know if it would be wise to go."

I scoffed, "I've been working with Nilsa on something that will take care of the problem."

"Nilsa? The Enchantress? You can't trust any Enchantress."

"Yes," I sighed, a puff of white air. I wondered if I was to be trusted. I was part Enchantress, after all. My supposed mother pulled the wool over almost everyone's eyes. "I know that, but she has a good plan."

"A plan for what?"

He pulled me to a stop. We stood a bit away from the sidewalk, tucked up next to a building. Though no one seemed to glance in our direction, I still felt watched. Goosebumps rose across my skin, and darkness cooled over my shoulders. "Asher?"

He emerged from the shadows, a heavy coat and hat tucked around him. He looked like every Ivar I had seen that morning besides the shadows that he pulled back like a dog on a leash. They buckled against his force before sinking back into him, their screaming faces marked with anger that they weren't allowed to kill. Asher took a shaky sigh at the work of keeping them contained.

"What are you doing here? If you get caught."

"I won't get caught, relax."

"No one has noticed? Are you sure?" I glanced around nervously again.

"You'll be surprised how busy everyone is and that most just keep their heads down and do as they're told, especially with all the massacres happening."

"What?" I breathed, "What's happening." Curse being stuck in this town. In that castle. How had no one spoken about any of this? Were they too self-centered to care or were they hoping if they ignored it that it would all disappear?

Asher crossed his arms and leaned against the building, "The Ivars are attacking Nightmare towns, taking them captive and killing those who are fighting back."

"Why are they taking them captive?"

He shrugged, “My guess is for slaves. Why else?” He glared at Keane.

Keane clenched his fists then took a breath, releasing them, “Ivars are dying as well.”

Asher’s jaw feathered, “Of course, Nightmares are attacking back. Rebel groups have heard what is happening and are trying to end it.”

“Those people who are attacking the Nightmares unprovoked are not Ivars. We vowed to protect Hatheya, and starting wars is not protecting it.” Keane’s voice was rising, “Ivars, just like Nightmares are being killed at every turn and we need to figure out why.”

I grabbed Keane’s shoulder hissing at him to be quiet and then at Asher who had loosened the reins on his shadows a bit. He looked exhausted trying to keep them contained, but if he wanted to walk around an Ivar town freely he had to deal with it. “Have you heard anything about Bexley?” I asked both of them, trying to hurry up the conversation before someone came looking for me and realized I wasn’t at the dress shop.

“No, he’s keeping a low profile at the moment,” Keane said, talking much quieter now.

“We should talk to Linda.”

“Who is Linda?” They both asked.

“Bexley’s sister. She lives near the candy shop.” I turned away, heading in that direction, with Keane by my side.

“What the hell is a candy shop?” Asher asked, slinking out of the darkened alleyway.

After asking an older man, who was hesitant about telling us where she lived, he directed us to a house that looked like all the others on the street. A pearly white house and large empty flowerpots filled with snow. But unlike the other homes, the windows were covered with heavy gray curtains, and a crudely written sign on the door said she was out.

"Looks like she's gone." Keane pointed at the sign.

"It looks like she doesn't want to be bothered." I banged on the door. "Linda?"

"If she doesn't want to be bothered, then why would she answer her door?" Asher said in a snark. He wiggled the door handle while I peeked through a small slit in the window, unable to see much besides a couch in a darkened living room.

"Perhaps we should try the back?" I stepped away from the window and started down the steps to check the back door.

"Ren, come on," Asher called softly over his shoulder.

"Did you just break into her house!" I hurried after him and Keane, closing the door quickly before we were spotted. "Why would you do this?"

"Because we needed inside," He answered casually.

Keane looked as paranoid as me, "No, we didn't. We needed to talk to Linda, not explore her home. If she finds us here, she'll tell the Ivar soldiers, and that's not us keeping a low profile."

"Calm down," He flipped through papers sitting on the table, "If she's hiding something about Bexley, it would be here. We'll take a look around before she's back."

"I'm not such a simpleton that I would leave information about my brother lying around for someone to easily find."

We turned quickly, staring up at Linda as she stood at the top of the stairs clinking her long nails against the railing in annoyance. She was middle-aged, with brown hair tied up in a bun on top of her head. Her gray dress matched the dreariness of her home. "You're not the quietest thieves, are you?" She descended the stairs and stood before us. Asher pulled his hat down further and turned away studying the artwork on her walls leaving Keane and I to stare awkwardly at her. She raised a brow at us, but neither of us said a word.

"So, you are here about my brother?" she finally asked after a moment. She sighed rubbing at the bags under her tired eyes.

Keane lightly punched Asher's shoulder, who was now playing with a trinket he found on the table. "Yes, but we didn't mean to intrude like this."

"Yet, you did anyways. Who are you?" She glanced between us.

"I'm Ferren and this is Asher and Keane."

She gave a slightly shocked look, "you're the ones that Bexley told me about. The human and the Nightmare." She stared at Asher and took a step back, "You're with the King."

"You had contact with your brother?" I asked trying to keep the setting calm. She looked ready to bolt at any moment, terrified of Asher and his dark eyes. He turned away again, and she seemed to settle down with his eyes off of her.

She smoothed her dress down nervously, "I received a letter a time ago. The Ivar already know and have the letter. I have not heard from him since." She said, clearing her throat and trying to wipe the look of fear off her face.

Asher had made his way to my side again, "What do you think of your brother betraying the King and fleeing like he did?"

She swallowed loudly and clasped her hands in front of her, "Disgraceful."

"Really?" Asher crossed his arms, "I bet he's one of the Ivars that's been taking the Nightmares. Torturing and killing them."

Linda pinched her lips together.

"That's what he did to Ferren."

"He thought she was involved in the killings of the Ivars and possibly the Nightmares as well." She responded coldly, eyeing me with the same disgust Bexley had. It must run in the family.

"He doesn't believe that now?" Asher asked.

She stayed quiet and shrugged.

"Who does he believe is responsible now?" Asher pushed.

"The King?" I asked, "We're not on his side either, Linda." I took a step forward, "We just want to understand what is happening in Hatheya."

She clicked her tongue, crossed to the couch, and sat down on the edge of the cushion. "Kandem is an evil man." She shook her head, "I've had little contact with my brother, but yes the King has to be responsible for the deaths. Bexley has been suspecting the King of foul doings for many years, but no proof, and of course, who would speak out against him?" Her shoulders sagged.

"Others believe the same thing," I said, "Bexley had people follow him, didn't he?"

"Yes." She wrung her hands together and cleared her throat again, "They're part of a rebel group. A group that plans on moving against the King. Nightmares and Ivars together."

"What?" Asher and Keane said at the same time. I gave a small smile.

"I heard of the rebel group of Nightmares, but not working with the Ivar." Asher scoffed and shook his head, "They've been pushing against the Ivar, saving themselves from getting captured not working with them."

Linda stood quickly, "Bexley didn't flee because he was afraid. He left because he could finally see the madness the King was creating. He could see how Kandem was manipulating both the Ivars and you Nightmares, pining each other against one another and sitting back watching the hate grow! I'm sure you've heard the rumors about Dentro still being alive?" She rolled her eyes, "Idiots all of them, but if that's true, then not even some Nightmares want that and not all Ivars believe in the way the Nightmares are being treated, that's why they're working together." She pointed at Asher and Keane "Isn't that why you're working together?"

"I guess so," Keane replied quietly.

"That's hard to believe after what Bexley did to me." I said calmly, "He was going to torture me and who knows to what end."

She gave me a soft look, "I'm sorry, but when one fears for their lives and desperately needs answers, they will do the worst, even when they are good."

I grinded my teeth together and turned away from her, feeling a powerful urge to slap her.

"Do you know where we can find this rebel group?" Asher asked.

She shook her head, "I'm surprised he even told me about it…"

"Do you know anything else? Asher asked, "Anyone we can meet with?"

She threw her head back and laughed, "No, I wouldn't ask him if I could. I don't want to be involved in this war with a dead man. Dentro is dead."

"But the King is not!" I turned back to her my fist clenched, "He has killed and will kill again and again until he gets what he wants! You agree that he is evil, perhaps just as much as Dentro!"

"And thanks to my brother, I'm now in the eyesight of that man. I'm sure I'm going to end up in a grave soon and it will be because of my brother. Because he couldn't keep his head down and do as he was trained to do."

"Kandem will bring a war that will never end," I said in barely a whisper.

"We are already in that war, girl. It's just finally coming to light. People are finally paying attention and deciding what side to take."

"And what side are you on?" I hissed.

"I just want to survive and be left alone and out of the middle of this."

"It's too late for that."

She walked back to the stairs, "My brother's letter, the one he sent about you, he was very brief about what happened. I, of course, denied it when soldiers searched my house and found the letter. I told them he was wrong that the King would never harm his people and that I don't believe Dentro is alive," her eyes flickered over to Asher. "But I know Bexley is right. Now that I have told you all that I know. It is time for you three to leave. You should have never come here. It has put a very large target on your backs and mine as well, but what's done is done." She walked up the stairs and didn't look back.

"Why tell us this?" I asked before she disappeared into her room.

She stopped in the doorway, "Because he said you were important somehow. Again, he didn't elaborate on the subject, but if he and the King want you, it must be true." She closed her bedroom door.

I sighed and plopped down on the chair, "This is a mess, one giant mess."

Asher was slowly pacing the room with his arms crossed and eyes swirling with darkness.

"They're all working their way to Dentro," I said finally. "The King wants the weapon; Bexley wants the King gone and supposedly peace." I snorted, "And Dentro, well, I'm sure he wants death for everyone."

"Do you actually believe that he is still alive? If he is, where is he?" Keane sat next to me watching Asher pace.

"Locked away in the tower still." Hopefully, we have time before the spell wears down and he can get out.

Asher paused and looked at me, "Do you know something, Ren? You say this like it's facts, not speculation."

"Perhaps I know that Dentro is alive, and that he is trapped in that tower at the moment, but I'm sure some want to get him out."

Keane looked shocked, "If they set Dentro free, he would kill the King and every Ivar there is. The King has to know that."

"We should go. I've already been away from the palace for too long." I stood and bolted to the door before Asher could stop me. Once out in the cool crisp air, I took a breath and let them catch up to me. I had to gather the courage to tell them more. "Now I am only telling you this because I fear more slaughter is coming and coming quickly. The King has found a way to control Dentro. I don't know how he plans on acquiring this item, but if he does, he will kill everyone who doesn't stand with him and will have most powerfully Nightmare doing his will. Anyone who gets their hands on this weapon will be powerful. Nightmare or Ivar."

"How do you know all of this?" Asher's face tightened with disbelief.

"My Father told me." Pain sprung through me at the mention of him. I blinked out the bloody image of his body.

Asher stopped short, "How long have you known this?"

"Since camp WinWord…I didn't know if I could trust you. Either of you."

We didn't speak until we edged the castle walls.

"There is one more thing you need to know," I whispered. "I plan on killing the King with Nilsa's help. I have a feeling I won't survive it with how many guards are always around him, but we have to try."

"When?" Keane paled.

"During the Festival."

"Are you insane!" He hissed, "He'll be surrounded by his men and on high alert." He rubbed the back of his neck, "That's what you're planning with Nilsa isn't it?" he grabbed my elbow pulling me

a bit further away from the castle, "You can't be serious about this Ferren."

"This could be our only chance." I chewed my lip, anxiety rising in my chest.

"Even if the King dies, which he won't, others that know about Dentro will just rise and take his place," worry pulled across Asher's face.

"I highly doubt Kandem has told anyone about the weapon." I pulled my jacket closer but couldn't ward off the chill that prickled across my skin.

"Where is this weapon?" Keane asked.

"In the tower."

"The King wouldn't be hunting down this tower if he didn't think he had a way in. One way or another, he will get his hands on that weapon," Asher's face was now dark as he studied me. I saw the questions that he wanted to ask. How much was I keeping from him, but he didn't ask.

"He already found it," I said, trying to keep the panic from my voice. "He killed my dad for information. I'm not sure what." I swallowed, "This land is dying and with it, the protection spell around the tower. Soon he'll be able to get out and the King could get in."

"Maybe that's why the King wants to find the tower? Maybe he's protecting us?" Keane looked hopefully at me.

I shook my head, "He's against Dentro being set free, but not against controlling every Nightmare he can. Maybe even wipe them out." I saw the conflict within Keane again. The pain of wanting peace for everyone in Hatheya, but maybe control was the only way for that peace. "They want peace too Keane, some do." I thought of the families in Sonder.

He nodded, "I know."

Asher seethed and ran a hand through his hair and down his face, "This is a lot to take in." He looked at me, again, "Every time I start to trust you, Ren…" He put his hat back on, "I trusted when you said you weren't Ivar, but then found out your father was Gannon," He spat the words. "Then now about the Tower and a weapon. Anything else you conveniently haven't told me?"

I swallowed hard, "Gannon was my adopted father, and I didn't know that until I was at WinWord. I didn't know any of this. I'm confused and…I'm just confused."

Keane had wandered away and stood awkwardly studying the wall. "You have just as many secrets, but we are all working towards the same things. Saving Hatheya, destroying Dentro, and stopping the King."

"No more secrets that could help us do that, then?" His shadows wrapped around my ankles for just a few minutes.

I nodded. "Help me kill the King?"

A small smile formed on his lips. "I'm not going to let you get killed. We need to be smart about this."

Keane reappeared at my side. "I don't think this is a good idea." He looked almost green, "I want to find out more information about his plan before we act." He pleaded.

I nodded, "He will be here before and after as well. We will find the right place and time to do it." I said. "And you two will find the rebel group and stop anyone else from finding that tower."

"I can kill the King faster and without having to get close. I'm not letting you do it." Asher grabbed my shoulders. "You will die if you try. I understand the need for revenge, but don't be stupid about this."

We stood in silence, the icy chill creeping in through my clothes. The only warmth I felt was his hands on my shoulders. I stepped back awkwardly and pulled on the golden locket with the old picture in it.

"What is that?" Asher asked, stepping closer to me.

"I found it at my cabin."

"That's- "

"Ferren! There you are!" Nilsa waved from the large doorway, "Get in here and have some tea with me before you freeze to death!"

I turned to go. Asher caught my arm and stared at the locket.

"Asher?"

He let go, "Let us meet with Nilsa, trust us to help with everything, trust us to keep each other alive."

I nodded slowly; we've helped each other this far. Now it was time to truly start trusting one another. "Okay, we'll all meet tomorrow. She'll come with me for a walk." I waited a second more before going after Nilsa with Keane behind me, mumbling that we were insane for even thinking about killing the King.

TWENTY

"It's much too early for a walk." Nilsa yawned, "And cold. Why did you insist I come with you when I could have been lounging in my bed, drinking tea and ignoring the world around me for a bit longer?" She huffed out a breath.

"Because I want you to meet my friends." I was annoyed by how I had to drag Nilsa from her bed this morning. She glared at Keane as he followed us from the castle.

"You have friends?" She laughed. I shot her a glare, "And how are we supposed to meet with them when we have a follower?" She glanced over her shoulder at Keane who was now walking close to us.

"He's one of the friends." I turned a corner and saw Asher leaning against the wall of a tea shop.

"Finally," He mumbled under his breath. "Keane, mind grabbing me something to drink?" He smiled mischievously, making Keane bristle a bit.

"Fine, anything for you ladies?"

"Oh yes, please!" Nilsa pulled her jacket tighter around her. "Anything hot and sweet." She winked at him.

"I'm fine. Thank you, Keane."

He glared at Asher before entering the shop.

"Wait a minute." Nilsa smiled, tilting her head to the side and looking Asher up and down. "You're that Shadow Nightmare that

Bexley caught." She gave me a light smack on the shoulder, "You said he was gone."

I rubbed my shoulder, "Now he's back."

She clicked her tongue, "I would keep you, too."

"Calm down Nilsa." I glared at Asher as he smiled at her, feeling a bit of jealousy in my stomach. I pushed it away, angry at myself for feeling that way. Sure, we were becoming friends, but that's it. Just like Keane and I were becoming friends, and I didn't bristle when she flirted with him.

Keane arrived back with the teas, "Alright, we better make this quick." He handed a drink to Nilsa.

"Agreed. I hate being out in the open like this." Asher took his drink from Keane. "Ren told us about you two planning to kill the King." He said casually.

"Did she now?" Nilsa took a long sip of her tea.

"They can help us; they want to help us." I shoved my icy hands deeper into my pockets.

Keane cleared his throat, "I'm not that eager to help, but we need to do something to stop him."

Nilsa pursed her lips, "We could use the help, I suppose. If they're useful, then we can keep them." She took another sip, her pink lipstick staining the cup.

Asher gave pause at her words then smiled at me, his eyes the color of the stormy sky, "Are we useful?"

"I guess we'll see." I smiled back for a second before feeling Nilsa's and Keane's eyes on me. "Asher is going to find others like us that want the King gone. The more people we have on our side, the better."

"We also need someplace to go after it's done." Asher said, "I'm looking into a camp with a rebel group that will hopefully take us."

"Why wouldn't they? Especially if we're successful." Nilsa tossed a lock of hair back that the wind had thrown into her face.

"I think I should be the one to do it. I can get my shadows close to him, and if you get him into a room alone, we can do it quietly and quickly."

Nilsa ran a polished finger around the rim of her cup, "No." Nilsa said harshly, "No one else but me gets to do it. Ferren will get him into the room alone and then I get the joy of doing it." She smiled wickedly.

I had to look away.

Keane clutched his stomach, "How you all talk so casually about murder isn't right."

Every morning after I awoke from a feverish Nightmare, I would hurry and dress before peeking out my door making sure it was Keane or Asher standing guard before throwing open the door and giving a sigh of relief that I didn't have to fake being happy or a stuck up airhead of a rich woman with fake confidence as Nilsa put it. The more time I spent here, the more I realized that mostly everyone faked their personalities, and they weren't as good at hiding their real ones like Nilsa.

"How did you sleep?" Asher asked, rubbing his eyes.

"Just fine, and you?" I noticed his tired eyes and dark circles. "Are you sleeping at all?"

He nodded and stiffened a yawn.

"You don't need to be here all the time; I can protect myself, you know." Keane was usually here in the morning while Asher came at night. When they weren't here, they were trying to find out more information about Bexley and the rebel group. I wasn't able to escape the palace all the time as Kandem had tightened the leash on me again and I felt more eyes on me. Some days it was better if I spent it behind my door unseen and quiet. I was beginning to go insane trapped like an animal here and couldn't wait for the festival.

He gave a slight grin, "I'm just here for your backup." He stepped into my room. "Keane isn't back yet."

My stomach turned. We always met at the same time every day to swap notes on what we had learned. "Where is he?"

"I'm not sure." He walked to the window, watching the workers in the yard preparing it for the festival that would soon happen.

"We should find him." I grabbed clothes and rushed into the bathroom dressing as fast as I could. I needed to tell Nilsa before we left so she could cover for me somehow.

"He might have found something. You can't just leave that would put the King on high alert. He'll be back." Asher said, still staring out the window. "We need to be patient." He said it tightly. I knew he had a hard time being patient as well.

I leaned against the bedpost, exhausted. The nightmares never seemed to stop, even during the day I felt them winding around my mind.

"What do you dream about?" I asked, watching his dark eyes spin like night stars.

"Nightmares don't dream."

"They don't?"

He pulled the curtain closed and turned to me, "I can hear you talking in your sleep sometimes. You're having nightmares, aren't you?" He stepped closer.

I looked at the fire. It popped and jumped around like a wild animal trapped in a cage.

"It's okay," he said gently.

I looked at him, shocked by the tenderness in his voice.

"I would think that any human that was stuck here would be consumed by them." He leaned against the other bedpost.

I licked my dried lips, "Do Ivars dream?"

He gave a soft laugh, "That's a question for Keane, but I'm sure they only dream of bright cheerful things."

I tried to smile. I wished I knew what I was. If I was part Nightmare, then why were my dreams torturing me like this?

"I once heard that Dentro was powerful enough to cause Nightmares to have night terrors. He would drive them to the brink of insanity. When you're not used to dreaming at all, then dream of him…" He let the words drift away. His shadows swirled at his feet.

"Asher," I wanted to tell him that I might be Ivmare, that I might be full Nightmare even. I wanted to tell him that I was being pushed to the brink by these nightmares, but my voice caught my throat. I don't know why I couldn't yet. Something was stopping me from being able to tell him. He accepted me as a human, but I still saw the conflict in his eyes when he looked at an Ivar. He was hurt when he thought I was Gannon's blood daughter and true Ivar. I didn't want him looking at me like that again, with so much pain and confusion. The way I looked at myself now. I twisted away from him as I realized we had been standing closer together. He wouldn't look at me if he thought I was Dentro's child. The child of a true monster.

"We should go, they're probably wondering where you are," He said after a beat.

"Let them wonder. I feel like taking a walk early today." I shrugged on my coat, avoiding eye contact with him suddenly felt awkward being around him. When did things begin to change with us? When had I grown to fear hurting him and less about fearing him?

We had been taking a walk every day. Even when the bitter cold wind drove others in, we walked along the streets talking about our plan with Nilsa and what we needed to do and sometimes we talked about the human world. About my small apartment and the camping adventures, I would go on with my father, which would bring me to silence. I would pull out my locket and spin it between my fingers, thinking of the cabin and the bookshelves. The smell of dried ink and old books.

Asher would slightly look at the locket until I tucked it back into my shirt. I asked him again why he stared at the locket, but he changed the subject quickly.

As we walked today, I studied the decorations around the town for the festival. They tried to draw attention away from the dying land with bright paper decorations and twinkling candle lights. They had ribbons around the gates, and paper mache moons. I tried pushing the dreams out of my mind. It was the same almost every time, a hand reaching for me, begging me to reach out and take it. I would wake up sick to my stomach, shivering and hot. What Asher said about Dentro tumbled through my mind.

"Are you cold?"

"What?" I tripped over a loose stone. Asher grabbed me around the waist. We took a few falling steps together before colliding into one of the brick buildings, "Has living in a palace made it difficult for you to keep an eye on your surroundings as I told you to?" He still had an arm around me. Leaning against the building pressed into him. I was suddenly aware of everything, his steady heartbeat, the air in my lungs, the wind pushing my hair across my face, and the woman standing at the window staring at us. "Are you going to let go? I think I can walk on my own now."

He slowly moved his arm and stepped aside to give us distance. I looked away, feeling my cheeks slightly blush, and saw that we were standing in front of the dress shop. The plump owner stood at the window smiling at us, then waved for me to come in.

Great, I thought, pulling open the door and putting a fake smile on my face. I guess I still needed to get a dress for the festival.

I choked on a laugh as Asher blanched at the god-awful dresses surrounding us with frills, bows, and huge hoop skirts that had to weigh as much as a small child. Others had blinding fuchsia ribbons and bright gems. Asher raised a brow at some that had such little fabric they left nothing to the imagination.

"I'll freeze to death if I wear that," I said as he eyed a slim dress. I gave him a haughty smile as his cheeks blushed quickly and his eyes bounced across the room avoiding me.

The owner approached me, "I thought you weren't a party dress type of girl?"

"It's for the Festival."

She nodded and circled me, staring at my body like she was doing measurements in her mind, "Still, I wouldn't have guessed."

"I want something functional. These dresses are too much. The weather is cold, and I would die if I wore one."

She frowned, "Are you planning on spending most of the time outside instead of dancing within the palace?"

I smiled tightly, "No, but I don't want to freeze if I just step outdoors." Or running for my life after we kill the king. I'll have some clothes stashed away somewhere, but I still needed to make it to the checkpoint that Asher found for us outside the city.

She pulled out a measuring tape and proceeded to measure every inch of me. Asher watched with an amused smile on his face as she walked once again around me, shaking her head making me feel self-conscious about my jutting ribs and bony back. My proportions didn't fit well together, which made finding well-fitting clothes impossible.

"Come back tomorrow!" She chirped suddenly, making me jump.

"Tomorrow?"

"That's what I said. I can't make your dress within this instance." She laughed, stuffing the paper with my measurements on it into her apron pocket.

"What type of dress will I be getting?"

"You will see. Now out, I need to focus." She ushered us to the door, "Don't worry, I will make your girl beautiful!" She winked at Asher who avoided looking at her.

"Oh, I'm not, we're not," she pushed us out, closed the door, and flipped the open sign to closed. "Okay then." I cleared my throat and looked at Asher. He gave me a sideways grin and started walking.

The rest of the day was spent watching people scurry around the palace and town decorating and cleaning. They strung up black lanterns cut out with stars and moons. Candles lined the dance floor and were placed on elaborate chandeliers. The town was decorating its windows to look like the night sky and an enormous banner was placed across the entrances of the palace that read, Festival of the Moon.

The one day a year that the palace doors and gates were open to every Ivar, not just the elite.

After a while, Asher had to disappear as more Ivar soldiers filled the town. Even Nilsa was preparing for the night. Probably sharpening her knives and dreaming about killing the King.

To my surprise, the Ivar Soldiers were out on the grounds, just in sight of my window. They all stood in a line facing a man who was clearly in charge, giving orders and reading off a piece of paper.

Keane was looking up at me. He blended perfectly in with all the others that stood in line with him. I gave him a quick wave, feeling relieved finally seeing him. He turned back and kept his eyes down. I watched them run through drills while I twirled my necklace in my fingers, thinking about it and Asher. I unclasped the chain and placed the necklace on my bedside table under a pair of gloves, wondering if Asher would say something about me not wearing it tomorrow.

He didn't, of course. I knew he wouldn't. He didn't even look at me as we walked. His mind clearly elsewhere.

The next day, Asher wasn't the one to walk me to the dress shop. It was a lanky, wide-eyed soldier who stayed a few paces behind me and never spoke. Even when I asked him a question, he acted as if he didn't hear. I scoffed and walked quicker to the shop, throwing open the door and letting it close in his face. I was angry at both men because they ditched me without letting me know what was going on. I planned on picking up my dress and then heading straight to Nilsa. Having a dress to show her was a perfect excuse to see her without the guards questioning why I was visiting her again.

"Hello!" the owner bellowed, "Come on back!"

"Stay here," I said to the soldier as I headed back with the woman.

"I placed your dress in the first dressing room, let me know if you need help."

I slipped the nude and black tulle dress on. It flowed to the floor and had a slit down the middle so I could easily walk. The top made me gawk. It was a corset that looked to be made of a deep black rock, but it was breathable and moved easily. The dress hugged my top tightly, following my curves, and dipped low in the back. Tulle sleeves hung off my shoulders and bellowed out like the skirt, and below that was a nude jacket that matched my skin tone almost perfectly. It would keep me warm in the wind. I wondered at the beauty of the dress and how she had managed to make it warm and beautiful.

"I still need to make a few adjustments here and there."

"It's wonderful. It's like armor, but lightweight. How?" I watched the light catch off of the swirling pattern of the corset.

She tapped her mouth with a finger and winked, "My little secret."

Smiling, I turned to her, "Thank you, I love it. I'm sorry, I've been so rude. I don't even know your name."

"Marsha."

"Thank you, Marsha, it's beautiful." I twirled in the mirror.

"It will catch the eye of that man."

I gave a quiet laugh, "What man?"

"Oh, you know, any man." She smiled and played with the skirt again. "Just one more thing." She pulled out a necklace and clipped it around my neck. It was small red pearls that flowed down like a waterfall of blood. "Perfect."

"Very." I turned again, watching the necklace sway like blood splatter. If this wasn't an omen of some kind, I didn't know what was.

TWENTYONE

As I walked back to the castle with the heavy dress box tucked under one arm, I couldn't stop picturing that necklace Marsha had given me. The flow of red pearls blinked into view every time I tried to shake it out of my mind. Of course, I had taken it. It was meant for me, in some dark way that necklace had found its way to me. I didn't want to die, of course, but Keane's worries had plagued me over and over and I was beginning to think about it more than the King's death.

I padded up to my room and managed to open the door without dropping the box, with no help from the guard, who kept his distance.

Throwing the box on the bed, I hurried over to the window I had left open for Eira and slammed it shut as the wind began to blow harder. It had been a stupid decision to leave it open for her today. The wind had blown my fire out and laced the room with unforgivable coldness.

Teeth chattering, I started another fire and watched the flame dance around madly until the hair on the back of my neck rose. I shifted slightly and pulled out the knife I had tucked into my shirt. I listened for a minute more, pretending to watch the flames. It was quiet, but something dark lingered around my room.

I turned, scanning every corner of the room. The fire cast wicked shadows around every piece of furniture. I calmed my breathing as I crept to the clothing hutch and flicked open the door. Empty besides clothing. I again moved, keeping my feet quiet, to the bathroom. A shadow moved just barely at the corner of the door. Fogged in dark shadows, I flicked my wrist, releasing my knife. It was embedded into the wall. The shadow lunged forward as I grabbed another knife from my side that was hidden beneath my shirt. I would have to thank Asher for them later. But before I could successfully flick the knife, the shadow slammed into me, knocking me to the ground. The knife slid away.

"Ren!" The shadow fizzled out like a fire being smothered. "It's just me."

I pushed to my feet, still eyeing the knife that now laid closer to Asher than me. "What are doing in here?" If he had been waiting for me, he would have let his presence be known the moment I entered the room. Why lurk in the shadows, blinding me from seeing him?

A loud knock came on the door, "Is everything alright? I heard a loud noise." Said the guard.

"Yes! I just tripped." I spat, not wanting to deal with this at the moment.

"Is there someone else in there with you? I thought I heard another voice."

I shot a glare at Asher, "No, talking to myself. I'm fine and would like some privacy, please!"

He sighed, and the sound of shuffling feet moved away from the door.

"Why did you attack me?" I hissed.

"I didn't attack you." He said, cocking his head to the side.

"You knocked me down." I retrieved both of my knives, wincing at the hole I had made in the wall. That would be hard to explain to the nosy servants who insisted on cleaning my already clean room every day.

"You threw a knife at my head and would have thrown another one if I hadn't." His eyes blazed with blackness.

I gave a disdainful laugh and relaxed my shoulders a bit as I saw a small piece of gold chain hanging from his pocket, "Why didn't you just ask about the locket instead of stealing it?" Leaving the bathroom, I went to the couch to decide between sitting or pacing. I locked eyes with Asher until he looked away, leaning against the couch, "How can you do that?" he asked quietly.

"Do what?"

"Look into my eyes. Nightmares can barely manage it, let alone a human."

I looked away, guilt threatening to bubble out.

"Ivars won't even look at me. They fear the endless darkness that could swallow them whole if I let it. But you, you can look at me and never waver."

"I guess I'm different," my voice hitched.

"Very." He took a step closer to me. His eyes began to swim with darkness, reminding me of the first time I saw him.

"Are you trying to scare me?" I stepped closer to him, trying to meet the intensity of his challenge. His eyes suddenly softened as I leaned forward, reaching out my hand to his chest.

"Ren," His voice was between a plea and uncertainty.

I grabbed the chain hanging from his pocket. "Why did you steal this?"

Flames of shadows shot from him, but he didn't move away. He reached up and grabbed the chain, our hands lingering together until I pulled back, letting him take the locket again. Asher was back to his stony mask. Shadows tightened in around him as if becoming a shield against me.

I turned to the fire, watching it instead of him as he clenched the locket.

"Did your father give this to you?" he asked quietly.

I bit back the dying image of him. When would those thoughts go away? They tainted every memory I had of him. "No. I found it after…after he was taken."

"Do you know who the woman is?" He gingerly opened the locket, trailing his thumb over her picture.

"I never got to ask him. I thought it was someone he cared for here?" I hugged my arms across my body, "But now I'm not so sure."

"Amber." He didn't move his eyes off the fading picture, "I never thought I would see her again."

I snapped my eyes to him, "Who is she?" I kept my voice level, not wanting his shadows to build a wall against me again.

He finally looked up at me, his eyes gray and longing. "You loved her?" I could see it, the pain that surrounded him as he looked at that picture. My stomach plummeted. The room seemed too hot and cramped.

He snapped the locket shut, "She's dead now, been dead for a long time."

"Oh…" I rubbed the back of my neck, unsure if I should ask, but it slipped out anyway. "What happened to her?"

He gripped the locket, "She was human."

I tried and failed to hide my shock, "Who was she to you?"

"Someone I cared about once, but they killed her, and I wasn't able to do anything about it." He sucked in a breath, "how did Gannon end up with this locket? Why keep it?" His eyes flamed at me, his shadows cold against my exposed arms.

"I don't know. Honestly." I took a step closer to him, reaching out my hand to grip his, but I hesitated as his shadows circled us. "Asher, I had it because I found it in the cabin. I was curious why he had it. That's all. I only wore it because it reminded me of him, of my home."

His shadows calmed, and I placed my hand on his. He loosened his grip on the necklace but wouldn't look at me. "What happened to her?"

He gave a sharp intake of breath, "I met her before the wall was built around Hatheya. I couldn't believe a human would want anything to do with me," his shoulders sagged his shadows fell in waves, but kept their distance from me. "I was going to run away with her from Hatheya, but it was against the laws of the Ivar for me to be in the human world and for her to be here. The night before the wall was complete, I found her torn apart." His eyes found mine. They were a dark gray. A storm that was about to die out. "You don't have to tell me anymore." I grabbed both of his hands covering the locket.

"Bexley found me there with her. He thought I did it. Someone tipped them off that I was sneaking away and where to find us." He shook his head, pleading with his eyes that I needed to believe him.

"I tried using my shadows, but I just couldn't I could feel nothing." He turned back to me, his face broken with pain, "Bexley whipped me that night in the Finara."

A gasped breath escaped from me. I remembered seeing the scars on his back when we were camping together. My dad told me that he remembered Asher being accused of doing something and that he had something of his to return.

"A few days later, I escaped, and the locket was missing."

"Gannon was going to return the locket to you. He told me he had something of yours but forgot. I don't think he thought you were guilty."

"He forgot?" Asher huffed out a laugh that sounded more like a choke. "I have missed this locket for years; I've thought about her almost every day since and how I couldn't protect her." He cupped my cheek, sending a shiver down my spine. "Then I saw you and I realized what you were and I- "

"Wait." I jerked away. "You've always known I was human?"

"It was pretty obvious." He smiled. A smile that made dimples appear on both sides of his cheeks and his eyes light up. My heart ached at his hope. He stepped closer, but I took a step back. His smile dropped.

"You like me because you think I'm human? Like her? Like Amber?"

"No, wait," His brow knitted, "Think you're human?"

"What if I'm not, Asher? What if I'm not a delicate little human that needs protection? Is that why you stayed with me? Because of guilt for what happened to her?" I put a hand up to stop him from coming closer. My heart hitched painfully in my chest as I repeated his words in my head.

He opened his mouth and closed it, "I never said you were, Ren. And if you're not human, then what are then?"

I scoffed, "I don't know. But I'm not her and I never will be."

The door pounded with a knock; I spun towards it. "I said I was fine!"

"Ferren, it's Keane," he breathlessly said through the closed door.

I rushed to open the door for Keane. He rushed in, stopping midway through the room, and raised a brow at Asher and me.

"Did I interrupt something?" He asked.

"No," I blurted, making sure the other guard was gone, and it was just the three of us.

Asher ran a hand through his hair, shaking his head at Keane. His eyes were back to dark black as he glided down in a chair. "I guess not." He tucked the locket into his pocket.

Keane hesitated for a moment before I motioned for him to hurry. "The King is sending for you. He sent a message that he won't be able to attend the festival and that you are to go to him tomorrow. The coordinates are somewhere in the rebel valley and from there, a guide will take you farther in.

"What! Why would he call on me?"

"I'm not sure. I intercepted the letter on the way to our general and only had a second to read it."

I started pacing the room, "This isn't good. I've been wondering why he's keeping me here, why in such comfort, why he killed my father, and what he could gain from me."

"Do you have any information that your father told you that he wants?" Keane asked.

"No," I stopped pacing, "Maybe?"

"What is it?" Asher asked, leaning forward in the chair. His elbows on his knees.

That I could be Mavi's or Dentro's daughter, but I don't know how he would have found that out. "I can't say."

Asher shook his head, "Ferren…If we haven't earned your trust yet, when will we? When we once again put our lives in danger for you?"

I turned to him seething, "I never asked you to put your life in danger! And last I checked, Keane was doing this for his family!

For the Ivars that know the corruption of the King! Not for me! What could I possibly gain from all this? I want to stop the King from killing others. Why are you doing it?"

He shot from his chair. "For Hatheya! For my freedom and for the other Nightmares. Are Ivars the only ones who are allowed to care about this place? About anything?"

"I don't know what is going on between you two, but this little tiff needs to end. We need to figure out what to do. If you go," Keane placed a hand on my shoulder, "Then I can request to be assigned to the escort and Asher can sneak along with us. Or if I get denied the request, well hey, it's not the first time I've gone missing before." He gave me a soft smile and squeezed my shoulder.

"I can't go to him. Who knows what is waiting for me there?"

"A way to get the weapon?" Asher asked Keane, more than me.

"Could be, but why would he need Ferren for that?" They both looked at me. I just shrugged. Even if I was Mavi's daughter, I didn't see how I could help with that. Especially if it was still locked in the tower with the most dangerous Nightmare, there was.

"Care to tell us your secret?" Asher said harshly.

"I don't see how it could help him, and I don't think he even knows it. My father kept it a secret for many years to protect me, and even if Kandem tortured him about it, he wouldn't have said a word."

"Are you sure?" Asher asked.

I didn't respond. I just shot him a glare. "Kandem needs to come here, send back word that I will be attending the festival, and then after that, he can escort me back to wherever he wants to take me."

"Don't you think he'll force you to go?" Asher asked.

"No, I have a feeling he wants me comfortable and trusting him."

"I feel that too," Keane agreed, "I'll have them send word. He won't be happy when he receives a letter instead of you."

"Good," I smiled at him.

"Asher, you should head out. More soldiers are coming in for the festival."

"Ya, in a minute." Asher opened the door for Keane.

Keane stepped out and waited for Asher who held up a finger.

Keane smiled and winked at me before closing the door.

"Don't," I said before Asher could speak, "Keane's right, bigger things are going on than our…tiff."

"I'm sorry, Ren." He scrubbed his face and leaned against the wall. "We all have a right to our secrets, but the thing is." He scrubbed at his face again, looking nervous. "I don't want to have secrets from you. I wanted to tell you about the locket and my past. And more if you want, but I don't know how to do that cause the last time I did that…Amber…" He exhaled.

My mouth hung open, and I found myself breathless, "I…Asher…there's so much…" I stumbled over my words, trying to grasp at my own feelings and what was going on in Hatheya and what I should tell him. Instead, I shook my head, wanting to step closer, but angry at his words of Amber and me both being human.

He nodded solemnly, "You don't have to say anything." He left with me, still trying to figure out what to say.

TWENTY-TWO

We didn't know how long it would take for the letter to get to him or even if he would make the festival, but we wanted time to plan if I was to go to him before he came here and that changed Nilsa's plan completely.

"Actually, killing him on the way there wouldn't be a bad idea," Asher said. "He points us in the right direction of the tower and where his men are, and bad things happen in the woods."

"And what are we supposed to do about his men?" I asked, "We can't kill them all. And the ones at the tower? If he did find it, then it won't stay a secret long, especially if Kandem dies."

"Well," Keane leaned forward in the white chair. We had made an exception this one time to meet all together in Nilsa's room instead of sending messages when we passed each other randomly. "Asher might have found a group to help us."

"Really?" Nilsa was laying across her bed, "They too want to kill the King?" she smiled.

"More than just that," Asher rolled his eyes at her, "They also don't want Dentro out. I had to feel out the group for a while, but I think they're our best bet."

"How many are in the group?" I asked.

"Not many." He was still not looking at me. It had been this way since the locket. I wanted to scream, but I also avoided him as well, because I couldn't stop thinking of the hurt in his eyes when he left my room.

Keane sat next to me on the couch balancing a cup of something minty and a plate full of small sandwiches that Nilsa had brought from the kitchen. "But, some Ivar with the King, given the chance, might turn against him as well. They could be afraid to do so, or some might not know what is going on. We need to give them that chance."

"I agree, but will they join the Nightmares?" I asked, stealing one of his sandwiches.

Keane smiled, "That's the best part about this group." He nodded to Asher to tell us.

"There's Ivars in the group as well." He snagged one of Keane's sandwiches and sat across from me, making my stomach flutter with a million different emotions.

Nilsa sat up clapping her hands, "Oh, how exciting. Once enemies are now friends."

"I wouldn't go as far as saying they're friends, but a common goal between them has helped them not kill each other," Asher said shoving the sandwich in his mouth and earning a glare from Keane as he defended another sandwich from him.

"Like us." She gestured an elegant hand around the room.

Asher and Keane gave each other a quick glance, making me fight a smile. They had moved passed pushing each other's buttons every time they were around one either, but Keane always seemed to be ready for a sudden attack from Asher and Asher rolled his eyes at Keane more times than I could count during a conversation. At best, they tolerated each other, which is probably what most of the people at the camp were doing at this moment. It was going to take years for Ivars and Nightmares to get along, and that's only if someone stepped in and helped fix the hate that was forever growing between them.

"They need to be ready to follow me and the King when he leads me to the Tower." I said, "Asher and you need to get them ready; we don't know when the King will come for me, but we have a very small window to get everyone ready and be prepared to travel."

"What if he's not taking you to the tower? What if he found a break in the realm and is sending you home?" Keane asked. "Maybe he wants to get rid of you."

"Then she'll go. Get away from all of this." Nilsa said matter of fact, "Wouldn't we all if we had a chance?"

They looked over at me except for Asher, who was now staring at his hands like they were the most interesting thing in the world. "No." I sat up a little straighter, "I wouldn't abandon Hatheya. If he takes me to a break in the wall, I'll do anything to stay. I promise." I was promising myself more than the others.

Asher finally looked at me. I couldn't tell if it was anger on his face or pity.

"Well," Nilsa twirled her hair, "That's daft of you."

I just laughed. I had gotten used to her sharp tongue and the fact she spoke her mind not caring about other's reactions. She had to play this fake little woman who held her tongue and was beyond bubbly all day long and when she could finally be herself, she completely let go. "Thanks, Nilsa."

"Just telling you the truth."

"I have to stay."

"For yourself or for revenge?" Asher asked, pain still etched on his face.

"Both," I said icily at his tone.

Keane and Nilsa flashed each other a look. They knew something was going on between us, but had stayed out of it, surprisingly.

Asher turned back to the window. I stood, readying myself to leave. The room suddenly felt too small for all of us, "keep your distance until the Festival. We don't want to draw attention to any of this."

"Agreed," Nilsa said, "stick to the normal and be happy, or at least pretend to be. Especially you, Ferren. You need to be excited about the Festival. It is why you denied meeting the King after all." She winked at me.

Keane followed me out, *escorting* me to my room. "So," he said awkwardly.

"Don't ask, 'cause I'm not telling you," I said, quickly cutting him off. "A lot was said, and I'm still…" I sighed dramatically as my emotions tumbled around again.

"Okay, whatever you say, but I'm here for you if you want to talk." He bumped my shoulder with his.

"Thank you, but there's nothing wrong," I said matter-of-factly.

He looked at me hesitantly. We said goodnight, and I locked myself in my room as I heard Keane letting a new guard take over the night shift. I couldn't wait till this was all over. It was suffocating, constantly being watched day and night, even by Keane. Nilsa was more occupied by Asher since I reintroduced them. Her eyes stalked his every move like a hungry animal. I blanched at the thought, pushing it clear out of my mind before I became heated over it. I had to keep secrets just like he did. He could have told me about Amber long ago, but he didn't. It was his right not to, but I still boiled over the fact that he liked me because I reminded him of his human love.

The Fallen Moon Festival was finally here, and my stomach was doing somersaults over maybe seeing Kandem today. There were plenty of pre-festival parties that had happened around town, but tonight the Castle was open for the town. The ballroom would be filled with drinking and laughing Ivars and a mountain of upscale foods. The town streets had been full of people dancing just yesterday, running up and down with sparklers and singing at the top of their lungs. I watched from my window smiling down at the children giggling in the garden until the chill of the night chased them all away and then moved to the edge of my bed staring at the dress I was to wear tonight, the blood drop necklace in my hand.

I had a nasty feeling that this was not going to be a good night and the necklace was a terrible omen, and yet, I dressed and clasped the necklace around my throat, watching myself in the mirror. I pinned my hair back, then undid it, letting my black hair fall across my face.

"Do you need any help?" A servant shouted through the door. She had knocked earlier, but I had ignored her and struggled to get into my dress alone. I opened the door and smiled, "I'm already!"

I took a breath before stepping into the large ballroom that was stuffed full of people and looked for Nilsa, Keane, or even Asher, just someone I knew, so I didn't feel so out of place standing there.

The place was decorated with large silver moons that hung high above us. Glowing lanterns and fairy lights circled us, making it just bright enough to see but kept the ambiance of romance. Large tables filled with food lined one end of the room and the other held a band that played loudly and excitedly. Everyone was dressed in lavished clothing dripping with jewels and champagne glasses in hand.

"You look lovely." Keane smiled, walking over to me. I sighed in relief as I saw him. He was still wearing an Ivar uniform, but his old one was traded out for a new and clean one. "And you look handsome. Have you seen Nilsa?"

"She was dancing earlier, then I lost track of her. Most of the men have flocked over to her."

"But not you?"

"She's a bit intense for me, to be honest," he pulled on the neck of the uniform.

I laughed, "I'm sure if others knew about who she truly was, they would think the same at times."

He returned the laughter, "I don't think that's who she truly is either."

I raised a brow at him.

"Just seems like another act," He shrugged, "Maybe I'm wrong."

"And maybe you're right. Time will tell."

"Do you think we'll have time?" His sky-blue eyes searched mine for my thoughts, "that's also a maybe."

"You're not really you anymore, are you? I don't feel like myself." He said stiffly.

A server swept by us offering us a drink. We shook our heads and stood in silence for a bit.

"I don't think I've ever known who I was. I've always just played the part that I was given." I finally said.

"And what role are you playing now?"

"Many at the moment."

"Perhaps you'll-"

"If you say find myself, I will walk away." I winced, "I'm not on an adventure to find myself and figure out what I want in life. My journey is to survive and not let the King kill a bunch of Ivars and Nightmares."

He gave me a grin, "sounds like a pleasant journey to me."

"I guess we'll see." I played with the simple black bracelets around my wrist, watching the dancers.

"Excuse me, I need to pretend I'm doing my rounds before someone notices that I'm just standing here. Keep an eye out for Nilsa."

"Is Asher with the group getting ready?"

"Yes, he should be."

Keane headed out of the ballroom, leaving me standing by myself again. I should have grabbed a drink just to busy myself with something besides picking at my dress. Maybe something strong would help calm my nerves?

I felt his eyes on me before I saw him. He was moving across the room. His dark suit matched his eyes, but as he neared, they turned a soft gray. "Asher? I thought you were with the group?"

He gestured to his suit, "Do you like it? Nilsa helped."

I looked around at the crowds of people. "This is too risky." But I was glad he was speaking to me.

His eyes moved across my body until he found my eyes, "We should get a drink." He snatched some drinks from a passing waiter and handed me one. It smelled of grapes and lemon, but tasted sweet in my mouth as I sipped it to calm my nerves.

"The group is fine; I know their location and they know not to move, so we can stay in touch."

"Still," I took another sip, "Is Keane aware of the change of plans as well?"

"No, I came to see you."

I cocked my head, "Why, what is wrong?"

"Nothing, I just…you…you look…beautiful."

I felt my cheeks flush, cursing myself for it. I still didn't want to be his human.

"The neckless fits you."

"Oh? It does?" I fiddled with it.

"Yes, it's powerful like you."

My whole body tingled, "Thank you." Maybe I shouldn't drink.

He took my glass from me and handed it to a server, then took my hand taking me to the dance floor. "We're less noticeable if we blend in and dance, which Nilsa also taught me to do."

I raised a brow in surprise, "that's why you've been spending so much time with her?"

He smiled, "Jealous?"

I cocked my head. Was he teasing me? I didn't understand what was happening. "Why did you want to see me?" I tried to keep in step with the dance but ended up tripping over my own feet or his. I wasn't taught to dance and the human world never had such parties, at least parties that they danced like this. Perhaps I should have asked Nilsa to help me as well.

"To tell you something."

"What is it?" I concentrated on the dance steps.

"It's about Amber."

I bumped into a woman and gave her an apologetic smile, "Oh?" was all I managed to get out.

Asher stiffened. His eyes darkened as he concentrated on keeping his shadows at bay. "Will you walk with me?"

I blinked at him, "Now? I have to keep an eye out for the King."

"After he speaks to you. I'll see you in a moment in the garden and if I don't, I'll come check on you."

"Why are you suddenly talking to me again?" I studied him.

"Because Keane helped me realize that I was stupid and should have told you this earlier."

"Told me what?"

He walked away before I could respond, spinning me out of the dance floor.

"I've seemed to have scared away your dance partner."

I turned to the King, masking my shock of his sudden appearance. I had hoped to see him before he saw me so I could school my face into one of my fake smiles easier than I had to do now. "I was worried you wouldn't make it. When did you get here?"

He smiled back, but it didn't reach his tired eyes. No, his eyes held the dark annoyance that put a genuine smile on my face, "Just arrived. I'm glad I found you in this crowd. I was worried I wouldn't be able to."

I caught myself before I rolled my eyes. I'm sure the throng of guards surrounding me at every moment helped him track me down easily, "I'm glad you made it. It would have been such a shame if you missed it."

He grabbed my elbow and shoved me into the group of spinning people, making them trip over each other. When they noticed who it was, their snarls quickly turned to smiles, and they moved away giving us space. His chapped hand grabbed mine and pulled me close with his other. He stumbled with the dance as he had a hard time putting weight on his left leg without his cane for support. He smelled of horse and aftershave that didn't sit well together. It made my stomach shift with nausea. I was glad I hadn't made my way over to the large food table yet.

"I'm quite surprised you wanted to attend something so festive after what happened." His voice was quiet in my ear. I looked over his shoulder at the band plucking away at their instruments.

Swallowing, my blood-drop necklace bobbed a bit, a reminder of Asher's words, *powerful.* I snapped my eyes to Kandem's face. He looked bored and tired. Deep wrinkles lined his face, even more than when I first met him.

"I've learned that you and Nilsa have become friends." His voice monotone.

"Yes, she's very lovely. Helped me enjoy my time here. I'll be sad to leave her."

"I'll speak to her and she will be coming with us."

"Where will we be going?" I asked cautiously.

"Let's not discuss travel tonight. Tomorrow, over breakfast, we can speak. It will be much quieter than."

"Can you tell me when we leave?"

"The day after tomorrow. We have no time to linger."

The song ended, but I didn't step away, "I know about the weapon, Kandem." I pulled away.

His eyes were dark, "Gannon."

I gave a slight nod, a small smile on my face, "Greet the other guests and I will be waiting for you in the library to discuss certain things alone, or I won't talk."

"What things?" He snarled.

I curtsied, "I will be seeing you."

He gave a slight bow, "Later than."

I waited a moment before I slipped out and went looking for Asher. I wandered into the garden, wishing I had grabbed a shawl or something to keep my shoulders warm. Wandering around the court I felt an icy chill run up my bare back and smiled at a shadow that curved over my shoulder, then quickly pulled back before it could turn vicious. I turned to see Asher standing a bit away in the shadows. There were no guards around, probably too occupied with the King to care about me at the moment. I breathed in the cool crisp air before wandering over to Asher. He held out his jacket for me, "You might be a bit cold in that dress."

I slipped it on as he led me down one of the garden paths, "What did you want to tell me?"

He ran a hand across his face; his shadows followed after us.

"Let's just walk for a bit," I said, enjoying the silence and darkness of the garden.

He brushed a bit of hair out of my eyes and nodded.

"Do you hear that?" I whispered.

His eyes scanned our path, "No."

"It's quiet. Isn't it wonderful?"

A crisp laugh escaped from his lips, soft enough that it didn't echo through the garden, but as if it was just for me to hear. "It's nice. I miss the woods and isolation there." His silent footsteps fell in step with mine. "But this is nice too," he said quickly.

I had to kick my dress out every time I took a step so that my leg would slide through the slit in the front to allow me to walk without my heels becoming tangled in the tulle. I should have opted out for flats instead, but then the dress was too long.

"I could cut that off for you," Asher said.

"Cut what off?"

"Your dress."

My face flooded with color, "I think I'll keep my dress on. It's much too cold to run through the garden naked." I couldn't help but laugh.

"No! I meant the bottom of the dress, just that fluffy part that is hard for you to walk in. Not the whole thing." He groaned and scrubbed his face with his hand, "I'm sorry."

"It's okay," I giggled, then turned away, stifling my laugh at the image of him cutting my new dress from my body, "I will keep the fluff."

He gave me a half grin and shook his head.

"So, are you going to tell me what you wanted to talk about, or are you going to make me guess?"

He groaned again and rubbed the back of his neck, "First, I want to show you something." He reached for my hand and then stopped halfway, waiting for me to take his. I gently slid my hand into his and let him pull me along. I tightened my grip on his hand as we turned down a smaller path that was covered in uneven terrain. The trees loomed above us, their branches woven together, creating a canopy and protecting us from the wind. "I wanted you to see this before the moon set tonight. Look, the falls have moonstones behind them."

"Moonstones?"

"They reflect the light of the moon. When the moon is the brightest tonight, right before it sets. It's like a flash of light."

We stood in front of a thin waterfall that cascaded down into a river. The falls seemed to glow against the moon. It shimmered with light and danced as the water fell to the stream. I gasped at the beauty. Then it darkened just as quickly as it had shone. Pitch blackness surrounded us. I gripped Asher. "When I heard it was the darkest night of the year, I don't think I realized just how dark." I couldn't see anything besides blurs of what I thought could be shapes around me. I turned quickly at a sound and bunked my head against Asher's. "Ouch

"I should have brought a torch for you. I can see, but I forgot you wouldn't be able to."

"You can see in this?" I grabbed his shoulder, thankful that one of us could see.

He placed his hands on my hips, "My shadows can see for me, and on this night I can see even better than normal. The Fallen Moon does truly belong to the Nightmares."

"Can all Nightmares see in the dark?"

"No, a lot more than not, though."

"What did you want to tell me about Amber?"

"Not about her, but about you, I guess." He whispered. "When I first met you, yes, I saw her in you. A human that needed help. Amber was." He took a breath, "Calm, quiet, and a much different soul than yours."

I hadn't realized how close he was to me until his warm breath tickled down my neck to my back. We stood still, like a frozen picture being painted right there in the dark. The only sounds were the trickling water from the falls and our intertwined breathing that raised goose bumps across my body. My breath hitched as he leaned closer, his hands slid under his jacket that was still around my shoulders to the middle of my back, pushing me into him. My chest was pressed against his, he leaned his forehead against mine. "I don't think of you as something frail that needs protection, though I will protect you. Protest all you like about that."

Smiling, I wrapped my arms around his neck. I knew he could see my smile.

"I don't know what you are, Ren, Nightmare, Ivar, Human, or something completely different. I care about you."

Our lips brushed gently against each other for just a moment. I felt him smile against my mouth. I moved to kiss him again. Deeper this time, to breathe in his scent, to feel him.

A spine-chilling scream echoed through the garden and off the mountain walls. We pulled away from each other. I quickly bunched up my dress to grab my knife that I had strapped against my leg. More shouts and screams poured through the trees; fire erupted in the distance. The castle was blazing with thick flames that grew franticly. They swiped at the sky and trees around them, taking hold of anything that would succumb to their touch.

We started back down the rocky path. I had to hold on to the Asher and let him guide me. My dress kept snagging on the bushes and rocks, making me stumble. "Just cut it off." I sighed in annoyance.

Asher grabbed the tulle and cut a jagged chunk off above my knee. It was easier to see as we closed in on the castle that was bright with flames. It illuminated the surrounding chaos with a twisting of orange and red light. People are running in all directions. Some were burned or choking on the smoke. The Ivar soldiers were trying to put the flames out while also trying to control the crowd and help the injured. I coughed at the flames and tried to wave the smoke away while we scanned the chaos for Keane and Nilsa.

"There!" I shouted to Asher and pointed to a soldier who was dragging a man to safety. Keane was wheezing from the smoke; his clothes were charred and his eyes bloodshot. I grabbed his arm once he set the man down. He looked up at us in relief, then sank to the grass, exhausted.

"What happened?" Snapped Asher.

Keane coughed again, "I don't know. Smoke started to fill the castle, and I was trying to get everyone out, but the flames came fast. I've never seen anything like it." He spat and tried to clean his lungs, "Where's Nilsa?"

I wanted to know the same thing, but with people moving around in such disarray and the darkness that pushed against us, it was hard to tell anyone apart.

A small group of women swiftly cut through the crowd and raised their hands to the flames, making a series of quick movements. Wind snapped in around us, making me fall to my knees at the sudden force. It spun around the flames, collecting them upward and spinning them around till they created a glowing tornado, then fell. I screamed, fearing that it would crash to the ground and swallow us in burning pain, but before the wall of flames hit the earth, it sizzled out into steam that covered us like a heavy blanket. I thought I had my eyes closed as darkness plunged in around us, but I realized the flames were gone and I was once again enveloped in the sickening darkness. "Asher?" I called.

"I'm right here." He grabbed my shoulder. "The Enchantress put out the flames."

"Those women were Enchantresses?" I breathed, still trying to shake what I just saw. "Was Nilsa with them?"

"No, I don't see Nilsa."

"Wait." Keane said from beside me, "You can see in this?"

Asher snorted, "Yes, can't you?" I could hear the mocking sarcasm in his voice, another jab at the Ivar soldier. The back-and-forth game they had going of who was better.

A small light appeared in one of the Enchantress's hands, then the other two hands suddenly glowed as well. A soldier approached them with a torch and extended it out to the flame until it lit. "Where's the King!" someone shouted. Murmurs rose from the crowd as more torches were lit.

"What happened!" another shout.

"This was an Enchantress's fire!"

Shouts of agreements.

"Damn it. It better not have been Nilsa." Asher seethed.

"Find her." I grabbed Keane, helping him to his feet. He swayed back and forth until Asher went to his other side and helped brace him.

"That smoke filled my lungs faster than what it should have. I was in there longer helping where I could, but that fire." He shook his head. "It had a mind of its own."

"Like a spell?" I asked, still watching the huddle of Enchantresses at the front of the group as they now spoke to a few Ivar. A soldier turned to the crowd and raised a hand to silence them. "Our first and only priority is to find the King and to get him to our healer if needed. But our Enchantress did not start this fire. If it was caused by a spell, it was surely that of a Nightmare's doing." More torches filled the sky.

"Or a rogue Ivar?" Keane, Asher, and I all glanced at each other.

"We should meet up with the group. See if they know anything about what has happened." Asher pulled on Keane, turning us away from the crowd.

"Wait," I stopped making Keane tumble into Asher, "take Keane there while I look for Nilsa."

Asher's face contorted into a look of concern, "You don't know where the camp is."

Keane cleared his throat a bit once more, "we should stay together. I can breathe easier now, anyway."

We both gave Keane a hesitant look, "neither of you can see well. It won't be easy to find her." Asher said.

"Can't your shadows find her?" Keane asked, taking back his own weight and breathing deeply, testing his lungs.

I heard Asher shift around for a moment, "No, there's too many people around here. They'll feel them, and I don't think it would be wise to spook an already jumpy crowd."

"They might think you're the one who started the fire," I eyed the Enchantress. Their hands glowed in a ball of fire, lighting up their faces. They were as beautiful as Nilsa. With striking, cut cheeks and curling hair that cascaded around their warm faces.

A soldier leaned forward with an unlit torch and gratefully accepted the flame before lighting others around him. People lurched forward, grabbing anything they could to hold the flames. They pushed and shoved against us until we were in a cluster of people reaching for the light.

People grabbed each other's torches and yelled for the light. It was a blur of panic, a mob pushed by fear leaping toward the only things they could see. The Ivar soldiers pushed them back, yelling for them to be calm. More torches were lit and handed to the soldiers who were trying to break down the crowd into groups.

An elbow slammed into my head, making me stumble and push deeper in the swarm of panicking Ivars.

They grabbed me like an ocean wave, knocking me about until I didn't know which way Asher and Keane had been. My voice was drowned out by others calling for their loved ones. The crowd shifted violently, knocking me to the ground. I covered my face and let my arms take most of the pain as people tripped over me in a stampede. I rolled to my side, trying to push myself up. The crowd shifted again, scattering in all directions. Screams filled my ears. I had to duck down again cover my head waiting for a moment to jump to my feet.

The familiar chill surrounded me, raking a hand down my back, making me cringe before I was pulled up into his arms. The smell of smoke and trees filled my lungs. My body sung at the pain exploding through me. How many people had trampled me?

"What's happening!" I yelled. The torches shifted violently around us in the soldier's hands. More torches filled the castle grounds, moving around with the screams of people.

Warm crimson splashed across us. I screamed and fell back into the throng of the crowd, clutching Asher before I could be dragged down again.

TWENTY-THREE

The Nightmares seemed to appear out of the darkness. Their teeth and claws caught any flesh they could reach. They were ready for battle with ragtag armor and weapons that were rusty and outdated compared to the swords that the Ivar soldiers had.

I pulled my long blades from under my dress as Keane drew his sword and circled to my back. Asher took half a step away from me. His shadows flowed freely from him. They bounced around, excited about the chance to kill. I wonder how long Asher would let them run wild till it began to wear on him. He had his sword as well, but the shadows were too exhilarated to be fully controlled right now. I saw the labor on Asher's face already as he focused on aiming just for the Nightmares attacking us and not the Ivars that bumped and jumbled around him.

I tried to breathe and not to focus on the fact that I was about to kill living creatures. That my blades would pierce their flesh and bone.

I couldn't kill a deer when I went hunting with my dad, but these were not innocent deer. These were creatures that tore through the crowd of Ivars with no emotions. They did not care about the screams of pain or if they slaughtered the old or the young. They hungered for blood, for the agony.

I grabbed a woman knocking her out of the way of a Nightmare. She fell to the ground sobbing with bone-breaking shakes. I tried pulling her to her feet, but she wouldn't move. I screamed at her to get up, but she curled into a ball, her large pink gown covering her like a blanket.

"Please, you have to move!" I cried, unsure if she could hear me over the sound of death. I pulled on her again, making her sit up. She grabbed my arm shaking hands, tears of mascara ran down her face.

A spear ruptured through her chest before I could pull her to her feet. She gasped, letting go, and grabbed at her chest as the spear was pulled back. She slumped to the ground, her eyes skyward and lifeless.

My eyes didn't linger on her body. My hand didn't hesitate to throw my blade at the creature that killed her. It stood grinning ear to bony ear, clutching his bloody spear. Its forked tongue licked his fingers that held the blood of his victim.

My arm jolted as I stabbed my blade into the creature's chest. Slicing through his feather-covered skin and into his ribs then his heart coming to a sickening halt. Terror filled his large snake eyes when he realized he was dying, and I could feel the guilt slide away from me as I pulled my blade from his body and turned to the next threat. I would deal with that later. Right now, I had to protect the innocent people around me. I had to survive in order to stop the King and Dentro.

It was a slaughter all around us. Screams echoed off the mountains as the darkness swallowed people, and the air smelled of copper and smoke. More lights flooded down on us. A group stormed out of the trees with their weapons raised. Shouts of anger poured from their lips. I gripped my knives tighter, slicing through the neck of a Nightmare that looked too human. I would see them in my dreams, their warm blood rushing over my hand and their body crumpling to the ground, but right now I saw the need for survival. My blades an extension of my body. I calmed my breathing and focused my vision on what I needed to do and not the guilt of what I was doing.

Don't look at the faces, don't see if they look more human or nightmare, just focus on survival. It helped me through it. It helped me shove the pain deeper and deeper away.

Metal hit metal. Screams of battle and cries of pain made my head pound. Light lit up the sky as buildings were set on fire. It made it easier to see, but someone was losing their livelihood or homes as more and more fires started.

"They're blocking us in!" I screamed. Fires encircled us as the arrows started to fly from the trees and the top of the buildings. They had to have planned for this night for months. Gathered every Nightmare that was willing to fight. They had made armor and weapons and waited till the silly Ivars had dressed up for a party and come without weapons. I screamed in frustration. I had seen a sketch my father had drawn of Ivars dressed as we were now, but there were weapons draped across them like accessories. Why had that changed? Did they genuinely believe they were safe, or did they become ignorant of the threat?

I slowed; my breath burned through my lungs and came out like a rattle. My arms shook as I raised a sword I had swiped from a fallen body and swung at my opponent; he stepped back with ease and grunted out a laugh noticing my exhaustion. My knees buckled as I stepped back, trying to get distance between us. How long had we been fighting? My body screamed with exhaustion, but I blocked the swing of his metal club and fell to a knee, grinding my teeth.

A sword swept through his chest, spraying blood across me. The creature fell to the ground, and I fell with him, my body sagging with relief. I was disgusted with myself for letting the exhaustion take over, for falling among the dead when I still breathed in life. I could feel my father's eyes on me, yelling at me to get up that the fight wasn't over. How many times had he pushed me to exhaustion and complete soreness that I could barely move and yet I always got up.

"Farren!" Keane grabbed my arm, panic coating his crimson face.

I tried to speak to tell him I was okay, but all I could do was grab him back and allow him to help me to my feet. "We need to retreat." He allowed me to lean into him.

Asher stood, blocking us. He was using his sword now. His shadows were still bouncing around his feet, but he didn't allow them to attack any longer. He and Keane were still okay. I was able to relax a bit into Keane's grip.

Others were retreating as well, pulling away into the darkness and fleeing into homes. The Ivars were shouting at each other, trying to regroup.

Drums pounded in the distance like a heartbeat. Covered faces appeared in the shadows. Pounding their fists against armor, their weapons against the ground, or even on shields that had the Ivar symbols scratched from the metal. I took a ragged breath and stepped back from the group.

I couldn't tell who or what they were, as their faces were blocked by masks of all kinds. Some covered their entire faces made from metal or wood, others were simple fabric tied so that I could only see glinting eyes.

Asher gave a relieved sigh, "They're ours!" He shouted. "They're here to help!"

"The rebel group!" Keane yelled, "Let them fight by our side!" He grabbed an Ivar soldier close to him. "Tell the others that they will fight by our side!"

He nodded and yelled at others. The word spread quickly, but the Nightmares didn't seem fazed by it, only threw the group a few glances before caring about their brutality.

The rebel group slammed their way into the fight, pulling people out of the clutches of the bloodthirsty creatures. It had become confusion about who was fighting who. The Rebels wore a simple blue band around their arms, but it was barely noticeable while fighting.

Keane took the opportunity of the distraction to pull me out of the battle and into a side street with others. We all panted and groaned at the exhaustion that plagued us. A low lamp light lit the grim faces.

"We need to go back out; we need to find Asher and Nilsa." My tongue felt heavy in my mouth, and my body ached for water, but I ignored the dizziness that swept over me with a spin. I would push through, I would dig deep like I was taught, and I wouldn't let Asher get hurt.

"I'll go," I felt Keane stand, "You stay here and rest, and when you can, move further away from the fight."

I scoffed, forcing my buckling knees to stand, "I'm fine."

"You're not used to battling. You're fatigued, and I can't protect you if you're out there."

"I don't need you to protect me," I snarled, "I've managed to handle it on my own for this long."

"No." Keane said forcefully, "I am the soldier here, not you, so do as I say."

I was taken aback by the brunt force of his voice and the commanding tone of his words. He was always soft-spoken and calm, but this was the soldier coming out, the man who had been trained for battle, bloodshed, and pushing himself until death.

I, on the other hand, hadn't kept up on my training and felt my body protesting just standing, "Fine," I said hoarsely, "But once I'm rested, I will be back out there if I have to. I will not run from this."

"Take this," an older man in a torn and burned suit handed him the lamp, "it's better if we don't have a light leading the Nightmares to us."

Keane squeezed my shoulder and gratefully took the lamp before running back into the streets. I looked to the sky, waiting for the sun to rise and shine down, lighting a path to safety for everyone. I didn't know how long it was till that would happen or if it would.

I took one more breath and headed out of the alley, back to the bobbing of torches a distance away. The shouts and screams curled around the streets and down the alleys. I raised my sword and screamed against my burning muscles, stabbed into a grizzly-looking

Nightmare that was taking a bite out of a woman. I swung it again, colliding with another sword. The creature roared, sending spit into my face. I shoved against it. Knocking it back then kicked it in the chest, sending it to the ground before driving my sword through its head. It squealed like a pig, eyes popping from his head. I swung the other way, stopping dead in my tracks.

The man with marble skin and silver eyes stood directly in front of me. I ran, jumping over corps and slipping on fancy silk fabrics. I kicked a Nightmares out of my way and slammed into those around me.

He was there in front of me again, pointing just up the road, "there," his voice was in my head. "There," he said fiercely, making me turn to look.

I saw torch lights. Nightmares grabbing at Ivars. Not just Ivars, but children. They shoved them into barred wagons or threw them over their shoulders and ran into the darkness.

I grabbed other Ivars as I charged my way to them. My exhaustion was forgotten. The screams of frightened children filled me with anger.

Others noticed what was happening and jumped in to help the kids. Others who had not been fighting rushed from their homes to help. Mothers with fire in their eyes no longer hesitated to battle with us. They grabbed the kids away from the Nightmares, screaming at the children to run. The carriage cage slammed shut and the snap of the whip made the horse bolt away. Ivars chased on foot and others tried to follow the Nightmares that took children into the woods. Nightmares that chose to stay were killed quickly. I knew they had stayed to give the others time to get away with the children and all I could do was pray that they could save the children.

I turned back to the others, sighing with relief as the sun seemed to be rising and the battle was thinning out.

I don't know when the fighting finally stopped, but it turned quiet at the castle, or what was left of it. It was now a burned, charred, and crumbling disaster that collapsed into the mountain. The water windmill was still spinning. Tossing debris around the water, making a loud crashing sound against the rocks.

I fell to my knees at the sight of the bodies. Ball gowns blew in the wind, clinging to the dead. Random high heels littered the area as if they had been kicked off as women fled. The sick scent of copper and smoke stuck to the back of my throat.

I felt tears and allowed them to fall. I wanted them to blur my vision to wipe out the view of bodies. To blur out the image of children, soldiers, red dirt, and slashed body parts. I think I threw up, but couldn't remember as I stood and walked across the battleground to a few wounded people and helped them move away from the stench of death.

I had been in a fight before, at the Ivar camp, but this was different. These weren't soldiers. They were just dancing and laughing with their families and friends. They weren't ready or prepared for what happened.

"Ferren!" I turned from helping a woman wrap her wounded arm in a piece of fabric and saw Nilsa gingerly walking toward me. She was wearing a strapless white dress that was cut low in the front and wrapped around her middle, making her look stick thin. It had a slight poof at the waist, and it was perfectly clean, except for the bottom of the dress that was dragging in the red dirt. I waited for her to make her way over to me. She brushed her loose hair out of her face and looked me over. If I looked how I felt, I'm sure it was horrifying.

"Are you hurt?" She asked.

I glanced down at my torn dress, my dirty legs, hands, and arms, "I'm not sure." My throat hurt to talk. The copper tang burned it when I breathed.

"Here, sit down." She grabbed my hand and led me to a yard that soldiers were using as a medical area. She handed me water and kneeled next to me.

"Where were you?" I asked after sipping my water, letting the coolness heal my throat.

She shook her head, making her curls bobbing around. "Not here."

I pointed to the castle. "They said it was an Enchantress's fire." More death lay in there.

She cleared her throat and looked around. The wounded were trying to help the wounded, and cries for loved ones sounded like ghost calls, weak and pleading.

She didn't answer.

"Nilsa!" I snapped.

"You need stitches." She pointed to my leg.

I had a long gash through my thigh, pain ruptured through me. How had I not noticed? I had put my dizziness off as dehydration and exhaustion, but I should add blood loss to that list.

"Let me find someone to help you." She jumped up quickly, leaving me to moan in pain. Now that I had noticed the cut in my leg, it throbbed.

One moment I was trying to pinch together the skin to stop the bleeding as it oozed out through my shaking hands, the next I woke screaming as someone held me down. Sharp pain stabbed into my leg. I screamed again as I smelled alcohol. My leg was on fire. My vision swam around me as black dots floated in front of my face before I passed out again.

TWENTY-FOUR

I awoke confused and groggy until shouts for bandages and clean needles fully awoke me. I was lying in someone's front yard surrounded by others who were being medically addressed or sleeping fitfully in the snowy grass.

Asher was leaning against a wooden fence next to me. His eyes closed and breathing deeply. His shirt was open, revealing bloody bandages that were tight across his shoulder and another one across his ribs. I watched his chest rise and fall until his eyes fluttered open and he winced, sitting up straighter.

"Are you okay?" He asked.

"I should be asking you that." My voice sounded too loud for my throbbing head.

He waved the question off. "How's your leg?"

I slowly sat up and examined my now stitched leg. That would explain the sheer pain I had. I thought it was a nightmare. I grunted and laid back down. "Where is Keane?"

"They took him to another location. He was injured badly and needed more help."

"Injured how? Is he going to be okay?" The jolt of panic made my head spin. I groaned again. I wanted to lie down in an actual bed and never move again.

Asher's eyes lifted to mine, "I don't know. They're working on him. I don't even know where he is."

My head throbbed. I needed water, "Are you going to be okay?" I asked again.

"Are you worried about my injuries or that I am a Nightmare in an Ivar town?"

I scanned his bloody body again, "Both."

"Some Ivars noticed that Nightmares were helping them in the fight and so they helped us. Most of the group left after the King's speech. We need to leave soon, Ren." His face pinched with concern.

"What speech?" I had hoped and prayed we had had a bit of luck and that bastard died in the fire or the fight. It would have made things easier for all of us.

"How's your leg?" Nilsa sat down next to me. She was now in a new set of clothes. A soft pink dress with ruffles draped over her shoulders. She must have borrowed it from a friend since her clothes, like mine, had been in the castle.

"Sore." I said, "Now about the speech." I looked desperately at Asher.

Nilsa raised a brow at me, "You didn't hear it?"

"If I had, I wouldn't be asking about it?" I snapped, shifting my leg to a more comfortable position as I sat up wishing I had some kind of painkiller or even some hard alcohol to numb my mind.

She narrowed her eyes at me for a moment then flicked her hair behind her shoulder, "He said that the Nightmares were out of control and that the Ivar territories were being attacked all over. The farms were being burned, just like Finara. They were attacking when we were weak, not caring about women, children, or the old. He said some Ivars have even turned their backs on their promise to protect and have fallen into the Nightmare's clutches swayed by the sick promises of power." She pinched her lips together and sighed before continuing, "He said that we can no longer allow them to poison Hatheya and they all must be stopped. He said he vowed to destroy their evilness, even if that meant ridding our lands of all of them."

I breathed out shocked, "He wants to kill them all?" I clutched Asher's hand tighter. It wasn't safe for him here.

Nilsa eyed our hands, "That's what it sounds like. The crowd cheered for his words. Some kept their head down about it. But after what we went through…what they all saw…"

Asher leaned forward, his eyes darkening on Nilsa, "Did you do it? Did you start the fire?"

She picked at her nails and then dropped her hands to her side quickly, "All those people died because of me," she choked out, burying her face in her hands, shaking.

I grabbed her hands, forcing them away from her face. Her green eyes filled with tears, but none poured from them. "Tell me what happened."

She clutched my hands, her manicure nails chipped and scratched, "I wanted him to burn, only him. But I-I was so angry. Everything got out of hand. The fire spread so quickly." She whispered. "He grabbed me and demanded I come with him. I'm sick of being his," she glanced around nervously, "I don't know what happened to him when the fire started, where he went, I didn't want him to find me, so I hid and then the Nightmare's attacked." She took a few breaths. "He wanted me to go with him. To the tower. He said he had others and needed more to help with the spell."

"What spell?" I squeezed her hands tightly, trying to bring her eyes back to me. I never thought that Nilsa could ever crumble so deeply.

"I asked if it had something to do with Dentro and he slapped me. He told me I was a stupid woman and shouldn't ask questions that could get me killed."

"Sounds like it has something to do with Dentro." Asher tried standing but only got to his knees before having to stop and take in a few pained breaths. "If he's trying to break the spell to get in, he'll put everyone in danger just for power."

I reached out to Asher trying to get him to stop moving to sit and relax but I knew we didn't have time, even with our wounds still fresh and burning, we had to stop Kandem.

I placed a hand on top of Nilsa's. She was still shaking and breathing deeply like she was trying to stop the tears that were threatening to explode from her. I squeezed her hand a bit and stood, pulling her up.

"We need to find Keane and make sure he is being taken care of, then we leave."

When we got to the large mansion that was housing the soldiers, my leg was aching and Asher was huffing short breaths so as not to strain his ribs too much. He looked deathly pale, even his eyes seemed to be fading into a pale sickly gray.

My heart pounded with anxiety. He needed rest.

I stopped short, grabbing Nilsa's hand, "Take Asher somewhere and wait till he is ready to travel out to the group."

"What? Why?"

The King had just limped into the house that Keane was supposedly in. He was cleaned up, smiling, and patting the backs of the soldiers that he passed.

Nilsa stared unmoving, her eyes reflecting a thousand emotions. I tugged on her arm, "go," I said sternly.

"We're not just leaving you," Asher leaned heavily on my shoulder. His weight was straining my injured leg, but I wrapped my arms tighter around him, breathing in his scent and calming my mind.

"He can't see either of you. And you're in no condition to fight right now, Asher." I passed him off to Nilsa, who was still shaking. I couldn't tell if it was from fear or anger.

"You shouldn't go in there either. Just come with us," Asher pleaded.

"We can't abandon Keane."

His jaw tightened, but he nodded, "Be smart, Ren. As quickly as you can."

I wasn't sure what the King would do when or if he saw me or even what I would do.

I swallowed and pushed my way into the house. It was swarming with Ivar soldiers. Some were tending to the wounded, carrying bandages, buckets of water, and bloody rags. Others were eating in any spot they could find. Sitting with their friends and talking quietly around their sleeping comrades, their faces tired and sullen.

I scanned the faces around the living room and moved to the kitchen, which was set up more to resemble an operating room than a kitchen. I quickly turned away as they brought in an unconscious soldier with a missing arm and a burned face.

"Excuse me?" I tapped on a soldier who was sitting on the stairs that circled up to the second and third floors, praying I wouldn't have to climb it to the top. I was already out of breath and my leg stung against the stitches.

"Mmm?" It was a woman whose face had been taped and wrapped on one side. Even her eye was covered. I tried not to shudder at the thought that it was missing.

"I'm looking for a soldier named Keane. Have you seen him around here?"

She glanced around tiredly with one eye, then shrugged.

I gave her a small smile and moved stiffly up the stairs to others who were sitting there. They seemed in better shape than the woman, and I repeated my question.

"He was with us at the castle," one said, the other two nodded. After a moment he said, "Yeah, he was staying in our quarters and training with us." He looked to his friends again for their nods, "I think he might be in a room upstairs."

"Thank you." I climbed the stairs to the second floor and began with the first door I came to.

At the third door, I decided I needed to rest my leg and solemnly pushed the door open, my heart stopping for a beat as I tried to calm my face from the shock that hit me.

Kandem stood next to Keane's bed, patting him on the shoulder and smiling down at him as he said something.

Kandem looked up, "Ferren!" He bellowed, quickly limping over to me and pulling me into a hug. "I have been looking for you! I feared you had been killed!" He released me.

I didn't know what to say for a moment and shook as he embraced me, his bitter smell filling my nose.

"I needed to stop here, check on my soldiers, and speak with my generals before starting my search for you again."

I looked him up and down. He had a few scratches on his hands and a bruise on his cheek, but otherwise, he was fresher looking now than when he was at the ball. "You look well," I said, "your soldiers tried to find you when the fire happened." I let the words hang in the air and watched as his eyes filled with annoyance.

"What a tragic thing those monsters did and then to attack when we're weak like that. They even burned our hospitals and killed one of the Enchantress." He said somberly, "I've heard that some Nightmares help us fight?"

I showed shock across my face, "Really?"

"You didn't know?" He eyed me.

I shook my head, my eyes wide.

"Did you not fight? Your Father told me that he had been training you since you could walk."

"Yes, but not for something like that. So…violent." Let him think of me as weak. Let him let down his guard and underestimate me. That would make his words spill out faster.

"I am grateful that you were not hurt. I tried sending my guards to look for you when the fire started, but they couldn't find you and then the attack happened," he seethed, "many died. My people have died in such a horrific slaughter."

And yet, you have come out unscathed. I wanted to yell, but others were in the room, others that were looking at their king like he was their protector, their only hope. I bit my tongue and looked down at the red-dotted carpet to keep from glaring and shouting at the people to wake up to see his lies and his darkness.

"Come," he opened the door, "we have much to discuss and to get you ready for the trip."

Keane shot me a worried look as I was shoved out the door after the king.

"Are you sure you want to leave now? At such a crucial time here?"

He sighed, his tired eyes drooping, "The battles have just begun, Ferren. I fear something else is coming our way, something I need your help with."

"Oh?" what sweet lie was he about to feed me?

He beckoned for me to follow him to a room down the hall where his general, Steerr, and Brice stood.

The new general who took Bexley's place gave me a quick nod. His face was too pointed, and his eyes seemed to dart around at every noise that echoed through the house. His bony fingers pointed at something on a map and Kadeem and him whispered quickly together.

Brice gave me a snake smile and slowly made his way over, looking me up and down, giving a small laugh, "Well, if it isn't the human. Oh, I guess I can't say that anymore," he winked.

I narrowed my eyes, "and why is that?"

He didn't answer as he flashed me another sneer.

"Ferren," Kandem waved me over, "we must tell you something and it might come as a shock, but you must listen." Kandem took a breath as if the words were heavy and sat down. "Your mother is alive."

TWENTY-FIVE

I blinked at him. Was he talking about Navara? Did he know for sure that she was my mother? How did he find out? Not even my father knew for sure. "Who?" I squeaked out, feeling disappointed at myself for sounding like that. I shot Brice a glare as his smile grew.

"You don't know?" Steerr asked. "I thought she knew of her mother?" He turned to the King, who ignored him even as Steerr crossed his arms and mumbled under his breath.

"Navara *is* your mother." His brow scrunched up. "Didn't Gannon tell you?"

"He said he didn't know who my parents were." I couldn't stand anymore; my bad leg shook and burned from my weight. I lowered myself into a chair, trying to breathe through the pain and shock.

He stepped closer to me, "I have spoken to Navara myself."

My jaw dropped, "how?" She was locked in the tower with Dentro. Dentro let her live? She was alive?

"At the tower-"

"At the tower?" I cut in. How was he still alive?

"Yes. You should also know a group of Nightmares have found it as well. They're trying to free Dentro. We're in constant battle; we're trying to keep them from the tower, from speaking with Dentro. They're hunting Enchantresses and forcing them to try to break the curse and free Dentro." He told Brice to get me water. I must have looked pale. "Navara has been a prisoner for too long. She has been abused and used by him and wants to help us truly destroy him."

I coughed out a laugh, "And you believe her? The Enchantress who betrayed Mavi!" Brice thrusted water into my hand, I took a sip and then thought better. I didn't trust anyone in this room.

Kandem grabbed a chair for himself, "I didn't at first, but she risks her life every time she talks to us, and I see the scars and bruises on her. The hate for him that is in her eyes. She told me about you. Told me about her child, who was whisked away by Mavi and given to Gannon. She was angry that he stole her child, but now she is grateful that you are not there, that you got away and don't have to be controlled by Dentro." He noted my eyes widen, "Don't worry, I didn't tell her that you were here or even who you are."

I swallowed, "And who does she say is my father?"

"Mavi," he said softly, "it was rumored that they were together briefly." His mouth twitched, "I never believed it, until now."

I sat still, focusing on my breathing, trying to mask my emotions, but I was exhausted in more than just one way and I needed to get out of this small room that was shoved full of people I didn't want to be around. My brain felt like it was on fire, shuffling through what Kandem had said. I was Mavi's and Navara's child! Not Dentro's and with that came a sigh of relief, "And why do you need me?"

He gripped his walking stick tighter. "She told me that if the spell that Kanna was doing had been completed, then Dentro would have been killed, not just trapped." He paused, letting me have a moment to take it in. "If she could get his blood and complete the spell, then it would still work. We could finally kill him."

"His blood?" I said slowly.

"His blood that flows through you, Ferren." He said it with too much excitement. His lips teased at a smile, making my stomach plummet.

"My blood!" I choked out.

Kandem nodded slowly. Steerr seemed to be suddenly distracted by a map and Brice stared at me, watching with the interest of a predator to its prey.

"How much of it?" I stepped away from him, eyeing the door.

"All of it…just as Mavi tried to do. Some of his blood still flows through the tower because of the spell Kanna did and with your blood added…"

"You want me to sacrifice myself to an Enchantress that could be good or maybe be tricking you? Are you all insane?"

Kandem raised a hand to quiet me, "I am no fool. If what she is saying is true, then another Enchantress or Enchantresses could do it, but we must be in the tower."

That is why he wanted Nilsa. He must already have a few Enchantresses with him already. "You want to go into the tower? Once you go in, you can't get out?"

"Not when that spell is broken by the new one. We will be able to leave."

Did he care about killing Dentro, or was it about being able to go in and get what he deemed was his? "And what will you leave with?"

He clicked his tongue against his teeth, "What do you mean?"

I raised my chin and leveled my eyes at him, "What if I don't do this?"

"We cannot force you to do such an enormous sacrifice." His eyes didn't match his soft tone. Was he truly still trying to trick me or was it a show for these men that stood quiet in the room?

I had to keep myself from scoffing at that. I was expecting to be jumped the moment my back was turned, to be dragged and drained at the tower and my screams and cries ignored by the sheep that followed King Kandem. "I know what you want from the tower."

His eyes flashed quickly with anger, "I'm sorry I don't know what you are talking about, my dear."

"I'm no fool either." I turned to leave.

"Have you seen Nilsa? I worry about her as well."

I stopped my hand over the door handle, "Perhaps she was killed, like my father." I tossed a glance over my shoulder at the King before limping back to Keane's room.

Keane gave me a cricked grin. I threw my arms around him and whispered in his ear, "We need to leave now. They're going to come for me." I pulled away, and he nodded.

"Where are you hurt?" I asked, looking him over.

"I was stabbed in the back. If it wasn't for Asher, I would be dead. He found someone to stitch me up, but they refused to help him. Where is he?"

I nervously looked around at all the Ivar, "Safe, I believe."

He swung his legs off the makeshift cot, wincing a bit.

"Are you going to be okay?"

"Ivar, heal fast. It's part of what makes us good at war."

"What of Nightmares?" I asked, thinking of Asher.

"I think it depends on them. I've never stopped to ask." He snorted.

I helped him stand and found clothes in the closet for us and quickly changed into a man's large shirt and pants that I tied with a strip of my torn dress then stepped out and handing him his before cutting my pants at the ankles and earning a look of horror from Keane.

"Are we stealing these?" He pulled on the shirt, flinching as his muscles flexed.

"If you would like to return them after all this is over, feel free to." I made him walk down the stairs alone and out the front door while I made my way downstairs a bit after him. Steerr was standing at the end of the stairs, looking up at me. His bony fingers tapped against the railing. Kandem stood among his wounded soldiers, smiling at them. His eyes flicked to me, "Ready to go?" he asked, making his way to me.

I didn't move. I could dash to a room upstairs, but I would be stuck. It was too high of a jump to make, especially with my leg barely holding my weight as is.

"Play nice." Brice's hot breath smacked my neck, making me cringe with disgust.

I stepped down to the King and his outstretched hand, a smile still on his wrinkled face, his soldier's smiling back and shaking hands. No one paid much attention to me as he led me outside and to a carriage.

The carriage lurched to a start at a steady pace. Kandem waved out the windows at passersby as if it wasn't a big deal that I was being hauled off to be sacrificed. I slid a hand over the side of my leg where my knife was hidden just beneath the fabric.

Brice eyed me and then turned to the window with a sneer, upset to be stuck in a small carriage right next to me. Steerr was on my other side and Kandem sitting straight across from me with another guard who refused to meet my eyes. I was sandwiched in and if I reached for my blade, Brice could quickly stop me from reaching the King. Not to mention the other three guards that were in the driver's seats upfront and those on horseback following after.

They needed me alive, but there were worse things they could do to me than kill me. I wondered if Kandem would be hesitant about spilling a drop of my blood, which could give me the upper hand in some ways.

"What will your people think about their king leaving them in such disarray?" We rolled out of the town. He didn't answer and didn't look my way, as if he couldn't hear me. "Did you plan the attack? It made such a good lead-up to that speech of yours."

At that, he turned to me with a smile in his eyes, "I'm glad you could hear the speech."

"I heard it second-hand."

"Perhaps from your friend, Nilsa? I do hope she is okay. She seemed a bit shaken the last time I talked to her."

"You mean threatened her and tried to force her to come with you, as you are doing to me?"

He relaxed back onto the bench of the carriage, "I do wonder what will happen to her when the town finds out about her causing the fire and killing so many innocent people. She is a Nightmare after all. Perhaps I should have mentioned them in my speech as well. Had them brought to me."

"And then what? Killed them? Don't you need the Enchantress to help you with the tower?"

He tisked at me, "Don't you worry about that."

"I'm the key component of your plan. I feel like I should have some insight into what I have to do."

He didn't answer, instead, he leaned his head back and closed his eyes, a small smile on his lips.

I snarled, wanting to reach for my knife and cut into the dozing king, but Brice was watching me. His eyes lingered on me for a moment, as if trying to read me. Trying to figure something out. I looked beyond him and out the window at the passing trees.

The road grew bumpy, and my stomach lurched as we hit deep divots and rocks, slamming us from side to side. It made me yearn for my car and paved roads.

We stopped for a break after what felt like hours. Steerr and Kandem slid out of the door, not allowing me out. I sat with Brice, glaring at me from the other side, another guard lurking outside peering in through the window from time to time. I fingered my knife, tapping on the blade wondering if it would be a foolish thing to use against four guards and the King, but maybe it was more foolish not to try.

Brice was stabbing the tip of his knife into the bench, making slivers sprout around the bench. I wondered if the king would make him sit on the splinted wood when we started up again. If on cue to that thought, the carriage door flew open and Kandem stepped in. I sat up, my muscles tensing.

This time the King slid in next to me sighing gruffly and yelling to his guards to go.

I angled myself away from the three and crossed my legs to bring my knife closer to my hand. My sore leg was screaming with pain from the pressure, but I embraced it, letting that pain keep me awake and alert.

Rain shuttered down on the carriage, and thunder rolled through the sky with lightning. I watched the rain splash against the trees, wondering how Gantrick was doing against the sudden flood of rain. Their town was a mess from a battle, their castle burned and broken, and now this. I leaned my head against the carriage, biting my rage at the King. The king who left his people to suffer and to figure it out on their own. Perhaps there was a better person there, leading them all, someone who wasn't out for their own good but for the good of the Ivars and perhaps the Nightmares, too.

I saw a flash of movement in the woods. Brice leaned forward, clutching his knife. I pushed myself back against the carriage wall and braced myself for whatever was about to happen next.

The horses screamed, and the carriage halted quickly throwing us around. I took the opportunity to draw my knife. A guard who was handling the reins fell to the dirt, an arrow stuck through his eye. Streerr cautiously looked out the window and then kicked the door open. His lanky body flew out the door, his blade catching a mace as it slammed down. He shook from the force, dodging away as the mace was raised again to strike.

"Get to the horses and get us out of here," Kandem ordered Brice. I slammed against Brice as he was trying to exit and fumbling with his sword. He tumbled to the wet ground with a curse. Kandem grabbed the back of my hair, pulling me back to the wooden seat. I slashed at his chest, making him release my hair.

Alarm flashed across his face as lightning lit the sky. I ungracefully slid out the door and into the slippery mud. A Nightmare grabbed my arm, pulling me up. I slammed my elbow into its green jaw, sending it sprawling backward. It gave me a confused look, rubbing its jaw, but didn't move at me again. The carriage door banged against my back; I stumbled forward, catching myself before face-planting, and whirled around just in time to duck and twist away from Brice's sword. I didn't have the reach with my knife like he did with his sword. I had to keep dodging away from him. The green trollish Nightmare lunged forward, stabbing a knife into his shoulder.

Screaming, Brice grabbed at the knife, his sword sagging in his limp arm. I struck my foot against his hand, making his sword clatter away from us.

He yelled furiously, pulling the knife from his shoulder, throwing it at the troll and rolling out of the way of another blade. It hit the skittish horses. The horse bucked and twisted around kicking Brice square in the back. He fell to the mud going still. The horses bucked around rocking the carriage and sending everyone jumping for cover whenever the horses came too close.

"Ren!" Asher stood atop a hill, clutching his bow. His shadows swept down across the ground, lurching up at a soldier. Once the soldier fell to the ground anguish marking his face Asher staggered falling to his knees breathing deeply. His shadows covered him in a cocoon, racing around him as if they were panicking, then settled into a rhythmic flow.

I ran to a leaning tree that I could easily climb up to Asher. I grabbed hold of the branches and pulled myself up until I could hook my leg around another branch. My body shook from the rain and snow and the stench of sourness and bitterness coated my tongue, making it hard to concentrate.

Asher's shadows settled down enough that I could see him. His face was still pale, and he was bleeding from the wound he had received in Gantrick. I reached a hand toward his shaking, outstretched fingers, barely brushing them before I felt my foot slip. He lurched forward, but I was already tumbling down into the swamp just below me. Muddy water covered my head and pushed its way down into my lungs. A hand grabbed mine, leading me up to oxygen. I gasped, coughing out the water. A knife was at my throat and another hand covered my mouth.

"Put the bow down! And tell your men to back away!" Steerr was clutching the blade pressed tightly against my throat so that a swallow would draw blood.

Asher was aimed at us, his bow shaking in his arms, his breath ragged in his chest. I wanted to yell that Streerr wouldn't spill my blood and not to give in and that even if he did kill me, maybe that was for the better because the sword would be locked away for good.

Asher lowered his bow.

"Good! Now your men!" I could hear the smile in Steerr's voice.

The others moved around to face Steerr their weapons out where he could see them.

"And now what?" Asher smiled, "Would you like me to do with *your* king?" Asher pointed to Steerr's side. The King was circled by shadows. "Seems like we should make a trade!"

Steerr hissed in my ear, "You'll kill him the moment I let her go!"

"I'll give you my word." Asher stood a little straighter, looking down on us.

Steerr gave out a quick laugh, "I will never believe in the word of a Nightmare!"

"You don't have much of a choice!" Asher walked closer to the edge of the hill eyeing his shadows. "They're growing restless. I would decide what you want to do, and soon."

Steerr shifted, making the knife nip at my skin and drawing blood. Asher's eyes flashed black his shadows shuttered. Steerr gasped and threw me forward. I fell once again into the bog of water, "kill him!" I screamed at Asher, trying to cough up the dark murk of muddy water.

He pulled back his shadow. They wound around his legs and torso. He seemed to relax, his face filled with color again.

Steerr had grabbed the king, helping him stand, while another had somehow gotten the horses to calm.

"You gave me your word, Creature!" Steerr was backing away with the King.

Kandem looked over at me. "You'll come to me eventually when you learn what is at stake."

I snarled at him, "I will never allow you to take my blood!"

"If you want to come with us and learn what must be done, then come. Come and see what true nightmare awaits if we don't control them. They will free Dentro at all costs, and only *your* blood, the blood of the *willing* and merciful, can protect this land." His face was full of desperation, "Please, Ferren."

"Willing?"

He nodded slowly, "willing. You will be soon enough; I can guarantee it."

Steerr helped him into the carriage quickly and slapped the horses with a whip.

TWENTY-SIX

I found Asher crouched down in the tree coverings. The others started to move ahead of us as I stomped over to him, not caring how loud I was and knowing it was annoying him.

"Why didn't you kill them! You had them! You could have stopped all of this!"

He sighed, looking over his shoulder, "I couldn't."

"Why? Because you gave that little snake your word? Has that ever mattered to you before?"

He flinched, and I cursed myself for my cruel words as I circled to his front. He stood clutching his side, his hand covered in blood.

"Just pulled some stitches." He winced.

"It's more than just that." I pulled his hand away, flipped up his shirt, and eased away the bandage that was covering a palm-sized gash along his ribs and another just above his hips. "You don't even have stitches. Did you let someone tend to your wounds when you got to the camp?"

He pulled down his shirt, wincing as his shadows circled his torso where he was injured. "I didn't have time. Nilsa dragged me off to get help, but I fell asleep and when I awoke Keane was there saying the King had taken you. This is the stop we were planning on attacking anyway if we couldn't get him at the castle. Most were injured in the battle. I only had a few to take with me."

I tried reaching for him, but his shadows wouldn't move and I pulled back hurt. "You shouldn't have come. You could have hurt yourself even more."

"The shadows help me heal; they take away a bit of the pain but while they're healing me, I have no strength to let them kill. I couldn't kill him." Rain stuck to his lashes as he closed his eyes and leaned against the tree.

"You were bluffing." My anger fizzled out.

Asher ran a hand through his hair then cringed at the pain of raising his arm, "I had to."

"He wouldn't have killed me…"

He narrowed his eyes at me and cocked his head to the side, "And why is that? Were they taking you to the tower?"

I dropped my hands, "I'll tell you at camp."

"Why not now?"

I gestured to his shirt dotted with blood, "Because you're bleeding and I'm starving."

He gave a soft laugh and nodded in agreement. Nilsa was huddled by the fire wearing a simple shirt with flowing sleeves and a pair of black leggings with knee-high boots. The surrounding men kept throwing glances at her. She would wink and smile at them, making them turn away with heated cheeks. Her red hair stood out among the muddy camp.

"You're alive!" She ran over to us, throwing her arms around me, then Asher. Their hug lingered a bit too long, making me burn of jealous just a bit.

"Thanks to Asher." I shook off the jealousy when he looked over at me, his eyes soft gray. He put his arm heavily around me. His breathing had turned ragged.

"He always seems to be saving someone," Keane moved stiffly to us, his crooked teeth showing in a wide smile. He clapped Asher on the shoulder and then apologized seeing Asher wince at the sudden force.

"I wouldn't have to if all of you wouldn't try to die so much," he scoffed teasingly.

Nilsa grabbed Asher's arm and laughed at whatever joke they shared between themselves. I sighed, watching them all together and realized that I suddenly had friends, people that I cared about and had been keeping secrets from. I had stuck so close to my Father's words of not trusting anyone I failed to realize that eventually I was going to have to trust someone with my burden and them knowing all of Kandem's plans required me to tell the truth about who I believed I was.

I cleared my throat, "we should talk." They all looked at me, "after Asher is stitched up."

"How is your leg?" Nilsa asked.

I had forgotten all about it. The stinging pain had gone down and though it was sore with stiffness, I was feeling better. I lifted my pant leg and looked at the long gash that was now a soft pink. The stitches no longer puckered out of a bloody infected-looking wound. "Huh, looks better to me."

Nilsa crossed her arms over her chest and eyed me, "It shouldn't be healing that fast, and really, for a human I'm surprised you aren't dead from it."

I pushed down my pant leg, "We'll talk, I promise, but Asher is more important right now."

Nilsa looked me up and down, then turned away with Keane as someone called that the food was ready.

I helped Asher find someone tending to the injured. My stomach grumbled with a sharp pain of hunger, "go get stitched up. I'll save you some food."

"Then you'll tell me whatever it is that you've been hiding?" He squeezed my hand gently, giving me a tired smile.

I nodded solemnly, "promise." I gave him a quick peck on the cheek, surprising him, and hurried to the food.

The soup was watered down, and the vegetables had no taste besides being dry and old, but I had two bowls of it and thanked the cook for the delicious meal that eased the pain in my stomach. Nilsa was surrounded by people laughing and swapping stories as always and Keane had gone to lay down his muscles sore and the wound to his back was healing slowly.

I scooped up another bowl of soup and headed over to Asher's tent.

Eira leaped from a rock she was sunbathing on and danced around my feet, looking hungrily up at the bowl I was carrying. "I was wondering when you would show up again." I ran a hand through her dirty coat. "You missed quite a lot."

She pawed at the bowl, spilling some over my hand, and quickly licked it up before I could wipe it away. "That's all you're getting." I stood and ducked under the flap, stopping short, "Oh sorry! I was just bringing you food."

Asher was shirtless and was just sliding on a pair of new pants as I walked in. I shoved the food into his hands awkwardly. This wasn't the first time I'd seen him without a shirt, but the scars across his back had stolen my focus from his broad chest. His tan muscles pulled against his stitches that were carelessly sewn into his skin. Whoever had done them wasn't experienced, and it would leave a nasty scar.

"I was just coming to get some, but I wanted to get dressed first." He gave a small grin and sat down on the cot, taking a small sip of the soup and then setting it aside.

I tugged on a bit of my hair, trying to avoid staring, but gave in and let my eyes crawl over him until I met his eyes. A hungry smile on his lips.

I wasn't sure who moved first. We stood just inches from each other. My breathing slowed, but my heart pounded as he stepped closer closing our small gap. He brushed the hair from my face, cupping the back of my head. I stood on my toes, leaning into his warm chest. Our lips met, taking my breath away. I wrapped my arms around him. He pulled me closer. I could feel his heartbeat against mine.

The tent flap opened. "Asher, are you up?" Keane walked in and turned around quickly walked out.

Asher sighed, making my hair flutter, "I'm going to kill him."

Even with the mood broken, I couldn't help but smile up at Asher, "We all need to talk, anyway."

He gave me a soft kiss before stepping back, his shadows curling in around his wounds again.

We found Nilsa first as she came bouncing to us with a smile plastered on her face. "Everyone is just so nice here. The Nightmares and the Ivars."

I eyed her, noting that I would have to talk to her later about her fake personality and that she shouldn't have to do that here. She was away from the King and the court. She noticed my look and dropped her smile into her Enchantress grin, winking at me.

Keane slowly walked to us, avoiding eye contact, his cheeks a slight pink.

Nilsa clapped her hands together, "All right, spill it, Ferren."

I took a slow breath, allowing my nerves to fall away, reminding myself I could trust them. I smiled at Asher, knowing everything was going to be okay, at least for a few moments. "I know part of the King's plan. Just a bit of it."

"Excellent," Nilsa said, "do share with the group."

"First, I need to explain why he needs me alive. I've been told that my mother is Navara and that Mavi is my father."

"Did the King tell you this?" Keane's face went gauntly.

"Him and Gannon. Gannon told me when I found him at WinWord, but that was just speculation."

"What does this have to do with the King taking you?" Keane asked. He seemed to be the only one capable of talking to me at the moment. Nilsa was looking at me oddly and Asher stood stoned face.

I started in on what I knew and what the King planned on doing to me, with my blood, but I was unsure if it would work. Kandem and his followers were taking a gamble with me. There was no proof and even though Navara had told Kandem I was her daughter; she could be lying. It was uncertainty that hung in the air for all of us.

"Kandem also said something about me being willing, though he didn't elaborate on that much."

"Why didn't you tell us sooner?" Keane asked.

"Because she didn't want to show her entire hand. She wanted to wait and see who she could trust or even if she had to," Nilsa gave me a supportive look, "I wouldn't want to admit that either."

"She's right," Asher finally spoke, "we all have things we'd rather not say, and being Mavi's supposed daughter can hurt more than help in some cases."

Keane nodded, "Lots of Nightmares would want to get their hands on you, try to break the curse, or just kill Mavi's offspring."

"And the Ivars could use this as a political ploy. Perhaps make you the rightful heir to the throne. That could come in handy," Nilsa tapped her chin and grinned mischievously.

"With a traitor for a mother? I don't think so and Kandem would never let that happen. Besides, I'm sure Nightmares and Ivars wouldn't want to see an Ivmare on the throne," I said.

Nilsa shrugged in agreement., "We need a little change in Hatheya."

"It sure does explain a lot," Asher said before he turned away, wandering back to camp.

My stomach plummeted, and I looked at Nilsa and Keane.

Nilsa hugged me, "Don't worry, Ferren." Then she headed after Asher.

"You never told him anything?" Keane asked, giving me a sad smile.

"I never told anyone anything, and he didn't tell me anything before yesterday either. Our relationship didn't start with honesty, it started with survival."

"It was going to come out eventually," he sighed, "we need to keep this under wraps."

"Agreed. The less the Nightmares and Ivars know the better."

"Let Nilsa and Asher know that."

"You still don't trust them?"

He winced, "Asher yes, because he cares for you, but Nilsa, she might use this to her advantage somehow." He looked away, "I guess being a soldier has taught me not to trust, especially Nightmares. We're all struggling with that, trusting each other and ignoring what has been forced into our minds since the beginning."

"Do you trust me? Now that you know what I might be? That I might be the daughter of Navara?"

Keane turned back to me, "Are you hiding something else from us from me?"

"No," I said sternly, but my voice broke a bit in desperation. I wanted his trust. I felt like I had just lost Asher's, and I couldn't lose Keane's as well.

"Then I trust you," he grasped my hands, "you're still Ferren. It doesn't matter if you're human or Ivmare, and I don't think that matters to Asher either. He just sucks at showing emotions."

A lump rose in my throat. We kept hurting each other because of our secrets, but a part of me felt as if I was protecting him with them as well.

"I have to go to Navara," I breathed. I needed to hear it from Navara. To look at her and see if I saw myself in her.

Keane didn't answer for a moment. His eyes flashed with a flood of different emotions, "That's suicide," he finally said.

I rolled my shoulders trying to shake off my stiffness, "I know, but I must do this. I need to talk to her."

"She betrayed your father, the king, the man who was trying to save Hatheya." He let go of my hands.

"Supposed, father. We don't know if that is the truth."

"And we don't know if she's your mother. Don't do this," he pleaded, "don't make a mistake that could cost you your life because you're curious."

"This is more than just a bit of curiosity!" Those at the fire turned to look at us. I avoided their eyes and stalked off with Keane on my heels, "I have to see her, I just have to, Keane."

He took a deep breath, "I understand. I wish I knew what happened to my family after we left. I don't know if they're alive or if they're hurt," he cleared his throat, "But I know what I did was right. I'm glad I left."

"We can try to find out if your family is okay. Maybe we can send someone." My heart ached for him.

"No, we need all our men here. We can't spare one."

I rubbed my eyes, wishing I could do something for him, wishing I could take away the pain that was deep inside him.

"I need to go on watch. It's my turn and you should get some sleep, then go talk to Asher."

I was sharing a tent with Nilsa, which wouldn't have been bad, but the tent was small enough without all her stuff thrown across the tent. She had clothes spread across my bed; books were spread out across hers. She must have looted houses to get these many clothes.

I took one look at the mess and went to find Asher.

"Asher it's me." I didn't give him time to answer as I walked into the tent.

He sat up as I walked in, then laid back down.

"I know you're angry at me for not telling you earlier, but Nilsa is right. I had to wait till I could trust you all."

"I know," he sat up again, grunting in pain, "I kept things from you as well."

"I'm going to go see Navara," I said quickly, seeing his hackles rising. He looked up at me his dark hair that had grown now covering his ears and dipped into his eyes. I expected his eyes to shimmer with his icy darkness, but they were gray like the sky when it was about to rain. "When are you going to go see her? How are you going to!" He had that same concerning voice Keane had.

"As soon I get supplies and some rest." I sat down on his mat, feeling every bone in my exhausted body aching.

He moved over a bit, allowing me to lie next to him. He wrapped his arm around me and I instantly fell into a dreamless sleep.

TWENTY-SEVEN

I was startled awake by Nilsa and Eira staring at me. "What the hell is wrong with you!" I reached for Asher instinctively, but wasn't there anymore. Eria flicked her tail and ran from the tent, sending up a kick of dirt.

Nilsa brushed the dirt gingerly from her skirt, "Keane told me that we're going to go see Navara."

"We?" I yawned. My day was already off to a poor start with aches from a stiff body and dread filling my very core for my plans to go to the tower.

"Yes. We." She eyed me devilishly, "You think you get to have all the fun?"

"Not the word I would use to describe this whole mess." I raked a hand through my tangled hair.

She huffed, "Well, get up. We have work to do, like finding your dear old mother."

I groaned before standing and following her out, blinking at the bright sun. It had been a while since I had slept through the night, and I felt a bit refreshed before the anxiety of everything hit me.

It took us longer than expected to find out where the tower was exactly located and that the King's men heavily guarded it and it seemed Hatheya was exploding into madness.

Some were like us, trying to stop the King and Dentro, others were trying to free Dentro, and others were taking advantage of the kingdom's weakness and doing whatever they pleased. Nightmares were still being captured and taken to an unknown location. Ivars were killed if they stepped even a little out of line. Hatheya was beginning to fall apart. The King was spreading the news that in order for peace the Nightmare's needed to be controlled and contained and that he was working on protecting the Ivars who continued to stand with him.

"How are so many finding out about Dentro still being alive?" A small goblin creature bit into a raw bird.

I looked away as blood dripped down his chin, trying to keep from gagging.

"Someone is spreading the news about him." Another Nightmare that reminded me of a broken doll with large frightening eyes spoke softly. She blinked slowly at me, waiting for me to speak.

Keane, Asher, and I had to move around in the group to see what the Nightmares and the Ivar were talking about in their separate groups. They didn't eat together. They kept their distance and still seemed jumpy about being in the same camp. I knew it would take time, but they needed to train together and learn to work together or our plan to stop the King and Dentro would fall short if they didn't trust one another.

We thought the battle at the castle would have bonded them, and it did for a bit, but they seem to break apart shortly after, "we're unsure of who is spreading it around, but it means we need to be more on guard, we trust no one with information that could be used against us."

"News from the group on the outskirts!" An Ivar woman ran over to us, handing me a weather-worn letter.

I stood and headed to where Keane and Asher were bickering about something stupid.

"We received a letter. Where is the runner?" We found another group mix of Ivars and Nightmares wandering through the woods and questioned them before they moved to the edge of farmlands scoping out a Nightmare group that had butchered and looted Ivars in one of their small towns.. They had an inside man who had worked closely with the King and knew how he planned and worked. They wouldn't reveal his name as we were not divulging all our secrets either, but they would tell us what he suspected.

If we wanted Ivars and Nightmares to work together, we needed to stop the violence, or at least some of it.

"He was attacked on his way here; I don't think he's going to make it." Keane crossed his arms and sighed. He was beginning to grow a beard, making him look older. His eyes were colder since we heard the news that no one could find his family. I knew the pain he carried around with him.

"Was he followed?" My heart clenched with fear.

"I sent out a few scouts and those that were already on watch didn't see anyone following him," Asher's tired eyes met mine. "We're not sure where he was attacked or why. When he made it here, he could barely talk and fell unconscious soon after."

"Did Nilsa attend to him?"

"With him now."

We went to the tent where we stored our maps and other letters and there, I tore open the envelope and let Keane decipher the message within.

Keane had been the one to come up with codes and taught it to us and two others at the other camp. I still struggled with it, but Asher seemed to pick up on it fast, which irked me a tad.

Nilsa ducked into the tent a moment later and came to stand next to me. Her hands and clothes were dotted with blood. She had been working on healing magic, but it seemed to be a laborious task.

"The runner?" I asked, making sure my voice was calm.

"He has passed on to the forest," she said quietly, "Some of the other Ivars have already begun getting him ready for burial."

After a moment, I told Keane to read.

After questioning one of the captives from the group that has recently pillaged the Ivar town Valit, he has admitted that he is getting his orders from Bhaltair, as are many others that are causing havoc among the Ivars and Nightmares.

They are being paid to cause disruption and to spread the word about Dentro's awakening, but he is unsure as to why Bhaltair wants chaos. He believes

Bhaltair might be working for someone and that is where he is acquiring the money to pay the men he had hired. We can confidently say that the captive does not know who Bhaltair is working for, nor does he know any more information about Dentro or the King. Questioning the second captive has confirmed the information above.

Never waver in the strength.

Keane tossed the letter down on the small table and sighed, itching his chin, "Of course, Bhaltair has something to do with this."

"Who would Bhaltair take orders from?" I turned to Asher.

He eyed the letter reading it over again, "Someone who has a lot of money. If he is having others raid for him and letting them keep all that they collect plus paying them to do so. Bhaltair is probably getting something more than just money for this." He tapped his fingers against the table.

"Someone with power and money."

Keane shrugged, "the King?"

"Or Dentro?" Asher said, "he was always obsessed with the stories of Dentro, the most powerful Nightmare out there. He told me once that Dentro would be the only one that he gladly serves."

"And maybe now he is. Dentro doesn't even need money to get Bhaltair to serve him, but how is he talking to him? The King still has the tower surrounded."

"Your guess is as good as mine," Asher continued to study the letter.

"Perhaps it's time to speak to Navara."

Asher scoffed, "And how do you intend on doing that?" He eyed me with concern even before I could answer. "Even if you somehow made it to the tower, how would you speak to her without Dentro? I know what the King told you, but can you honestly believe that man?"

"I know what I have to do, Asher, and I will not let you stand in my way." He had been trying to talk me out of this since the beginning. Only Nilsa seemed to understand my need to talk to her.

"You're being reckless." He slammed his fist down on the table.

Keane's hand went to his sword, then quickly fell back to his side as he shook his head at Asher. They had talked intensively about me going there, but Asher was still against me going.

"I've had scouts at the tower, and they have seen Navara in the window of the tower every evening. They have also learned the guard's schedule. It is a two-day walk to the tower from here."

"What scouts? Keane and I haven't approved scouts." He shot a vicious glance to Keane, who shrugged, "Is that why you insisted we come here? To be closer to the Navara and the tower? You're putting us in danger of being so close!"

"We all must approve this, that is what we agreed upon," Keane said calmly, but his eyes burned.

Nilsa crossed her arms and shuddered, "I knew I felt darkness around us."

I leaned against the table, sick of the argument already. "We need to keep an eye on him, and you were all too afraid to do it. We *cannot* let others risk their lives for us constantly. I need to go to Navara and see what the King is planning and I'm not waiting any longer. I'm done discussing this."

"We're not!" Asher huffed, now gripping the table.

"I don't need to be babysat or told what to do." I left the tent and went back to mine to calm my mind. Nilsa still never picked up her stuff, and I had to shove it out of my way to get to my bed, but to be fair I was only in here half the time, the other half I spent in Asher's. I slept better there. It seemed the dreams didn't follow me into his tent.

When the sun was low and shadows were cast around the trees, I readied myself to head to the Tower. I counted my knives twice and sharpened the blade I got from Evir, then I strapped on my sword and paced for a minute deciding if I wanted to take my bow or not, in the end, I decided to leave it and headed to meet one of my scouts that was coming with me. She was a small Ivar with thick blonde hair and freckles that covered her face and arms. She always looked like something bad just happened and she had to break the news to me.

Her eyes held sadness in them that I never asked about, and she never said.

"Ready?" I pulled my black wool jacket around tighter as the night had grown foggy and bitter cold.

Missy crossed her arms and huffed, "Your men told me that I shouldn't take you and that if you're insistent on it, then they'll go with you, so they can protect you." She rolled her eyes.

"Protect me?" I made a disgusted noise and clutched the hilt of my sword, wanting to hunt them down and use the newly sharpened blade on them.

"I told them you didn't need their protection and if you wanted them to come, you would have told them to come." Even when she was angry, the sadness within her couldn't be hidden. I wonder if she wanted to be a scout so she could stay away from others since she looked at us as if death were just on our doorstep.

I turned to Nilsa, who was seeing us off. She wanted to come, but I didn't want her getting hurt, plus she had a lot to do around camp. "You didn't tell them when we were leaving, did you?"

"Nope." She pulled the hood of her coat up, sighing at the wind as it threw dirt at us.

Seething, Missy and I walked on into the fog-drenched forest, staying slow and cautious. After a moment, I tapped Missy on the shoulder and stopped. I listened for a moment to the forest noises, the crickets, frogs, and other animals that Missy said wouldn't hurt us as long as we stayed away. I sighed in frustration at the familiar slide of coldness crossed over my legs. "Asher!" I hissed through my teeth, "Keane!" Shadows moved away from us. Missy cussed under her breath and walked away, probably upset that we didn't know we were being followed earlier. I cursed at myself for that. The only reason I knew they were because of Asher's shadows nipping at my heels. "What are you doing here?" Neither one answered. "Go back to camp."

"No, we're here to help you," Keane said. His figure appeared from the darkness with Asher right behind and Eira following close by.

"Fine, just don't get in my way or question Missy and me. We know what we're doing, and we don't need either of you getting in our way. Understand?" I said sharply.

"Yes, you're in charge," Keane raised his palms to me, nodding quickly.

"Keep your shadows in check, Asher. I don't need them following me around like a lost puppy." I was upset he followed me, but I was also a bit relieved he had come. My shoulders relaxed, and I was comforted by his presence.

"Sounds like someone needs a nap before infiltrating an enemy camp," Asher said smugly.

My mouth gaped for just a moment before I snapped it shut and laughed as a smile crept across my face.

I could tell Asher was trying to pull the shadows away, but after a bit, he gave up and allowed them to annoy me. I didn't quite understand their fascination with me. Perhaps it was attached to Asher's emotions about me that made them hover.

After two more days of walking, we finally arrived at the tower. "Look." Missy pointed up.

My stomach dropped when I looked up. From the trees, a tall crumbling watch tower touched the clouds. The tip of it reminded me of a blade that would cut the sky wide open. A large platform encircled the middle with open windows. That must be where my dad would have stood when he was on watch. He had described the tower as a lookout post for only the brave who could handle the wind and the cruel heat of being so high up. It was why the castle was called the Tower. The rest of the tower reminded me of needles. It was crude sharp angles that all pointed to the Heavens. The shorter towers were bunched together tightly with slit windows on every layer. There were no bridges or archways, no beautiful designs on the outside like the other castles I had seen here. It was a smooth brick that no one would be able to climb. No windows large enough to fit through. The side of it was crumbling, vines stretched across it, strangling the grimy bricks.

We followed Missy's lead as she led us around large boulders and into a little covering among fallen branches and overgrown weeds. We crouched in close together, our eyes on the darkness ahead.

The small town around it was cold and forgotten. Houses were leaning or broken, children's toys abandoned, a graveyard a walk away was flooded and sinking. The tents of the Ivar soldiers were among them, looking new and too bright for such a bleak and broken place.

"I can feel him," Asher's voice was tight. Sweat was building on his brow, his hands shaking.

Eira passed back-and-forth panting and yipping.

"Shut that thing up before I do it," seethed Missy, hand on her dagger.

"Eira," Asher grabbed her. She struggled in his hands, nipping at him. He quickly let her go. "Go," He waved her off, "go!"

She ran in a circle a few times, then sprinted off into the darkness.

Asher took a shuttering breath and leaned his head against the log, his eyes distant and foggy.

"Are you going to be okay?" I placed a hand on his arm, drawing his gaze away from the castle. He didn't answer, but slipped his hand into mine and looked back.

"I know you can do this, but I just want to protect you. Don't ever run away without telling me again. Please," he whispered.

I squeezed his hand, "I promise to tell you the next time I run straight into danger."

"What window does she go to?" Keane asked, his breathing turned deadly calm. He was expecting problems at any moment. His knuckles were white from clutching his knife.

"We need to move to the back of the castle, next to the cliffs." Missy said, "It's a tight fit in the cave I found. I don't think all of us will fit."

"Is that where the King spoke to her?" Keane asked.

"I'm not sure."

Keane leaned forward, studying the grounds around the tower. "Those aren't the King's men," Keane said tightly, "They're all Nightmares."

"What?" I looked back at the tents and the people walking the grounds. "I thought the King and his men were here?"

Missy quickly pulled out her spyglass. "They were the last time I was here; they were all on edge looking as if haunted by ghosts."

"Perhaps that couldn't handle being around Dentro any longer." Asher was breathing heavily now.

"Or they were attacked," Keane pointed to a large fire. "That's not for warmth, it's for burning bodies."

I gulped loudly in my ears. Asher looked ready to pass out. He didn't look this ill after the fight in Gantrick.

Keane looked worriedly at him. "Are you okay?"

Asher gave a quick nod.

"Missy and I will go. You two stay here and keep watch. Keep your eyes out for anything." I let go of Asher's hand..

"I don't think you two should do this," Asher whispered hoarsely.

Keane took the spyglass from Missy. "This is one of those rare times I have to agree with Asher. Something isn't right."

"Nothing is right here. Nothing." I said harshly, "which is why we must speak to Navara and try to figure out how we can change it."

We had to scale a cliff in the dark, groping at the jutted-out rocks and the indents for my foot to slide into. I bit my tongue to keep from screaming as my hand grabbed onto something slick. It lashed out and bit my wrist, sending pain through my fingers. I had to shake out my hand as they kept falling asleep, making it hard to grab onto the rocks.

I looked down at the campfires that were far below us and gulped. The world tilted and spun around me. I pulled myself closer to the rocky wall and took a breath. We were now sliding sideways across the cliff then had to go down a bit until we were next to the window Navara was hopefully going to be at.

I lowered myself down into the cave, stretched out my tight muscles and took some water Missy offered me. "She should be here soon."

We sat huddled together in the small cave; our hoods pulled low over our brows. Missy sat so still at times that I thought she was asleep until she would spin her knife.

Part of scouting and spying was waiting, and I was bored out of my mind. I wished to move, to stretch, even climb the cliff again if it meant I could do something besides sit here and wait for something I wasn't sure would happen.

A candle flickered in the window. I sat up straight. A ghost of a woman appeared, holding a candle. Her features were blurred in the small window. She leaned forward, the candle under her chin highlighting her now visible face.

"Is that her?" I breathed.

She had shining white hair like mine and thin lips. She scrunched her eyebrows together for a moment until her eyes landed on me, then she tilted her head toward us and smiled softly at me. I wish I could see her more clearly, see the color of her eyes, if she truly had such sharp cheekbones, or if that was a play of candlelight. I wanted to be closer to her, to hear her voice and take in her scent. Was this what everyone thought when they saw her? Was she truly this alluring, or was it her power that drew people in?

Hello

I jumped a bit; a voice had echoed in my mind.

I can speak to you within your mind as long as I can see into it.

"See into it?" I looked at Missy. "Can you hear this?"

She gave me a sideways glance, "Hear what?"

"She's talking to me in my head." I put a shaky hand on my temple.

Missy raised her brows at me then looked at the window, "Is it truly Navara?"

Yes, I am. Her voice was soft, like a passing thought in a dream. It was almost comforting.

"She said yes."

"She can hear us, both of us?" Missy said in awe. "I've heard of powerful Enchantress being able to communicate within people's minds. Some believed they were going crazy hearing voices in their heads telling them to do things."

I swallowed; I didn't like that thought at all. "You've spoken to the King?" I asked.

I have.

"What did you speak about?"

You.

"Do you know who I am?"

Yes, she sat down. *I knew it the moment I felt your presence.*

"Who am I?" I leaned forward trying to see her more clearly. I wanted to see her eyes when she said.

She placed a hand on the window and smiled sadly, *My daughter, my child.*

She leaned her forehead against the window. *I knew one day I would see you again. I only held you once. Right after I gave birth to you. I held you, then Mavi took you from me.*

It took me a moment to talk again. The image of her clutching me in her arms, tears streaming down her face, filled my mind. I wasn't here for this. I wasn't here to reconcile our relationship or ask her about that night.

"The King said that you no longer serve Dentro." I hated speaking his name so close to his tower, like if I said it too loud it would summon him to the cave.

I was angry at Mavi for taking you, for ripping you away, but the abuse that is within this prison…I'm now thankful that he did it. He saved you from the pain of the torture and torment that Dentro has inflicted upon me for so many years. Her voice pulled. *When I told him I was pregnant, he was angry. He beat me until I bled and yet I still served him. I loved him. And then when I held you, something changed. Suddenly I could see his poison, and being trapped in here with him has been my hell. It has broken me, and I wish to only set things right so that I may finally rest.*

"How can you prove that you're telling the truth?" She looked like me, she had the same hair the lips, and her smile was what I saw when I looked into the mirror.

I don't serve the King or Dentro. I will tell you what the King is seeking from me.

"How did he speak to you without Dentro finding out?"

Dentro is busy planning and building his army. And I talk to Kandem the same way I'm talking to you now.

'Planning what?"

He does not say, but I can only assume it is not good.

"What does Kandem want from you?"

The Sword.

"No. That was destroyed."

"What is she saying?" Massy asked.

I held up my hand to silence her.

She shook her head. *The King has a piece of it. He feels the power that pulses from it. It makes him hungry for more.*

"What?" That was impossible. "How?"

A piece was broken during the battle. That is all I know. He only showed me a glimpse of it, but I could still feel the power and sickening stench that poured from it.

"He said he needs me, my blood" I ignored Missy as her head snapped to me.

Oh, my poor child. He has been speaking to the other Enchantresses. She put her head in her hands and shook before looking back at me. Her face crumbled in despair.

"Why does he need me if he can have the Sword? He could control them."

Because the tower is weakening, the magic of hope and protection that Mavi used from the land is dying like everything else. I can feel our land weakening and the King wants to stop it and he believes if he kills Dentro then the land will begin to heal, but I fear he will also try to kill all the nightmares when he gets the sword…He believes your blood will kill Dentro.

"And will it?"

I believe it could.

"So, it's true…my father is Mavi?" I felt my anxiety relax a little. To not be Dentro's child was a weight off my shoulders.

She nodded.

"Is there any other way for him to get the Sword?" I asked before emotion took over my clear thinking.

No, and an Enchantress from Kanna's and my bloodline must do the spell.

Nilsa! Then I quickly pushed the thought away. What if she could also read my mind and not just speak into it?

"The King mentioned something about me being willing blood."

Yes, you must willingly sacrifice yourself, as Mavi did, in order to have your blood be pure and healing. She sighed. Mavi wasn't just killing Dentro, he was ridding the realm of the sickness that was eating the land. The anger and the fear flooded the land and it will only become worse since there is no hope in the land any longer. The King is not being the light the Ivars need to thrive.

"If I did it… it would bring light into the realm again?"

Yes, she said sadly, *but you can't do this you would die, and the King would slaughter all the Nightmares, and I will not lose you again. Let that be selfish.*

"Is there no other way? A leader that could bring light?"

It would help very little; the land would still die and break, just slower. The cliff shuttered as darkness slammed against the castle trying to get out. I grabbed onto a rock and pulled out my knife. It was the same coldness that came from Asher's shadows.

Navara stood and looked down. *Run my daughter!*

I looked down and saw the pale ghost of a man standing at the bottom of the cliff. "We need to leave."

Missy was already on her feet. I felt a wave of relief that someone else was finally seeing him as well.

"Who is that?" I asked Navara.

Danger, you need to leave. Quickly. Dentro is looking for me. I have to go.

"But I have questions!"

Go, my child.

She was gone in a flash. Missy pushed me onto the cliff and ordered me to go. My mind was still buzzing with all that Navara said and that I had looked into my mother's eyes. I had seen her smile and heard her voice.

We didn't stop till we were back at the covering with Keane and Asher. The earth shook and broke as darkness pelted against the castle.

"What is going on!" I shouted.

"It's Dentro!" Keane helped me to my feet.

Asher pulled me into his arms. He was drenched in sweat and rapidly breathing, "What happened? Did he discover you?"

"No, I spoke to Navara. I saw her." Her voice was still floating in my mind like a ghost.

"Tell us when we get the hell away from here!" another earth-shattering roll of darkness hit us. Asher's shadows pulled towards the Tower like dogs on a leash. Sweat was now pouring down Asher's face. "Now!"

Keane was knocked to the side by another quake that came from the ground this time. He rolled down the hill and Missy slid down after, grabbing him by the wrist and stopping him quickly.

Soldiers shouted and raced towards us.

I pulled my sword and headed down. Asher was now pacing, seeming to be yelling at his shadows.

The earth shook again and then started to sink; I stopped on a jutted-out lip of rock.

"Sink Hole!" I yelled to them. It was quickly growing. They backed up against the slick dirt edge. Missy dug her blades into the mountain and Keane grabbed a vine. The soldiers shot arrows while backing away, confused about what to do. They turned and ran back to safety.

Missy and Keane began to slip, Asher couldn't make his way safely to the rocks to help me pull both up and his shadows weren't helping. I reached Keane, prepared to take his weight and pull him up.

Missy took an arrow to the shoulder, causing her to drop the hold on one of the knives. She clutched to just one and a sliding rock under her feet. A Nightmare stood at the edge of the hole, smiling triumphantly. I tried to pull Keane up fast. Another arrow hit her back. Screaming, she let go of the knife. Her foot slipped, and the earth swallowed her.

"No! No! Missy!" I was screaming for Keane to hurry up for Asher to get a grip on himself and to help Keane; then we were running.

TWENTY-EIGHT

We spent two grueling days traveling back to the camp in complete silence. Asher's shadows swarmed around him angrily and Asher seemed to be whispering to them. We had a brief conversation about what my mother said, then back to silence.

It was weird looking at her. I felt a connection to her. The way she looked at me, the way she talked. Keane said he understood that and that he felt a connection with his family. Asher just shrugged and said he wouldn't know.

"What did she say about Mavi? Is he your father?" Keane asked.

"We didn't have much time to talk, then everything went to hell real fast."

"And what about the 'willing blood'? It sounds like the King can't kill you," Asher said.

"No, but…" I scrubbed a hand across my tired face and rolled the thoughts around in my head. If sacrificing myself would rid the world of Dentro and perhaps heal the land of Hatheya, maybe it would be worth it. What was one life to save thousands? War was a whisper in the wind for both Ivar and Nightmares. When that would come to pass was still a question.

"But what?" Asher asked, "Don't tell me you believe Kandem is telling the truth about being able to kill Dentro with your blood?"

He shook his head and placed his hands on my shoulders, making me look at him. "Don't even think about doing that, I won't have you running off to kill yourself, especially since we don't even know if Kandem is telling the truth."
I tried shrugging off his hands, but he gripped me a little tighter, "No, Ren. Please."

Keane had started walking away, giving us room. The plea in Asher's voice must have made him realize Asher and I needed to talk. We were a hill away from the camp now and once we were there I planned on shuffling away to my tent to process what happened at the tower and to mourn Missy. I barely knew her, but she still deserved someone to mourn her death.

"Ren, please." He hugged me. It took me a minute to relax in his embrace. His heart was still racing. A slight shake in his hands. Being that close to the tower hurt him somehow.

"I'm so confused," I whispered, pulling him closer.

Asher kissed the top of my head then quickly pulled away, "Keane needs us," we ran swiftly over to where Keane was hiding behind a tree and waving us over.

"It's Bexley and Zyra," he said as we reached him.

In the camp, Bexley stood with a handful of Ivar soldiers and our group. They seemed to be having a civilized conversation at the moment, but all of them were straight-backed and on edge.

"What is he doing here?" I checked our surroundings for any archers.

"His sister did say he claimed to be with a rebel group, both Ivar and Nightmare."

"That's still hard to believe," Asher said, "But we do seem to outnumber him. At least what is visible" His shadows scurried along the ground checking for any other unknown soldiers. After a moment, Asher stepped out into view and casually walked over to Bexley. "Nice to see you again," Asher flashed a devious smile, earning him a frown from Bexley.

"You," Zyra stepped forward, "you're the one traveling with the human."

I took that as my cue to make my appearance, "and you two were the ones who tried to torture me for information I didn't have," I said snarled.

"Awe, Keane, I wondered if it was you who helped them get away," Bexley eyed Keane and me as we made our way over to the gathered groups, ignoring Zyra and me glaring at each other.

Keane didn't say a word as we stood before his old general. He didn't waver his gaze either as Bexley looked him up and down then turned to me, "Still alive, I see."

"Should I not be?" I said haughtily as his brown eyes pierced into me, searching for information.

"I heard word from one of my spies that the King wants you dead."

I shrugged, "In a way, yes."

He arched a brow but didn't inquire more as we were surrounded by others who eyed us both with great caution and curiosity.

"Why are you here?" I brushed some dirt from my jacket, trying not to seem too shifty while looking over his soldiers. They wore the Ivar uniform, dark helmets, and masks that covered their faces, only their eyes were seen. That wasn't part of the Ivar uniform. I looked a bit closer at one. He shifted his gaze away, but not before I noticed his pupils were more like a goat's than a human's, and another soldier's proportions were off. His arms were much too long and extra fabric had been sewn on to help cover them.

"So, your sister was right. You're working with Nightmares."

"You spoke to my sister?" His face flashed fear for just a moment, then the calmness took over. "When? The last I had heard she had been taken by some of the King's men."

"When we were in Gantrick."

"Yes, I heard you were there," he mumbled, running his eyes over the three of us.

"We are against the King and Dentro." I stepped forward raising my chin, "Are you?"

"Yes, we are." Bexley raised his chin.

"Then let your troops rest and we can talk in the tents." Smiling, I walked away, feeling the shift of power coming my way. "Why didn't you tell me there were Nightmares among them?" I asked Asher.

"I knew you would see it eventually. You're getting better at noticing your surroundings." He gave me one of his lazy grins. I hurried into the tent, ignoring my suddenly quickening pulse, and quieted my mind. I needed a clear head to talk to Bexley and Zyra.

"Do you know what has happened to your sister?" I asked Bexley when they entered.

He shook his head, "I assume the worst at this point."

Keane cleared his throat, "Have you heard anything surrounding my family sir-" He caught himself. Relaxed his shoulders and now looked like Bexley's equal, not one of his foot soldiers.

Bexley noticed the shift in him, though his face didn't reveal how he felt about the change in Keane. "I haven't heard anything specific about yours, but I did hear some went into hiding and others," He paused for a breath, "others were slaughtered by Nightmares if they didn't pledge to Dentro. Those still loyal to the King are also rounding up those who have been said to be against him. I'm sure to be killed in a much more private place. The King is trying to stop those who are speaking out against him."

Keane just gave a quick nod and swallowed.

"I'm sorry soldier," Bexley gave him a hard nod and Keane returned it.

"I should get Nilsa? She should know about what is happening as well. She has family." He left quickly, without meeting any of our eyes.

"Tell us what you know about Bhaltair," Asher said, causally shifting the tension in the air.

"Awe yes, a few of my men have seen him collecting, as they like to put it, Nightmares. We haven't been able to get close to the camp where they're taking them, though. Too many guarding it."

"Dentro's doing," I stated more than asked.

"Yes, I believe so, but he is still trapped in the tower. How his followers intend to get him out is unknown to me. Do you know?" He looked at me like how my father would when I had done something wrong and wanted me to tell him the truth.

"Why would I know?" I said calmly.

Zyra hissed through her teeth, the first noise she had made since entering the tent, "Do not play dumb with us, girl. We are fighting against the same evil and need all the information we can get."

Asher laughed coldly, "And if you had the same information would you share it with us if we asked?"

I stepped between the two as Zyra stepped closer and was thankful that Keane and Nilsa had come in. They paused at the entrance, reading the sudden heated tension that filled the small space.

"Perhaps we need to show our good graces before asking for something from you," Bexley said, "We didn't meet on good terms nor left on them either."

"Do I get a double apology, then?" Asher rolled his eyes, "Perhaps a sorry we flogged you for being a Nightmare?"

Bexley coughed out a laugh, "If I remember correctly, you killed quite a few of my troops and broke one of our most strict laws of not crossing the realm border multiple times putting humans at risk for the sake of," he scoffed, "love."

Asher flew across the room in the blink of an eye, grabbing Bexley around the throat and knocking him to the ground. Zyra drew her sword; Keane drew his, knocking it against Zyra's before she could run Asher through. Nilsa started yelling at both Bexley and Asher as they rolled across the ground, fist flying.

I sighed heavily, exhausted from the days of travel. I wasn't worried about Bexley. If Asher wanted him dead, his shadows would be helping not running across the ground and the sky begging to join in. "Enough!" I screamed at the top of my lungs, sick of them acting like children. The shadows shuttered above me, shaking the tent. I looked up at them as silence fell around me, and then they darted out, striking everyone to the ground except Asher and I. Keane rolled to his side and groaned, "Why the hell did you do that!"

Asher, now with a bloody nose looked over at me. I stood wide-eyed, staring back at him. He shrugged and looked away, "sometimes they have a mind of their own." He wiped his bloody nose with his jacket sleeve.

"Are you okay Nilsa?" Keane asked, helping her to her feet.

She just nodded, looking at me like I was the one who did it. Perhaps my yelling agitated them, but I never felt like Asher would lose control over them.

I cleared my throat, "okay now that we've got that out of our system, are we ready to talk like adults?"

Bexley straightened his clothes and rubbed his neck where Asher had left bruises. I had to hide my smile. He did deserve it, after all.

"Perhaps we should cool off for a bit before talking about war and such," Nilsa fluffed her hair, making sure no knots were tangled in it.

"War?" Bexley pressed a handkerchief to his bloody lip.

Keane must have filled her in on what my mother had told me. I hadn't said war, but Dentro was building an army.

"Why do you think Dentro is taking all those Nightmares?" I said, "He's building an army."

"And how will he command this army within his prison?"

"The Tower is weakening."

Bexley rubbed his beard, "just as our land is."

"His power was able to get out of the Tower. I felt it. We all did," I noted my friend's grim faces.

"When?"

"We were at his Tower just recently."

"What!" Bexley bellowed, "You fools! Why would you go there? The King-"

"The king no longer has control over that territory." Keane stepped in. "They were attacked; I saw with my own eyes. They were burning Ivar's bodies."

"And what of the King?"

"Unknown. We need to send out our spies and see if there is any word about his whereabouts."

Bexley nodded, "Zyra, get on that! We have no time to waste."

She darted out of the tent and started yelling for others. I would hate to be on the receiving end of that bark.

"If the King is dead, at least it will be one less problem for us," sighed Nilsa, a small smile on her ruby lips, her eyes dancing with the thought of death.

"I doubt we're that lucky," I said, "Kandem is smart. He wouldn't get caught so easily."

"And what did the King want with you?" Bexley said, "he had men combing Hatheya looking for you."

I tapped my fingers against our map table, "I'm Gannon's granddaughter, and when Gannon was forced to come back, they thought they could use me as leverage to get him talking. They thought he could know something important."

"Yes, my spies told me he was back, but not as a prisoner. That he was freely walking around in their camp and whispering with the King," he scoffed, his eyes laughing as my cheeks burned with anger.

"Free to those who didn't know what was going on. The King wanted Gannon to feel like he was free and safe as he did to me in Gantrick, but he wasn't. The King killed him for information." I slammed my hand down on the map table, "I don't care if you believe me or not."

"Who told you the King killed Gannon?" The laugh was now gone from his eyes.

"Gannon did with his last breath." I glared, his dark eyes turning haunted like mine as he nodded.

"What will we do against his army?" Nilsa said, breaking the silence and reminding us of many deaths to come.

"Which one? The Kings or Dentro's?" Bexley asked, his hands behind his back and his gaze in the distance, his eyes turning with a million ideas and plans that he needed to execute to have his soldiers prepare for battle. Keane and Zyra's eyes were the same, the faces of soldiers ready to take down death.

"Both, I guess," she said, playing with the cuffs of her dress casually.

"We need to build ours as well," I said.

Bexley gave a quick laugh, "With whom? Not everyone who is not with the King and Dentro will fight. We're on the losing side of things. Unless.."

I turned to him waiting, my face set into a scowl already knowing where this was going.

"If we persuade the King to fight with us, we could destroy Dentro's army."

Asher snorted, "You're kidding, right? You want to fight alongside a man who would gladly slit your throat with a smile on his face! He wants to enslave all Nightmares just as Dentro wants to enslave all the Ivars. They're both evil in their own ways."

"Maybe we wait for them to fight each other and take down each other's defenses, lay a path for us to move in?" Keane inquired.

"We will still need an army to finish off theirs," I said. Then there was always Dentro to worry about. The unkillable creature could wipe out an army that stood in his path. "If we kill the leader, though, who will his followers turn to?"

Bexley said, "If we're able to kill the King, that would liberate quite a few to fight with us without fear of them being called traitors to the King. Their families wouldn't be in danger either." His eyes flashed to Keane for a heartbeat. "But everyone must know why he was assassinated and by which side. If we do it without anyone knowing it was us, they'll think it was Nightmares of Dentro's. They'll pull farther away from helping Nightmares and more towards his cause and not ours."

"We need to spread the word as much as we can about Kandem's intentions," I said, "they also need to see Nightmares and Ivars working together trying to help the communities that have been hit by Dentro and Kandem."

"It's a dangerous time to be doing that." Bexley braced his hands against the table, his eyes distant, "but it could work to our advantage. If they see we're the only ones helping rebuild what the others destroyed, then they'll see that they have-"

"Hope," I interjected, "hope for both the Nightmares, the Ivars, and for Hatheya."

"And what do we do about Dentro?" Nilsa was now lounging in one of the creaking wooden chairs.

"We'll figure it out." I avoided Asher's raging eyes, "Let the others know they'll be camping together for a while and if you have any other troops, Bexley, send them words ASAP."

We left it at that and headed our separate ways, my aching body begging for a bit of rest, but my mind wouldn't let me relax. I laid on my bedroll, tossing and turning, wondering if my life mattered that much. If I had to sacrifice myself to save Hatheya, it would be selfish not to. I scrubbed my tired eyes, deciding to take a walk to the stream.

The bite of the cool water felt refreshing to my dry and chapped lips and face. I sat on one of the larger rocks listening to the babbling brook, trying to block out the noise of the camp and focus just on the sound of the woods. The birds had become more and more quiet. Hatheya seemed to grow sicker. We had found many dead and decaying animals that had succumbed to the sickness of the land as well. My heart ached for this forgotten land, for the selfishness of my wanting to live and not instantly give my life for it. How had Mavi done it? How had he willingly died? Was such a thing possible?

I snapped my head up at the approaching sounds of footsteps.

Nilsa stood next to me, "may I sit?"

I swallowed the lump in my throat and nodded.

"Were you crying?" She kneeled next to me.

Had I been? I wiped my face, "I splashed some water onto my face earlier."

She didn't believe me as her eyes searched mine, giving me a sad smile.

"Did you need something?" I didn't mean to sound cold, but I had too much to deal with at the moment.

"No, I saw something and followed it over here. Now it's gone, but then I saw you and thought perhaps it led me to you?"

I scanned the area, "what did you see?"

"I'm not sure, but I think it was a spirit. Enchantresses are the only ones who can see them, and they come to us for help or to help us when we need it. I have never seen one before, but my grandmother has and would tell me stories about them and how she helped them move on."

"Why would it bring you here?"

She studied me for a moment, "Ferren, if your mother truly is Navara then you are half Enchantress."

I sat up straighter, "I guess you're right."

"There are many types of Enchantresses. Some are warriors and possess battle magic like me, others are connected to the earth and can make beautiful things from it, though they haven't been able to do much for a long time. We all possess a little of it all, but one is stronger than the others."

"And you think even a half Enchantress could possess something like that?"

"I'm not sure. I've never met a half before and if you do possess magic, it wouldn't be as strong, though with your father being who he was," she whispered, "then you could be just as strong. It's something I would have to ask my family about. Any half Enchantress or those they expected to be half Enchantress were killed."

"Right, Ivmare…How could we find out what power I might have?"

"You'll figure it out in time. It just starts to appear, like mine is warrior magic, but lately, I've been a healer," she smiled haughtily.

I looked her over. She wore a lilac dress, dark coal around her eyes, and flat ballet slippers, she didn't look anything like a fighter, but her powers had burned down the castle and the look she always held within her eyes screamed to be let free that fire in her as well.

"Why do you still act like you're back at the castle? You can be yourself here."

She looked down at her dress and shoes, "I guess I don't know how to be myself around others. And I saw you and knew you had to pretend to be something else too, so it was easier to show the real me, the same with Asher…we're all just pretending to be something else."

"I guess you're right."

"Tell me why you were crying?" Nilsa slid up on the rock.

I pulled a blade of grass from the ground and wound it around my fingers. "I'm too selfish to do something that will help Hatheya."

"Oh? And that would be willingly sacrificing yourself?"

I buried my face in my hands cringing at the words, "I have to die."

"It is not selfish of you to want to live, Ferren," she said softly, laying a hand on my back.

"It is when my death can save this realm," My hands muffled my words, but I didn't lift my head I couldn't look at the dying realm around me that I could stop. "Navara said it would have to be an Enchantress from her bloodline and well…" I finally looked up from my hands at her.

"Me? You want me to do the spell?"

"You would have to."

"We're barely related."

"Nilsa, I think this is the only way."

She sighed through her nose, "I will research everything I can, but I must get the text that holds her original spell, and that will require me to go back to Finara, to where my grandmother hopefully still is. She might have some knowledge of it. Or even another way to do this without you having to die."

"I'm not holding out hope for that. I can't."

Her eyes watered, "would that make me a murderer again? To kill you."

"No," I clutched her hand, "you would be a hero for what you will do."

"So, you've made up your mind then? You're going to do this?"

I stared up at the sky, unable to look at her, "If we can't find another way, then I'm going to have to. I'm going to have to die."

TWENTY-NINE

"Sad," Nilsa was flipping through an old Enchantress history book, desperately searching for anything about the spell.

"What is?" Keane leaned over to look at the intricate swirls and markings on the pages.

We all sat around a fire eating dinner, our cold hands wrapped around bowls of soup or plates of slop that had to be farther stretched with the arrival of Bexley and his soldiers. Food was the one thing I missed about being trapped in Gantrick. It made my mouth water just thinking about it.

"How history is always forgotten. How, if we don't like it, we ignore it or change it or destroy it." She flipped the pages, "Do you know most Enchantresses can't read this language anymore? The King didn't want us to have our own language. He wanted us to be part of the Ivars and a lot of the Enchantresses agreed, so they changed their books and destroyed the old ones."

Zyra nodded, "my grandmother told me that many books were destroyed when we started to split apart from the Nightmares, not just books, but art as well. The Nightmares did it too."

"My father said that he always thought that Kandem would be an excellent king, that he was a fair man and cared for his people." I cleared my tight throat, trying not to let tears into my eyes, "but that he had changed, that he reeked of evil, and corruption and he didn't know why…"

Keane ran a hand across his chin, now covered in stubble, "People change, and not always for the better."

"No," Zyra said, "This…this change within the King is different. I saw what Gannon saw," she stared down into the fire, her eyes dark and pained, "it reminded me of an infection. His cruelty started slowly, then took over completely. I wanted out of the service of him. I wanted away that's when Bexley told me he felt the same, how the King would become worse if we didn't do something to stop him."

"What if we can't?" Nilsa closed her book and traced a finger across the runes on the front. It was a short, thick book that she would tuck into the pocket of her dresses and periodically pull out to read. Her new comfort blanket it seemed.

"Think of something happier, Nilsa," I leaned against Asher trying to steal some of his warmth as the wind started to pick up. "Let's go pretend our lumpy cold cots are fluffy warm beds," I smiled.

She smiled back, tucking the book away, "Then fill our bellies with watered-down soup pretending it's delicate sweets that will keep us full."

"Now that sounds amazing." Keane grinned, his eyes far away surely dreaming of food it seemed we would never see again.

"When this is all over, we can sleep in a big fluffy bed again, eating sweets and–oh.." She looked away from me.

Others continued the game of fantasy, raised laughter flowing through the camp. It was a welcome change from the melancholy nights. Asher pulled me in tighter, as he laughed along with the group. He didn't seem to catch Nilsa's sudden change in emotion. I would have to tell him tomorrow about my decision.

Asher didn't look at me as I told him and Keane what I had decided and continued to sharpen his knives.

"Ferren," Keane shook his head then turned to me, "what if Navara and Kandem are wrong?"

"Or you know, lying?" Asher huffed, stabbing one of his knives into a wooden chair till the wood splintered. I had brought Keane and Asher into the map tent and broke the news to them. I was afraid that if I told Asher alone, I would talk myself out of it or would break down crying trying to explain everything to him.

"That's one of the reasons Nilsa is going to be doing some research. We won't do the spell until we have the information."

"All the information," Asher stood and finally put the knives away.

"The most we can find, yes."

Keane grabbed me and hugged me tight, "I feel like I'm saying goodbye to another family member."

I hugged him back, "We have time, I'm not doing it until Nilsa gets the spell," we let go of each other.

Asher gave us a quick look before shaking the jealousy from his face. It almost made me smile, but I scolded my face. He was not in the mood for teasing.

"What do we tell Bexley?" Asher asked coldly.

"Nothing. We keep this between the four of us. The fewer people that know, the better."

"Dentro is going to send people after you and try to kill you before you can do this." Asher stepped closer to me, his dark eyes pleading.

"Do you think he knows?" I asked.

"He might."

Keane's face was pinched, "definitely need to keep this on the down low then. Hopefully, he doesn't know."

"I'm sure Navara told him," Asher breathed.

I shot him a look, "why do you think that?"

He just shook his head, "Don't be fooled by her. You're smarter than that."

"Even if she told him and is playing us, the sacrifice is still worth looking into and seeing if it can save Hatheya. Nilsa needs to travel back to Finara and see if she can find her grandmother. That's where we need to start anyway, by trying to rebuild and gather help from. If we go there together, we'll keep eyes off of Nilsa and let her research what she can."

"Does she still think they're there?" Keane asked.

"Yes, her family has worked with the King for many years, and she doesn't think he would touch them and anger the Enchantress clans."

"Unlike my family," Keane said under his breath.

Asher gave Keane a quick pat on the back.

"We need to tell Bexley we're going to Finara," I rubbed the back of my neck. I hadn't slept last night, but tossed and turned. Even the warmth of Asher's body next to mine couldn't cast away the anxiety running through me.

"I'll talk to him," Keane ducked out of the tent.

"I'm worried about him." My arms fell slack at my sides. My body felt heavy. "Maybe he'll find out something about his family when we go to Finara?"

Asher shook his head quickly, "Pray not. If we can find something out that means others could too, they could use his family against him."

"Like they did to my father," my lips curled at the thought.

Asher stepped closer to me, "Ren-"

"No," I said quickly, "Don't let your heart lead when in battle. I always thought that it was cruel when I saw that written in my father's journals, but I understand it now."

"We're not in battle right now," he pulled me into his arms, encircling me with warmth. My body sagged against his and tears pooled in my eyes. "I'm so scared. About everything," my tears streamed down my cheeks, wetting his jacket.

He pulled me closer, running a hand through the back of my hair, "I am too."

I sniffed, pulling back just enough to look up at him. His eyes were heavy with worry, "I can't lose you, Ren. I'm terrified of losing you and here you go, running off into danger, trying to kill yourself."

"I don't want to, but I have to," my voice clipped.

"No," His hands slid down my arms to my hands. He gripped them in his, running his thumbs across the backs. "You don't. We will find another way. I promise you I will do everything in my power to find another way." He quickly pulled me forward his lips parting mine as he kissed me deeply. My breath hitched as kissed me again, hungry and desperate. "Ferren, I need you." He said with his lips against mine. He took a breath and pulled away.

My head spun with lust. I didn't want him to pull away. I wanted him closer. Wanted to feel safe, to feel wanted, and I suddenly realized that we never had a date. We never got to sit down some place quiet and learn everything about each other. More tears filled my eyes. I wanted him to feel safe and wanted by me as well. I didn't want him thinking of death or losing me.

He brushed the tears from my eyes, "I'm going to protect you."

I cleared my throat, "I'm going to protect you too."

He looked shocked. Then he gave a shy smile before pulling me back to his mouth.

THIRTY

The sun seemed to disappear overnight. It stayed cold and windy. Rain poured down, stifling any hope of having a fire and warm food. Even when the rain stopped, the wind remained. The grass and flowers withered and died from the sudden burst of coldness and darkness.

"Dentro grows stronger, and our realm's hope is fading," Bexley shook his head, spraying water around the tent. I bit out a curse as cold droplets hit my face.

We were all bitterly cold and sore, our clothes seemed to never dry, making the grumbling around camp constant. Keane seemed on edge and pushed the training harder, saying the rain and wind would be there when we fought and to get used to it. I had to agree with him. I can't count the number of times I was forced to camp out in such weather as a child. At least we had a few tents, but it didn't completely keep the cold from seeping into our bones.

"Our horses need food. They're starving," Zyra said.

"Much like everyone else," snorted Keane, "most of the animals we find are rotting from the inside out, not even the Nightmares can eat them."

Asher made a gagging sound, "Sorry to disappoint, but not all nightmares enjoy the taste of rotting infected flesh."

Keane winced and gave Asher an apologetic look.

Zyra rolled her eyes, "We need to find better shelter, an abandoned town perhaps and food before we all die."

"My, you're such a downer," Nilsa flowed into the tent wearing an off-the-shoulder top corset she cut from one of her dresses and made the bottom into a heavy cape and a long skirt with high slits up the side. Gone were the bows and lace that used to drench her.

Bexley and Zyra stared at her as if they didn't know who she was.

"Aren't you cold?" Keane asked, eyeing her legs sticking out from the slits as she sat, then quickly looked away, his cheeks flushing pink.

"No," she snapped her fingers and fire appeared in her hands, "I'm quite warm, actually."

Zyra curled her lips back, either in disgust or jealousy. I was so cold I would gladly step into the fire just to feel warmth return to my body.

Zyra said, "Put on actual clothes before we ride to Finara."

Nilsa ignored her lounging back in a chair as if nothing in the world was wrong. I, on the other hand had knots in my stomach about what we would find in Finara regarding Nilsa's and Keane's families. I was worried about leaving Asher behind, but we needed someone here to help manage the camp, and I knew how Asher felt about Finara. Just at the mention of it, his eyes would burn with anger.

"Let's hurry up!" Zyra threw her pack over her shoulder, "we have a long ride ahead of us."

I frowned, following her out. When we told Bexley we were going to Finara to see if Nilsa's family had any information about the spell Kanara had placed on the tower, he thought it was a good idea, but insisted Zyra join us, and perhaps we could recruit others to our cause. It wasn't a bad idea. Zyra wasn't my first choice to come with us, but she was a hard worker and passionate about wanting to heal Hatheya, so that made up for some of her intense personality.

Asher sighed and stuffed his hands in his pockets, looking around as we approached the horses.

"No sign of Eira yet?" I asked solemnly. The little fox never returned to camp after the trip to the tower and it was beginning to worry both of us. Asher had gone out a few times to look for her, but had no luck. I could only hope she wasn't sick like so many other animals around here.

"I knew I should have made her stay here instead of following us to the Tower." He patted the horse's side, "She'll find us when she's ready. Come on, I'll help you saddle your horse."

I gave a small laugh, "Already done, but thank you," I expected him to smile back or even say a quick quip about it, but instead, he sighed and closed his eyes for a second. "You don't need to worry about me. I'm going to be fine."

"I promised to protect you, and I can't do that if I'm miles away." He cupped my cheek, his chilly hand sending a jolt through me, "and if I recall, you promised the same thing and you can't do that if you're miles away."

I couldn't help but smile again, my cheeks and neck burning red, "I feel like no matter how far away you are; you'll always find a way to protect me."

He grinned, "Never forget that." He pulled me into a hug, warming my body instantly. I sighed, trying to let go of the fear that was eating away at me, and I felt him do the same.

It was a long tiring trip back to Finara even with the horses. We kept quiet and pushed through until we had to rest the horses, hunt, and sleep, then we were back to racing through the dying and foggy forests. My face burned from the wind, my body ached from riding and my heart never stopped pounding with adrenaline even when I slept. It felt as if my body was pumping anxiety through my veins instead of blood.

I didn't know if I was anxious about Nilsa's grandmother telling us I had to die or that she had no knowledge about any of it. I just wanted a straight-forward answer from someone we could trust, then maybe my heart would calm down a bit.

We left the horses deep in the woods next to a stream and a bit of shelter then continued on foot to the town. Our breath curled around us from the cold, the icy rain pelted us as we finally made it to the town. Houses that once stood tall were scorched, reduced to nothing but splintering wood. Bloody spots covered the roads, windows were smashed, and stores were broken into and cleaned out. It was silent and felt hollow.

"The houses have crosses in their lawns," Nilsa pointed to a few.

"They're marking how many died there," Zyra remarked quietly.

There were so many grave markings across the lawns that my stomach turned. "How can they be doing this? Both sides are doing this…"

"Keep your head girl," Zyra said, eyeing me, "we're here to show them we're strong, a united group that can lead them to peace."

I gave a quick nod as we darted through the town until we came to a burned building where we hunkered down for the night. Tomorrow we were to find food and any living sympathizers to the Nightmares and see who we could get to come back with us or even stay here and fight for the town if there were enough people.

I stared up through a hole in the roof and watched the dark skies flash with lightning. I tossed and turned, feeling dread seeping into my body. Something was wrong. I scanned the house, checking in with Zyra, but the ache didn't dissipate. It felt like one of my nightmares. The dark figure hovering over me reaching his hand out.

I didn't sleep. Dark circles hung under my eyes and dark thoughts hung in my head. The only saving grace was the appearance of the sun.

No one strayed from their houses. They were shut closed against the wind and unwanted guests. We checked empty homes, scavenging what food, blankets, and clothing we could. If we saw a person, they were quick to run in the opposite direction, not giving us a chance to talk to them.

"Nilsa!" A demanding whisper came from a dark home with broken windows and a burned roof. "Get in quick!" snapped a woman with the same red hair as Nilsa and crow's feet around her eyes.

"Mom?" Nilsa gasped, rushing to her.

Her mom shoved her inside and harshly did the same to us.

"What do you all think you're doing? Walking down the middle of the street like that! You're all going to end up dead!" She was a tall, thin woman with fierce eyes. She wore a heavy black sweater that hung loosely on her frame and a skirt that was tied with a belt around her waist.

"Mother, please, we need your help," Nilsa grabbed her mother's hands and looked shocked at how bony her wrists were.

She pulled her hands away and tucked them into her sweater, smiling mournfully as Nilsa.

"Nilsa?" An old brittle woman stepped out from a room, her face beaming. She was leaning heavily over a cane; a gray shawl hung over her hunched shoulders.

"Grandmother," Nilsa hugged the woman tightly as her mother continued to shake her head.

Nilsa turned to us, "This is my grandmother, Agatha, and my mother, Nelly."

Hello, we all said awkwardly. Agatha smiled at us, but Nelly just frowned. Worry lining her face.

"Did you offer them any tea or food?" Agatha said, hobbling into the kitchen with her daughter on her heels.

"Lovely mother you have." Zyra peeked out the window and locked the door.

Nilsa pursed her lips and glared.

"Here," Nelly laid a tray of old berries and thin slices of meats down on the table. Agatha slowly lowered herself into a chair and patted Nilsa's hand.

"I was so worried about both of you," Nilsa said after she took a breath, "I've been with the rebels and unable to look for either of you."

"The rebels?" Her mother scoffed, "So you can also end up dead like so many others?"

"Nelly," Agatha scowled, her wrinkled face looking frightening.

"If we don't stand up and fight, we'll end up dead anyway, or ruled by a dictator wishing we were dead," I said harshly.

"I thought you were dead, Nilsa." Nelly turned her back to me, "I didn't know where you were or what was going on. Then they came. Those Nightmares, they killed so many…so many we knew, and the King was hunting down any rebels that even whispered about wanting Ivars and Nightmares to be together."

"I'm so sorry, Mother," she wrapped her arms around her crying mother, "but Ferren is right, we need to fight. You used to tell me about how you felt like a slave to the King, that you dreamed of being free and now is our chance to become what we once were when Mavi ruled."

"The clans will spread the word," Agatha said sternly, eyeing her daughter, "we will as well."

"Where are the other Enchantresses?" I had seen a few here when we were first taken and a few in Gantrick, but I was sure there were more.

Agatha sighed, "Scatter here and there. Some fled to the mountains after the King started using us for his needs. Others hid, afraid of their powers."

Nilsa smiled sadly at the old woman who looked pale but determined, "Grandmother, I was hoping to look through some of your old books."

"And why is that?" Nelly asked, wiping away her tears with a handkerchief Keane had given her.

Nilsa didn't respond as she helped her grandmother up and they slowly padded down a short hallway. I hoped Agatha and Nelly wouldn't have to flee their home. Agatha wouldn't be able to escape. I swallowed, hating myself for thinking that, but this was the reality we lived in. We were all prey and the strong had to try to protect the weak.

Nelly turned to us, her face full of anger and fear.

"Well," I said, trying to sound casual, "is there anyone here who could use our help?"

"Or those willing to fight with us?" Zyra ask.

Nelly pursed her lips with contemplation.

"If you tell us, we can get out of your house," I picked at some of the food on the platter until I gave in to my hunger and shoved it into my mouth instantly feeling guilty that I was taking food away from them.

She sighed, "As much as I would like you all to leave my house, I can't send you out there. The guards probably already know you're here anyway and anyone you talk to is in danger."

"We were careful and avoided any main roads and clearings. You are safe from the King," Zyra said, her voice sharp.

Nelly bristled, "It's not just the King that we fear you stupid girl. I know Dentro will soon break free from his prison. I can feel it." She sunk into the chair; her face suddenly exhausted.

Zyra stepped forward and I quickly stood, blocking her path. "Why hasn't Kandem done anything? He says he wants to protect the Ivars from the Nightmares, yet keeps abandoning them."

Nelly started shaking, "he's taken anyone who can fight and told me and my mother to stay here. My house has a protection enchantment on it. He said he would be back for us." She fidgeted with the handkerchief, "I'm not saying he is a good man, but he is the lesser of the two evils at the moment," she looked up at us, "I swear I have seen Nightmares and Ivars here, together." She raised her hand to stop me from talking. "They have taken those that I know have been working against the King."

"Nightmares working for Kandem?" I scoffed.

"I have seen it with my own eyes," she seethed, "something is not right."

"No Nightmare would work for him," I shook my head and leaned back against the plush couch. It was a small home with worn furniture, not a place where I thought two Enchantresses who worked for the King would live.

"Are we still so split down the middle that Ivars and Nightmares can't work against their *kings*? Isn't that what you're doing?" Nelly looked triumphantly at that. She crossed her arms and stuck her chin in the air, "That's what you're all doing, just in different ways."

The spies confirmed that the Ivars were Kandem's, and we assumed all the Nightmares were Dentro's, but I don't remember a report about that being true.

Zyra caught my eye. We needed to discuss this away from Nelly, then send a spy out to see if we could get information soon. If Kandem could convince Nightmare to work with him, then we would have problems. "Nelly, we need to find others that are willing to join the rebels. We want the Nightmares and Ivars to live alongside each other and to stop the dying of Hatheya, but we can't do that with how few there are of us."

Her eyes fell away from my face and to the floor, "I don't know…"

Zyra huffed angrily as she returned to her spot at the door, periodically checking out the window, with Keane doing the same.

"It's okay to be afraid," I said, "I don't blame you or anyone who is. You're afraid for Nilsa and for others you care about. I understand that." Fear was constantly in the pit of my stomach, threatening to take over and force me to give up. I was tired of death.

Nelly suddenly stood, "Don't act like you understand the wall they put up between us human."

I flinched at her cruel words and wondered where she had learned I was from the human world.

"I was raised in an Ivar realm, but I am a Nightmare, and I have heard the stories from my mother of what happened when Mavi died and how she was ripped away from her friends who were Nightmares. How the divide started slowly then became harsh and cruel, how the Enchantresses became servants and slaves of the King, how Ivars were forced to be savage to Nightmares when Mavi made them to be protectors of all. It has broken my heart more times than you know. You know nothing human."

I launched toward her, making her stumble back, "I do not come from a peaceful realm! I have seen misery and bloodshed. I've seen people divided from what they look like, and for what they believe, I have seen riots and destruction over it. Nelly, I am not from a fairytale land." Taking a breath, I stepped back before more anger erupted..

Nilsa and her grandmother were standing in the doorway. Nilsa was clutching a few books, looking between her mother and me. Agatha hobbled forward, wrapping me in a hug. I stiffened and then sank into her. It had been so long since I'd had a motherly hug. My eyes stung with tears. A sudden pain for my parents hit me. My mom would hug me like this every day. I pulled away feeling as if I would crumble at any moment if I allowed myself to spiral down in those emotions and avoided looking at anyone, suddenly feeling awkward about my display of emotions at a time like this.

Nilsa stepped forward, "I found some books that might help us, though it is going to take some time reading through all of them," she didn't look too hopeful saying this.

My shoulders sagged, "All right, we should get going."

Nelly grabbed Nilsa, "You should stay here," her eyes pleading.

"I can't," Nilsa looked down, "I have to help them."

Nelly laid a hand on her daughter's cheek before pulling her into a hug and quickly letting her go, "You be safe, you hear me? You will come home."

"Come with us," Nilsa said, "you're no longer safe here." She looked from her grandmother to her mother, her eyes wide with panic.

Agatha shook her head, "No, I need to find the other Enchantresses. Call them to help us. Go, child, we will be fine."

Nilsa gave them another hug tears sliding down her cheeks.

"I need to stay with my mother," Nelly said, "I will help her. Now go before someone finds you here."

THIRTY-ONE

We carefully slinked out the back door and wound around the streets, seeking those who would join our cause, but most kept their doors tightly closed against us.

"Hello," said a voice.

I pulled my daggers, turning to the sound.

They stepped into the light, their hands up a dark hood over their face, "I am not going to hurt you. I saw you sneaking into town earlier and wanted to talk."

Zyra scoffed, "Who are you?"

"My name is Flynn Bowen; I was a trader here in the market."

"And now?" I asked, "What are you?"

He gave a soft laugh, "Now I help those who don't necessarily like what is happening within our realm."

I sighed at his answer, "What is it that you don't like? Give a straight answer. We don't have time for games."

"We want change. Neither the King nor Dentro is who we want to lead us. We're tired of the divide and the cruelty from and to both sides," he put his hands down, "I know you are Zyra's, second in command of Bexley. I know that you and he are rebels of Hatheya and we would like to join your cause," he gave a small bow.

"There are others?" Keane asked.

"Oh yes, many. We have tried our best to stay hidden. There are even some still working with the King. They tell us when raids are going to happen so that we can move around more easily."

"And where are all these people now?" Zyra growled.

"Come, I'll show you," he stepped away.

"And how can you prove this isn't a trap before we follow you?" Zyra's voice was still rough.

He turned back to us, "I can't."

"You just want us to blindly follow you?" Nilsa shook her head and grabbed Keane who was holding her satchel of books, "that sounds like we're going to end up dead.

"I'm trusting that you are who I think you are and that you aren't leading death to my friends. It's your decision if you want to trust me the same way."

"Let's go," I stepped forward, intent on following him.

Zyra grabbed me, "Are you stupid or just have a death wish?"

"Nilsa and Keane will be our lookout. If we're not back soon then assume us dead and get back to camp."

"What if they torture you for information and you give up the camp and everything we know?" Zyra's grip tightened.

"Then you come with us and if they look like they're about to capture us, stab me," I said flatly.

"Don't think I won't," she said through grinding teeth.

"Ferren," Keane sighed.

"I'll be fine. This might be our only chance to find others that will help."

"Quickly," Flynn said.

Zyra harshly told Nilsa and Keane what to do and glared at me as we followed Flynn to a bakery. "In here and down the stairs," he waved us in franticly.

Down the stairs was a cramped room consisting of five others, a small table, and a candle that didn't produce much light. "This is not all, but they will contact the others for you. It's too dangerous to have everyone meet."

"Flynn," a fair-haired, rounder woman gripped him tight as he pressed a kiss to her temple.

"My wife, Sasha."

"Hello, you must be the other rebels?" She grinned at us.

"Ferren and Zyra," I said.

Flynn finally flipped his hood off, revealing a mop of brown hair and a short stubble of a beard. It was too dark to see much of anyone's features.

"We're so excited to see you both," Sasha handed us glasses of water and I gulped mine, letting the cool water run over my chapped lips and dry throat. Zyra gave me a shocked look, glancing worriedly at her water. She thought it could be poisoned. I gulped the lump that rose in my throat and could feel my father rolling in his grave at my stupidity. Think before you act.

I handed back the now empty cup, "Thank you," I said tightly.

Zyra handed hers back, "not thirsty."

Sasha just nodded and smiled at both of us.

"Let me introduce you to the others," Flynn moved to a middle-aged man with dark skin, "This is Mavric, a farmer."

"Retired now that they burned down the farm," he said gruffly.

"Laker, another market worker from here."

Laker nodded to us. Her face pinched together nervously. She was an older woman with short blonde hair and perfectly oval eyes. I'm sure before all this worry about Hatheya she was a beautiful woman, but now she looked sickly and overworked.

"And these two are Casflix and Jovie. They're both Nightmares," Flynn smiled.

"Jovie from Sonder?" I stepped closer to the tall woman, who was hidden in the shadows.

"Indeed," she purred, stepping into the flickering light and flashing her yellow teeth at me, "wonderful to see you again."

"I have to say I'm surprised to see you again."

She clicked her nails together, "Why is that? Do I not look the part of a rebel?"

I cleared my throat and stepped away, trying to get a look at Casflix. A fishlike creature with bug eyes and a small mouth. He blinked his giant eyes at me. I felt my skin shiver from the way he looked at me, like I was lunch.

"We want to help in any way we can," Sasha said.

Zyra stepped forward bracing her hands against the table the candle glowed eerily against her face, "war is coming, and we need soldiers. Do not come to us unless you are willing to die for your cause," she glanced around the room, eyeing each of them. "We are gathering troops to not only fight against the King but also Dentro."

"How do we stop Dentro?" Mavric asked, "Not even Mavi could stop him."

"We're working on that," I blurted.

Zyra threw a glance over her shoulder. We still hadn't told her how we were working on stopping that, but the fewer people who knew, the better.

"How?" Jovie was now back in the shadows with Casflix.

"We'll tell you when we have all the answers," I responded.

Jovie fluttered her eyes, "And when will that be? After we go to battle with Dentro and all die?"

"No, I- I will do what needs to be done before then."

She clicked her nails together again, but thankfully, stayed quiet. I could feel concern and doubt rising in the room. "You must trust me," I said, keeping my voice level and powerful.

"I do," Flynn chirped, his wife nodding along with him.

"We need a safer meeting spot," Zyra said, bringing them back to her, "go and get everyone who will fight with us. Gather weapons, food, clothing, and medical supplies, and at all times be prepared to fight. We don't know what Dentro is planning or how much longer the tower will hold him, but once he's out, hell will be unleashed upon Hatheya. The King will not hold back once that happens either."

"We can't simply abandon our towns," Laker said. "If we do, many more will die."

"What if we strike first? At least at the King? Weaken him so we can take back a bit of our towns and be more prepared for Dentro?" Mavric asked.

Zyra shook her head, "we will lose more soldiers that way. We're hoping the King will take the brunt force of Dentro's attack."

They all nodded except for Jovie, "we just wait around until then?"

"We do not have the numbers to fight anyone head-on. And most Nightmares don't have the proper training to fight in a war."

"And the Ivars do?" Jovie scoffed, "Didn't they stop the mandated training?"

Zyra crossed her arms, glaring at her. Exhaustion wore heavily on her face, but she squared her shoulders. She was much shorter than everyone in the room, but at that moment, she seemed as if she was towering over them all.

Flynn lit another candle as the other one started to die out. "We're all required to train. Nothing as intense as it was, but battle is bred into us. We pick up on how to train faster, how to handle weapons, and survive. It's how Mavi made us all." She flicked a nervous glance at me. I wasn't sure how to dilute the tension within the small room. Talking of war and fighting wasn't something that put people at ease, especially when we didn't know what our enemies were doing.

"We need to handle this quickly," I said, "Zyra's plan of branching out and finding others willing to fight is the best option at the moment." I turned to Zyra, "Make a plan of where to meet and quickly." I didn't want to have Keane coming looking for us. We told them we would be quick and then find them near the horses.

A round of agreements circled the table before we left the stuffy room.

"Thank you," Flynn said. "You have our trust and I hope we have yours?"

Zyra eyed him carefully before responding, "If they come through for us, then perhaps."

He smiled, but it didn't reach his eyes, "remember you are asking us all to put our lives on the line, and though this cause is something we all believe in, it is still hard to die for it without a second thought."

"Thank you," I gripped his hand, feeling elated at finding help, but a crushing sense of fear suddenly washed over me.

I swallowed and looked up at the sky as morning was trying to break free of the darkness. His words burned my soul. How true his words rang in my ears over and over as I followed Zyra back through the town and to the horses. So many people were going to die. They were going to die for something they all believed in. So many had already died. As soon as we found out if my sacrifice would truly stop Dentro, I would do it. No more second guesses, no more selfishness. I needed to do it to save many.

"Why are you pouting?" Zyra asked, "We did what we came to do and yet you look as if your dog just died."

I studied Zyra's back as she walked with such confidence. Never stumbled or looked afraid. I had heard the camp whispering about her, how she became one with whatever weapon she was using, as if it was a part of her. She clawed her way up to captain next to Bexley and the King. She did it on her own, too. None of her family held sway with the King.

I cleared my throat, "Zyra, are you afraid of dying?"

She stopped walking after a moment but stayed silent, looking deep into the trees. I narrowed my eyes at where she was looking, but couldn't see anything. I gripped my knife, readying myself for an attack.

She turned around, her eyes searching mine, "I think I have become friends with the thought of death taking me. I have fought many battles and have been wounded to the point where I thought I was going to die, and I was scared, but as time went on, I finally gained peace with death. I don't let it control my actions or thoughts."

I looked down at my worn shoes, afraid she could see into my desperate soul.

"Are you afraid?"

"Yes," I croaked out ashamed of my unsteady voice.

"I do not have the right words to help ease that burden. It is something everyone in a war must go through. Hopefully, you find peace," She turned back around.

"Me too," I whispered into the wind.

Nilsa emerged from a hidden cove, "finally."

"Town seems quiet still," I looked over my shoulder.

"Good," Nilsa said, "perhaps, that means they're okay."

"I'm sure they are," I squeezed Nilsa's shoulder; sorrow laced my eyes.

"What happened? Did you find others willing to help?" Keane asked.

Zyra mounted her horse, "hopefully we can rely on them."

THIRTY-TWO

*N*ilsa tried to read the books as we traveled back to the camp, but the weather was harsh and made us keep our heads down for most of it, but as soon as we got back she was in our tent pouring over them as quickly as possible.

I slid off the horse, grunting in pain and handing the reins over to a Nightmare that was tending to the other horses, grateful to be off the saddle. I didn't see Asher as he rushed over to me and grabbed me into a hug. "I told you I would be okay," my voice was muffled by his chest.

He let go, "everything went okay then?"

I nodded tiredly, "I'll tell you all about it in the warmth of the tent."

We laid on his cot facing each other as I told him about Finara. He traced his hand up and down my spine and kissed my neck, making me smile. I had to shove him away to tell him to finish my story about Finara.

"It was eerily quiet there."

"Most are in hiding."

"No," I leaned my forehead against his, "most are dead."

"I'm glad Jovie is fighting with us. She knows a lot of Nightmares and can sway them to our side. I'm glad she's alive." He swallowed tightly.

I brushed his lips with a light kiss, "Me too." For Asher's sake, I was glad someone he knew was still alive. Someone he knew before our lives turned to horror.

We only had a little time together before we had to meet with Bexley, and I quickly checked on the camp and how everyone was getting along. There were still a few that were weary of each other, but other than that, it seemed to be running smoothly even with Bexley. I hated to admit it, but it was probably Bexley who had helped it. He knew how to deal with soldiers.

Bexley laid out a map and we all scrunched together over it, pointing out towns we needed to scout and what places would be the most beneficial to us as well. I ignored the guilt that we would only go to those who could help us and ignored many of the smaller territories. I hoped they were smart enough to flee when they saw danger.

"The farms have been decimated already," Bexley said when Keane suggested them. "We passed them on the way here. Nothing left to save."

The ground shook, sending us sprawling to the ground. The tent collapsed over us, wrapping suffocatingly around me. I slipped my knife from my boot and cut my way out of the fabric, quickly scanning the shaking camp. Trees cracked to the ground, their rotting trucks and roots unable to handle the force of the shaking earth. Shouts of commands were drowned out by death cries as the ground cracked and shifted. Black shadows rolled across the sky in magnificent and terrifying clouds, turning dark. I squinted, waiting for my eyes to adjust before standing.

I stumbled back, the wind no longer the reason for the bitter cold that sank into my bones. "Asher!" My voice ripped at my throat, "What is happening?" The clouds pooled down to the ground, grabbing at the campers and tearing them apart from within. Their bodies convolute violently, every poor oozed blood.

"Asher! Keane! Nilsa!" I ran from the hungry darkness tripping as the ground shook again. Nilsa stumbled into me. Her face was horrified and panicked, "Are you okay?"

"Asher!" she pointed over my shoulder. Asher stood still, staring at the wall of shadows as it edged closer to him.

Keane grabbed Asher, trying to pull him away, but his shadows leaped at him. Keane jerked away, yelling at Asher to move, but he wouldn't.

I ran to him, grabbing his arm, but he pushed me off, "No, they'll hurt you!"

"What is happening?" I was beginning to panic trying to grab ahold of him, but his shadows would leap toward me like they did to Keane. "Move Asher!"

His shadows pushed him forward. He reached out, catching his balance with his hand brushing the darkness. He froze, dropping his hands to his sides, took in a breath, and smiled ruthlessly at me before walking forward.

"No!" I lunged to grab him; Nilsa pulled me back before I could touch him.

The darkness swallowed him. The earth shook again. Nilsa and I stumbled away from the darkness. More trees collapsed; the earth split around us. We jumped over the cracking ground, tumbling in mud that sprayed us in the face.

I wiped it from my eyes, gaping at the sudden stillness. The darkness was replaced by a dimming sun. Nightmares and Ivars stood around, confused and frightened.

"What the hell just happened!" Bexley yelled, "Zyra, get me a body count! Keane find Ferren!"

I stood up slowly, I was breathing too fast, and my heart pounded out of my chest. It took Asher. It took him. Keane was at my side, helping me stand.

"Did Asher do that!" Bexley was in my face. "He walked straight into that thing."

"No-no, he fought it," I swallowed. My throat burned from screaming.

"That's not what I saw," Bexley grabbed my arm, dragging me out of the mud pit Nilsa and I had landed in.

Nilsa shoved Bexley aside, "Leave her alone."

I couldn't breathe. My mind spun. Nausea burned my stomach and my eyes blurred. I stepped out of the suffocating circle of people and tried to take a breath. "Asher couldn't have caused something like that. That- that.." I shook my head, stepping farther away from them. "Dentro."

Bursts of concern came from what was left of our group. "He broke out of the tower!" someone asked.

"That's not possible," Zyra said. She pressed a cloth to a cut above her brow, wincing as Keane helped with another cut on her lip.

Bexley stood over me, his eyes seething, "the moment he touched the darkness, it went away and him with it."

My nails bit into my palm as my eyes hardened against his, "you think I know what just happened? You think I understand any of it?" My heart pounded with rage. I wanted to scream until my throat bled, I wanted to gouge out Bexley's incriminating eyes as they bored into Nilsa, Keane, and me. "You know that was Dentro. We all do."

"No one else could have controlled that many shadows," Keane's eyes were wide as he scanned the trees for the powerful enemy.

Bexley turned away from us, "Regroup! Pack what we can! We move out within the hour!" His commanding voice reverberated through the camp.

"What about Asher?" I circled to his front, "are we just going to abandon him?"

"My soldiers are not going to go on a death mission to bring back one Nightmare, a Nightmare that potentially brought that death wall here."

"I am not one of your soldiers to command, Bexley. I will go if I please." I stepped up to him, my nails bit into my palms.

Bexley shot me a disdainful look, "We cannot just have people riding off whenever they please and to wherever they want. We need to have order here."

I didn't like how I was being treated as his to command, one of his soldiers. "Don't forget that half of these people are ours. We put them together before you even showed up, so how I look at it, we're the same here."

Zyra snarled at me, but I ignored it.

"Ferren," Bexley took a breath, "what if it's a trap?"

"Then we will deal with it," I snapped, "let's go Keane. See if anyone will help us. Remind them how much Asher helped them."

"He'll be okay," Keane said, taking hold of my arm, "he's strong."

"Stronger than Dentro?" I shook him off and wandered to my tent, anxiety ripping through me. Another worry was placed on my mind, and I was beginning to crumble. I was tired of holding back the pain, the fears, and the exhaustion that had held my body since I stepped into Hatheya. I fell to my knees. The cold ground bit into them and I let a sob break through my lips. I didn't care who heard me. I buried my face in my hands. He had smiled. He smiled when he went into the shadows. A cruel smile. I didn't understand it. He should have fought, but he just stood there waiting for it to take him.

"Oh Ferren," Nilsa gingerly placed a hand on my back. I curled tighter around myself, remembering how Margret tried to comfort me when my father died and suddenly felt guilty that I hadn't thought of her since leaving. I didn't know if she was okay.

Asher could still be alive. I could still save him, but I didn't have much hope. He could be dead right now; he could also be being tortured. My tears spilled at that thought, my body shook from exhaustion. I sat up on my knees and took a breath. My face was caked with dirt and tears. Nilsa grabbed a rag and handed it to me. Her face was blotchy from crying as well. Keane was sitting next to her, his eyes dark, and tear-stained, but he looked more pissed than sad, "we'll find him," his voice was hard.

"And what if all we find is a body?" I didn't want to say that I didn't even want to think about it, but I had to ask if I couldn't hide that fear. Flashes of my father's bloody, broken body on the ground kept recurring. I couldn't see that again, especially to Asher, or else the little part of me that kept me from destroying myself would break.

Keane kneeled before me and cupped his hands around my face, "he saved me from Bhaltair, and I will save him from this."

"We all will," Nilsa wiped her tears away. Even with her blotchy face, she was still stunning, and I suddenly felt self-conscious about the dirt covering my face.

"Why didn't he fight?" I whispered, afraid that Bexley or Zyra were listening in.

They glanced at each other worriedly.

"It was Dentro's doing," Nilsa finally said.

"Definitely," Keane said sternly, "I trust Asher."

I wiped my face with the rag Nilsa had given me and stood trying to say something confident to them or reassuring, but I couldn't speak without my voice giving away to tears, so I instead just nodded. Keane pressed me into a hug, wrapping his arms around me tightly. "I promise you we will find him, and we all will survive whatever is coming our way."

I pushed away, "You know that can't be true. I won't make it."

He stared down at the ground, "give Nilsa time to go through the books."

I sighed heavily. We didn't have time, not if Dentro was out.

"Do you think Kanna even told Navara the spell or Mavi?" Keane asked.

"I'm unsure. It's difficult to create a spell, especially one that involves a sacrifice of blood. It's unnatural even if it was meant for good. If she said one word wrong or moved her hands wrong even in the slightest, it could have been catastrophic. She would have had to practice it, had to have studied hundreds of other spells selecting the right wording and actions." After a moment, she stood and started pacing, "There are other Enchantresses who are sent away. She could have sought one of them out to help."

"Why were they sent away?" Keane asked.

Nilsa pursed her lips, "she could have needed one who was experienced with that type of magic and somewhere she could practice the blood protection spell."

"Practice?" Keane's eyes widened, "on other people?"

"I'm hoping she just used animals, and she wouldn't be able to try all of it. Obviously, animal blood wouldn't heal or help our land."

"No," I wrinkled my nose and rubbed the dirt from my face, trying to distract my mind from the images that came along with those thoughts. "It was a pure spell; she wouldn't have done that; Mavi wouldn't have wanted that."

"That's true," she tapped her chin with her long fingers, "that's part of the reasons those types of Enchantresses are sent away…killing innocent things takes a toll on you. It starts to sicken the mind, starts to kill the goodness within."

"Navara has to know something about the spell. She was spying on them for Dentro."

Keane stood, "she could be the only person that does know."

"Do you think that is how Kandem found out about it? When I questioned Navara about it, she said he had to be talking to the Enchantresses. Maybe the ones from the mountains?" My legs had stopped shaking and my mind became clearer. I needed to get to Asher, which meant I needed to shove my fears and emotions down.

Keane closed his eyes, "If he has, then we have no chance of getting to them," he opened his eyes, "they're either now guarded by his soldiers or all dead."

"We need to find out soon," I said, "and figure out how to get Asher back."

THIRTY-THREE

"Why did it only take Asher?" I was pacing in the new map tent that was significantly smaller, and I could only get three or four steps in before having to turn around, but at least we could fully stand up in it. "It doesn't make any sense." It had been a week now, but I felt like it had been months since Asher had been taken.

Keane leaned back in his chair, "maybe he wanted Asher's power?"

I nodded; Nilsa had mentioned that before. That shadow power could be taken away by another who possessed the same power but was dangerous and resulted in death for usually both the individuals, but Dentro was strong; he could do it. I felt bile rising in my throat again. A cruel image of Asher's body, broken and bruised slammed into my head. I took a shaky step forward, trying to rid the image out of my mind. We didn't know if he was alive or not, but there were things worse than death that could be happening to him right now. I had wanted to run straight to the tower and search for Asher, but word came from our scout that the Tower doors had been opened and that hundreds of Nightmares had migrated to it. I would be dead before I could even get close to the tower.

"Maybe Dentro took him to get at you?" Keane rubbed his tired eyes. I had kept him up most nights. I couldn't sleep and he would sit up with me by the fire until I finally convinced him to get some sleep. Nilsa was just as anxious as I was as she read the books until her eyes blurred. Even now, she slept at the table with a book as a pillow. I'm sure she had read until sleep finally pulled her down.

My head pounding, my eyes heavy with exhaustion. I ran a hand through my hair and started to untangle it just to give myself something to do with my hands. I didn't know how Nilsa kept her hair so curly and perfect in this wind and with nothing to bathe in besides a cold little river.

"Stop pacing, you're making me anxious," Keane stood and stretched.

"Sorry," I stopped and leaned against the table sighing, "I want to go to the tower."

"Ferren, we've talked about that. We wouldn't make it."

"We're pretty confident that is where Dentro keeps those he captured. Shouldn't we be working towards rescuing them?" Bexley and I had spoken in circles about it, but he said the same thing Keane did. Dead before we would make it. They hadn't packed up and left like they wanted since they were still scouting where to go that was safe and what damage the earthquakes had caused. It was looking grim everywhere.

"With what army?" Keane pressed a hand to his eyes, "I hate waiting and watching as much as you do, but we can't be rash.

I started to pace again. Keane gave me an exasperated look as Bexley and Zyra entered the tent with grim expressions.

"Nilsa," Bexley said, his voice tight, his eyes lined with dark circles.

Her head snapped up, sleep still in her eyes.

"I need you to look at some of our soldiers. They've fallen ill."

"What is it? What is wrong with them?" I asked.

"We don't know." Bexley cleared his throat, "we need to hurry."

Nilsa, Bexley, Zyra, and others hovered over an Ivar soldier. Zyra and Bexley had cloths covering their noses and mouths. I stopped at the edge of the tent, suddenly feeling exposed. Should I cover my face like them? What did the soldier have?

"I've never seen anything like this," Nilsa said in a gasp.

I stepped in closer, peering over Zyra's shoulder. An Ivar woman lay on the ground, coughing violently. She shook as if cold, but her brow was slick with sweat. I took a step back and pulled the collar of my sweater over my nose. Black blood was coming from her nose, her eyes were bloodshot and foggy. I wasn't sure she could see anymore. Her veins seem to be trying to push their way out. I swear I could see her heart beating in her chest.

"I can try to take away some of her pain but," she flinched away as the woman started coughing again. "I'm not a healer Enchantress and I can't heal whatever this is." She hesitated to approach the ill woman. "Are there others?"

"Yes, another Ivar. He became sick shortly after her. We're unsure when she fell ill. Her tent mate said she complained of feeling sick just a few days ago but didn't mention it again till she couldn't move."

"And her tent mate? Is she feeling ill in any way?" Nilsa finally laid a hand on the woman and mumbled something under her breath as a soft glowing light pulsed from her hand. The woman shuttered then fell into a deep sleep, her breath ragged.

"I questioned her, and she seemed healthy. No complaints, but I've quarantined her just to be safe. The other soldier hasn't fallen quite as ill, but seems worse every day."

We moved to the other tent Bexley had set up in the quarantined area. "Hello," He coughed out. His eyes were clearer but still red, and he was sweating heavily in the cold. A rag with black blood was clutched in his hand. I saw Bexley eye it and his brow crinkled in sorrow.

"Can- you- help?" The Ivar looked at Nilsa with pleading eyes.

"I will try." She kneeled next to him. She tied a bandana around her nose and mouth. "We need to warn the others around the camp about the sickness and have them report any symptoms of feeling sick." Nilsa wiped her hands roughly on her skirt.

"They already know, and they're scared that it's Dentro's doing. They blame him for our land dying as well." Bexley sighed deeply, running a hand down his beard. "I have also found animals around that have black blood leaking from their eyes and mouths."

"Did they eat any of the animals?" Nilsa asked, still wiping her hands.

"No, we didn't touch them and the two that are sick weren't with me at the time."

"Ivars are part of the realm," I said more to myself than to others, "maybe as the land dies it starts taking them as well."

"If that's true," Zyra said, "then none of the Ivars are safe unless we stop the land from dying and everything in it."

Bexley was stroking his beard and nodding, but his eyes were distant, "perhaps, we don't have time to wait. We need to stop Dentro before the Ivars die out."

"What about the Nightmares, won't they get sick too?" Zyra asked.

"I'm sure they will," I responded, "But Mavi's blood is in this land, and in Ivar's, you're more connected to the land than they are."

Nilsa and I finally made it back to our tent. I sat down and kicked my boots off, sighing with relief as I laid down.

"Do you think you'll get sick?" Nilsa asked worriedly.

I didn't want to think or worry about another problem we had to face. Another thing that seemed impossible to fix. "We can't worry about it right now," I finally said.

"Maybe you won't get sick as fast since you're Ivmare?"

I nodded, "I'm more worried about Keane," Nilsa and I had told him what was happening, but other than that we couldn't do much, so he went off to his tent with new anxieties.

Everyone's face was coated in worry. Worry about when or who would be next to get sick and what would happen if we couldn't fight.

Bexley was more worried about his soldiers getting sick. Nilsa could only take away a bit of their pain at a time.

"She's going to die soon," Nilsa said as we walked along the creek the next day collecting water.

I stayed silent but linked arms with Nilsa.

"Her name is Brit." After a minute she said, "I can't heal her, and I just have to watch her die and soon I will have to watch others die as well." Tears streaked down her face.

"We could stop him; you could do the spell."

"No," she said sternly, "we still don't know if that would work or if Navara was lying."

She sighed deeply, "I don't enjoy taking care of the sick. I know I need to, but I am not skilled with that type of magic."

"I know," I mumbled.

"Have you felt any type of power in you? Anything at all?"

I shook my head; I had completely forgotten about it with everything going on.

Nilsa looked a bit disappointed but didn't say anything else about it.

We told Bexley we needed a way to the Enchantress in the mountains, telling him as little as possible and Zyra even less. I looked at the high frosted mountains that seemed distant enough to be in another realm. Were we really going to go tramping over there on a false hope? We couldn't send a spy for us; what would we tell them we were looking for without explaining it all and we couldn't count on them not to spread the word then everyone that wanted Dentro dead would want me to kill myself and everyone who wanted Dentro alive would want to kill me to keep him alive. Either way, a lot of blood and chaos.

Keane gently shook me awake, "What is happening now?" I stretched my back, making it pop, and noticed I was still in my clothes and boots. I must have fallen asleep talking to Nilsa.

"The King has been spotted marching towards the Tower."

"Are you sure?" I sat up and waited for the dizzy spell to subside.

"A scout came back with the information just a minute ago. We're moving camp today. Zyra and a few others have already headed out."

I had heard rumors about Kandem wanting to attack Dentro at the Tower, but I didn't think he was serious. "Does he have enough troops to even stand a chance against Dentro?"

Keane shook his head, "no, at least not what the scout saw."

"It doesn't make sense why he would go to Dentro. He's crazy, but not stupid."

"Bexley said the same thing. I think it's weird too, but maybe this will help us weaken both sides."

"More like slaughter on one side." I grabbed some food before heading to the map tent with Kenan. Our rebel camp had grown quite a bit from when it first started. Zyra and her scouts had found 200 others who wanted to help us, but that wasn't anything to Kandem's army and Dentro's. We needed to find those that had been captured by Dentro and the Kandem. To reach out quietly somehow to the Ivars stuck within the King's army and see if any would choose us instead. How many were choosing Kandem because they felt like it was a sure thing, and our little rebel group was doomed?

The sun was high above us, but the icy wind still whipped around us, unforgiving and bitter. I slept until early noon and still felt exhausted. It didn't help that I always felt hungry. We all were hungry.

The map tent was the last tent still up. The others had been taken down and dozens raced around preparing to leave. I swallowed the last of my dry bread and stepped into the tent.

"Finally," Bexley growled, "I'm glad you finally woke her."

"She needed rest." Keane's voice came out cold.

"Rest is a luxury we do not get." The bags under his eyes were growing darker, but he was still well put together even if his uniform was wearing thin, but his shoes still were shined, and his beard was trimmed.

I didn't run a comb through my hair or change out of my wrinkled clothes before coming here. I didn't care. No one cared what you looked like when a war was coming. At least I didn't. "If

Kandem attacks Dentro and Asher is there at the tower, he could be killed. Every Nightmare that has been taken could be there and in danger. Kandem doesn't care if they're innocent or not, he wants to kill all the Nightmares."

Bexley started to roll up the maps and place them inside the saddlebags. "It has to be a ruse. The King isn't foolish enough to take on Dentro yet. He'll wait till Dentro shows his hand and his power before thinking through what to do. I have worked with the King for many years, and he is a smart and strategic man."

I walked with him to the horses, helping to saddle them, "should we still move camp then? If-"

"Yes, we've already stayed here too long."

"I need to go to the tower; I need to see if Asher is there and anyone else that could fight with us."

Bexley stopped buckling the saddle, "And what if they're all dead?"

I turned away, tightening the saddle on another horse. I refused to believe that.

"We should first find out if the King has kept any of his captives alive. It's more likely he has more than Dentro. It's wiser to do it that way than go off to Dentro lovesick and angry. Control your emotions, then act. You are to go to the mountains after we move camp. That is what you wanted, that is what you will do."

I blanched, lovesick? I might never get a chance to grow that with Asher if he's dead. Heat rose to my cheeks; I wasn't sure if it was from thinking about Asher or from thinking about him dying.

With my clothes packed, I strapped on Evir's knife and the sword I'd somehow gotten back from Gantric. I sometimes wondered if it was important to the soldier who dropped it if he had named it. I sheathed it. It felt heavier at my side today than in the past.

I didn't like the thought of going to the mountains. It felt like I was leaving Asher behind, but I knew he wouldn't want me to put my life in danger for him. No, I was putting my life in danger to see if I could save everyone else.

My tent was down and packed away, my bag was strapped on a horse. All that was left was to find Keane and Nilsa. I wanted her to ride with Keane and me.

"Riders coming in!" Shouted a voice. It took me a minute to find the voice high in the trees. A Nightmare with bat-like wings and the face of a man sat perched in the covering of branches. He pointed to the west and shouted again, "Riders coming in! Ivar uniforms!"

I pulled my knife. We weren't expecting anyone to come to the camp today. If they were deserters of kings, how did they find our camp?

"How many!" Bexley shouted back, coming up beside me with Keane.

"I count five!"

"Five that he can see," I took a breath gripping my knife tighter.

Others around us prepared for the Ivars, grabbing weapons and steadying the horses. Bexley ordered some to continue to be ready to head out but to be prepared for a fight.

Slowing their horses to a stop in front of us, a rider jumped down and raised his hands showing he had no weapon in hand or around his waist.

"Brice," I snarled, stepping forward, "What do you want?" He was no deserter of Kandem's. I could smell the love and loyalty he had for his king on him. "How did you find us?" I signaled to the bat creature that was still hidden in the trees to be looking out. If Brice was here, surely Kandem wouldn't be far off.

Brice smiled broadly as if we were old friends, "Now Ferren, no need for hostility. We are unarmed and come simply to talk."

"Then talk quickly before I show your friends your insides." I raised my knife to his stomach, "how did you find our camp?"

"A mutual friend told us."

I felt the others stiffen behind me. What traitor did we have in the camp? No one had been taken by the King in our camp. Only Asher had been taken, taken by Dentro, we had assumed. "Who?" I breathed.

Brice's smile widened, "the King would like to know if you have come to your senses."

"About?"

"A willing sacrifice."

I moved closer to him, my blade now pressed against his chest; the other Ivars shifted on their horses unsure of what to do. I knew they had weapons somewhere hidden, but I had a line of weapons at my back as well. "Who did Kandem talk to to find out about that? Does he have the spell?"

Brice held my gaze, his smile gone, but he didn't step back from the cold metal pressed on his chest. "He spoke to a very knowledgeable Enchantress."

"An Enchantress from where? Who would know about such things? Know the exact spell?"

His eyes flickered, deciding what his king would want him to tell me. What did this so-called olive branch they were extending entail? "I already know he spoke to Navara. Anyone else?"

"No."

"He doesn't tell you everything." I pushed the tip of the blade in just enough to puncture into his uniform, "Did she tell Kandem the spell and explain every little thing to him?"

His smug smile fell away, his jaw clenched, "You are welcome to come with us, to speak to the King and ask him any questions."

"Would he answer honestly, Brice? Or would he continue to lie as he always does?"

He raised his chin and snarled, "He wants you to do what is right, what would save us all."

"Then what? Kandem takes complete control and kills every Nightmare? What of the children should they be killed too?"

"He will keep those that have sworn their lives to him."

"As slaves!" I pushed the knife in and felt it connect with his skin. He winced, but didn't make a move.

"Dentro will do the same to us," he said through his clenched jaw, "Dentro will never stop. He is as powerful as Mavi was perhaps even more so. You won't just be stopping Dentro, you'll be saving our realm. The lives of every creature within this realm."

"I've already heard all of that." I played it in my mind repeatedly. I was desperately trying to save everyone. A part of me wanted to go with Brice back to Kandem and get it over with. Take Dentro out of the equation and then let Bexley try to figure out the King. I lowered the knife. Maybe I should? Maybe this was the only way that I could save them, save Asher. It was a better plan than wandering through the mountains while everyone else died and suffered.

"One more question. Answer honestly, then I will go with you."

"What." Keane bellowed, "Ferren?"

Brice smiled again, making me want to stick him with my knife.

"How did you find us?"

He opened his mouth, his eyes wide, no words came out only a cough of blood. I stood there stunned for a moment wiping his blood from my face. An arrow was lodged in his throat. The horses screamed and bucked around, the Ivars on them drew their hidden weapons, and Bexley shouted orders.

I spun around to face Keane and Nilsa, ready to yell at whoever released that arrow. Nilsa's face was pale. Keane grabbed my arm, pulling me into the circle of our allies. I drew my sword as Nightmares collided with the King's men. Twenty against five. It was a quick kill; in the blink of an eye, the Ivars fell. The camp erupted into a fight at our new threat.

"Ferren Vair!" The Nightmare that sat on a large horse didn't seem to have any eyes. Its head curved into dark horns, its face was smooth bone except for the deep groves in the middle and his sharp mouth. "We will bring blood down upon this camp unless you listen to the words of our master!"

Bexley raised his hand, signaling for our camp to hold as the other Nightmares seemed to freeze at his words.

"You have heard Kandem's message, and his promises now listen to the true king's message. You will come to the Tower alone, or the Shadow Nightmare will be killed along with every Ivar and Nightmare our king has collected."

"Dentro has Asher?" I wanted to fall to my knees to scream. To hear it be true was a stab to my heart.

The Nightmare smiled, flashing its pointed teeth, "Yes, the weak one, he told us everything when our king spoke with him."

"Lies!" Keane barked.

"What did you do to him?" I choked, "What did Dentro do to him!"

"He showed him who the true king was and that all should kneel."

"What does he want with me?" I rasped.

"I do not question my king on such matters."

"How long do I have?"

Keane grabbed my shoulder, turning me to him, his eyes wide with worry and panic, "He'll kill you."

"How long do I have?" I pushed Keane's hand off, turning back to the large creature and his horse.

"Find a fast horse," the Nightmare laughed. "Take the Enchantress!" He roared at the others behind him as he turned his horse and rode off.

A Nightmare galloped forward, reaching down, trying to grab Nilsa. She screamed, pushing back; a flame shot from her hand. The horse bucked, knocking the Nightmare to the ground. Keane thrusted his blade into the fallen Nightmare before he could stand. "Fire now!" I shouted at Nilsa. She pushed her hands forward with a quick motion and muttered something I couldn't understand. A wall of fire leaped out from her hands, sending the horses into a fit. Knives and arrows flew at them as well. Some finding targets and others the earth and trees. They fled to the forest except the bone man who was a distance off smiling at me, "The Enchantress's family is also in your hands!" He kicked his panicking horse off into the covering.

Nilsa's eyes were wide. Her breathing came out short and quick. I feared she was going to collapse, but she took a breath, shaking off the panic that coated her face, and replaced it with bitter anger. Flames still sparked at her fingers. "What does he mean by that?" She turned to me.

Keane went to grab Nilsa's hands but saw the sparks, "we'll go to Finara. We'll get them to safety."

Nilsa barked out a cold laugh, "They're as doomed as Asher."

I walked away from them as Keane tried to tell Nilsa something encouraging. Brice's eyes stared unseeing into the sky. I waited for Kamden to come marching over to me, anger in his old eyes. To be taken away from here and be sacrificed. I was willing to do anything at this point. Asher could already be dead, but I wasn't going to risk anything.

"Are you going to go to the Tower?" Nilsa stood behind me, her eyes looking up at the treetops away from the bodies and scorched earth.

I didn't know what the hell I was going to do. It was all on my shoulders to figure it out. There was no true right decision for anything. I was going to be someone's villain and someone's hero in the end. "I need to find Kandem. If he has the spell, I can end this right now."

"They will still all die. Every Nightmare that follows Dentro will lash out. They will see Dentro as their fallen god, a creature whom they must avenge."

I threw my knife at the tree trunk, and the blade sunk in deep with a loud thunk. "Then what should I do Nilsa? Tell me what to do?" My voice was hollow, filled with pleading instead of the rage that I wanted. I felt weak and exhausted. I was one person, one average nobody who didn't want any of it, but I was also the only one who could deal with it so I would suck it up like my father always told me to do when I was exhausted and carry on, if not for myself, then for the others that needed me to be strong. "Get me a horse, a fast one."

"We need horses," Keane cut in. He raised a hand to silence my protest, "I'm not sending you in there alone. I don't care what Dentro's messengers said."

I ran a hand through my tangled hair, "No, I need you and Nilsa to find the King, find out what he knows and how he knows it. Nilsa's right. We need to bring Dentro down from his thrown before we kill him, or else Nightmares will riot, which means I have to go to the Tower now and see if I can save Asher and Nilsa's family."

Keane scratched the back of his neck and shook his head, "I can't let you go there alone."

"And I can't put you two in danger." My hands shook. The thought of them being taken like Asher had frightened me. My stomach curled at the thought of them going close to the tower and being in danger. I looked at Keane, his bright blue eyes shown with defiance and fear, "Please don't follow me, Keane, please."

He raised his chin, "I will go with Nilsa to the King, but as soon as I find the information we need, I will come find you and Asher."

I tried to smile at his honor, confidence, and determination, but I couldn't shake the descending trepidation that loomed over us.

"Ferren," Bexley called me over to a large trunk he was standing beside. I peered over his shoulder as he lifted the lid and pulled out the dark black uniform of the Ivars. "You will need this."

It was heavier than I expected as I lifted it to take in the silver threads that arched around the shoulders and ribs. The leather was cold, but dark fur lined the inside protecting my skin from the chain-mail that gave it its weight. I didn't want to take off Asher's wool jacket, but it wouldn't fit under the armor. I reluctantly shrugged off his jacket and slipped on the armor. It was a bit big on the shoulders and hit just below my knees, but it would work. I still had movement without it bunching up. I flipped the hood up, feeling the sliver threads beneath my fingertips, and took a shaky breath. My father had worn a uniform just like this, a symbol of his love for Hatheya, a symbol of his honor to protect it. I wish I could have seen him in it just once. To see the pride and honor that he once held.

Bexley looked me up and down, "just one more thing." He took out his knife and with a quick motion he cut the thread that stitched out Kandem's initials. He pulled the strings out as best he could before returning his knife to his side, "That will do."

"Thank you," I said hoarsely, then cleared my throat, "watch over them." Nilsa and Keane stood by the horses trying to help calm the chaos of packing and wounded soldiers.

He gave a soft laugh, "I will try, but they are both hardheaded and will do what they need to do, even if that means putting themselves in danger. Much like you."

"I'm doing what I think is right."

He closed the trunk with a thud, "the Ivars are taught to follow what feels right within themselves. To look at the situation and all the outcomes, to judge what would be best for others, even if that means doing the harder thing."

"Like defecting from your king and helping in the rebellion?"

He sighed deeply, "it took many years for me to realize what was happening was wrong. I had grown up watching it, accepting the hate that we were supposed to give to the Nightmares, but I always felt the burn that something was wrong, that we were wrong." He helped me re-strap on my sword, "I would listen to the stories of Mavi and how he wanted peace in Hatheya for all, not just Ivars not just Nightmares, but all of us who walked within this realm, so I started to change the way I thought, the way I looked at others and the way I acted. It was difficult to watch the King becoming more and more angry at the Nightmares, becoming darker. I don't know what happened to him."

"Some people change for the better and others fall into the darkness of the world. We are responsible for our minds, for our actions, and his actions had led him down a dark path."

"You are heading into the very pit of darkness Ferren, don't let it corrupt your mind," He clasped me on the shoulder, "never waver in the strength."

THIRTY-FOUR

Nilsa threw her arms around me, "I can still come with you," she whispered.

"No," I hugged her tighter, "Dentro wanted you for some reason, so you need to stay far away from him, from the tower." I let go. Her eyes gleamed with tears.

"I hate the heroics you're trying to run off and do, but I thank you for trying to save my family."

"You don't have much hope, do you?" My hands hung slack at my side, my shoulders seemed heavy.

She wrung her hands together and looked away, "I wish I did, and I wish I could lie to you and say that I did," she finally looked at me, "but I will not send you away with false hope. Just be smart, be safe, and know that you might be walking into a tower filled with death. You have to be prepared."

I straightened my back and took a breath. I had to be a soldier through and through.

Keane brought over a horse, "others said he is the fastest we have and the bravest."

I took the reins, "we will see each other again." I mounted the horse.

"Yes," Keane said sternly, "we will."

Nilsa gave a sad smile but nodded.

I didn't look back as I kicked the horse into a gallop. The cold wind dried my eyes and chapped my lips, but I didn't tuck down into the collar of my armor. Instead, I looked out across the tree-filled landscape at the clouds in the sky threatening snow, and the dying realm. I would survive this. I will fight for my life at the tower, for Asher's life and when I have knocked Dentro from his throne and Kandem from his, then I will let my blood flow through this land. I swallowed a laugh that bubbled in my throat. It was a beautiful thought that I could save them all, save my father's land, but I barely knew how to keep myself alive and I was about to face Dentro, the king of death.

I pushed until the darkness swallowed us and I could no longer see what lay ahead. I risked a small fire to help fight off the frigid cold. Snow had finally burst from the clouds and came down in a flurry. I only rested for a couple of hours trying to sleep or eat, but I tossed and turned my mind creating nightmares of everything that could go wrong when I got to the tower.

As soon as the sky started to brighten, I was off riding again. The sky stayed cloudy and cold as I pushed on through the wind and snow.

I was almost there. I could feel the sickening power pulsing off the tower as it came into view above the treetops. The horse bucked, throwing me to the ground. Air was knocked from my lungs, making me gasp as I rolled to my hands and knees. The horse nervously pranced around shaking his head, and eyes wide.

"Shhh, calm." I tried reaching out to the frantic animal, but it dodged away. "Okay." I put my hands up, showing him I wasn't going to grab at the reins. The tower was so close, just a couple of miles a quick ride and I would make it before the sunset, that was if I could calm the horse. I lunged forward, grabbing the reins as the horse reared up. I grabbed the reins tighter and pulled the horse farther away from the tower. He calmed down and followed me, but his eyes were still wide with panic. "You feel that too?" I ran a hand down his neck, "Don't worry, I won't make you go." I quickly grabbed the food and Asher's sweater from the saddlebag, "go!" The horse took off, leaving me standing in the falling snow.

The snow never relented as I marched to the tower. It grew thick and heavy around my feet making every step slow and painful. The Tower came closer inch by inch and soon I could see the castle covered in ice and frost.

I collapsed to the ground. I needed to breathe for a moment. It was quiet, so quiet. The abandoned town that was at the base of the castle I had once seen Nightmares occupying was eerily still. Had they taken refuge inside the collapsed houses? Or had Dentro sent them away?

I looked to the heavens and closed my eyes. Gentle snowflakes landed across my lashes. The cold air burned my ragged lungs. Asher's jacket was soaked with snow, weighing it down, but I couldn't feel the cold through my armor. I pulled off my gloves, grasping at the snow. It bit into my chapped fingers. I sighed at the pain. It helped take away some of the defining silence and foreboding thoughts of death. I stood, taking another shaky breath. I could not die here. My death was meant to happen somewhere else. I pulled my sword and walked down to the broken town.

I saw a few Nightmares peeking out from the broken houses, hissing, and growling at me, but they didn't emerge. Dentro must have sent orders to let me pass, but I still gripped my sword with white knuckles and tried to be aware of my surroundings. It was hard to look away from the castle.

The dark door loomed in front of me. I pulled my hood up farther and walked forward. The door swung open with an icy hiss. I stopped in my tracks and raised my sword.

A dark claw reached out gingerly and beckoned me forward. I stood there with my sword in my hand, unsure of what to do as it waved me forward again. I tried to see who or what was attached to the claw, but the castle was as dark as a tomb. Not even the sun that was sinking could pierce the darkness.

I was Ivar. Was born with braveness and strength within my very core. I knew how to fight, and how to survive, and I would save those who needed me. I would never waver in the strength.

I stepped into the darkness and only glanced back once at the snow-covered mountains and the setting sun before the door slammed shut behind me, sinking me into the blackness.

A small candle was lit, lighting the face of a mangy dog with sunken eyes and missing lips. It handed me another candle, forcing me to take one hand off my sword.

I shined the candle on the creature to get a better look and instantly regretted it. It was half dog, half tree beast, with spikes jutting from its back and furry scabs covering it. It walked on all fours, but if it stood, it would have surely been nine feet tall. I took a cautious step back from it.

"This way," its voice sounded like breaking trees and firewood cracking.

I took slow steps, following the Nightmare down a large hallway. The windows had been boarded up, blocking out any light that would have helped me see where I was walking. The air was musty, and dust clung to my lungs.

Farther down the hall, a candelabrum hung above a door. The brightest thing I had seen since walking into the castle. The light should have been a comfort, but it only brought on anxiety. With every step that brought us closer to the door, my heart pounded. I gripped my sword and took a breath. I was prepared; I would be brave, I repeated to myself repeatedly until we walked under the light and through the doors.

More candelabrums hung high above us. The long walls were covered in windows all boarded up with rotting wood. The pillars were crumbling and dusty, but the intricate designs of pictures still stood out on them. One was of a battle atop a hill. A figure stood at the very peak, sword raised, and another was that of a broken throne and bodies lying beneath it.

My eyes slid away from the stone pillars and to the end of the curved room. Shadows swarmed around a silver and black throne. *I will not waver in the strength.* I would not give Dentro the satisfaction of seeing me afraid.

The beast leading me stopped and bowed deeply, "My king, I bring the girl." He stepped away from me and melted into the shadows that the candles couldn't reach.

I couldn't keep the small gasp from happening as I saw who else was standing at the edge of the shadows. Navara wasn't looking at me. She kept her eyes on Dentro, her hands clasped tightly in front of her thin frame. I wanted her to look at me, to see me, her daughter standing right in front of her, to give me a reassuring nod, a small smile. I craved anything that would reassure me, even if it was from a mother I barely knew or trusted.

I peeled my eyes away from her and to the shadowed throne. His hands curved around the arms of the throne. I had expected claws or talons, but they were clean and polished, not even callused. I stepped closer never letting my sword shake or drop. The angry shadows around him lifted slightly, showing his legs and torso. He wore black pants and shirt. A deep blood-red cape that hung off one shoulder. I crept closer. The sickening smell of blood and rot filled my nose. I stopped on the bottom step leading up to the throne suddenly remembered my nightmares. Being trapped in a dark throne room, staring up at the dark king that was blurred. Blood rushed through my head. He had been in my dreams.

"Why won't you bow to your King?" His voice was distant and blurred I strained my ears to hear him. Had he spoken, or was it in my mind?

I shook off the haze that came after his voice, "You are not my king." My voice was too loud. It bounced off the walls and rang in my ears.

He tapped his fingers against the throne, "You will. I will bring you to your knees. Every breath you take will be filled with screams. Your blood will be upon my crown, your crimson corpse will lay hollow at my feet." He stood quickly, making me drop the candle. I gripped my sword with both hands and stood ready for anything.

"I feel the fear pulsing through you. It makes me hungry for more." He stepped down two of the stairs, leaving only three to separate us. "But I require you at the moment,"

"What do you want with me?" I was sweating in my armor. My hands were slick in my gloves, but I set my jaw and glared up at Dentro. I will not die here, not by his hand and not for his purpose.

He gave a click with his tongue, "selfish women. Shouldn't you first ask about Nilsa's frail grandmother? Or what about your shadow Nightmare?" He sounded disappointed, "Mavi would have asked about them first and not have cared about himself. Perhaps more of Navara's blood runs in you than his."

Navara looked down, her lips pressed tightly together, her hands shaking.

"Would you like me to tell you what became of them? Of anyone I took, or are we still focused on you?"

"Where are they!" I snapped. The calmness in his voice sent waves of anger through me.

"Nilsa's grandmother is still alive for now, though very weak. Poor thing. And Asher," his voice bitter on the name, "Was never truly alive." He took another step down.

"What?" I felt a coldness ripple through me, "You took his shadows, didn't you? You killed him."

With a crackle of laughter he took another step down, "There was nothing to take, they were already mine."

"Where is Asher!" I swung my sword to him keeping him from taking the last step down.

"I always hated that name," his shadows faded away, his face coming into view.

My sword fell to my side. I couldn't breathe. I gasped for a breath, but nothing came except a silent scream as I looked up at Asher's face, at his dark eyes that swirled like the night sky.

"I prefer to be called Dentro." He spoke with Asher's lips. His voice. The way he tilted his head and smiled Asher's smile. It was him. My shadow Nightmare.

"Why do you look so surprised?" he scrunched his brow.

"This is a trick; it has to be a trick." The room spun and my legs threatened to give out. "You can't be Dentro. It's impossible. You've been trapped inside this tower since Mavi and Kanna died.

People would have recognized you! Kandem would have recognized you!"

"No actually," He took the last step down and circled me, "I have been locked *out* of the tower since they cast that horrendous spell, and like everyone affected by it I forgot where it was. I fought my way out and sadly half my shadow power was locked in here and the other half with me. Sickening to be without all my power, but I spent my time waiting, waiting for Kandem to fall to the sickness of the sword he stole, waiting for the Hatheya to break and bleed, waiting to find my tower and it to open once again and in my waiting I happen to find another shadow Nightmare, horribly weak, I took his body and his shadows. I have become used to this body now. I've grown to like it and I know you do too," he winked at me.

I wanted to vomit, scream, cry, and throw something. This had to be a lie, it had to be a trick. It had to be. I raised my sword, swinging it at his neck. His shadows dived in front, knocking me to the ground and sending my sword flying across the ground. I stood up, screaming in anger.

He sighed deeply ignoring me, "I do need to send thanks to Kandem for finding my tower and castle again and for starting the sickness of the realm. I didn't know how long I would have had to wait if he were a righteous king. I was beginning to worry the sword wouldn't affect him." He smiled at me, "Oh, I see the confusion on your face. You poor, simple women. I will explain everything over dinner, but first," he snapped his fingers. The dog beast brought out an old woman. She was wobbling and panting, blood dripping down her head and arms.

"Agatha! What did you do to her?" Asher grabbed my shoulder while digging his fingers into me before I could run to her.

"I was ecstatic to find more of Navara's and Kanna's distant family," he snapped his fingers again. The dog creature rose to his full height, grabbing Agatha in its claws.

I screamed again, pulling against the shadows and Asher, but it was too late. It roared and with a sickening snap of bones, Agatha fell to the ground. "No!" I dropped to my knees. I promised Nilsa. I tried to give her hope. What a foolish thing I did, "You killed her!"

Asher looked offended, "I did not. He did," he pointed to the dog, "If it would make you feel better you could kill him. I won't let him attack you."

The dog creature looked down at me, panting. I stood. "You killed her." I pointed at Dentro. He knocked my hand away from his face and gave me a disgusted look.

"Fine, believe what you want," He sat back on his throne, "Navara, show your daughter to her room and get her dressed for dinner. We have much to talk about." He looked me up and down as if I was what was for dinner.

"Asher," I growled.

He raised a hand to stop me, "Please, it's Dentro. It's nice to finally be me again."

Navara stepped to my side and patiently waited for me. I couldn't look away from Dentro, from Asher, or whoever he was. Navara gently touched my arm. I turned with her back to the hallway and silently followed her to a room decorated with dark leather furniture, a moth-eaten rug, and a large bed fit for royalty. I glanced around the room again. The entire room was fit for royalty. Moonlight streamed into the sitting room through the large, uncovered windows, illuminating the grand furniture and gold fireplace.

"Dentro's room is the one right across the hall," she whispered.

I finally turned to look at her, "You knew…you knew who he was."

She shook her head, "No, I haven't seen Dentro for a very long time and I didn't know he took a new body."

"When I spoke to you, you told me he was in the here at the tower. You lied to me." I couldn't look at her. I couldn't swallow how stupid I had been to believe her. Asher told me not to believe her. No. I slumped down in a chair. No, Dentro told me not to believe her.

I let my sword fall to the ground. I was exhausted and overwhelmed. "Leave me alone."

"Ferren, please, I didn't know. I was trying to warn you of the King."

"What good did that do me?"

She kneeled in front of me, "I will get you out of here. I will find a way to send you back to the human realm, where you can be safe."

"Get out of my room," my voice cracked.

She stood slowly, "There is a dress lying on the bed that Dentro would like you to wear for dinner. I will be back later to do your hair if you would like?"

I didn't respond and let her walk out the door in silence. The door clicked and I heard a lock turn into place. As soon as I heard her footsteps leave, I jumped up and looked out the window. I knew we had to be in the highest part of the castle, not including the look-out tower that loomed far above us. I looked down at the forest and the town that seemed to come back to life. It was once again crawling with Nightmares.

I would be getting out of this castle one way or another, and I wasn't going to be using Navara's help. Asher, or Dentro. Whomever he was had taken me by surprise had blurred my mind of thinking straight. I should have darted out the door as soon as Navara led me from the throne room. I had my sword, my strength, but seeing Asher hearing him talk that way numbed me.

I leaned my head against the glass and closed my eyes, trying to imagine that I was back in my father's office in the window and that I wasn't locked away in a castle by someone I had trusted, someone who hadn't made me a fool. Tears slid down my cheeks. I didn't try to stop them, didn't wipe them away. I had cried when Asher was taken when I thought he was dead, and now what was I crying for? My broken promise to Nilsa? The betrayal of a man? No, he was a Nightmare. He was my worst nightmare. I opened my eyes, staring at my reflection. And I was going to be his.

ACKNOWLEDGMENTS

Firstly, I would like to thank my mother, Haley, for helping me with editing multiple times. From my first draft to a published book, she was by my side cheering for me, along with my father, Dan, my husband, Russell, and every family member who was constantly excited for me. There are too many names to write, but thank you all for the support. I am very lucky to have such a supportive family.

Thank you to my beta readers who took time out of their lives and helped me edit and gave me confidence that this book was worth publishing.

Thank you to my amazing arc readers who were the first to leave reviews and helped hype up this book.

And finally, thank you to the readers who picked up this book and gave a new author a chance. I hope you fell in love with the world and characters like I did.

Shayha Obert-Hickey is fueled by a lifelong love for storytelling and reading. She has now published her very first dark fantasy novel, The Realm of Nightmares.

She was born and raised in Wyoming and instead of writing about cowboys and Yellowstone, her heart is full of fantasy stories that she grew up reading late into the night. Now, as a wife and a mother of two, she has accomplished her dream of becoming a published writer.

If you would like to get updates on the upcoming publication of her next novel, please follow her Facebook page, Shayha Obert Hickey-Author, and Instagram Shayha_books.

Made in the USA
Columbia, SC
22 July 2025

924a8389-bb67-45ce-9a65-d7edff22b610R01